"SNIPER'S MOON is psychologically acute, rich with suspense and black humor. A first-rate police thriller. Stroud's talent is undeniable."

—Jonathan Kellerman

"A standout, with an ingenious plot, suspenseful pacing and strong, gritty dialogue."

—*Publisher's Weekly*

"Quite simply . . . the best debut cop novel since Joseph Wambaugh's The *New Centurions* . . . an absorbing page-turner."

—The Flint Journal

SNIPER'S MOON

SNIPER'S MOON

CARSTEN STROUD

BANTAM BOOKS
NEW YORK • TORONTO • LONDON • SYDNEY • AUCKLAND

SNIPER'S MOON

A Bantam Book
Bantam hardcover edition published November 1990
Bantam rack edition / February 1992

Grateful acknowledgment is made for permission to reprint lyrics from "Heartattack and Vine" by Tom Waits copyright © 1990 by Fifth Floor Music, Inc.

ISBN 0-553-28752-4

Bantam Books are published by Bantam Books, a division of Bantam Doubleday Dell Publishing Group, Inc. Its trademark, consisting of the words "Bantam Books" and the portrayal of a rooster, is Registered in U.S. Patent and Trademark Office and in other countries. Marca Registrada. Bantam Books, 666 Fifth Avenue, New York, New York 10103.

Linda Mair

for going the distance
with style and wit,
as she does in every story . . .
and for bringing me
all the cold Beck's
it took to keep me at it—

Thanks. Here's to you.

—CARSTEN STROUD
Thunder Beach

ACKNOWLEDGMENTS

Nobody reads this part, but I want it down on the record that some of the best work in this book is there because my editor at Bantam, Beverly Lewis, went far beyond the call of duty, reading and re-reading various incarnations of this book, thinking about it, engaging with it, in a way, and with a kind of grace, that few writers are lucky enough to encounter. If you like this book, you should raise a glass to Beverly Lewis.

If you hate it, blame me.

I also want to thank David Reid, ex-SWAT sniper and my good friend, for keeping my sights in line; David Forbes of the Royal Bank, for trust and good faith; and, of course, Betsy Cenedella, who, as usual, kept me from making a complete fool of myself in print more times than I care to recall.

And . . . finally . . . thanks to the men of the Seventh Cavalry, First Air Cavalry Division. When the time came, the black hats paid the reckoning. On the nail.

"You got to tell me, brave captain,
why are the wicked so strong?
How do angels get to sleep
when the devil leaves his porch light on?"
—TOM WAITS
"Heartattack and Vine"

SNIPER'S MOON

PROLOGUE

John Keogh was a man without metaphor. Madelaine was his wife and her body was as well known to him as his own; a sequence of sensations and images, surfaces, tastes, scents, warmth in the hollow places of her neck, the rising of muscle and bone along the line of her shoulders, her black hair with a soft light in it fanned out across the white sheet in the pale-blue glow from the window, her voice a wine-scented vibrato, sharp and somehow dizzying in the darkness of their room. Keogh was on his right side, close to her hip, aware of her heat, his left hand on her chest so he could feel her voice, her left knee touching his thigh. The sheet, rumpled and twisted from their movements, was now pulled away to uncover his wife from her breasts to her knees.

Something about the openness of it, the dark shadow at the base of her rounded belly, her strong tanned legs apart, her heavy white breasts with the nipples hard and violet in the slow blue light—all of this made Keogh hard again, slowly, in time to his pulse, the way hardness comes back to men in their forties.

Madelaine felt him at her hip.

"Well, Johnny . . . this is a compliment."

Keogh was past talk. He was feeling a violence that was disturbing to him. He did not think of himself as a man with

1

passions. Men with passions seemed weak to him. He dealt with them every day, down in the city, men who had a hundred reasons for the damage they did, every one of them rooted in passion.

Madelaine took him in her left hand.

"After twenty years and a child, Johnny?" Her smile changed as Keogh moved his hand down over the soft swell of her belly, through the delicacy of her hairs, sliding a finger into her, the heat and the silkiness making his heart pound in his thick chest.

For a long moment she moved against his hand, her legs stretching and opening. When she pulled him down to kiss her, Keogh could feel the nails on her right hand cutting into his neck. There was a singing of blood in his ears. Then she was up and gone, taking the sheet with her, leaving him sprawled stupidly in the middle of the empty bed, on his back, watching her as she went to the glass doors that opened onto the backyard. Blue light from the swimming pool poured in through the sheer curtains. A blue aura shone around her hair and her hips and her shoulders.

"Johnny, you look like a moth pinned to a card. Get up and come for a swim." She turned, pulling the sheet around her, and opened the glass doors.

"What? Skinny-dip? Madelaine . . . come back here. What about the Bukovacs?" Keogh was sitting up now, fumbling in the tangle of bedclothes for his pajama bottoms, finding them, tugging them up and over his hips and his erection. The sight of this made her laugh, a sharp clear sound that went right across their yard.

"Madelaine! Come inside!"

She laughed again and, turning, let the sheet fall to her feet. She stepped out onto the damp stones of the patio. Keogh stood there for another three beats, staring at his wife's naked bottom, watching her as she went on tiptoe across the flagstones and out onto the lawn. Halfway to the shimmering blue of the in-ground pool, she turned and waved him on.

The sight of his wife standing naked on the family lawn,

in the middle of the family lawn furniture, the outrageousness of the thing filled him up and pulled him out the door. Natural velocity carried him to her, standing there in the blue light, her tanned body marked by white breasts and the violet delta below her blue-white belly, her hands on her hips, smiling at him and feeling the cool night wind on her skin. Keogh came down the steps and across the lawn to her, stepping on the cuffs of his pajamas, the grass wet and slippery between his toes.

"What if they see us?" he whispered, looking over toward the dark bulk of the Bukovac house beyond the cedar hedge.

"What if they do? Irina runs around her backyard in a towel all the time. I've seen you lusting after her, you hound. This just makes us even. Come on."

She took his arm and led him over to the tiles at the edge of the pool. All the lights were on. The water was as clear as the air above it, tinted a tourmaline blue by the round porthole lights set into the pool walls a few inches below the surface. Keogh and his wife stood by the waterside for a while, arms around each other. Keogh was thinking about the water. It would be cold. Leaves had blown into the pool. There was a cluster of them in the deep end. He'd have to get them out with the vacuum. God, he thought. Romantic sonovabitch, aren't you?

"John . . . I got a letter from Frank today."

Keogh felt a dull surge of old anger. Oh, yes, little Frankie would be sure to write his mother. Where was a letter for his da? No no. Go straight to mother. Standard for that boy.

"Well, is he doing all right?"

She thought about it for a while.

"Yes. Well, he says he is. It's over a month old. Military mail. It went from Danang to Honolulu. He doesn't say a lot. That boy from Union City? He's related to your desk sergeant?"

"Nicolucci?"

Madelaine shook once under his arm. He pulled her closer.

"He stepped on . . . a Betty Crocker? Something like that?"

"A Bouncing Betty. A kind of bomb they put in the ground."

Keogh had been learning the names of a new war. His son was twenty now, a rifleman in the Sixth Cavalry. Keogh had read all about the Tet offensive, about Hue and Khe Sanh. Cronkite had talked on the news about America losing this war. He got secondhand stories from other cops about Arc Lite creepback, and hearts and minds, and body counts. It seemed a damned stupid little war to John Keogh, fought on the far side of the moon for thieves and criminals.

Well, his own war hadn't made much sense either. Sticking a flag on Suribachi—they'd asked those men to do it again for the cameras. Half of Iwo was still in Japanese hands. Most of the men who raised that flag were dead in a week. And Kwajalein was worse, except there'd been no cameras.

Madelaine was silent for a longer time. Keogh could feel her thinking of Frank over there in a strange country, a country where they put bombs in the ground and called them cute names. He stroked her hair and she turned to hold him. She looked down at his waist.

"Johnny . . . what happened to Steve and the Twins?"

He smiled, a slow revelation of ragged teeth in a face full of planes and angles.

"They're in there somewhere. Whyn't you go look for them?"

Madelaine pushed him hard toward the water. He staggered at the brink, waving his arms, getting his balance.

He recovered and lunged for her. She darted away around the edge of the pool, hair flying, on her toes, slipping away from him, Keogh coming after her, a lumbering heavy man coming down hard on his bare heels. He had just turned forty-eight. His wife was forty.

They played at the poolside for a time, Madelaine pretending to elude him, Keogh lurching after her, regretting all the cigarettes and some of the red wine he drank at the B and V in Hunts Point.

Finally she slipped by and stepped lightly up onto the diving board. Keogh, breathing hard, came up after her. She walked out to the end and did a ballerina spin.

Keogh stood and looked at her for a while, taking her in, remembering all the things there were to remember about this woman. Her dark eyes, the sounds of her various voices, her tanned and untanned secrets, and her way of going.

She knew he was admiring her. She felt a rush of strong emotion for the man, for the years they had seen together. For his fidelity. Solid John Keogh, honest as stone, serious and steady. He'd loved her for twenty years in his slow tidal way. She thought of him as inexorable. He was like that on the job, so they told her. She tried hard not to know anything about his days or nights in the city. What was the point of the two of them knowing such things?

Tonight had been a fine moment between them. They had not fought. They had talked about Frank and they had not fought. She was happy for both of them. Madelaine turned to face the water. Stirred by a night wind, the water burned tourmaline and cerulean blue. It shone up at her, ruffled and restless and glittering.

Keogh looked down at the water. The leaves, that cluster of dead leaves . . . something . . .

Madelaine arched, an alabaster figure in the blue-green light.

The cluster of dead leaves . . . too brown for high summer. Keogh tried to see through the wavering light. Not leaves . . .

"Madelaine . . ."

Birds. Dead birds. Four of them . . . Why?

"Madelaine—the lights!"

But she was already in the air.

Twenty-two years later . . .

CHAPTER 1

Friday, August 17
2200 hours
The South Bronx

A sniper needs a gift for stillness, a way of moving through violence as a full moon glides through a black volley of storm clouds. The gift is hard-earned. A Remington rifle weighs close to ten pounds. It has a heavy stainless-steel barrel and holds four .308 rounds in the magazine. Frank Keogh keeps another one in the firing chamber, for a total of five. He has never needed more than two.

The Leupold scope adds some weight. The Starlite scope weighs even more. He doesn't use that much. The city puts out a lot of light. Always enough light to shoot by.

Frank Keogh has learned to carry the weight of this weapon on bone, hard into the hollow of his shoulder, his cheekbone welded to the stockpiece, the forestock resting on the bone of his upturned palm. When the hammer comes down, flesh gives way. Bone was something Keogh believed in. Bone was stronger than flesh.

Frank gave up cigarettes when he took this assignment. Breathing is everything for a sniper. Frank always thought of wings when he was trying to be still, a slow sweep of great wings as his lungs filled and his heartbeat slowed.

Through the bright image in the scope, he could see a wolfish boy pacing back and forth in the harsh fluorescent light of the gun shop, in a barren concrete room filled with racks of rifles and shotguns, battered old Garands and surplus M-14's, a rifle Frank used to take to bed with him. The wolfish boy looked vaguely Latin, his sharp face puffed and slick with rage or fear or something chemical. His right eye was swollen and green, the cheek beneath it scored and raw. In the circular image of Keogh's scope, the boy's edgy movements were exaggerated and twitchy, as if he were hearing from some animal mind in his head and the animal could feel the halo-weight of the scope on him, feel the weight of the 148-grain round resting in its chamber down the twisting tunnel of the rifle barrel a hundred yards away across the wide Bronx street full of police cars and media vans and armed men.

Frank Keogh had his left elbow braced on the back of a wooden chair in the darkened attic of the Pretty Kitty Pet Shop. The chair was in the center of a cleared circle, six feet back from an open window, with a good sightline across Third Avenue to the Bolsa Chica Gun Store where the wolfish boy was pacing. It was one of those luminous August nights in the South Bronx, when the air is scented and thick with heat and diesel smoke.

Keogh had his legs spread around the chair back. His upper body was welded into his rifle, part of the machinery. Keogh's thick blue-black hair had grayed at the temples. His pit-bull Irish face was creased and tight, with a fan of wrinkles around his right eye at the scope, a glimmer down deep in his eye where the image of the boy across the street lay like a silver coin in blue water.

Frank Keogh was John Keogh's son, rough-skinned and solid, with a wide salt-and-pepper moustache, long fine-boned hands. He was thickening at the waist; the blue pinstripe pulled tight across his back. He had one blue eye, his sighting eye, and one green eye. People who met him found it hard to look at him straight. They switched their connection from one eye to the other, off balance, sensing a certain distance in the man.

The image in his scope-sight played in silence for Frank Keogh. By a Department order, police snipers are not allowed to monitor any conversations between the street cops and a barricaded target. This target had some hostages, and they had brought in Art Pike, the negotiator for the 40th Precinct, to handle the thing. Pike had been talking to the people in the Bolsa Chica for a long time now. Keogh didn't have to hear what was going on to know it didn't look good.

There were five people in the front room of the gun shop: three yellow-skinned Haitians—two of them young and female, and a third, a man, lying on his belly at the foot of the long glass counter, his hands bound, blood running freely from his left ear, his eyes half open and dull. And the two others, the targets, Keogh's target and Pat Butler's target, both boys armed and pacing, both of them haggard and raw-looking in black jeans and plaid shirts and the kind of head scarf they call do-rags in the home neighborhoods. Both kids were members of a Marielito street gang called the Ching-a-Lings, with a home base up around the 46th Precinct, along the Harlem River. This wasn't their territory. But they had problems of their own up in University Heights, a gang war, troubles with the Vietnamese. They put themselves into it down here, looking for cash and weapons, and now Keogh and Butler were going to take them out.

They had themselves barricaded in the Bolsa Chica Gun Store with their three Haitian hostages, one of whom they had beaten almost to death in the first few minutes of the incident. That was Ton-Ton Toussaint, an old Papa Doc enforcer who had probably gotten no more than he had earned over his fifty years. But then there were his two young daughters. They'd been helping him in the shop during the afternoons.

A radio car from the 40th had seen the boys go in, seen the weapons. They called in a Signal Thirteen and pulled a hard U-turn to go mix it up, the way street cops will, trading on nerves and luck, doing business the way they always did business in the Bronx. The time on the screen was 1652, almost five o'clock.

It went badly. Two officers went down in the first thirty

seconds. The career sergeant went first. His name was Kris Paznakaitis, a black cop big and gristled like old beef, two kids and a wife in Park Slope. He had the Greek name from a man his mother once knew, and a Greek name on a black cop was all that came out of that. Kris was known in the Bronx as The Paz. The Paz died when a gang kid named Zon put two into him from an alley as the patrol car pulled up. The Paz got out of the car with most of his stomach gone and tried to get off a couple of shots, but then he was down on his back, staring up at black birds wheeling in the dusty blue, his breath sounding in his ears like a knife on stone.

His partner in the car was a cop named Patsy Laputa. Taking shit for the name of a Spanish hooker from day three had hardened her, so she managed to get her Smith & Wesson up and coming around, before Zon got the barrel in the open window. They both fired at the same time. Her round plucked at Zon's collar. Then she was dead.

Another female cop, on foot patrol, got there just in time to put five rounds into Zon's back. He was running for the door of the low concrete building. His friends slammed it shut and hammered down the crossbar. Zon got his in the doorway, settling softly into a pile of candy wrappers and his own intestines.

The hot shot went citywide from Communications. At 1655 hours, cars started to arrive from the 40th, the 42nd, the 44th, along with Street Crime Units, a couple of unmarked detective cars, and one Neighborhood Stabilization Unit with three stunned rookies and a veteran sergeant named Weisberg, all of the cars canted this way and that on the sidewalks and curbs around the old Bronx Borough Courthouse.

Communications put out a No Further a couple of minutes later, and the officers on the scene put down some ragged but effective suppressing fire while two harness guys from the 40th dragged Patsy and The Paz out of the fire line. In a minute or so the word got around that they were both dead. Everybody settled down to the business of killing the gang members still inside the Bolsa Chica. The

Remingtons came out of the trunks. People put their Kevlar on. The gunfire took on a regular rolling rumble. Chips of concrete block started to fly off the front of the store; white dust settled on Zon's body. The plate-glass window came down with a satisfying jangle. Slugs started zipping and zanging around in the interior of the gun shop, powdering the walls and shattering the glass cases.

Finally, the patrolwoman who had killed Zon in the doorway managed to make herself heard over the radio. Hostages, she said. Three hostages, you sons of bitches. There was a general "whoops" around the perimeter.

Weisberg, the veteran who had pulled up in the NSU car, slid down the fender of his car and laid his overheated Smith on the tarmac. His three rookies were huddled at his feet, staring up at him with that odd combination of flat fear and anticipation that rookies get in situations like these.

"Well, kid," said Weisberg, looking at the closest one. "What do we call this situation?"

"Ah . . . well, this would be your barricaded EDP, sir?"

"No, kid. This would not be your barricaded EDP. This would be your basic shitstorm. Get up in there and see if somebody has called the ESU guys yet. Let Keogh and Butler take these assholes out."

"Yes, sir," said the kid, going for the radio. Over in the Bolsa Chica, the two Ching-a-Ling boys had reloaded and were putting out side windows all around the block. A charge took out the NSU bubble light, and red glass came raining down on Weisberg's hat.

"We having fun yet, kids?" said Weisberg.

Weisberg couldn't hear the answer. He figured it was no.

Art Pike was still talking nearly five hours later. Keogh was getting tired.

It was 2200 hours by the Hamilton watch Keogh wore on his right wrist so he could check the time without moving his rifle. Pat Butler, his partner, would usually have been up here with him, working as a spotter and talking to

Pulaski over the radio, but the unit was short a shooter
tonight, so Butler was somewhere in close, up on a rooftop,
using the M-16 with the laser sight, and Keogh was alone in
the Pretty Kitty with his Remington rifle and the smell of
pet food and nothing to keep him company but the
cross-talk on his headset and a spider the size of a lawn
sprinkler up in the corner of the window.

Pulaski had issued a couple of Stand-downs. Pulaski was
down in the street in his kelly-green Plymouth—Bert
Pulaski, lord high ruler of the Bronx ESU sector, right now
the only member of the unit who could hear the conversation between Art Pike and the boys in the gun shop. If
things went sour it would be Pulaski who got onto the
lockout channel and said "green light" to Keogh and Butler
somewhere out there in the dark. The first clue Art Pike
would have that the talking was over would be when the
brains hit the walls.

Keogh's assignment was the taller of the two kids. His
name, according to one of the biker squad guys from the
46th, was Flavio Rodrigues, known as Slide on the street, a
kid with a long and depressing sheet: weapons and assault
charges, sixteen months at Spofford and the Great Adventure before his eighteenth birthday.

Slide was holding a heavy-caliber stainless-steel Smith &
Wesson in his right hand and talking into a telephone held
in his left. In the scope image Keogh could see the heat in
the kid, the wet shine on his bony face and the way the
cords in his neck pulled tight as he screamed into the
phone. His black eyes were large and red-ringed. Now and
then he would be silent for a long while, apparently
listening to the voice of the negotiator. And from somewhere out in the dark Butler would flick on his laser sight
and a disc of ruby-red light the size of a half-dollar would
appear on the boy's plaid shirt, or on his forehead, like a
Hindu mark. The thin red beam would show up in the
smoke of the city, coming from somewhere off to Keogh's
right and down in the street. Butler liked the laser sight.
He liked the psychological effect it had on targets. What he

was doing with it was against the rules, but rules didn't mean a hell of a lot to Pat Butler.

As for the talk that Keogh couldn't hear, he had no real desire to hear it. It would only assign an emotional value to the target in his scope, narrative details that would raise his heart rate and affect the scope picture. It was strange to see the cross hairs pulse in the exact rhythm of his heartbeat. He knew the target's name, and the name of the other boy, Jesus Goncalves. Goncalves was sitting on the floor of the gun shop, just out of Keogh's line of fire, holding a Browning nine-mill on the Toussaint family, speaking soft Spanish obscenities to the two girls. Butler had a line on him. Butler was putting the laser on him as well, and on the wall behind the boy.

What the hell was Butler doing?

The ruby disc went straight up, then down to the right at an angle, up again at an angle to the right. Vertically down two feet. What . . . an "M"?

Keogh grinned and watched the letters forming.

"O"
"T"
"H"
"E"
"R"
"F"

The radio crackled into life. "Echo to Single Six, K?"

Echo was Pulaski. Single Six was Butler.

"Ahh . . . Single Six, K."

Pulaski's voice was tight and hard. "Butler, quit fucking around. They'll see the fucking thing!"

"Come on, boss—these assholes can't spell."

"Just stop jerking around."

"Ahh, that's a roger, boss. You want my advice, boss?"

Pulaski was silent for a while. He was probably listening to Pike and the boys in the Bolsa Chica.

"Yeah, Butler. What's your advice?"

"Sir, me and Frank over there up to his ass in Kibbles 'n Bits, we got both these assholes dead in their Reeboks right now. We could punch their tickets right now, neat and clean—we all go home happy. Whattya say, boss?"

Pulaski thought it over. Keogh put his cross hairs right over the middle of his target's upper lip and let his breath out slowly.

"Negative, Single Six. And try to remember that everything you say is being recorded, hah, Pat? Pike's doing okay. We're gonna give him a chance."

"Fine, boss. Single Six out."

Butler. Typical Butler. A big rangy brush-cut blond about Frank's age, a blunt-faced man with a tobacco-stained gunfighter's moustache and a heavy build running a little to fat. Butler liked the gunfighter look. He had a thing about Pat Garrett, the lawman who shot Billy the Kid. He wore pointy-toed snakeskin cowboy boots and a big Ruger, a single-action .44. The gun was sheer theater and it drove the Department crazy. Still, Pat was a good hand with his M-16 and there was a general feeling in the squad that Butler could use whatever he felt like for a sidearm. In all the years that Keogh and Butler had been working together in various units, Butler had never fired his Ruger in a street fight.

And there was Pike. Things got tangled if you let personalities get into the line of fire. Pike was a good man, a friend of the Keogh family for thirty years, a thin angular man with a face like a Chippewa hatchet and a taste for bagpipe music. He played the Great Highland in the pipe band and kept a neat little bungalow on Staten Island with his wife and three teenage sons, none of whom wanted to be cops.

So Pike was not the kind of man who could easily watch as two boys went down before his eyes in that boneless way they do when the .308 round arrives like God's particular grudge. They go directly to the floor when it hits, not back or up or fighting and spinning, just down to the ground as if suddenly reminded of gravity, feeling the pull of black soil, the sudden silent blow in the chest or head, the spreading icy nerveless tide outward from the entry wound, blunt trauma and hydrostatic shock racing through the water-laden tissues of the body like a tsunami, the synapses crackling like sparks from a fire against the rising darkness of the mind.

Keogh had seen it all, seen the muzzle gases and the recoil of the weapon and the image clouding and jumping, the heat and the flame from the muzzle erasing the scope picture, and there would be only a fragmented series of images, the target going down, tissue and blood still rising in the air, a pink foamy cloud, tissue on a back wall or spread around the floor like a scatter of taillight glass . . . and perhaps that single ruby-red dot the only still point in the room, perfect, round, crystalline, still, the color of new blood.

Days after a clean surgical kill, Frank would feel a stillness in him, a kind of sweet sadness.

Frank never talked about this feeling. He wondered sometimes if Butler went through the same thing. But he never had the nerve to ask him.

"P.B.R. Street Gang. This is Almighty. Come on?"

Butler's voice in his headset. Butler breaking all the rules again. Keogh recognized the lines from *Apocalypse Now*. Butler liked to run strange lines past Frank and see if he could connect them.

"Yeah, this is Street Gang. We're not supposed to be talking."

"Yeah, yeah, Frank. I think this is a sideband. Anyway, fuck 'em. Frank, I got me a dickless tracy up here—she wants to meet you. Say hello to Ruthie." There was some static and whispers. Then a woman's voice.

"Hello, Street Gang. Hello . . . Detective Keogh?"

"Jesus. Use my name in the clear, why don't you? Who's this?"

"Ruthie Boyko. I'm with the Four-Oh. Where are you?"

Christ. "Never mind, honey. Where's Butler?"

"Just a minute. Pat . . ."

"Hey, Street Gang. Don't be such a prick, huh? Listen, you picking up anything from Pike over there?"

"I'm not trying, Pat. Why?"

"Well, it's coming to me that old Art's forgotten who signs his paychecks. I think he's getting emotionally involved with these little shits. Pulaski thinks so too. He's already on to the Zone Commander. You know what the assholes want now? They want somebody from the TV news to go over there, tell her all about how we're fuckin' around with their rights."

"Pickett won't go along with that."

"Maybe. You see how my guy's been keeping low out of the window line?"

Keogh had already noticed that.

"Yeah. I see him over there with the Browning. Slide, he's all over the place, but your man stays put."

"Yeah, he do, don't he. What's his name, Hay-soos? Hay-soos wanted to go take a piss about a half-hour ago. Pike says to him no, he should stay where he was. He should not stand up, is what he says."

Keogh thought that over for a full minute. Pat waited quietly.

"You think Art's Stockholmed?"

"Hey, he's a family man, Frank. He's got kids of his own."

"So. I've got a kid too."

"Yeah, but yours is a pain in the ass. Man, Frank, you oughta listen. It's enough to make you hork. Pike's got Moxie and Pepsi bringing 'em burgers and fries from the White Castle. Only thing is, Hay-soos has the hammer back on that Browning. I can't quite make it, but Arnie is over in the command van and that's what he's saying."

"Has he got it aimed? Has he got a target?"

"Oh, yes. You see the broad with her back to the counter?"

Keogh went back to the scope. Ton-Ton's daughters were side by side near the shattered glass counter. The older one looked about eighteen, dark and pretty in a sky-blue jumper. Her eyes were fixed and hunted, staring at something down and to her right.

"Yeah, I see her. I take it Hay-soos has that Browning on her."

"That's what Arnie says. So I get in anything less than a perfect head shot, he spasms, the piece goes off anyway. She gets it in her baby-blue jumper. We gotta get Pike to move him out, change the picture over there."

"How we gonna do that? We're not even supposed to be listening to this stuff."

"Ruthie here's gonna tell Art that I'm somewhere else. You see the ARCO station over there?"

Keogh could see it, a hard white island in the dim Bronx street.

"Yeah. How's she gonna convince Pike that you're not where you are?"

"Arnie's gonna go over there with the spare laser. He's gonna start dicking around with it, get it onto Hay-soos so that Pike'll see it."

"What? If Pike moves him, we do a bank-shot? We don't tell Pulaski? We just pop the guys?"

Butler's voice was low and soothing, his three A.M. deejay voice.

"Hey, Street Gang. Pulaski wants to see what happens. If Pike moves his guy, for *any* reason, that'll do it."

"Okay, Almighty."

"Hey. Flights of angels, Street Gang. K."

Butler clicked off. The quiet came back in on Frank again, and with it that odd sense of isolation and distance, as comforting to him as the feel of his mahogany stock and the smell of silicon grease.

The scene at the Bolsa Chica hadn't changed. Keogh's target, the kid named Slide, was leaning on the counter with most of his attention on the black phone in his hand. The heavy Smith was in his right hand, inches away from one of the hostages, the muzzle of the weapon level with her left earlobe. Now and then the kid would slide the barrel through the thick glossy black hair at the back of her neck. Butler's target was still in his position down by the window, only his head visible to Keogh. Unless he moved out of there, they were all blocked. There was no point in killing one gunman just so the other one could take out all the hostages.

Keogh's headset was actually a spotter's set. It probably had a channel for the hostage line. He thought about it for a while, watching the scope image. What the hell?

He flicked through six channels. There was a burst of Spanish, a long unlikely curse in a shrill adolescent voice. This was it.

". . . *endejo!* Fuckin *la-jara*. You lissen to what I'm telling you. I'm telling you we been fuckin talking and we don't see no fuckin television pussy coming over here. You got yourself one more minute and then we shoot one of these *negritas* here, you hear me?"

Pike's voice was the classic airline captain's drawl, all patience and serenity and the sweet cadence of reason.

"Son, we have that young lady on the way right now. What you don't want is to do something all of a sudden that will take us all the way back to the get-go again. We have a good understanding here, you and me. I have troubles over here too. I have a lot of people around me who are not thinking good thoughts about you. They don't have your best interests at heart, and you don't want to give them an excuse to step in and screw up what you and I have been working on, do you? Now, you all must be pretty hungry over there. I know I am. I mean, look at the time. It's Friday night, son. You could be at home watching 20/20 right now. Watching Barbara Walters. I personally think Hugh hates her, but what the hell. That's what we should be doing. You said—"

"You fuckin don' tell me what I said. I tellin you those fuckin cops jus started shooting at us—all we doin is trying to buy some stuff, and now we got my friend shot in the back and the only reason those faggots out there ain't shot at us is because we got these people. You get that TV pussy in here, all of the whole city is gonna see how the fuckin NYPD set us up and tried to kill us and all we done so far is justifiable and nothin but self-defense. But you been promising that TV pussy for two hours and so far I don' see *shit*!"

"Well, son . . . it's a matter of you helping me and me helping you. There's been some bad blood on both sides and there isn't anybody who wants there to be any more. . . ."

Only about twelve million people, thought Keogh. By now this hostage was national, out on all the up-links. People would be sitting in their rec rooms sucking back the brews and saying, yeah, yeah, shoot the fuckers.

". . . So the way it is," Pike went on, "is that you give us some help with Mr. Toussaint there, and then in comes your TV crew and everybody. But how's it gonna look, one of your . . . one of the people in your care in front of the cameras, lying on the floor? Bleeding. His hands are tied. That's not going to be too good for your image, is it, son?"

Image. Well, that was something the kid could connect with. Even the most zoned-out maggot in the South Bronx could relate to image.

In his scope picture, as if he were floating just outside the barred window of the gun store about twenty feet in the air, Keogh could see the effect the word *image* had on the boy. He stopped shifting from foot to foot and focused on some point in the middle distance, his face clearing and smoothing out as he left the irreducible now and drifted into dreams.

Keogh could see the dream shaped in sweat on the boy's wolfish face. Donahue. Winfrey. Cameras. The whole 1,500-watt benediction of white light and there he is in the magic center square saying, well, you know, Phil, we was just out shopping and these cops, man, they start shooting and well, you know the ress is jus like the movie where my part is played by Emilio Estevez and we good buddies now, we go to the Copa and all. . . .

A red disc was crawling up Slide's shirt, two inches from his throat. Arnie Sayles and his spare laser, down there at the ARCO station. Keogh watched the thin red beam as it swept across Third. Slide was still dreaming about being in

the spotlight, and here it was, all coming true. Only in
America, thought Keogh, smiling in the dark and leaning
into his Remington. Now let's see if Pike moves anybody.

Keogh switched back to his tactical line. Pulaski was
already on it.

"Archangel, K? Frank, what the hell are you doing?"

Shit, thought Frank. Pulaski. Pissed.

"Ah, I read you five by five, Echo."

"Where the hell were you?"

Keogh jiggled the headset and rubbed the mike. "Don't
(CRACKLE-HISS) catching all the (RUMBLE-POP) possible trouble with this head (CRAACK-POP) but am reading
you now, boss, K?"

"Horse shit, Frank. If you been listening, you know we
might have a little problem here with Pike. Just stay on
your man, because you could get a green at any time, K?"

"Ten-Four, Echo."

Pulaski switched off.

The beam was still moving. Arnie Sayles had got it off
Keogh's target and now the point of red light was sliding
across the gun shop to where Jesus Goncalves was sitting
just out of the line of fire. All that counted now was a
change in his position. Keogh had Slide covered, had his
cross hairs on Slide's upper lip. If Pike saw the laser and
decided that he had to move Goncalves, then Pike was
Stockholmed and there would be nothing left to do but
cancel two tickets. Pike would get a year on a rubber gun
squad, where he could work on remembering who he was
and what his actual responsibilities were.

Well, hell, thought Keogh. Who doesn't get it wrong
sometimes? Keogh had been in the NYPD since 1969, and
most days he could hardly tell the good guys without a CAT
scan.

Arnie's touch with that laser sight was positively surgical.
It floated and flickered down the walls of the gun shop like
Tinkerbell looking for Peter Pan. Finally Sayles got it
settled into Hay-soos' hairline, where it nestled into the
blue-black waves an inch above his right eye.

Slide was still on the phone to Pike. He hadn't seen the laser moving. But somebody must have seen it.

Slide stopped talking and bent his head over the phone. You could see him listening. Then he looked up at Goncalves. Arnie must have seen it, because he shut the beam off. Slide blinked, as if he had seen or imagined that he had seen something strange in his friend's hair. Then he waved to Goncalves. Keogh could see what was going on from across the street. Pike was asking to talk to Hay-soos. Pike was asking. Pike.

Pike was moving the target.

Pike. You poor dumb bastard.

Now Keogh began to pay the freight for listening to the negotiations. The boy in his sights had a voice and a name and even that flash of avarice, that adolescent flush when he began to see himself as someone with a future, as someone with an image. All of this rushed in on Keogh and he felt his blood begin to race in his jugular and his cross hairs began to jump.

Pulse.

Pulse. Pulse.

Pulse pulse pulse . . .

The target—Slide, the boy—the target was moving. He was moving away as Jesus took the phone. Jesus had the Browning and he was out now where Keogh could see the black bulk of the weapon with its hammer back and the muzzle now pointing at the floor as Jesus came across, actually pointing at his own right foot. Then Slide was crossing in front of Jesus, his head turning, looking back at Jesus, perhaps feeling that the silver thread connecting him to glory, to Oprah and Phil and Geraldo and nights out with Emilio, all of it was down that wire, and then Jesus was on the phone.

Jesus said something to Slide. Slide looked at Jesus. Arnie had put the laser back on, and now a red disc was sitting on Jesus, on his upper lip. It twisted as Jesus turned to look back at Slide. Slide's hand came up, pointing. He was shouting something.

Jesus started to bring his Browning up.

Keogh's headset crackled. "Green light, Frank. Green light."

And now Keogh went up on those great wings of breathing, floating like a falcon outside the window of the Bolsa Chica, out in the blue silence of the moment, up into that cold blue space where the actual killing got done, where Keogh could watch the streets and the blocks and the borough itself receding into grids and rectangles and chains of lights and everything was perfectly . . .

The Browning was the problem.

. . . circular . . .

Jesus knows. Jesus has felt the laser on him. He knows.

. . . like a full moon . . .

The Browning—the muzzle of the Browning was moving toward Ton-Ton's daughters, in an arc. Jesus' face was closing up, his shoulder and his right arm bracing and stiffening, the muzzle coming up. . . .

Keogh's target did not know. Not yet.

But Jesus knew. He knew everything.

Bank shot.

Keogh moved the Remington. The luminous disc of the scope blurred and danced, a streaking light, and then there was Jesus in his sights, Jesus with his Browning coming up and his arm bracing, his muscles tightening, aiming at the back of a girl's head. Keogh watched his cross hairs slither up the boy's torso.

A puff, a breath, a jet of pink foam exploded out of Jesus' forearm, midway between his wrist and his elbow. Jesus' arm began to shatter.

Keogh's thumb and fingers were locked around the stock, the weapon carried on bone, his breathing like a sweep of wings. He fired.

The weapon rode back into his shoulder, hard and solid. Jesus was still trying to get the Browning to fire, not knowing that his arm was gone, not yet getting that message from his nerves.

Keogh's .308 round took him in the soft channel under

his nose, in the place where a mother might have touched him to say hush, sleep now. It hit him with 2,200 foot-pounds of energy. It went through his skull at 2,600 feet per second. It came out the back of his neck in a meaty red ball, a spray of pink foam.

The Browning was in the air, spinning—Jesus' hand and three inches of wrist still attached—then falling, bringing the shattered arm over in a red arc. In Jesus' mind the synapses would be flaring and arcing, blue sparks in the gray cloudiness of his brain. *Fire I'm firing. Fire.* He went down to his knees and fell forward onto the grimy tiles, his eyes wide, seeing wonders.

Keogh was already moving the rifle, trying to find Slide. He wasn't there.

Keogh felt a burst of fear. His scope wavered. There was a flutter of hand in the circular image. Keogh followed it down.

Slide was falling, the Smith floating out in front of his chest, drifting away from him as he fell. He was still looking at the empty air where Jesus had been standing, where Jesus had been trying to bring up his weapon. As Keogh watched, another round hit Slide in the soft part of his throat. It passed through without changing his fall. Slide went down below the window line and Keogh lost him. There was nothing in his scope but a section of dirty linoleum tile, the toe of a woman's shoe, and a perfect ruby-red oval in the center of the circle.

Keogh held the image for ten seconds. And then he straightened up in the chair and pulled the Remington off the chair back and set it down on the floor beside him.

Bank shot, Butler had said. Butler took out Keogh's man. Keogh took out Butler's man.

Five people had died on Third Avenue in the South Bronx on this soft summer evening. Various people had various reactions. Most of the eastern seaboard got the news. There was good up-link feed of crowds, of RMPs and ambulances. There was even a long shot of Frank Keogh in his blue pin-striped suit, rumpled and ruddy and looking—if he had known it—very much like his father. He was carrying his Remington down the stairs of a store with a sign on it that read PRETTY KITTY PET SHOP.

A lot of people saw that image on television, people all over the East. Some of them were friends of the Keogh family, or men who knew Frank, or people who had known his father back in the old days.

Up in Albany, in a blue room smelling of wintergreen, a man watched Keogh come down the stairs on the eleven o'clock news. He watched it again on the CNN newsbreak at one in the morning. Then he picked it up again on the news final off the Albany station, and by that time he had his VCR set up to tape it. He taped the whole thing and then he took the cassette out and held it in his hands and thought about the Keogh family for a long time while the anthem played and armies marched and wheatfields waved, and he was still watching the screen when the picture snapped off and the screen was full of white flarings and black fire from the burning of suns a universe away.

CHAPTER 2

Saturday, August 18
1130 hours
Lawton, Oklahoma

As soon as he turned around and saw that trooper strolling in through the door, Sonny knew he and Lucas should never have brought Lyle into it. Lyle was family, for one thing, and it split a man's concentration to have family around when guns were going off. Also, Lyle had a tendency to talk down to people, even to Sonny, who may have been younger but who was a hell of a lot bigger. Lyle would say things like: They had no right to shoot someone just because the man didn't want to let go of something they were trying to steal.

Sonny would let out a long breath and wait a bit and then he'd say—looking into Lyle, as if by the force of the looking he could get some part of this man back into the world— Lyle, we got the weapons and the guy doesn't, so while that may not be right, it sure as hell is something the guy has to consider, and if he considers that somebody's property is more important than his life, then the guy is out of touch with what's real and it could be argued that he ought to get shot just for being so damn contrary and bloody-minded. Lucas Poole would just sigh and drink his beer.

But Lyle would just stare out into the middle distance, as if he could see things Sonny couldn't, and say: Well,

24

drawing down on a man didn't have anything to do with rights, and Sonny's argument was tautological and anyway robbery was more of a privilege, like drinking single-malt or being born in Charleston.

The whole debate bothered Sonny, because he wasn't the kind of man who liked to shoot people either. He would if he had to, if somebody was shooting at him, or if a little surgical gunfire could increase the overall level of cooperation in a payroll office or some such. Sonny had hoped the issue wouldn't come up in this particular operation, but of course it did as soon as that trooper went all slitty-eyed and started digging down into his holster for a sidearm the size of a Sunday pot roast. Cracker farmboy, the poor bastard—Oklahoma being your mainly agricultural state—and of course there he was, old Lyle the Philosopher, having his metaphysics put to the question, standing there in the middle of the First Commercial Bank on Cash Street with farmers and office clerks lying every which way on the floor, and Lyle holding this big black German assault rifle called an HK-91, the kind of piece that looks like you could stitch your name into the belly of a full moon with it, but Lyle was just standing there holding it like it was something you got for opening a savings account, his suntan disappearing into his shirt collar and spent .308 casings lying around his feet like peanut shells.

Fortunately for Lyle's spiritual growth, Lucas Poole, the back-up man, stepped around from behind the vault door and regretfully blew the trooper out of his snakeskin cowboy boots, and a couple of minutes later they were flying down Six Killer Road in a powder-blue Chevy pickup.

Eufemio Broca was at the wheel, a Tex-Mex half-breed with a poorly developed sense of self-preservation, and Lyle Beauchamp crouched down on the passenger seat thinking about those two weasel-slim lawyers back in Charleston who'd slipped his used-car dealership right out from under him, which was how he had gotten into this situation. In back was Sonny and next to him Lucas Poole, down on their bellies in the flatbed, peeking out now and then over the tailgate at ten miles of two-lane blacktop toward Lawton, Oklahoma, with the road as shiny as a lizard-skin belt under that blue-white Oklahoma sun and the hammered-flat red dust farmlands stretching away all around.

Lucas Poole was a friend of the Beauchamp family going all the way back to their Charleston days, a big, black, slab-sided man with eyes that turned down and some gray in his short cut, forty-two now, old for a professional in his field. Sonny was waiting for Poole to say something about Lyle. After they had figured out they were pretty much alone on Six Killer Road, Poole leaned across toward Sonny to say a couple of things on that topic over the wind rush and the howl of the truck tires on the blacktop.

"A full clip of three-oh-eight, Sonny. Took him a full clip to shoot out the camera back there. Man, I got to ask you, why's he here? He has money problems, you lend him some. Lyle's not suited to this kind of work."

Sonny looked past Poole's shoulder. Was that a road over there, across the field? Looked like it could be a road, next to a line of sagebrush about a hundred yards off to their right.

Sonny knew Poole was right about Lyle. Back in Lawton, Lyle's only job was to take out a video camera with his Heckler & Koch. It was a job that Lyle had lobbied for and gotten. He had practiced with the thing out in the back country north of Lawton. It should have been a simple job.

But Lyle had emptied a full magazine in three-round bursts, hitting the camera on the last round. At less than thirty feet. Man. Somewhere there was a videotape that would give the FBI a good laugh, Lyle shooting away, with his piece jumping around in his hands like a pike he couldn't get into the boat. Sonny looked over to the rear window of the pickup. Lyle was staring back at him, his mouth and his eyes doing disconnected things, his pink skin going red as he watched Poole and Sonny talk, guessing the issue, his thin blond hair slicked back with Dippity-Do.

"Lucas . . . I give you my word: Next time, he's in the car or something."

Poole's face got more creased.

"Sonny. You don't need this boy diddy-bopping around in our lives. He's no help to anybody and he's just embarrassing himself. You're not helping this man here. You're just going to make him think he's an even—"

Poole's face went through a couple of changes and his skin went from black coffee to coffee and cream. A small red poppy-flower appeared on the front of his white polo shirt, an inch to the left of the little alligator. There never was the sound of a shot, Sonny was sure of that. Poole came forward into Sonny's arms. Across the flatbed there was a ragged round hole in the steel sidewall. Far across the field on their right, a white car was racing parallel to them, sunlight glinting off something. Then the passenger window blew in, spraying Lyle and Eufemio with bits of glass, and Sonny saw a puff of smoke coming from the white car.

That's shooting, thought Sonny, dragging Poole toward the front of the truck. A hundred yards if it's forty, and a moving target. Poole was on his face now in the dusty bed of the pickup, his big hands caught under his belly, looking up at Sonny with one clear brown eye, a little blood running like syrup from the side of his mouth. Eufemio Broca turned to look at Sonny through the rear window. His thin Indian face was tight and hard but he was calm. He was saying something, but the wind was making too much noise. Sonny crawled over to the window just as another hole appeared in the side of the truck with a sound like somebody hitting a garbage can with a ten-pound sledge. Lyle ducked down into the passenger footwell, leaving nothing between Broca and that sharpshooter in the chase car but dusty air. Poole was still looking up at Sonny, his teeth red with blood, his lips moving. Broca reached down between his legs and brought up a massive Smith & Wesson revolver, aiming it out the side window over Lyle's hunched back. An impossible shot, thought Sonny, but full marks for balls.

There was another lick of red flame from the far side of the field, and the rear window exploded out in a web of glass powder and tiny rainbows. A second later Broca's Smith went off with a solid bass boom, driving his shoulder back.

Broca put out three more rounds, not hurrying, using his right thumb to cock the piece, getting his sight picture lined up. Squeezing it off. Each time the Smith fired, dust would jump off the dashboard and the roof of the cab. Finally, Sonny remembered the Heckler rifle down behind the front seat and he got up on his knees to fish for it in the well, scraping his forearm on shards of glass in the window frame. He saw two more puffs of flame out of the corner of his eye and all the nerves along his right side tightened up. The chase car was matching speed with them to give the shooter a steady target. A hole appeared in the passenger door and a shred of blue denim flew off Broca's right shoulder.

He shook his head a little and squeezed off two more rounds. Sonny scuttled back to the rear of the truck, dragging the assault rifle and the canvas bag full of magazines.

Poole levered himself up on his left elbow, his eyes half closed, his hard black face looking gray and wet. One hand came up, away from the wound, five fingers spread, the red stain shining against the pink palm.

The gesture made Sonny smile. Five bucks he couldn't make the shot. He grinned at Poole and slammed the magazine home.

There it was. A patch of white paint about the size of his thumb, a good hundred yards off to the right, racing along a dusty side road, matching their speed. Something tan-colored was sticking up on the far side of the chase car. The guy was probably sitting up on the passenger window ledge, his leg wrapped in the safety belt, his gun sling twisted around his left forearm, using the roof to steady his shooting. Another flicker of red from the tan smudge, and another sledgehammer strike somewhere up front. Maybe a lever-action Winchester.

Sonny got up into a crouch, taking the swing and jolt of the road in his knees, bringing the Heckler up to his cheek, getting the sight picture. He set the butt hard into his shoulder and let out a slow breath, trying to get it right. Broca had stopped shooting and was busy keeping the truck on a solid line. For Sonny, the world got very silent. It narrowed down to a red spike in a black iron channel and a blurred tan patch. Slow. Squeeze.

He fired. In three-round bursts. The white patch disappeared in a haze of muzzle gases and flame. The rifle kicked a little. Four more bursts. He rolled away to the front of the flatbed, braced to take return fire. He could see the white patch waver. It slowed, jumped some obstruction, flew into the air. Dust hid the rest.

Broca hit the accelerator hard. Nobody else did anything for a minute. Sonny lay on his back in the truck bed and watched a bank of high clouds wheel into the east. Poole lay down again and closed his eyes. Lyle pulled himself up into the passenger seat and looked down at his brother. Sonny's shaggy blond cowhand moustache was white with road dust, his blue eyes rimmed in red. Sonny smiled back at Lyle and pulled himself to the window.

"Eufemio, you can get to the Red by going through the Double Dee at Devol. We have to get under some trees—there's a chopper at Fort Sill and they'll have it up by now."

He could feel Lyle's silent reproach but he ignored it.

"Lyle, you turn around and watch for the side road. It'll be nothing but a cut in the brush, so look sharp."

Lyle waited a bit, establishing his independence with a sullen twist in his lower lip. Then he turned away and stared off up the road. Sonny resisted the temptation to smack him in the side of the head.

Broca got them to the banks of the Red River. Off to the west the sun was huge and red. The cottonwoods by the river had shadows a half-mile long. They put the truck under a stand of cottonwoods and carried Poole down to the riverbank, where he could see across into Texas. Dry grass lined the banks. They stripped off Poole's shirt and laid him down on his back in the cool mud.

Lyle stood back about thirty feet, up at the top of the slope, turning away and facing east. He had his hands stuck into his pockets so hard they jerked at his suspenders.

Sonny knelt down and looked at the hole in Poole's chest. It was ragged and full of old blood. It looked like a well dug in black earth. When Poole let out a breath, the wound bubbled and sucked like a mouth. Over Poole's head, Broca was looking grimly down at Sonny.

Sonny had taken a war-surplus field dressing out of the truck. He stripped it out of the net wrap and sprinkled sulfa powder into the wound. Then he pressed the thick cotton pad over the wound and Poole moved his hand to hold it down. He never opened his eyes. Sonny stood up and moved away toward Lyle.

Lyle didn't turn around, but he knew Sonny was coming up. He spoke when Sonny was close enough.

"Well, we're into it now, right, Sonny?"

"You could say. You all right, Lyle?"

"I feel a little sick. I could throw up but I don't have anything in my gut."

"That's natural—it'll pass." Sonny wasn't sure how to ask what he had to ask. He waited for a long moment. A slow wind stirred in the wild flowers at their feet. From the top of the slope they could see ten miles of prairie rolling away under a blue velvet sky. The air smelled of river mud and sweat and gasoline, but under it there was something cold and clear.

"How's Poole?" asked Lyle.

Sonny shrugged. Lyle felt the movement in the gathering dark.

"Well, I guess I'm into it now, little brother. You got me fucked up real good there. Poole killing that trooper and all—"

Sonny felt the anger and tried to ride it.

"Lyle . . . as far's the law's concerned, we all of us shot that poor son of a bitch. And you ought to think about where you'd be right now if Lucas hadn't done what he did. You'd be on your back in a tin bunk with nothing on but a toe tag and a shocked expression. Well . . . The question now is that I gotta know what you're planning to do from here."

Lyle turned to face Sonny. The setting sun shone on his face so that there was a hot yellow spark in his left eye but his right eye was black and empty, as if his brother were half skull.

"Ah, shit, kid. I know what a pain in the ass I've been. I know it was me who fucked up in Lawton." A wetness came into the eye with the yellow spark, making it glitter like a tiger's eye. Sonny felt a rush of affection and love for this puzzling man.

Lyle shook his head and laughed. "Sonny . . . I don't know what it is with me. I'm just trying to get in step with the planet, you know. But I keep getting the wrong song. The song wrong? I guess I'm gonna go the distance with you, if I'm still welcome. I mean, with you, well, there's always a chance we can work this shit out, right? Sonny?"

Sonny felt the weight again, the weight of Lyle's hapless trust and his vulnerable bravado and the years they had seen come up and go down like a stand of winter wheat.

Sonny tapped Lyle on his puffy cheek.

"Yeah, big brother. We'll ride this out. Frank and Jesse Beauchamp, right? You relax here. I gotta go see to Lucas."

Lyle nodded, and as Sonny went scuttling down the slope Lyle turned back into the east, as if he were trying to see all the way to the Carolinas.

"That's a through-and-through, Lucas," Sonny announced, down on his knees at the riverbank, looking into Poole's gray face. Poole inhaled slowly, testing.

"You're a lying hound, Sonny. I can hear my own air hissing around. I got a sucking chest wound. Don't talk down to me."

"Hey, you just got a hole in you, neat as a cat's asshole. Got your ticket punched there, Lucas."

Broca was standing behind Poole with the Smith in his right hand, staring hard at the back of Poole's head.

Sonny slapped Poole on the leg.

"Long way from Charleston, Lucas. Now, we can do a couple of things here. Eufemio can wait till full dark, take the truck into Burkburnett. He's got some relatives there. He says we can stay with them a while, couple of weeks. Let the hounds run by. Get you healed up. His uncle's a vet, used to working with animals like you. I've been through the bags. We got close to a hundred eighty thousand there, some bearer bonds, cash from the grain pool and the cattle auction yesterday. I say we cut Eufemio in for a full quarter. He's been a good hand. You got any problem with that, Lucas?"

Poole grinned at Sonny.

"That greaser stands there behind me with that hogleg cannon in his tiny little fist and you think I'm gonna dicker with him? No. He's in for a quarter and welcome to it. Now, Lyle I got a problem with."

Sonny's smile dropped a couple of degrees.

"Lyle's a Beauchamp. He was in from the start. He got us into the accountant's office in Duncan. He drew the map of the bank in Lawton. And he did take out that camera."

Poole snorted and winced. "Eventually."

Sonny put his head down, sighed, and looked past Poole to Broca.

"Well, he did take it out. You gotta admit, him standing there pumping away with that piece, it gave the customers something to think about. Anyway, we agreed up front to put him down for a full share. Job cost is sixteen thousand, plus I say we give another five to Eufemio's family for putting us up. Leaves us maybe forty thousand each. Now . . . Lucas . . . we got to ask you a hard question."

Sonny was silent for a long breath. The river beside them ran broad and brown and deep under the violet sky. A soft wind played in the cottonwood leaves. Poole's eyes softened. He looked up at Sonny's face and seemed to wait quietly.

Finally, Sonny spoke.

"Well . . . you got yourself a tricky wound there. It could go green on you. Eufemio's uncle is a vet but there could be . . . It could come to it that you gotta go to a county hospital. We don't know any tame docs around here. Some intern is sure to file on you. Now you know how pissed the local mounties are gonna be with us. They'll be all over Tillman County, Comanche County, Cotton County, and north Texas, all pumped up with themselves and looking for some dog to kick. They catch you, you being a gentleman of color, well, they might be pretty bad-tempered with you. Give you a very bad time in some roadside toolshed. It happens. You remember what the Wisconsin troopers did to Charlie Delaney?"

Poole's face shut down.

"You leave me with a weapon. They can take their chances. I'm not going in again. Not now. Not later."

"You know, I figured you'd feel that way. But it could be, you're not up to holding a weapon. It could be they'd get you while you had other things on your mind. You say you can take your chances with Eufemio's uncle . . ."

Poole smiled at Sonny. "Or . . . I could stay here."

"Yeah. By the river."

Poole was quiet for some time.

"It's a pretty spot, Sonny."

Broca was right behind Poole, the Smith raised a little.

"Got to rest somewhere, sooner or later, Lucas."

"Yeah . . . all God's chillun."

Two minutes passed. Lyle was watching them from the top of the riverbank.

Finally, Poole shook his head.

"I'll tell you something, kid. No way I'm bailing out before I see Charleston again. Anyway, these cracker sons-a-bitches, they'd let their hounds dig me up and chew on me. I'll take my chances with the Frito Bandito and his *tio* . . . but you promise me one thing, Sonny."

Broca walked away and sat down under the trees.

"Yeah, Lucas?"

"We don't do any more work around here. Let's go north somewhere, back to civilization."

"Anywhere in particular?"

"Don't you know somebody in New York? Who was that guy, was in your block at Santa Fe? The Jew?"

"Myron Geltmann. He's gone north. Got a job with his son-in-law. Industrial maintenance work. Strictly up-and-up, Lucas."

Poole's red grin was sly and slow.

"Industrial maintenance. Gets into a lot of buildings, does he? I'll bet you my left testicle Geltmann's been taking notes, has an easy three hits all lined up, just waiting for an enterprising bunch of guys to come along. Come on, Sonny . . ."

Sonny thought about it. Poole was probably right. Geltmann had spent a life in and out of prison, setting up jobs for other men to do, taking his share in foreign banks. He was an old man now and not likely to take well to working for his daughter's husband.

Poole said, "I hear those New York cops can't shoot for shit, either."

Sonny looked up the bank at Lyle.

"We'd have to take him, Lucas."

Poole groaned. "Why the fuck would we want to do that?"

"He's a television star now. How long do you think Lyle would hold out with the *federales*? They'd hook him up to Ma Balls and crank out your mother's name and the home phone of every guy ever gave us a drink of water from Arkansas to the Canadian border. Lyle comes with us."

Poole looked at Sonny. Sonny stood up.

"Sonny, you should never have brought Lyle into this."

"Yeah," said Sonny, smiling to himself, his face hidden in the darkness. "I was just thinking that a while ago."

Sonny looked up the riverbank where Lyle was standing with his hands in his pockets and looking out across the Red into Texas, his head cocked to one side, as if Lyle could hear something in the wind and the water that Sonny could never hear.

For a moment Sonny's chest was full of a strange hollow fire and he could smell a salt sea and feel the spray and there was that old spice-ridden rot-scented wind from the breakwater and the sweet scent of the marshes, and in his mind the amber sun shone on the spires and roofs of Charleston in the late afternoon and there were lamps along the boardwalk and there were casement windows full of a warm yellow light and music came across the bay like goldfish rising in a pool.

Lucas was breathing hard.

"Yeah, Lucas. Maybe we'll go to New York. They've got an ocean there, don't they? I'd like to see the ocean again."

CHAPTER 3

Tuesday, August 21
1500 hours
New York City

There was a slow rain coming down the day they gave Laputa and Paznakaitis the Honors. Keogh and Butler were in harness for the first time since the last cop funeral. They were sitting in one of the Charlie Unit cars, a dark-blue Plymouth Fury. Keogh had a thing for dark blue, and this squad car was one of the last of the '83 Police 440 Interceptors, really a traffic car, but Pulaski owed Keogh for a couple of collars Keogh had given Pulaski's nephew, so when the car came through from Motor Pool, Keogh called in the favor.

The rankers and the pipe band guys were standing around outside the church. It was still hot and the air was like sea water. Butler had the passenger window rolled down and he was waving his hand back and forth in the air. Then he'd bring it in and show Frank how the damp had made the blond hairs on his wrist wet where it stuck out of the sleeve of his blue dress jacket. Out on the steps of the church perhaps a thousand cops from the NYPD, from Yonkers and State and all over the East were standing around smoking cigarettes and saying hello to people they hadn't seen since they'd buried a Bronx detective a couple of years back. For cops, it felt kind of like a racket, sad but solid-feeling, with the brothers all around and that slow rain.

Keogh was still in that guilty euphoria he always felt after a shooting. He felt bad for Paznakaitis and worse for the female cop who had died behind the wheel of her squad car, never even getting a shot off, just calling in a Ten-Thirteen when that Marielito had turned the muzzle around on her. Keogh had dreamed a little about it on the night it had happened, tossing and rolling in his wife's brass bed in their house up on City Island.

Butler and Keogh were supposed to be out on the sidewalk with the rest of the boys, but sometimes they made the other cops nervous. There was a kind of distance in the job that the ordinary patrol cops felt even if they couldn't describe it. Snipers. Enough of the harness guys had seen some hard-corps duty in Vietnam, and even now they found it difficult to be friendly to snipers. Keogh and Butler were names in the Department, and being a name was not always a good thing. There were a lot of cliques and jealousies in the NYPD. Everybody wanted to get onto Citywide Emergency Services. Outsiders saw it as a glory detail.

Keogh was quiet for a long time, content to watch the crowds and looking forward in a passive way to the ride out to Cypress Hills and the moment when the pipe major would play "Lord Lovat's Lament" and the Marine Hymn and, finally, "The Last Post." The music would drift over the fresh-turned earth on a hillside slick with mist, the smell of cut earth and grasses, the jingle and stamp of horses and the murmur of talk from the long blue ranks, over the flag rolling in the breeze like a sail for Paznakaitis, the sailor going to sea. Butler waited a while, watching the rain on the windshield and the blurred figures. He was at heart a happy man and it was against his nature to settle into the kind of Irish melancholy that Keogh drifted into after a killing. After a few minutes he pulled a silver flask out of his tunic and unscrewed the cap.

Keogh watched him take a long pull, the liquid running

into Butler's thick blond moustache, his unshaven throat working as the liquor went down. Butler finished with a long sigh and handed the flask over to Keogh, who took it without turning his head and swallowed a long draft. When he put it down, Keogh's eyes were running.

"Jesus, Pat. That stuff is awful."

Butler looked a little hurt.

"Well, maybe it is. But it's good too."

"So why're we drinking it?"

Butler thought about it while he had another long pull. "Maybe it's bad in a true way."

Now Keogh turned to look at Butler, his one blue eye very blue and his green eye as green as new grass.

"It's bad in a true way? Pat, what the fuck does that mean? What the fuck is that?"

Butler tried to look at Keogh in the way his priest looked at him when Pat told him he was still screwing around on his wife. Butler liked his wife, but that wasn't the point. Life was short—that was the point.

"Frank, I gotta say this: Your language skills are really deteriorating. Fuck this and fuck that. It's not dignified. It's not a good example to set for your youthful partner here. You're polluting my mind."

Butler was one year younger than Frank Keogh.

"You're not answering the question. You're also bogarting that bottle."

"Hah! Tastes like shit and such small portions, too—is that it? I'm saying that Cuervo Gold is bad in a true way, a way that's true, you follow?"

Keogh took the flask.

"No, I don't follow."

Butler gave him a look full of compassion and condescension. "You know, I try and I try and you never seem to learn a damn thing. How many years have we been partners, Frank? Including ESU, and forget the part where you got me stuffed into Communications for a year."

Butler watched Keogh work it out as a squad car from Midtown North went whooping by with the rack flashing, a couple of black-gloved cops staring out the sidescreen at the church where Paznakaitis and Laputa were being cut adrift.

"Technically, you weren't my partner in Bronx Vice. I was working strictly with Pulaski then—"

"Hah! Nobody works 'with' Pulaski. We were *all* working *for* that son of a bitch, and anyway, why you hanging me up on 'technically,' you prick?"

Keogh laughed. "You told me my language skills were deteriorating. I was trying to be accurate. Okay, so we've been 'associates' for, say, three years in Bronx Vice—"

"Plus we worked together on the Lazado thing—"

"Shit, Pat, *everybody* on the job did the Lazado thing. And now we're, what? Two years in this job?"

"Yeah, more like three. Plus one year you worked Citywide Armed Robbery while I was UC with the Joint Task Force over on Fifty-seventh."

"What the hell *were* you doing there, anyway?"

Butler gave Keogh a long smug look over his ragged yellow moustache. "Can't tell you that, buddy. Sorry, but I just can't go telling any hairbag who has a thing for undercover work. So we're looking at all-told maybe six years you and me have been side by each in this rat's-ass city, right?"

"Yeah, so . . . ?"

"So . . . you ever screw around on Tricia?"

Tricia was Patricia Corliss-Keogh, an O.R. nurse who worked at Bellevue. Tricia was a sore point for Keogh. She was working shifts and he was working thirty-six-hour on-calls and they had a thirteen-year-old kid named Robbie, who . . . No, damn it, he was fourteen now. Well, thought Keogh, that's the whole thing right there. They were goddammed strangers rooming in a bungalow up on City Island. Keogh couldn't remember when it had stopped bothering him, the way you can't hear a machine until it stops.

Keogh hesitated. "No. Not once."

Butler looked sideways over at his partner.

"You're lying to me, right?"

"Maybe."

Butler slammed his fist into the padded dash of the squad car. A glow-in-the-dark statue of the Virgin Mary flew into the air. Keogh caught it in his right hand.

"But I *knew* you were lying, right?"

"*If* I'm lying, then yes, you knew I was lying."

Butler waved that away. "So . . . it's bad that you lie to me, because you and me, we've been through the program and we ought not to be lying to each other, but—now get this, Frank, because it's gonna be on the final exam—it's *good* that you've got somebody like me to tell these lies to who knows you're lying and you know he knows you're lying so your lie is really the *truth*. You follow?"

Keogh did follow. The fact that he did follow was another thing that was worrying him. "Yeah. So . . . ?"

"So! That's how something can be bad in a true way, like Jose Cuervo Gold tequila is bad, only it's bad in a way nothing else is bad. In a way nobody else could mistake for something that's just fucked up, or done badly, or faked out, or just not a true thing, a thing that would be true even if all the lying sons of bitches in the world said, hey, man, no, that's not the way it was. It's bad in a true way, like you are, Frank. You're the genuine article."

There was something in Pat's voice that was different. Whatever it was, Keogh wasn't up to it. One thing you can count on, thinking deep thoughts can only lead you downhill. He tried to look at Butler as if he could give him cancer if he got it right. Butler was used to that look.

"Pat, you've been into the Hemingway again."

Butler looked hurt. "Don't you start into me about that again, Frank. Ernie's my role model."

"Pat. Pat Pat Pat. Ernie ate his twelve-gauge. What kind of role model is that?"

Butler thought about it for so long that Keogh was beginning to think Butler wasn't going to answer. He rolled down his window and the noises of New York came into the car like an aural tide, the low roar of the traffic and the permanent murmur of wind and rain and tires, the sound of people walking by on the sidewalks, the distant rising call of a siren. Across the street the big pipe major was working up his Great Highland bagpipe. Keogh could hear the first atonal flats and wheezes from the instrument. How could something so ridiculous have the power to cut through your heart like a hot wire?

Finally, Butler said, "How old are you, Frank? Forty-one? Forty-two?"

"Forty-two."

"And how old was Ernie when he bailed out?"

"What is this, *Jeopardy*? Wait, Robbie's had him in English . . . Nineteen sixty-one, I think it was . . . Ketchum, Idaho. Ernie was sixty-two or something. Poor bastard."

"Poor bastard nothing. He was a hell of a writer. Just that the job got to him. He was . . . He had no shell left. He was nothing but an egg without a shell anymore."

"Yeah. We going somewhere with this?"

Butler sighed and looked across the street at the church. There was a pale-yellow sheen on the west wall of the church, a shaft of misty sunlight through the clouds. People were coming out of the doors, and the rankers were forming up again. The pipe major had the bag under his left arm, the bellows full, his heavy bearskin angled, the chin strap tight into his chin. Behind him two drummers rumbled into a muffled roll that carried across the avenue and echoed off the walls and windows. The high hysteric skirl of "Over the Sea to Skye" rose into a low gray sky. A sergeant called the cadence. Out in front a long black hearse floated at the curb, a twist of fumes like lace fluttering from the tailpipe. Now the doors were full of blue and black and gold. A heavy wooden casket was carried out of the doors, followed by another, like trees borne downriver in a flood. Bright bursts of flowers rode the flag on each casket. The faces of the pallbearers were pale blurs. Each of their badges was wrapped in a thin black ribbon. They came slowly down the worn stone steps into the gray light of the afternoon.

Butler pulled on the flask. "What's the point? I don't

know. I'm seeing this kid, Ruthie Boyko. She's the one was at the shooting. The PW? She says the thing you gotta do is talk this stuff out. Like it boils over if you don't. She talks all the time to that stress counselor?"

"Owens."

"Yeah. They got stress classes in the Academy now too. Ruthie says it keeps her from going crazy. She thinks Pike oughta go see him. If he had, maybe Pike wouldn't have screwed up last week."

"You think when you shoot, Pat?"

"What . . . no. Can't do that."

"You ever feel . . . good? After it?"

Butler looked across at Keogh. "You know, the thing is, it's like with Ernie. We're only in the forties. We gotta be careful. It's early days for both of us. That's the point. We gotta watch ourselves. That's all."

They rolled out onto the Williamsburg Bridge, a mile of cop cars and black Fords, the light changing as they came down into the dense streets of Brooklyn. The cortege rolled along Broadway under the weight of the rusted El, past the shops and the empty lots, the red brick and twisted wooden frame homes, up onto Myrtle, into Queens and the cemetery at Cypress Hills.

Keogh and Butler stood at attention with the rest of Charlie Unit and the members of the 40th Precinct while the piper played "Amazing Grace." Troopers fired their M-14's into the air. A pile of raw earth was covered with a sheet of plastic grass. Typical, thought Keogh. Nobody wants to see things the way they are. So where was Art Pike? The thought came to the surface and he looked around at the cops, the women, at the press of media people whose hands were busy with cameras, the chatter and the occasional flare of lights, but Pike wasn't around anywhere. Now the PBA man was giving Paznakaitis's widow an envelope, and the chaplain was talking into the wind and the slow rain. The valley of death. Fear no evil. Thy rod and Thy staff. Comfort me.

Now the stillness was broken and the solid thing the crowd had been started to break and drift. There was another cortege forming for Patsy Laputa, who was to be buried near her sister in Forest Hills. Butler and Keogh walked in silence back to the blue Plymouth. When they reached it, Butler opened the driver's door for Frank and handed him the keys.

"You mind going back without me, Frank?"

Keogh looked over Pat's heavy shoulder. There was a uniformed policewoman waiting at the side of a 40th Precinct squad car. She had her hat off and Keogh was struck by the dark eyes and the broad white forehead, the flat calm and steady regard in her eyes, the softness in them. She smiled a slow smile at Keogh. Blue-black hair in a corona caught the soft light of the emerging sun. Keogh nodded at her, and the smile went away. She looked at him steadily and without expression for a long moment. With a sense of something breaking, Keogh looked away. Butler was waiting for his answer.

"This is Ruthie Boyko, Pat?"

Butler raised his shoulders and let them drop. His grin was wry and pulled down slightly to the left.

"Hey, Frank. Life's short."

"Where's Junie?"

"She thinks I'm going to the racket at the Armory tonight. Told her I'd be late. Front for me, she calls?"

Irrationally, Keogh felt an electric jolt of some indefinable emotion. Not anger. Something close.

"Pat. You seen Art Pike around today?"

Butler shook his head no. "Haven't seen him since that thing at the Bolsa Chica. I hear he's in a bad way. Why? You worried about him?"

Keogh realized that he was, that he'd been worried about Pike ever since he squeezed off the first shot at that Ching-a-Ling kid . . . what was his name? Jesus. How's that for humanity, Keogh? Kill the kid on a Friday. Forget his name by Tuesday. Butler was right. He was the genuine article, a genuine prick. Pike had left the scene, riding in the back of the Zone Commander's Chrysler, Keogh standing in the glow of the video lights, holding his Remington in his hand, watching the back of Pike's head as he was driven off. He had started worrying about Pike then. And he had, of course, done absolutely nothing about it. Typical.

Butler could see this. He stepped closer, put a hand around Keogh's neck, and shook him gently. Butler's hand felt hot and corded, a bear's paw.

"Hey, Frank . . . you'll see him at the party for The Paz tonight. I envy you, man. The Guardians, they're putting on a hell of a show. Even the white peckerheads are allowed to go. Gonna be a hell of a go-round. Goddam Zulus know how to throw a racket. You go, you'll see Pike. You'll get pissed. Pike'll chew you out for popping one of his charity cases and getting him promoted to One Police. Chrissake, Frank. Cheer the fuck up, will you? You could be going where The Paz is going."

Butler gave him a final shake and turned away down the slope toward the blue-and-white. Keogh called out to him: "Hey, dickhead. We're on duty tomorrow twelve hundred on the hour. Tomorrow, Butler. You don't show up for Pulaski's Film Festival, he'll have Steve and the Twins for a paperweight."

Butler reached the squad car and looped an arm around Ruthie Boyko's shoulders. His breast bars glittered above the gold badge on his dress blues. "Steve and the Twins? Where'd you get *that*? Go with God, my son."

"Yeah," said Keogh, watching them climb into the squad car, watching Ruthie Boyko sliding in beside Butler. "I'll try, Pat."

The blue-and-white burbled out into a line of blue sedans and Cadillacs trying to get out of the cemetery. Keogh stood there on the rolling green slope with the wind moving softly through the trees around him, hearing the murmur of low talk, the crowds breaking around him and flowing down toward the parked cars. It looked to Keogh like a Mafia funeral. He was trying to figure out why Butler's infidelity was bothering him so much.

He and Butler had been through some hard years in the NYPD. There was an unspoken agreement in the life that what a man has to do to get through is what he has to do, and you don't ask him to change. Butler seemed to take some comfort from thrill sex in various Brooklyn motels. He did what he could to keep Junie from knowing about it, and he was always home when he had to be. And Frank had his own problems.

"You're Frank, right?"

Keogh turned around to see three men standing a little way up the hill. Two of them were almost twins, slender and reedy in three-piece banker's suits. One had a hawkish face and the liquid eyes of a gun dog. The other man was trim and meticulously turned out. A slick, it seemed to Keogh. A lawyer, maybe.

The third man looked like a fifty-gallon drum, short and solid and beefy. A red pirate beard obscured most of his face. Hard and slightly cold blue eyes glittered in his puffy red face. He looked like a man who drinks but doesn't get drunk. He was wearing rough blue denim and biker's boots. In his left hand was a police motorcycle helmet with a California Highway Patrol crest.

Keogh said nothing. He raised an eyebrow, not too interested in a chat right now. The men came down the hill toward him.

Redbeard stuck out his hand and said, "You gotta be Keogh. I'm Burke Owens. This is Paul Young. And Lyman Hunt."

The hand was out and steady as a spar. Keogh decided to take it. Owens's grip was dry and a little too firm, as if he'd taken a course in neurolinguistics and had gotten an A in First Impressions.

"Owens? The stress counselor?"

Owens leered at Frank as if he'd said something funny.

"Yeah. Don't get all defensive, Keogh. I'm just here to say goodbye to The Paz. You know the doc here?"

Dr. Paul Young was taller than he had looked up the hill, a couple of inches taller than Keogh or Owens. He took Frank's hand and folded both of his around it to shake. His eyes were clear and flat and unblinking. Like a couple of wet stones in a puddle of water, thought Keogh. Lyman Hunt kept himself out of the conversation but he watched Frank the way a keeper watches the tigers.

"I've heard of Detective Keogh," said Young, in a voice that seemed to come out from under his vest. "I understand you used to work with Kris Paznakaitis in Schaeffer City."

So what. "Yeah, who told you that?"

Young seemed to ignore the tone, but his eyes receded a little.

"Your boss. Lieutenant Pulaski."

"You talking to Pulaski about me?"

"Is there a problem with that, Detective Keogh?" Owens was watching the exchange like a boy who has put two liquids in a beaker and doesn't know what will happen.

"I get up to John Jay now and then, doc. You been running a bunch of lectures up there, part of the sergeant's exam course. What the hell you call them?"

"Mental Disorders and Crime. A Comparison of Psychotic and Nonpsychotic Homicides. Also, Case Management of Psychopathologic Offenders Through Psychopharmaceuticals. I think I saw you at one of them last month."

"Oh, yeah. I caught the one about how Thorazine is God's answer to the question why am I such a sadistic prick."

Young smiled a slow and oddly charming smile.

"I take it you're not a fan?"

"Nothing personal, doc. Better Living Through Chemistry, right? It just gets on my nerves when guys in your profession turn up as gunslingers for the defense. Guys like you got some asshole off a murder charge—what was it, involuntary somnambulism? Fucking sleepwalking. I got no problem with whores, doc. I just don't like seeing killers walk on technicalities."

Young's smile never wavered, a professional's mask.

"Really. It seems to me more killers walk because of the incompetence of arresting officers in the presence of the Fourth Amendment. But I know the case you're talking about. It was a Canadian case, I believe. As it happens, I agree with you in that matter. There should have been some argument for diminished capacity that could have resulted in a period of psychiatric care. I can only say that psychiatry is an art, not a science. Rather like police work. I admired your . . . precision, in the confrontation last week."

Another so what. "Thanks. Is there something I can do for you, or are we just in a pissing contest here?"

Owens laughed at that.

"Jesus, what a prick you are, Keogh. Pat said you were cranky. We're just passing through, thought we'd say hey. Don't get your tutu in a tizzy, Keogh. Boys, we gotta go. You coming to the Laputa thing, Keogh?"

"No, no . . . there's a racket for The Paz downtown." Keogh looked down and back up.

"Look . . . Dr. Young. I'm sorry if I got a little rough there. It's been a bad week."

Young made a dismissive gesture. "Nothing done, Detective Keogh. Sorry if I gave offense. Burke, we'll see you at the car."

Young and Hunt walked away down the hill, Young a gray insect picking his way through the grass, Hunt seeming to glide an inch above it. Gold glimmered at Hunt's left wrist.

Owens stayed where he was. Now we get to the point of this, thought Keogh.

"Who's Hunt? I know Young."

Owens watched them walking down the hill. "Hey. Fuck 'em. They're shrinks. I was talking to Butler."

"Where you know Butler from?"

"He helps out with the stress classes. He never tell you?"

Frank didn't answer. There was always something to a guy you didn't know to look for.

Owens waited and then said, "Look, Frank. Can I call you Frank?"

"Yeah. What can I do for you?"

Owens was quiet for a while, looking for words.

"This scene here, it's a hard thing. I know you had some service time. I did too. You were in the Sixth, right? Tet, Hue, Khe Sanh relief?"

"How'd you know that?"

"Well, come down to the question, I read your two-oh-one file. You look good. Purple Hearts. Couple Citations. A Bronze."

"There's a reason for you fucking around in my file, and I'm gonna hear it, right?"

"Yeah. Look, you know what I do for the Department, huh?"

"Warm fuzzies and touchy-feelies. Also some chanting and you help the guys get in touch with their mantras."

Owens took it with a sheepish smile.

"You don't trust the whole program, do you?"

"Do you?"

"No . . . That's the point. I'm no Paul Young. I can't even figure out how I got into this thing. I came out of the Green Machine, couldn't seem to focus on anything. Bunch of friends also out, some of them in that gork farm in Honolulu? I started going to see them. Helping them, in a way. It gave me something to do. I don't know . . . The rest just happened. Lots of guys like you in the department, ex-vets. One thing led to another. You ask Butler, he'll tell you, there's a minimum of bullshit in the sessions."

"Sessions? Is this the part where you roll out the full-sized color picture of the encyclopedia and I get to see how it would look on my shelf?"

Owens seemed to shut down for a minute, going deep into some interior place. It was as if he'd emptied out and drained away and there was nothing in front of Keogh now but a straw man. Then he opened his eyes and there he was, back again. It was an unsettling effect.

"You're really giving me the whole nine yards, Keogh. Why the fuck you so defensive? Is it because you don't want me to find out how much you enjoy taking out these dickheads?"

Butler. It would have to be Butler.

Owens held up a hand.

"No, it's not Butler. Not directly, anyway. But I'm talking to you because I got asked to. By Pulaski, if you wanna get technical. All the guys in your unit have been in the shit for some time now. You've rolled on a lot of calls. I'd like you to think about coming in. We got a whole floor above the DEA offices on Broadway. A bar, a good pool table. Nobody has to do anything. But if you feel like it, you can kick around some shit, see if you feel better. There. That's the pitch. You want it in leather or cloth?"

Keogh had to smile.

"Leather. Plus the Great Books and the Synopticon."

"You actually gonna come in?"

"Hell, no . . . but I can see you're just doing your job."

Keogh put out a hand. Owens shook it hard and grinned back at him. The hillside was almost empty now. The coffin waited above the grave inside a silver rectangle. Four young men in gray suits and black shoes stood at the side of the grave. They were all looking at Keogh and Owens. The four men wore identical sunglasses. A gust of wind flipped up the plastic grass cover and a plume of rich black soil eddied around their feet.

"Gotta go. Thanks for trying. Tell Bert . . . tell him whatever you want. Give my regrets to the shrinks. Tell them I'm sorry I was such a prick to Young."

"Hey, fuck them. They're consultants. What do they know?"

Keogh smiled and turned away down the hillside. When he got to the car, Owens was still standing there halfway up the hill with the open grave at the top and the four gray men in a row, and now the wind was pulling at the mound of earth and brown whirlwinds of grave dirt were flying.

Keogh looked away and started the car and accelerated out the paved drive and thought about nothing until he reached the Williamsburg Bridge, and then he was up and out over the river, and under the wheels there was the sound of drums.

CHAPTER 4

Tuesday, August 21
1930 hours
New York City

Voodoo ricochet is how Keogh thought of New York City in times like these. One way or another the city has just handed you a hard time—it's killed your dog or your job has been fiscally reallocated (you're fired) or you've shot up a kid who needed to be shot up and an old friend of the family gets his hand nailed to a desk in the fourteenth circle of hell downtown—and you're driving back over the Williamsburg Bridge, you're coming up to the crest and there it is, there's the Emerald City itself, New York New York, with the clouds and the slow rain pulling back over Queens and a low red sun burning purple and rose and delicate pinks on the underside of the clouds. There's the whole city, backlit and glittering with lights from the Battery to the Triborough Bridge, the World Trade Center towers, the Chrysler Building, the Empire State, the chisel-headed Citicorp tower, and under your wheels the light is catching waves and eddies in the East River, Roosevelt Island looks like a barge full of jewels, there's a solid ribbon of taillights going uptown on the East River Drive, and all the cross-streets are jammed with trucks and cars and incipient psychopaths . . . and here it comes, the voodoo ricochet of New York.

51

Keogh loved being alone in the Plymouth, with the radio switched to the Midtown precincts and the air conditioning on and maybe something by Jimmy Smith on the FM, feeling the weight of his Browning and that gold shield on his chest with the breast bars piled over it, the city lights playing on the hood of the car like kerosene flames, sky-blue and ruby-red and acid-green. He never felt more like a city cop than when he was alone in this over-powered car and he was in uniform, the cabs butting around him, the citizens staring as he rolled by them, the muted thunder of tires on the bridges . . . and the talk on the radio is the usual Midtown fever dream, the harness-cop tango coming over the set.

South Boy South Boy, K?
South Boy, Central?
South Boy, a barricaded EDP at the Holland House.
Oh, great, Central. We got a callback?
Callback you wanna callback, South Boy?
Roger, Central.
South Frank, K?
Just a minute, South Frank. Can't you see we're talking to South Boy here? South Boy, you gonna clear for this run?
Negative, Central, we made that run four times today.
Whoa now. You refusing a run, South Boy?
South Frank, Central!
Yeeess, South Frank, you got something to add?
Roger, Central. We're at the Holland. We're holding two and we could use a slim jim, K?
Oohh, *you're* at the Holland. You got two in custody, South Frank?
Ten-Four, Central, plus we need a slim jim?
South Boy, K?
Ten-Twelve, South Boy. South Frank, what's the slim jim for? You locked outa yer car again?
(STATICSTATICSTATIC) . . . ahhh, that's a roger, Central.
Way ta go, Charlie . . .

Eighty-six the cross-talk, boys. Okay, South Boy, you gotta slim jim for South Frank?

Hahhahhahhah . . .

Putzes . . .

Ahh . . . that's a roger, Central?

Was that South Boy?

Fuckin' A . . .

Roger, Central. Tell South Frank we got an ETA of maybe five minutes, K?

South Frank, Central, K?

Jussaminute, South Frank. South Boy, what's the holdup? You're showing you're Ninety-eight at the Port Authority, so how come you're five minutes away from the Holland, K?

Ahh, we're on a Fifty-three at Eighth and Forty-third, Central, K?

You're on a Fifty-three, South Boy?

Roger, Central.

When'd *this* happen, South Boy?

Just occurred, Central.

South Boy, this Fifty-Three involve any Department vehicles, K?

Aahhhh . . . that's a roger, Central.

Harharhar . . .

South Boy, you crack up your car?

Negatory, Central . . . We were rear-ended.

So you're not goin' to the Holland with a slim jim?

Aahh . . . that's Ten-Four, Central.

South Frank, Central?

South Frank.

Ahh . . . cancel the slim jim. We got inta the car.

Roger, South Frank. You still holdin' two?

That's a roger, Central, K?

(BEEPBEEPBEEP)

South Boy, South Frank, South Charlie, this is from Ten desk. We have a Ten-Thirty, a past assault just occurred at Bryant Park. EMS is on the way. Three male blacks, one possibly armed with a revolver. First male black six feet, clean-shaven, blue track jacket, black jeans, sneakers, may be armed. Second black five seven, heavy build, beard, gold earring, plaid shirt, jeans, red sneakers. Third black five ten, thin, red head-scarf, sunglasses, gray pants, black shoes, last seen on foot southbound on Sixth at Fortieth.

South Frank, Ten-Four.

South Charlie, Ten-Four.

Street Crime Five, K?

Ah, Central, we're holding two. Request backup. We think these are your guys. We're at the Chock Full o' Nuts, Herald Square. Suspect is in the bathroom here, K?

Roger, Street Crime. Is the perp armed?

Roger, Central. Manager here says he has a gun.

Roger, Street Crime. South Boy, South Charlie, and South Frank are on the way. All units, we have a gun run at Sixth Avenue and Thirty-fifth, the Chock Full o' Nuts. See Street Crime Five on the scene.

South Adam, Central, K?

South Adam?

Central, request a sergeant to Eighty-Five us at one-three-five-seven the B-way at Thirty-eighth.

Roger. Any sergeants on the air to meet South Adam?

Same same, they used to say in Vietnam. Numbah One G.I. all same same. It was always *dee dee mau* in Vietnam and it's always *dee dee mau* in New York. Listen to the poor sons of bitches. Keogh could see them now, hard young guys and beefy older cops, cops in blue and cops in plainclothes, and the portables, the PWs, everybody on the tips of their toes in Midtown and it wasn't even . . . Shit, he'd forgotten to call Tricia. It was almost eight o'clock and he was supposed to call her right after the end of the funeral. Keogh was off the bridge now and he cranked the car hard around onto Allen Street, looking for a phone. He was checking his side mirror as he turned. Three cars back there was a gray Benz with tinted windows. Something about the way the driver jumped as Keogh cut right stayed in his mind. Keogh got the car into a clear lane and accelerated north toward Houston. The Armory was over on Fourteenth Street. Things were supposed to get off the ground at eight.

Down in his animal brain, Keogh had marked the gray Benz. Most cops do that, out of habit or just as an exercise. Something—some car or the way a person is walking—will catch their attention. They'll open a file on it in some part of their mind, go on about their business—talk to you, buy a drink—but that file is now open and they're watching. The gray Benz went straight across Allen. Keogh watched the driver in his rearview, feeling a little paranoid and a little foolish. Well, as they say, even paranoids get hemorrhoids. Okay, so the Benz went right through Allen. If he's tailing me, I'll see him again north of Rivington because he'll go around on Delancey and come north to . . .

Frank, Frank, yoo-hoo. Earth to Frank.

Frank here.

Frank, Frank, Frank. Why in Christ's name is some guy in a silver Benz gonna be following you?

Well . . .

How long since you've been in Vice? How long since you were in Holdup? How long since you have done anything even remotely cop-like except you get dressed up in your blue pinstripe (about which we have to talk, but later) and you go up to a roof or something, and when your boss says Green Light, Archangel, you blow some poor Puerto Rican junkie into the next dimension? The point is, Frank, are you so hooked on being a cop that you're gonna start fantasizing about how some guy in a silver Benz who probably just happened to fart when you looked at him is now streaking up an alleyway knocking Dumpsters full of addicts out of the way so he can swing around behind your sorry ass on Houston Street and *follow* you! *You*?

Ah . . .

Ah nothing. You're a sniper—that's what they made you. You're not a cop now.

Yes, I am. I'm—

Your father, now. *There* was a cop. Your father—

Hey, okay. I'm not being followed by a Plutonian in a silver Benz. But leave my goddammed father out of this.

Call your wife.

Oh, shit . . .

The third pay phone that Keogh stopped at, on Houston at Broadway, was working. It did not have a bullet hole in the dial. It did not have a condom stuck on the speaker. The cord was not severed. When he picked up the receiver he got a dial tone, and when he dialed, with some of his mind on his parked squad car and another tiny part of it looking for a green dwarf in a silver Benz, he actually got a ring.

"Hello." It was Robbie.

"Robbie, how are ya, kid?"

"Fine, Dad." Flat voice. He could have been talking to the operator.

"How was swimming, Robbie?"

"Fine."

"You get your grade?"

"Yeah."

Keogh suppressed his anger. Somehow he felt that a kid ought to try to be polite to his father. But every time he felt like yelling at Robbie for being so flat on the phone, he'd begin to feel like his own father. And he had not liked his father. *Did* not like his father, even now.

He forced some warmth back into his voice.

"Good work, Robbie. I knew you would. They give you the crest?"

"Yeah."

"Yeah? What're you going to do with it? You going to frame it?"

"Why would I want to frame it?"

"It's a joke, Robbie. It's your first trophy—you oughta frame it."

Damn. That sounded like sarcasm. Robbie apparently thought so as well.

"Yeah, Dad. I'll frame it. I'll put it in the den with all your shooting awards. Dad, I gotta go now."

"Wait a minute. And watch your tone, Robbie. Is your mother around?"

"Nah. She went out."

"She say where?"

"Yeah."

God*dam* little smartass.

"So . . . ?"

"So what?"

"Look, Robbie. Don't dick around with me. I'm sorry I hurt your feelings about the badge. I'm *glad* you won, kid, really I am." Defensive. He was standing here on Houston Street in the middle of a heat wave, talking to his own son on the phone, he had to go to a racket for a cop who was killed with a year to go for early retirement, he was sweating and dirty and tired and he was back on duty tomorrow, and here he was trying to get his own kid to be nice to him on the phone. Families could make a eunuch out of a man faster than any other piece of machinery in the world.

"Mom said to say she was at Mrs. Zuniga's place if you want to call her there later. Also, Custer is gone."

"Custer? How'd he get out?"

"I don't know."

You let him out, you little bastard.

"Robbie, he's not supposed to go outside unless somebody goes with him."

Robbie was hardly listening. In the background Keogh could hear people cheering and some announcer saying, "That's right, Pat, a *brand new car* and nine thousand six *hundred* dollars" and more cheers.

"Robbie. Turn off the TV and go look for Custer."

"I can't, Dad. I gotta—"

"Just find him, kid. Goodbye."

Keogh resisted the temptation to slam down the phone. He was delighted to see a couple of cocky Hispanic teens leaning on the front fender of his car. Delighted.

The racket for The Paz was being held in an old Armory, up on the third floor. The huge wood-lined room was packed with detectives and uniforms, black guys and white guys and a few women. It was strictly Members of Service Only, a restriction enforced at the door by a black patrol sergeant about six four with a deadpan face and tribal scars cut into his cheeks. Keogh knew the man. They'd worked together in the 25th years back. His name was Weeks.

Weeks's face split into a fifteen-hundred-watt grin as Keogh appeared in the doorway. The music was a physical force, a solid wall of Cajun zydeco music. Weeks had to put his mouth down to Keogh's ear just to make himself heard.

"Great to see you, Keogh. You got your hat on wrong! You gotta wear it backwards!"

Weeks took Keogh's uniform cap off and set it back on Keogh's head with the peak at the rear. Keogh shoved the big black man away and laughed. Weeks's hat was on backwards as well. Here and there around the room, a number of white and black cops were wearing their hats reversed.

"All these guys from Schaeffer City?"

Weeks shook his head.

"Nah . . . some of them're fakers. But you and me, we oughta keep the tradition alive."

Schaeffer City was the nickname of the 25th Precinct, a tiny Harlem precinct at the top of Park, in the East hundreds. It was a hard precinct when Keogh had been assigned to it as a rookie out of the Academy. This was back in 1970. Keogh's father, John Keogh, was at that time a major force in Seven Zone Homicide up in the Bronx, a department star. He'd used all of his influence to get Frank put into one of the roughest precincts in New York, just to prove to himself that he played no favorites. The 25th was a small area but it covered a lot of projects and tenements. There were a lot of stairs and rooftops and fire escapes to patrol, a lot of overhead threat.

One day, one of the 25th's patrol cops was walking out onto a fire escape. He was wearing his peaked cap according to the regs, and the peak blocked his view of the stairs above him.

There was a guy on the catwalk just above him. He put a bullet through the top of the cop's hat.

The cop didn't die. But everybody in the 25th got a special dispensation to wear their hats backwards from then on. It had become a precinct tradition. Keogh left his hat on backwards, shook hands with Weeks again, and pushed his way into the crowd.

The cops were ten deep at the long bar. Keogh saw twenty people he knew in the first thirty feet. Somebody handed him a yard of Harp and somebody else slammed him on the back and made him spill half of it down the back of the man in front of him—who turned around to complain. But it was Slick Ryan, one of the Charlie Unit members, and somebody else handed Keogh another yard of Harp, which he tried to drink while Slick dragged him out of the crush and over to the corner where most of the rest of the Emergency Services Unit team was gathered around talking. They saw Keogh coming over and gave him a round of applause.

Slick Ryan was a lean six-footer, a genial cop out of Narcotics who got married and divorced with metronomic regularity. Slick had also been in Vietnam. His friends had gotten a jeweler to make up a special medal for him, which he was wearing tonight above the rest of his breast bars. It was solid gold, an engraved picture of a bottle of Ba Mu'oi Ba beer with a scroll around it that read REAR-ECHELON MOTHERFUCKER. Slick delivered Keogh into the group.

"Hold on to this guy, will ya? I'm going to look for Finn."

Finn Kokkannen was the unit's surveillance expert, a small-arms specialist who was also one of the unit's two female officers. Charlie Boudreau was there, a heavyweight black sergeant from Lake Charles, Louisiana, and Nate Zimmerman, thin-faced and darkly bearded, and Arnie Sayles, another black patrolman assigned to the ESU just two months back. Arnie Sayles just wanted to get through this tour without killing anybody and go back to Queens Auto Squad, where he got to drive around all day looking for stolen cars and play the trumpet in the passenger seat. Sayles was, for that matter, a very good trumpet player.

Through the blast of music from the far end of the room, where a lanky black cop with Academy insignia on his collar was working as DJ, Keogh raised his Harp and toasted The Paz. They drank it down in silence.

"Anybody seen Art Pike around?"

There were a lot of shrugs and guilty looks.

Sayles said, "I heard he got sent downtown."

"Oughta be here tonight, though," said Keogh, looking around the crowd. "He knew The Paz from Knapp."

Kris Paznakaitis had made something of a name for himself during the days of the Knapp Commission corruption hearings back in the early seventies. The Paz was just a patrolman then, working on the PEP anti-drug teams up around West 116th Street. The paranoia of the Knapp witch hunt got so bad that lawyers were dragging up any cop who was seen anywhere around street drug dealers. Since it was hard to bust pushers without getting close to them, Internal Affairs had dragged The Paz down to One Police to explain himself to a kid from Harvard who was working for Knapp, trying to make his own reputation.

They say you had to be there, but it's easy to imagine the scene when a skinny white kid with an excess of belief in the protection of the law started to tear into this thirty-year-old veteran black foot cop. There were a couple of gofers from the Chief of Patrol's office, a bull from Internal Affairs, and the delegate from the Patrolman's Benevolent Association whose name was Art Pike, at that time a uniform sergeant at the 26th in Harlem.

Anyway, it seems the lawyer saw himself as something of a legal Doberman. He went straight for the throat, ragging The Paz about his record of assault charges, the street pushers he'd put in the hospital, the nice house he'd managed to buy for his family out in Tenafly. He'd asked him the kind of questions that any normal man would knock a man on his ass for. But Pike watched The Paz just sit there, a black rock in a rose garden, answering every question calmly and sweetly. No matter what, the lawyer couldn't catch him on a thing. The Paz rode him to a draw. So they all stood up and told The Paz he could go.

The Paz then pulls out an arrest warrant for this kid and busts him right there. On three traffic violations from his student days at NYU. The lawyer left in cuffs.

Art Pike had seen to it that there was no reprisal. The Paz was one of the few honest cops who got tangled up in the gears of the Knapp Commission and managed to come out the other end of it with his self-respect intact.

So, it seemed to Keogh that a racket for The Paz would be one place where Art Pike would be tonight. And he wasn't, at least not yet.

It was natural for them to get into telling war stories about The Paz, and they spent a couple of hours watching the crowds of patrol cops and detectives and remembering stunts The Paz had pulled during his twenty years as an NYPD cop.

Slick Ryan, back now with his arm around Finn Kokkannen, told about the time The Paz was holding a perp on a jostle charge, pickpocketing on West 125th Street, when two armed robbers came racing out of a liquor store and damn near ran him down. The Paz hated foot chases, and he was already cuffed to this skinny pickpocket, but he took off after the robbers, gun out, pounding along 125th Street, with this kid flying like a banner from The Paz's left arm. In those days you could shoot a fleeing perpetrator, so after a block or two The Paz said fuck this and took aim at one of the perps, the one with the cash bag.

The pickpocket starts tugging at The Paz's arm.

The robbers are still racing away.

The pickpocket is whining and struggling.

So The Paz brings his sap out, knocks the pickpocket unconscious, and then puts a thirty-eight round into the right buttock of the man with the cash bag, who goes down in a tangle. The Paz dragged his unconscious prisoner a full block, cuffed the wounded robber by the ankle to the unconscious pickpocket, and dragged them both to his call box.

Well, there was the time The Paz put Mace in the Zone Commander's squad car heater.

Or the time The Paz shot eight wild dogs in a half-hour one night shift. They'd been attacking kids in the neighborhood. The Paz took them out on foot. Crazy bastard.

There was the Myth about The Paz. One day he was in the squad car when he got a call about a jumper hanging from the ledge on top of the Godfrey Nurse Houses. He gets to the call, sees a guy hanging by his hands from the roof, about ten floors up. The Paz goes up to talk to the guy. He sits down at the edge of the roof, about five feet from the guy, with his big polished boots hanging over the edge, his hat pushed back, as if they were having a picnic. The guy starts to tell The Paz his story, and it is a very sad story. The Paz can understand why this guy wants to jump. But he talks the kid into changing his mind. As he's trying to get the kid up, the jumper tells The Paz that his life's nightmare has always been to die in a fall. The Paz promises him he won't die in a fall, that he'll be all right.

The jumper is sweaty. It's a hot June day.

His wrist slips out of The Paz's grip, and he starts to drop. The kid is looking up at The Paz as he falls. His face says everything he's feeling.

So, the story goes, The Paz did the only thing he could do. He pulled out his thirty-eight and shot the kid through the head. The kid was dead when he hit the sidewalk.

Most of the harness cops in the 26th figured that if the story wasn't true, it ought to be.

Keogh listened to the talk go around, thinking that it was funny how cops buried their dead. They talked them into the ground, sorting out the myths and the legends, seeing the cop alive again, in the days when he or she was on the street, chasing the perps and talking the talk. Ten years, twenty years, a life.

Mike Bukovac and Bert Kowalczyk showed up around ten that evening. Charlie Unit called them Moxie and

Pepsi, from an old *National Lampoon* parody of *The Lord of the Rings*. Moxie and Pepsi had been a pair of venal and drunken hobbitlike creatures, nasty, brutish, and short.

Well, Bukovac and Kowalczyk weren't short.

They even looked alike. Six four, three hundred pounds, both of them could press four hundred pounds and do a fifty-yard dash in under ten seconds. They wore their hair cut close to the scalp. Bukovac had a zigzag pattern cut into the black hair at his temples. Kowalczyk's hair was cut into a Mohawk with a short tufted tail hanging down over his collar at the back. Bukovac wore a gold earring. Kowalczyk wore a diamond stud. According to some of the patrolwomen who had been in a position to find out, Bukovac had a tattoo on his cock: PROPERTY OF UNITED STATES MARINE CORPS.

Actually, the story ran, it was USMC. You could only read the whole thing if it was angry.

Moxie and Pepsi were trying to set a personal best record for this year: They both intended to sleep with every patrolwoman in each of the Bronx precincts; age, color, race, creed, physical condition, and marital status no object.

Finn Kokkannen, the small blond sports-model female cop who was Charlie Unit's technical surveillance expert, was keeping a chart back at their squad room on the top floor of the 46th Precinct. No name was written down unless Finn had managed to find at least two independent sources who could confirm their claims. Moxie Bukovac was slightly ahead, but Pepsi Kowalczyk had asked for a recount, maintaining that Moxie had paid Finn to put his sister's roommate's name on the list, and Moxie's sister's roommate wasn't really a cop; she was a forensic technician who worked at the Police Labs. So far, Moxie and Pepsi had made claims for a total of 109 female cops this year.

Finn had only been able to confirm seven.

Keogh was at the urinal down the hall when Bukovac loomed alongside, blocking out a fair amount of light.

Bukovac and Keogh had grown up, in different eras, on the same street in Mount Vernon. Keogh remembered

Bukovac as a good-natured and seriously oversized toddler who was always climbing the hedge-fence from his own backyard to go swimming in the Keogh's pool. He couldn't have been more than five or six when Keogh's mother . . . Well, Keogh had no problem with Mike Bukovac personally. Keogh's father had even gotten Bukovac into the NYPD. It wasn't the kid's fault that every time Frank looked at Bukovac he had to think about Bukovac coming over the hedge to swim in the backyard pool, and that meant he had to think about that goddammed pool.

Well, they'd sold that house the year he came back from Vietnam, he and his father, and they'd packed all of her things. And anyway, that was more than twenty years ago.

"You know, Frank, I got a call from Art Pike's wife when I was back at the station."

Keogh felt a surge of anxiety. "Marian? She okay?"

Bukovac was looking down at himself as if he'd never seen it before. He was a little drunk.

"Yeah, sure. Well, no. Maybe not. I mean, she seemed okay. But she wanted to know if we'd heard anything from Art, you know. Was he with us . . . was he riding with us to the racket? I told her no, we hadn't seen him."

Keogh zipped up and stepped back.

"She say how long since he's been gone?"

"Yeah. He saw the funeral on the news. I got the impression he was hitting the Red Stripe pretty good. Pike, he loves his Red Stripe. Anyway, Marian says he went out when they played Taps."

"He say where he was going?"

"Not according to her. Frank, he's not on duty right now, is he? I mean, he sorta fucked up over that hostage thing. He's gotta go see the stress counselor twice a week. He's on the rubber-gun squad for a year. He's fucked as a cop. I'd take that hard, man."

"What's he done, take his piece somewhere?"

"They took that away from him, Frank. No . . ."

Bukovac got very interested in his hands, rolling them

together in the bright-pink liquid soap, keeping his eyes down, not looking at Keogh.

"No what, Mike?"

Bukovac looked at Keogh in the mirror, and Keogh realized that Bukovac wasn't that drunk. His eyes were cold clear blue and his face was pale.

"You don't wanna go starting some shit, there's no reason, you know? It's just that he . . . Well, you know he's big into hunting. He and your dad . . ."

Shit! Everything seemed to come back around to his father these days.

"Just fucking say it, Mike."

"Marian, she comes back into the den from the kitchen, you know, Pike's not there. So she goes looking. Well, he's not anywhere. But she looks in that basement room, you know, where he's got all his trophies and shit. And he's taken that wop shotgun he was always so proud of."

Oh, Christ, thought Keogh. "The Beretta? Bukovac, you dickhead, why the fuck didn't you say something?"

Keogh was already on his way out the door. Bukovac shuffled after him down the hall, through a crowd of cops.

"Hey, slow down, Frank. Me and Bert already been looking. That's why we're late. Already been to the Four-Oh and everything. I was gonna tell you, soon's the music slowed down. Hey, Frank . . ."

Keogh was down in the elevator and into the Plymouth and hard into a U-turn on 14th Street about forty-five seconds later. Bukovac would get some guys out looking, but Keogh already had a theory. He got the car to First Avenue and drove north with the flasher in the window and the high beams on. As he pounded over the iron plates at 23rd and First, it occurred to him that it would be nice if he could get some help from Butler, but Butler was probably well into it right now in some Queens hotel room.

His mind was out in front of him, trying to see into the next hour. He never looked back.

CHAPTER 5

Tuesday, August 21
2300 hours
The South Bronx

The Bolsa Chica Gun Store was sealed up and black, a low bulk of concrete in the yellow downlight from a street lamp. Somebody had nailed plywood up over the shattered front window. A yellow police ribbon had been stretched across the front of the store in a crazy zigzag pattern, like a bolt of lightning. It was close to midnight when Keogh pulled up across the street from it. He shut down his lights and sat in the darkened car, staring across Third Avenue at the buildings along the row. There were a couple of blue NYPD barricades set along the sidewalk. The Pretty Kitty was closed, and most of the shops were shuttered against the unpredictable Bronx night. No one was on the street. There were seven cars parked here and there along both sides of the block. The huge ruin of the Bronx Courthouse cut into a dark sky. The clouds had all rolled away into Long Island Sound. The air was clear and still.

Art Pike's family station wagon was parked fifty yards up on the east side of Third.

Keogh couldn't see anyone in the wagon. He sat in the car for about five minutes, thinking it out.

He could do the smart thing, ask for some backup from the 40th. Have a couple of squad cars do a sweep. Maybe get Central to call Butler on his pager.

Down the street the neon sign above the Blue Flame Bar was sending a frantic blue light over the street. The front of the Bolsa Chica changed from black to indigo-blue to green to red as the sign worked its way through a sequence.

The problem with calling Central was that if Pike was in the area with an unauthorized shotgun, then there'd be no way of keeping the thing small. There'd be a full report to the Chief of Detectives and the Chief of Patrol. Pickett, the Zone Commander for the Bronx, would see to it that Pike got the whole nine yards. He'd be Section Eight, retired, out.

Or worse. There might be criminal charges. The press was always on the scanner. There'd be a truckload of media jackals all over the block. A circus. PSYCHO COP LOOSE WITH WEAPON! POLICE TAKE DOWN ONE OF THEIR OWN.

Or . . . or Keogh could just get out of the car and stroll over to the gun store. Say: *Art? Art?*

You in there, Art?

Keogh was tempted to drive away slowly and let Art Pike work out his own problems. Just go on up, catch the Cross Bronx to the Bruckner. City Island was no more than fifteen minutes away. Tricia would be asleep in that big brass bed. She'd smell of shampoo and Shalimar perfume. The house would be dark and safe, but she'd have left the fluorescent light on over the sink, and a couple of sandwiches in aluminum foil on the counter. When he got into bed she'd be wearing that pink cotton thing that always rode up around her hips. Under it she'd be naked and warm.

Keogh tugged out his Browning and flipped the magazine into his lap. By the yellow light of the street lamp he saw the glint of brass cases. The gun was heavy and warm from the heat of his body, black and solid as stone.

Maybe Custer had come back. Custer would be waiting on the lawn, at the foot of the steps, that dumb-happy look on his face, waiting for old Frank to come home.

Keogh shoved the magazine up until it locked. Then he pulled the slide back and ran it forward quietly. He could feel the slide pick up the top cartridge and run it into the chamber. It set solid and final. The hammer was back. He flicked the safety off with his right thumb and put his left hand on the door handle.

The glass of the side window was swelling inward, breaking up, the plastic safety sheet stretching, ballooning inward like the fat belly of a crystal Buddha.

There was a huge yellow-red flare of light from the darkened doorway of the Bolsa Chica. Keogh's left cheek stung with cold fire. Bits of glass were spinning, flaring, blowing past his eyes.

Keogh went flat to his right, belly-down on the front seat, the frozen burning spreading from his left cheek down into his neck. He fumbled at the door handle on the passenger side with his left hand, his right arm with the Browning pinned under his body, his knees jammed into the wheel. He got the door open.

There was another flare, and now he could hear the blast, the deep resonant boom of a 12-gauge shotgun. Spread, spread, Keogh was thinking, trying to remember. Pike was a hunter; he'd have double-ought buck—what was the choke on that Beretta . . . ?

The front of the car was full of wind and metal shot. Keogh felt shot lift his hair, felt another cold blow in his left calf.

Scrambling and sliding over glass and metal, Keogh tumbled out onto the sidewalk. Damn, Keogh was thinking, he'd helped Pike clean that goddam weapon; he'd stood around in Pike's basement *admiring* the thing.

Keogh was outraged at the basic unfairness of the situation, lying in God-knew-what while a close family friend turned Keogh's favorite squad car into a colander.

"Pike! Pike, for chrissakes! Will ya stop? Will ya fuckin' quit shooting at me! It's Frank!"

Keogh scrambled over, to get the engine block and the wheel rims between himself and that shotgun.

There was a thin cry from the interior of the store, a voice barely recognizable.

"I know who I'm shooting at, you bastard!"

Drunk. Drunk and maudlin. Crazy-drunk and wild.

"Pike, what the hell are you shooting at me for?"

Pike was smart. He fired again, lower, at the pavement fifty feet in front of the car. Boom, and another red flare from the doorway. Grazing rounds came skittering over the roadway an inch off the ground. The curb stopped most of it, but Keogh heard his left front tire go. God*damn* it!

"Pike, you fuckhead! You're gonna bring the whole Department down on us."

"*Fuck* the Department! Fuck you—"

Keogh was looking around for another position. It was never a good idea to lie around in one place when people were shooting at you. Light infantry tactics. Fire-teams. Hey, no problem. All he had to do was get the fire-team to lay down suppressing fire, get some smoke down on Third. Throw a little M-79 action into the bunker, use the 60 to chew up the concrete. Two squad will maneuver right. Three squad flank left. We'll call Six and get some arty. Couple of Tomcats. Tactical nuke.

"Pike, Pike, you gotta stop this. Two or three rounds, they're gonna ignore that. You keep on banging away with that thing, somebody in this neighborhood is gonna call the cops. Will you just quit this shit and come out of there?"

Keogh's portable radio was in his briefcase in the trunk, along with his Remington and Butler's pistol-grip Ithaca 12-gauge. Keogh had the idea that trying to get the trunk open would have a negative effect on his health.

There was crackle from the police radio under the dashboard. The tinny voice carried in the still night air.

"Four Frank, K?"

"Four Frank, Central?"

Great, thought Keogh. Four Frank covers this sector. Somebody has called the cops.

"Yeah, Four Frank . . . we've got a report possible gunfire in the area of Third and One Hundred Fifty-ninth."

"You got a callback on that, Central?"

"Pike!" Keogh yelled. "Are you listening to this?"

"Negative, Four Frank, no callback. We'd have to do a Bell trace to get the number."

No answer from Pike.

Four Frank's voice was bored and cranky. "Nah. We'll slide over there, take a look when we're clear here. This Ten-Eleven is Ninety-Z, K?"

Audible alarm. They'd be here in three minutes.

That pretty well tears it, thought Keogh. The only chance he had of keeping this thing small was to get over there right now and get control of Pike so that by the time Four Frank got here, he'd have some story worked out. Couple of drunk cops, accidental discharge. If he knew the cop in Four Frank, he might be able to get the whole thing—

"How's it feel, Frank?" Pike's voice was shaking with self-pity and rage.

"How the fuck do you think it feels?"

"You know me, Frank. Come on, talk to me. Negotiate with me, Frank. Use your charm. Talk to me while those cocksuckers get a sniper onto the roof. Pour your fucking heart into savin' my ass. Just when you're getting somewhere, they'll put one right into my face."

This was horse shit. Time to do something.

"Pike . . ."

Boom. Another shot. The car rocked on its springs, and the rear tires exploded. The Plymouth settled into the gutter.

This guy's killing my car.

Keogh was firing over the hood, sideways across his chest, the Browning in his right hand, the left bracing it. Fuck this.

Keogh put nine rounds into the black rectangle of the doorway. The Browning kicked and bucked. He kept squeezing the trigger; the slide chattered back and forth. His left ear rang with the sound of the explosions. Bits of stone flew off the doorframe.

Give Pike something to think about—take his mind off his career problems. Pike was finished anyway. The idea was to keep him alive.

Keogh came around the front of the car low, on his toes, racing for the side of the gun store.

Well, the idea was to keep Pike alive without being killed himself. That was the idea. If Pike wasn't dead already. Keogh was almost all the way across when a blue-white flare appeared in the black hole of the door. Buckshot skittered like marbles over the pavement. Keogh felt fire in his ankles. He stumbled, cursing, and put another five rounds into the doorway as he ran, telling himself he was only trying to keep Pike off balance and away from the door.

No, it didn't look like Pike was dead. This was putting a severe strain on their relationship, this business of shooting at each other. It was hard not to take it personally. Keogh reached the side of the gun store with his chest burning and blood running down the side of his shirt. His uniform, his best dress blue with his gold shield and the breast bars—it was a sorry-looking mess. Fourteen rounds at 60 cents a round. Plus the uniform.

"Pike, you know so far you cost me eight-forty for the nine mils and an easy six hundred for the dress blues. They're tailor-made, you know?"

Silence.

"Pike?"

Silence.

No. There was a car coming up Third. He could hear it, hear the tires on the road.

Oh, shit.

This was the part he hated most. Back in Vice, there was always some fired-up youngster who was aching to go in first, go through the door or down the alley. Even in the ESU, Keogh was usually on sniper post. Moxie and Pepsi usually did this part.

Keogh released the magazine and slipped in his spare. "Pike?"

A cone of white light caught him broadside.

"You there. Drop your weapon!"

Keogh looked across the street. There was a squad car parked next to his battered Plymouth. They had the spotlight on him. He couldn't see the cops, but he could feel their guns on him. He shifted around to show the badge on his chest. "Turn that fucker off! And stay where you are. You better call your sergeant."

"Keogh? That you, Keogh?"

"Yeah. Who're you?"

The voice was vaguely familiar. He could see the cop crouched at the side of the blue-and-white.

"Jack Weisberg. Who you got?"

Weisberg was the veteran sergeant running the Neighborhood Stabilization Unit car. He'd been here last week.

"Weisberg, you're not in an NSU car?"

"'Fraid so, Frank. What you got in there?"

Great. Weisberg was here with a couple of cherries from the Academy. There was now zero chance to cover up this shit between the old boys.

"I got Art Pike in here."

There was a long moment while Weisberg took this in. "Who's holding him?"

"Nobody. Pike's a little upset."

Another silence.

"Pike do that to your car?"

"Yeah. One of your babies know how to cover?"

Weisberg looked down at the two recruits crouching at the side of the car. The skinny kid from Jersey, Cicarelli, was pale and sweating. But the broad looked okay.

"Yeah, I got a PW here—she's okay. What you want?"

"I gotta go in. The back door's sealed shut."

"Yeah. Wait a minute."

All through this there had been no sound from the interior of the Bolsa Chica. Keogh had a vision of driving up to Pike's house in Staten Island in that pale hour before dawn and knocking on the door with the Scottish lion rampant, and one of his sons opens it up, looking sleepy and rumpled and the first signs of panic in his eyes.

Weisberg pulled the girl to her feet. Her name was Kholer. The skin was tight over her cheeks and her green eyes were wide, but she felt steady. "Just keep your weapon on the door. Cicarelli, you cover the alleys."

Kholer asked about backup.

"Not yet, kid."

Weisberg came across at a run.

Keogh looked back at the NSU car. "You tell 'em to get backup?"

Weisberg was a career sergeant. He'd spent his whole life in patrol. He smiled at Keogh.

"What, you wanta make the morning papers?"

"We may do that anyway."

They went in after Pike.

Art Pike was in the back room of the Bolsa Chica Gun Store, up against the farthest corner, down on his rump with his knee drawn up and his hands around the shotgun. It took them about three seconds to pick him out with Weisberg's flashlight, Weisberg holding it way out from his body, both of them tight as drumheads waiting for that big white flare and the shitstorm of pellets to come out of the dark.

Keogh and Weisberg picked their way through the litter and garbage on the floor. Weisberg kept the flashlight on Pike as they came across to him. Pike's eyes glinted, wet and glassy, as he watched them approach.

He had one shoe off, and the sock. His right toe was wedged into the trigger-guard of the glossy black shotgun with the intricate wooden stock. The muzzle of the shotgun was shoved up under Pike's chin. His hatchet face and his white forehead slick with sweat made him look like something trapped in a box.

Pike's voice was calm, conversational.

"Frank, you call that a tactical entry? You came in like a pizza boy looking for a washroom."

Keogh squatted down about ten feet from Pike.

"You cocksucker. See what you did to my uniform?"

Pike gave him a weary smile. "Did you know those kids, Frank? Did you listen to me talking to them?"

Keogh sighed. "Art, it was a bad situation. Two cops down."

"You know why they hit Ton-Ton's, Frank?"

Weisberg tried moving in a little.

"Weisberg, you come any closer, I'm gonna ruin two grand worth of Jewish dentistry."

Keogh had to laugh. "Hey, aim lower then. Pike, you have to stop taking life so seriously."

"You oughta take it a little *more* seriously, Frank. One of them had just got out of Spofford. You know what happened there? He got buggered in E wing. Raped. Four guys, Frank."

"Art, life's hard. We all get porked in E wing one way or another. You think at all how this is gonna look to your own boys?"

Pike seemed to grow smaller, tighter, paler.

"Why should life be any easier for them? What's the point, anyway? I'm history, thanks to you."

Keogh nodded once, cocked the hammer on his Browning, and shoved the muzzle deep into the side of his own neck.

Pike stared blankly at him.

Weisberg set the flashlight down on a desk with the beam on Pike and Keogh. He moved carefully to the left.

"Pike, I'm taking myself hostage."

"Shit, Keogh."

Keogh raised his free hand.

"No. Fuck it. You're right. Life's a hand job. Howdy Doody had wooden balls. Mr. Greenjeans is dead. This year only one swallow came back to Capistrano, and somebody ate it. Sinatra is starting to look like Jabba the Hutt. I dropped three hundred bucks on a metric tool kit and bingo, we don't go metric. There isn't a single white rhino left west of the Mississippi."

"Keogh, just shut the—"

"No way. You go, I'm going with you. You know how much real football was in the last Super Bowl? Actual action? Ten minutes. I think Tammy Faye *still* loves that son of a bitch. You know that thing cats do—they get all bristled up and stare out into the hall where the lights are off and you're all alone in the house? I think they do that on purpose, just to fuck us over. The other day I was leaning over the sink while I was shaving and I saw my face in the water—you know, with the flabby cheeks all hanging down and the lips all wobbly and the ears flopped over—and it hit me that that's what women have to look at when you're on top of them and that's why they close their eyes—"

"Frank, put the gun down. Your dad—"

"Hey, fuck my dad. *You* put the gun down. Put it down or pull the trigger, Art. I'm getting depressed just thinking about all this shit—like why do they have to wear short pants to play hockey? That just looks stupid. Little knobby knees hanging out. I hear they wear garter belts to hold 'em up. You know what Oprah's name is backwards? Harpo. Makes you think, doesn't it? Whales have five fingers in their flippers. That means they were here and they said, 'Hey, fuck this, guys. Back to the beach.'"

Pike's hands were slipping off his knees. His grip on the piece was loosening. There was dead silence from behind the flashlight. Close, thought Keogh.

"Who ate the first oyster, Art? And what happened to him? If they made a movie of Joan of Arc's life, would the theme song be 'You Light Up My Life'? Why does Mickey Mouse always wear white gloves? What's he trying to hide? Do fish fart? If the guys who beat up Dan Rather thought he was some guy named Kenneth who knew what the frequency was, did Kenneth think that was funny? If you and me are both Catholics and we die tonight, does that mean we both go to Purgatory together? If so, can I sit in the front? Why do guys always say 'oh, God, oh, God' when they're going to come? Does God give a shit? If God is eternal, who pays His rent? If the sea gives up her dead, who's gonna want to have lunch with them?"

Weisberg came in out of the dark so fast it scared the hell out of Keogh and he almost pulled the trigger on the Browning. Weisberg got his hands on the shotgun, tugging the muzzle out. Pike's knee came down. There was a huge flare of blue-white flame. Weisberg and Pike were silhouetted in the glare, a black shape. The sound of the shotgun was deafening in the tiny room.

Keogh scooped up the flashlight from the desk where Weisberg had left it. Dust was drifting in the cone of light. Weisberg was pulling Pike to his feet, the shotgun in one hand, Pike in the other. Pike's eyes were closed, his mouth slack, his face bloody.

"Is he hit?"

Weisberg shook his head and raised his right hand. There was a lead-filled sap in it.

"Nah. I just cracked him one. He'll be okay."

"What about you?"

Weisberg shook his head again. "Well, I'm deaf, I think. Fucking thing went off right in my ear. That's okay, I like it like that."

Keogh scooped Pike up in a fireman's lift. Weisberg picked up his flashlight and they headed for the door.

"You like being deaf?"

"Yeah. I don't have to listen to you talking."

They came out into a glare of spots from two RMPs. The PW named Kholer was waiting on the sidewalk.

Keogh carried Pike to the NSU car and dumped him into the back seat. Weisberg was putting the Beretta into the trunk. He slammed the lid down and stared at Keogh over the roof of the cruiser.

"Well, do they?"

Keogh didn't get it right away.

"Do they what?"

"Do fish fart?"

Keogh thought about it for a while.

"Depends on what they eat."

"Yeah," said Weisberg. "It would."

CHAPTER 6

Keogh and Weisberg tried to keep it simple, but the complications were out of control. Communications had taken a legitimate gunfire call, so Weisberg's Four Frank car was in the computer as RMP on the scene. Pike was looking at something a little more serious than a Command Discipline. Unlawful discharge of a firearm was a felony, even if Keogh refused to file an Information. Charges and Specifications had to be backed by an Information from a witness. But then there was the damage to the car, the presence of other officers, the injuries sustained by Keogh. His neck and ankles had been peppered with glass and buckshot fragments. Section 265 paragraph 25 of the Code required a physician to report any gunshot wounds to the police. Keogh had fired his own weapon, and he had been heard firing it. So he had to file a PD 424-151, and that report had to go to the Chief of Patrol.

So Art Pike was alive and that was the best thing you could say about it. Weisberg and Keogh both figured that Pike wasn't in "a culpable mental state," so he might be able to get away with a plea. But he was through in the NYPD and it was up to the Sergeants Endowment to save his pension.

It was two in the morning before Weisberg and Keogh

77

walked out of the emergency unit of Lincoln Hospital. The Cicarelli kid had gone off duty at midnight, but the green-eyed PW had stayed around to see what happened. She was sitting at the wheel of the NSU car when the two tired cops came down the driveway. The streets were empty, but there was a distant rumor of cars and trucks from Bruckner Boulevard. A low crackle of cross-talk came out of the radio. Keogh looked around for his Plymouth. Then he remembered.

Weisberg saw the look on Keogh's face.

"Hey, Frank, don't worry. I was shocked, Frank, shocked to see what senseless vandalism had been perpetrated on a Department vehicle. Myra here wrote up a vandalism report and had Popeye's come and get it before the Duty Captain got a look at the buckshot tattoo. Myra'll take care of it."

Keogh leaned down to look at the girl behind the wheel. She wasn't a girl.

Myra Kholer's summer uniform was under a certain amount of strain keeping Myra under control. Her look was straight-ahead all-Kansas, the classic strawberry blonde with green eyes. No makeup, her hair up in a roll, but wisps of it floated like tinted smoke around her temples. She gave Keogh a maternal look and put out her hand. Keogh took it through the window. It was dry and strong.

"Popeye says he's got all sorts of Plymouth parts in the back lot. He'll have it back to you by Thursday."

Jesus, thought Keogh. How old can she be? He tried not to look up at Weisberg. He could feel his reaction to her in his hip pocket.

Weisberg inhaled the night air.

"Well, it's beddy-byes for me, Frank. This car's off Central. Why don't you let Myra drive you home?"

Keogh had called his house several times. The phone was off the hook. That usually meant he was up shit creek with Tricia. Maybe Robbie had done his usual number on her. Robbie seemed to be in some sort of competition with Keogh for Tricia's loyalty. Tricia had the idea that Frank was trying to turn his son into a robot. Frank felt that she was trying to turn her son into a daughter.

"You don't mind?"

She seemed surprised he would ask.

"No. No, sir. I'd be glad to. You're up on City Island, aren't you, Detective Keogh?"

Keogh opened the door and climbed in. When his back hit the seat he felt a wave of exhaustion and depression roll over him. "Yeah, City Island. And call me Frank."

They were going north on Third, heading for the Cross Bronx with a full moon riding the low Queens skyline. She put on the broadcast radio and found some slow music. They rolled up the broad avenue listening to Duke Ellington do "Willow Weep for Me." Myra wasn't saying anything, but she was restful and calm, and now and then she would look over at Keogh as if there were something she wanted to say to him. Keogh's neck was stinging, and his ankles ached, and he was worried about Art Pike and his family. And Tricia. And Robbie. And himself.

He was worried about himself because he was forty-two years old, tired and banged up and not at all sure who the hell the good guys were and damn sure he wasn't one of them. Because it was all he could do to stop himself from asking this PW here in the car with him to go somewhere and buy him a drink.

The nights were always like that, those hours after midnight and before the sun came up to show everybody where the boundaries were. Being a cop had meant years of living in that hour-of-the-wolf zone and it was hard not to learn to love it, not to want it to go on forever. He had always felt how easy it would be to slip all his cables, to drift away, to cut himself free of all the attachments that rubbed and limited him. The kid, a home, the place in the Catskills, the constrictions of being a good man and a good father and an honest friend to his wife. He knew he still loved his wife. Whenever he was facing something hard in the job, like having to go into that store after Art Pike, he would have a vision of somewhere safe and Tricia's soft eyes and her cloud of auburn hair and her familiar body, the history they shared—all those things would come over him in a sentimental tide and he'd feel a sick ache in him for all the possibilities for happiness that he had personally slam-dunked into the trash can over the years. And yet, when he was with her, with Robbie around the house, all he wanted to do was get back into a job, get the adrenaline hit, be on the street and free. It stung him that he couldn't or wouldn't be graceful about his own life and the things he had spent years trying to build up and hold on to. There was an absence in him, a distance. He was born a sniper. He was too weak for anything more immediate. The thousand-yard man.

They got to the Cross Bronx. Myra looked at him.

"Well, here's where we go right."

There was an obvious question in her voice. He felt the possibility in it.

"Or here's where we go wrong. . . ."

"Don't be so intense, Frank. I just don't want to go home and count ceiling tiles right now. I could use a drink, and if you'll forgive my saying so, you look like you could use one too."

"I'm married, Myra."

"Jesus. The conceit."

"Yeah. One drink?"

Myra's smile was slow and wry. "At a time?"

At a roadhouse in Yonkers they talked, until it closed, about the Department and the job, about Art Pike and the city, about Keogh's family and Keogh's wife. Myra had two brothers and she believed that the best way to raise boys was to pay as little attention as possible to what they said and have a little faith that sooner or later their brains would kick in and their hormones would settle down.

It was talk-talk. Keogh could do it, too, and he did it well, but he knew where he was headed. Her face was flushed, her hands busy with her Stoli. Several times she touched his hand or leaned over to make a point. He was acutely aware of her body, the fullness of it and the secrets of it.

Her scent was soap and leather and something spicy. They talked for an hour in a red leather booth at the back of the roadhouse, with Yonkers cops and State Police guys off duty and a couple of NYPD guys from Highway, but most of them just came by to say hello and they were left alone when it counted, because those were the rules of the game and every cop in the place had a stake in the game. She got up to go to the bathroom and came back with keys.

When she came into the bedroom, he was already in the big double bed. She had a terry robe on with the hotel crest. She was damp from the shower, and pink. She sat down on the edge of the bed, leaned over to kiss him.

He reached up to pull her across him. Her scent was strong, and her breath warm on his lips. He held her like that, her body across his lap, her arms around him. He felt her tongue, a tentative flicker. She had a delicacy and a graceful way of opening without urgency. Keogh moved a hand down over her shoulder, taking the robe away. In the soft light from the lamp her breast was heavy and marked with a pale tracery of blue veins. He brushed a finger carefully and lightly across the small brown nipple. She stiffened, and he felt her nails in the small of his back.

Keogh heard the percussion of his own heart, felt the blood in his thighs and his throat. He hurt with the pressure of it. She could feel him under her hip, and she laughed softly into his neck. She shifted and the robe came off her shoulders. Her breasts were soft against his chest. He could feel her nipples on his skin.

She was strong and young. When he pulled her down beside him, she untied the cord holding her robe. Her body was marked with white, and where it was tanned she was the color of sherry. When he moved his hand down her belly, she smiled again, and her mouth glided down his cheek to his neck. He felt her tongue on the wounds. She was gently, delicately tasting him. Tasting the blood on his skin.

She tugged at the sheet between them and rolled away onto her knees. The robe came off and she was naked, her strawberry hair down and loose, an umbra; it looked like mist in the lamplight. She pulled the sheet away and looked at him. He took her hand and she came down beside him. Her body was cold and damp from the robe, her scent and his scent and their scent very strong in the silent room.

CHAPTER 7

"Pike . . . Pike . . ." The voice was soft as rain.

"Pike . . ."

Pike was in a dream. At the bottom of his bed a square of bright light floated in the air, a field of restless and ceaseless movement, sparks of color and explosions of darkness playing across a luminous blue-green surface, and in his ear a surge of noise in which he could almost hear voices whispering, hushed conversations, muted muffled cries that sounded like warnings or lamentations, a breaking wave of sound that rose and fell in a slow syncopation.

"Pike . . ."

In the dream the light from the square felt like a river on his forehead and his cheeks, cooling and soft, and under the surge of sound he could hear the working of his own heart, a steady bass beat, and under that a demiquaver of loss, a half-tone of sadness.

"Pike . . . wake up, man. We have to talk."

Pike heard the voice but he didn't want to surface. The dream was safe; being in it was like lying at the bottom of a pool and watching a kind of moonlight glittering on the surface of the water.

"Pike . . . goddammit."

83

Pike lay on his back at the bottom of the pool and watched the light playing on the surface. In the light he could see shapes and images and transitory flashes of shimmering motion, and the voices became the voices of boys in the distance, and the radio noises like static from distant planets, gunfire, shattering glass in slow motion, rainbow pinwheelings, tiny ruby-red pinpoints of light and the boys going down, and around him in the darkness men working their weapons. . . . *Pike* . . . one voice now, rising out of the tidal welling of noise . . . *Pike* . . . A sliver of blue-green light cut his eyes and the pain brought him up. . . .

"Pike. Art . . . come on, talk to me. . . ."

Pike came up slowly, coming up toward the glittering light above him, coming up to the sound of a voice he knew. . . .

"What is it? They have you sedated?"

A dark room. Where? The hospital . . . Now it came in on him: the gun shop and the snipers, and the funeral on the TV news, and Keogh talking to him with a Browning shoved into his throat.

"What . . . who's that?"

"Art. It's me."

A dim shape in the darkness, standing at the foot of the bed, behind the square of bright light. The television. Slick Ryan? Frank? Pulaski? It looked like it could be Pulaski. But wrong. Somebody . . .

Pike felt the earphone in his right ear and heard the sizzle of static. The stations had stopped transmitting and now there was nothing on but snow and static.

"Jesus . . ." Pike's mouth felt as if someone had filled it with earth. "What . . . time is it?"

The voice came out of the darkness from somewhere behind the television.

"Hour of the wolf, Art. Sometime after four in the morning."

Pike tried to lift his head off the pillow. His arms and legs felt like helium, but his head was a stone.

"Take it easy, Art. Go slow."

Pike relaxed into the pillow and pulled in a long ragged breath. The room smelled of Lysol and . . . earth? Cut turves of new earth. Something sharp and earthy.

"I thought you guys had all gone home."

"We're back. We're *here*."

"So . . . what happens now?"

There was a pause, as if his visitor was trying to figure out how to answer the question. Pike took it for sympathy.

"Look," said Pike, "don't patty-cake me. I could give a fuck for the Department."

"You feel resentful, I can see that. It's natural."

Pike felt the water coming up around him again. He used the voice as a way to stay above it.

"Well . . . one way or the other, I'm out. Pickett'll see to that . . . and . . . you guys. The club."

"We had nothing particular against you, Pike. You really left us with no choice."

Pike tried to speak. His voice was a dry rustle.

"You could use something. Here . . ."

He moved forward out of the dark. Blue-green light played along the side of his face and on his outstretched left arm. There was a white cup in it. Pike felt a strong hand on the back of his neck. He came up to the cup and drank. It burned down, a slithering ribbon of chilled flame he could feel all the way down into his belly. There was a pattern of some sort on the side of the Styrofoam cup. Flowers? Leaves? Purple against the shell-gray of the cup.

The cut-earth smell was very strong now. The man stepped back into the darkness. The television screen flared and flickered, green fire and black snow.

"Thanks . . . Jesus—scotch?"

"Glenfiddich. Just the best for you. For auld lang syne."

"Yeah. Absent friends. You hear that?"

"What?"

"I don't know . . . water. Something's dripping some-where. Get the light, will you? Maybe I got a tube pulled out or something. I can smell, like medicine or something. Smells like Listerine or something."

Silence from the dark.

"Hey, can you? The lights?"

"No, Art. No lights."

Pike felt a weak pulse of anger. It tired him. He felt the water rising around him.

"What're you, Con Ed? Gimme a light."

"No, Pike. Best not. We have things to do."

The voice was soft as rainfall on a garden. Pike couldn't get the smell of earth out of his nostrils. He ran his tongue over his lip and now he could taste it. His heart began to flutter like a fish.

"Things to do? Listen, why don't you just go home. We all had a bad night. You don't sound so good yourself." Pike moved his right hand, looking for the call button. They usually pinned it to a patient's pillow or the top of his sheet. He couldn't find it anywhere.

"Look," he said, feeling afraid and not knowing why, "I don't hold this against you. You were just doing what you get paid to do. Man, I never meant what I said. I don't take it personally. It's just The Job."

"My . . . a speech. I hear you saying this, Art. I hear you telling me. This is good stuff. It's a breakthrough. Are you looking for something?"

Pike stopped moving. The button was not there. Someone had moved it. His heart rate went up a notch.

"Could use a nurse, man. You see the buzzer anywhere?"

"You need a nurse? There's a nurse right here. Can't you see her? Your own private nurse, Art."

The television on the articulated arm began to move. Pike had to work to get his head to move, to follow the fan of blue-green light as it traveled across the floor and up the side of the other bed in his room. Halfway up the side of the bed, the sheets were covered with a pattern of . . . purple flowers? Leaves. Ribbons of purple and pools of . . . a blue-white hand, an arm. The light rose up across the terrain of the hospital bed like a full moon rising over a snowfield. In the middle of the bed a woman lay on her back, one knee up, her head turned toward Pike's bed. On her belly a glistening mound of purple and pink bubbled out of her. The smell of cut earth was everywhere.

Pike went down like a sounding whale to reach his voice but there were strong hands on him and the smell of cut earth and the hands pulled him up and out of the bed toward the square of blue-green light and he died a while later with his eyes full of dazzling lights and in his ears the hissing surge of static and whispers, and in his mouth the taste of cut earth.

CHAPTER 8

**Wednesday, August 22
0730 hours
City Island, the Bronx**

Keogh's day started with a phone call from Lieutenant Pulaski. Tricia woke him by dropping the phone onto his stomach. He was dreaming about Art Pike. Pike was naked and floating on a blue pool, his hands behind his head. There were cops all the way around the pool, like a squad muster. Pike was telling Keogh about his father, about what a good homicide cop his father was. Keogh was trying to get Pike to listen to his side of it. But Keogh's throat muscles wouldn't work and he couldn't speak. Pike's thin old-man's body floated on the clear water like a bundle of dry sticks.

The water around him was turning red when something hit Keogh in the stomach and he snapped awake. Tricia was standing at the end of the bed, holding a black coffee and looking at him with that weary tolerance that veteran wives get when they think the husband has been drinking too much. Keogh's first thought was that she had seen marks on him. Myra had tended to scratch. Then he felt a rush of self-hatred and disappointment. Now that he was back in his own bed, the whole stupid stunt came back in hard-focus clarity and it looked as glamorous as a crime-scene shot.

"Bert on the line. You have a good time last night?"

Tricia was holding her body in that half turned-away style she had when she was angry and worried. She was wearing a long white cotton nightgown. Keogh could see her full hips and her long legs in the sunlight from the window, a shadowy arc of breast. Her auburn hair was up and her face was scrubbed and pale, her voice bruised.

"I called a coupla times, babe. Robbie tell you?"

"No. Robbie was out at the pool last night. How could he take a call?"

"What, am I lying about it? Jesus, babe. I . . . we had kind of a bad time with Art last night."

She looked at his neck, at the dirty bandage there.

"You get into a fight with Art?"

"Yeah, in a way. Let me talk to Pulaski. I'll tell you about it in a minute. Okay . . . ?"

Tricia looked at Keogh for a while, something cool and disconnected in her eyes. Then she nodded and walked away into the bathroom. Keogh picked up the phone.

"Frank?"

"Bert. What's up?"

Pulaski hesitated. "I got the sheet on you and Pike. I take it you're okay?"

"Yeah. Got some buckshot. How's Art?"

There was another long pause. "They're looking at him now. What time'd they let you out?"

There was some guilt here. Keogh and Myra had used a Department car for decidedly undepartmental business. Keogh could ride that out, but they might hit Myra with a Command Discipline. And Pulaski was a pretty strong Catholic.

"Around two. Got a drive."

"Yeah. Weisberg said. Pat was trying to get you."

"Pat. He finally come up for air?"

"Yeah. What was he, screwing some broad?"

Pulaski made no fuss about off-duty diversions, as long as nobody slacked off on the job and no damage was done to The Department. Pulaski always saw the NYPD in capital letters. Keogh answered carefully.

"I heard he was in Queens, at the thing for Patsy Laputa. That would have gone late."

"Yeah. You talked to anybody yet?"

"About what?"

"Never mind. When you going to be in?"

"Twelve hundred, the usual. Why?"

"Weisberg says you got yourself pretty fucked up. He wanted me to give you a few days. Maybe you want a break? Talk about it. You gotta go through the usual PD four-two-fours. Talk to Ballistics and Internal. You guys are all supposed to get post-traumatic stress . . . what the hell they call it? Goddammed Commissioner is all worked up about it. Got to take care of you little dickheads."

"Bert. I hate all that touchy-feely warm-fuzzies shit and you know it. I'm fine. I'll be in. Okay?"

Pulaski grunted and the line went dead. Keogh got up slowly and wandered into the shower, hoping that Tricia was already down in the kitchen. He ran a long hot shower and scrubbed himself brutally.

Tricia and Robbie were sitting at the kitchen table eating Eggo waffles, Tricia wearing her uniform. Robbie never looked up from his "Silver Surfer" comic.

Robbie was fourteen, thin and bony and long-legged in a scarecrow sort of way, with vivid black eyes and a shaved head. He wore an earring, and according to Tricia, he had a tattoo of a skull on his upper arm. Keogh was not supposed to know about it so Keogh never had to discuss it with him. Robbie's skin was pale and blue-tinged and he wore a permanent look of distracted contempt for Keogh and everything Keogh thought was important. Keogh was damned if he knew where it came from. And he was through trying to charm his way back into Robbie's good graces.

But he made it a point to get through breakfast without a scrap. He had enough to think about.

"I'm on twelve hours again today, Frank. Can you be home tonight?"

"Pulaski's got something going on. I can maybe get off around nine?"

Tricia got up with the dishes. Robbie never moved. Keogh said nothing. In his mind he had knocked the kid onto his ass on the floor and Robbie was now scrubbing the sink. But he said nothing. Tricia would get in the way, and they'd fight, and while they were fighting, Robbie would get up and wander outside and that would be another day on the list of bad days with Tricia.

"You're going to have to look for Custer."

Custer was usually on the bed when Frank woke up.

"Yeah, I saw. Did Robbie look for him?"

"He looked for a couple of hours. And I've called the pound. I've been driving around calling him, but he won't come unless it's your voice."

Keogh took his plates over to the sink and picked up a dish towel. "Okay, I'll take a cruise around the Island, but he'll come home anyway. He's just in one of those moods."

Tricia wiped a soapy hand across her cheek. She looked up from under at Keogh and whispered, "He's horny, if that's what you mean." Her smile was sudden and open and it cut Keogh deep. "Remember 'horny,' Frank?"

Robbie released a theatrical sigh and pushed himself away from the table. "Jesus, you two."

Tricia laughed and looked at Robbie with such intense maternal affection and warmth that Keogh felt a kind of envy for her, for her ability to love the unlovable. It was one of the graces she possessed, to love and to be tender toward people who gave her less than she gave them. It was the vulnerability in her that had attracted him in the first place. She was strong enough to go unguarded through her loves. You could hurt her and she would not instinctively hurt back. Keogh felt she was a better person than he was, but he also felt that Robbie needed a serious boot in the ass for taking advantage of Tricia's good heart.

Keogh put his arm around her and pulled her in close to him. He found himself kissing her neck, breathing in her scent, aware of her body. He realized he was hungry for her, more than he had been in weeks.

She leaned into him and reached up to put soap suds on his nose. "Nice to see you, stranger."

"Nice to see you too," said Keogh, feeling like a cockroach on her shoulder.

"Frank, what happened . . . with Art?"

Frank told her as simply and undramatically as possible, leaving out most of the gunfire.

She listened quietly but with fear showing in her eyes, seeing more than he was telling her.

"Where is he now? Is Marian with him? I'll call Marian right now. She's going to be a wreck, Frank. What'll happen to them now? You're not going to charge him?"

"In Lincoln for observation. Marian was with him last night before he went to sleep. No, I'm not going to charge him. Neither is Jack. But he's out—he's off the Job. I think he'll maybe get off with a Command Discipline. Depends on Pickett. It's a Zone Commander's decision, and Emil's fucked up enough on his own, he'll be glad to see somebody else screw up worse than him. And the Sergeants Endowment guys will go to bat for him."

"Poor Art. So close to getting out with a clean sheet. Why was he so angry with you?"

Telling her why would mean talking about pulling the trigger on a couple of teenage boys, and teenage boys were tricky to talk about around her. She brought everything back to Robbie. And he never liked to tell her too much about exactly what it was he had to do for a living. She knew, but they never talked about it.

"Well . . . he kinda figured we were a little hasty in that Bolsa Chica thing. He was kinda upset about it."

She looked hard at him.

"What about you, Frank? Are you all right?"

She touched the bandage at his neck. She put an arm around him and kissed him on the cheek. Under her hands he felt the scratches that Myra had put there.

"Hey, babe. I'm a rock, huh? I'm fine."

"Yeah? I think you're lying."
Well, thought Keogh, she's got that right.

Pulaski shoved the cassette in and hit the PLAY button so hard the machine rocked on the rollaway cart. The huge Sony monitor flared white, snapped into a dead black with violet sparks. There were nine men and two women of Charlie Sector Emergency Services in the squad room on top of the 46th Precinct house. Slick Ryan, Moxie and Pepsi, Finn Kokkannen, Charlie Boudreau, Arnie Sayles, Nate Zimmerman, Joe Langosta, and Peggy Zacco, a blonde from Naples and the unit's only Thai-boxing specialist. They were leaning on desks, slouched in battered oak chairs, standing along the back wall. Pat Butler was sitting up front, playing with his stainless-steel Ruger single-action. He had his blue cowboy boots up on Pulaski's desk. He looked like a Panhandle sheriff and he seemed very pleased with himself. Keogh stayed at the back, drinking a cup of industrial-strength coffee out of a pig-shaped mug.

The room smelled of cigarette smoke and gun oil and Endust. A shaft of August sunlight the color of old bone lay in a hard square on the wooden tiles. There was no talk.

In the way of cops, Keogh's go-round with Art Pike had not been mentioned. Nobody wanted to talk about a cop who had lost it. The idea was to step around it and go down the road and not get any blood on your own file.

Bert Pulaski was a big wide-bodied bullet-shaped man with a Marine crew cut and a red face. He always wore a two-piece suit and shiny black uniform shoes. He looked like a tall toad with heartburn. He was staring at the screen as if it was going to tell him the answer to every question that had ever kept him up at night.

An image snapped onto the screen. There was a time marker running in the lower right-hand corner of the frame. The picture was black-and-white, almost a sequence of still shots taken every half-second. The viewpoint was high and the angles were distorted, fish-eyed. It was the interior of a medium-sized bank branch. People were moving around at desks and tellers' stations. Five tellers were visible at their stations behind a long counter. Out in the public area a few citizens, farmer-types in jeans and western shirts, were waiting their turn. Double glass doors at the front. Cars parked outside. A bright white glitter off the windshields.

As the people in the bank moved, they seemed to blur and re-form. A gesture became a fan of gray mist that suddenly hardened into an arm or a head turning. Mouths moved in silence. At 1130.07.09 hours by the time marker, three men came in the front door carrying weapons. They moved fast. They were not wearing masks. One of them, a big black male, had sunglasses on. The other two were white, one rangy blond and a second man, shorter and running to fat. The short man was carrying an automatic weapon.

"Watch the guy with the Heckler," said Pulaski into the heavy silence. "I've got something to say about him. Keogh and Butler, you watch this."

The big black man and the blond went through the bank in a very thorough professional way, herding the tellers back, getting the citizens down on the ground. Their movements were efficient and cool but they worked fast. There was no bank guard. Nobody was giving them any trouble.

The short man with the Heckler put his legs apart and braced himself. He pointed the weapon right at the camera and everybody in the room felt the chill that comes when something like that is pointing at you.

The man was holding it wrong, too tight against the ribs but not firm in the hands. At 1130.19.03 he started firing at the lens.

There were three fast flares from the barrel. The man rocked on his feet, and you could see the muzzle climb. The picture shook with the concussion, but the image stayed.

You could see the shock wave run through every citizen in the bank. Farmers on the ground flinched and tried to dig into the terrazzo. The tellers at the side bunched up and you could see their mouths working in soundless screams.

The man collected himself, hands unsteadily fluttering over the weapon. The muzzle rose again, and there was more white flaring from the weapon. Three flares.

"*What* an asshole," said Butler, mesmerized.

"Those are three-oh-eight rounds," said Slick. "A twenty-round magazine. He's got it on three-round bursts."

The blond man was visible in the lower circle of the fish-eye. He was staring at the short man with the Heckler and you could see that he was disgusted. But his hands were full of cash bags. He said something but there was no sound. The short man fired again. And missed.

"Nine down. Eleven to go," said Moxie, grinning.

"Shut up, Mike. The black guy killed an Oklahoma trooper about thirty seconds from here," Pulaski snarled.

The man fired in two more three-round bursts. You could see his face clearly, see the fear and the anger in it, and now and then you could see him look down to where the blond man was racing through the cash drawers, as if he expected the blond to come over and show him how to do it.

There was a figure at the door, a boy in a trooper's Stetson; he was looking back over his shoulder. He did not seem to know what was going on in the bank. The short man fired again, holding the weapon into his shoulder, aiming it like a bolt-action rifle. His shoulder rocked with the recoil and more white flame exploded out of the barrel.

The man at the glass door hesitated.

"Well, he musta heard *that*!" said Slick.

The short man was still firing.

The big black man appeared in the lower frame, holding a shotgun. The trooper started to come in through the doors, loose and tentative.

The frame went black.

Pulaski got up and hit REWIND.

He turned toward the silent room and lifted up a sheaf of papers on his desk. He set a pair of half-lensed glasses on his nose and looked out at them over the tops.

"First thing, the trooper's name was Bunny Keegan and

he was twenty-four. He took a full load in the stomach and died three hours later in the Comanche County Hospital. This happened on Saturday. The FBI guys sent this video to Langley and the spooks did a computer enhancement run on it." He held up an enlarged color shot of the short man. It was a printout on dense computer paper. It was a pretty good likeness of Lyle Beauchamp. It showed the fear in him, but it was Lyle. You could pick him out with the shot.

"Only benefit of the space race. There's no clear shot of the other two guys. The FBI has been circulating this picture nationwide. Some county bailiff in Charleston is the cousin of the senior agent there, and he was having lunch with him. Sees the computer thing of this guy on the duty room wall. Apparently he was in on a seizure of this guy, had a used-car dealership in Charleston. He IDs the guy as one Lyle Benning Beauchamp, D.O.B. ten May—you guys better take this down—D.O.B. ten May, one nine four three. No priors but a long sheet for credit. Also busted for drunk and disorderly. Various small-time shit."

The unit was looking at him expectantly. There had to be more. There was.

"Seems Lyle here has a younger brother. This is his shot. He's done state time in Utah and California." He held up the classic full-face and profile of Sonny Beauchamp.

"He's a professional armed robber. FBI says he's dangerous, armed. Anybody recognize him?"

They all stared. Pepsi finally said, "Yeah, I think so. I think . . . it's football, isn't it? Guy maybe played . . . Jesus, let's see—"

"Two years middle linebacker with the Dolphins, back in the seventies. Never amounted to much. Got into this with another guy after he got cut. They say he's a pro. He never shoots unless you shoot at him. People in Lawton said he was very polite."

Butler laughed. "Right up until he pops the cop."

"Witnesses say it was the black guy did that. We don't know who he is yet, but we got a short list of people Sonny worked with or served time with. FBI is going over the possibilities. You're getting all the files on this."

Keogh spoke from the back of the room.

"Why us? If anything, this is something for Citywide Armed Robbery guys."

"Texas Public Safety guys got into the border towns. They found a stolen pickup in some place called Burkburnett, Texas. Little old Mexican lady was driving it. Forensic found blood on the flatbed. They gave her a pretty hard time. Finally she says maybe the guy who gave it to her is going to New York City."

There was an unspoken "so?" hanging in the room.

"So . . . we're trying to be ready for anything. Duffy—you know Duffy from the Feds—Duffy wants us to keep an eye out. This Sonny guy, he's a hell of a shot. They were running down toward the Texas border and a couple of Comanche County troopers were chasing them on a side road. Now get this. . . ." There was definite admiration in Pulaski's tone.

"Two cars going parallel down some potholed cracker roadway. A pickup truck and, one hundred yards away on the right, a state car with one of the troopers up on the doorframe, firing at the pickup with a lever-action Winchester. He must have hit somebody. There was blood on the flatbed."

"Nice shooting," said Butler.

"Yeah. So somebody on the flatbed gets up and lets fly with the Heckler. Puts a whole magazine out. He hits the trooper car in the grille and the windshield. The front tires go. The driver takes a round in the left lung. The car rolls, and the next time they see the pickup, some Mexican granny is driving it into the Helpy-Selfy in Burkburnett, Texas."

Pulaski looked up as two men came into the room, a black man in a gray two-piece suit with a detective sergeant's badge, and a second man, white, also in a good suit, also showing his gold shield.

"Yeah, just a minute, Zeke, Butch. So . . . we figure

the shooter sure as hell wasn't this Lyle guy. It's one of the others."

Keogh nodded to the two newcomers. He knew Zeke Parrot and Butch Johnson. They worked Homicide at the 46th.

They both nodded at Keogh and walked over to stand next to him. Butler waved to them and turned to Pulaski.

"Duffy give you a lead on why they might be in the city? We got a shitload of perps to watch out for on the wall back there, boss."

"Duffy says the FBI ran a list of known associates. Sonny Beauchamp did farm time with a guy named Myron Geltmann, and Geltmann is now working for a company in the city called Pelham Bay Industrial Services. They clean offices and residences. Very Upper East Side stuff."

"Ahh . . ." said Butler.

"Yeah. So they're putting Surveillance onto this Geltmann guy, just to see who he's talking to. Twenty-four hour. And Armed Robbery wants us to be ready if they need us. They don't want to take down a guy with a Heckler without some help from ESU."

That figured, thought Keogh. Armed Robbery guys were cowboys but not kamikaze cowboys. The Heckler alone would make anybody with an ounce of sense very nervous. It made Keogh nervous just watching the video. More than anyone else in the room, Keogh knew what it was like to take automatic weapons fire. It feels like you're a radish in a Cuisinart, steel coming down all around you, shreds of leaves, red dirt exploding out of the ground, the air full of rushing noises and the solid chunking sound a round makes when it hits bone and flesh.

"Finn, you're surveillance-trained. I want you to go work with Surveillance on this. They like you—you hang around with them. No contact, understand. When you get any sign of either of these Beauchamp guys, we hear directly from you."

Slick Ryan grinned at Finn. Pulaski dropped the papers on his desk. "The rest of you guys, go suit up. We're going up to the range and do some standard assault scenarios. Be at the portcullis in fifteen minutes with your gear. Keogh and Butler, you stay here. That's it."

The room cleared out fast. The two Homicide detectives said nothing. Butler came back to Keogh.

"Zeke, Butch. Always a treat. Frank, you look okay. I heard you had yourself a little adventure last night."

Pulaski walked over to them. There was something on his mind. It was clear from the set of his mouth, and his face was pale. Butler saw this too.

Pulaski looked down at his shiny black shoes and then looked up at Keogh. Keogh's stomach did a slow roll.

Tricia? Robbie?

Was it his father? His father worked Homicide, worked the same desk that Zeke Parrot sat in, back when it was the Seven Zone. He looked hard at the two detectives, and they looked hard back at him.

Pulaski cut into this. "Frank, I want you and Pat to go along with Zeke here."

"Bert . . . what is it? Is it Tricia?"

Pulaski's face went through a number of changes.

"No . . ." He nodded to Zeke Parrot. Zeke's brown face was drawn and tired. He pushed himself off the back wall and came up to Keogh. Butch Johnson came up on Keogh's other side.

"Frank, cut the shit. Just cut the shit."

Keogh stared at Zeke.

"Fuck you. Has something happened to my wife?"

"You're good," said Butch. Zeke looked down and then up, moving in closer to Keogh, looking down at him.

"Okay, Frank . . . what time did you get home last night?"

Zeke's eyes were yellow around the iris. He seemed braced for something, as if he expected Keogh to turn violent. Keogh got it then. He'd been on the other side of scenes like this, so it was the mirror trick that had put him off, like when you drive up to a familiar intersection from another direction and you don't recognize it right away.

"You want to Mirandize me, Zeke?"

"You want us to, Frank?"

Keogh waited. They watched him wait.

"I got in about five in the morning. Ask Tricia."

Butch Johnson was writing in his memo book. His salt-and-pepper hair was cut so short Keogh could see the pink of his skull shining in the sunlight that came through the dirty windows. Butler opened his mouth to say something, and then shut it.

"We did," said Zeke. "She confirms that. Jack Weisberg says you left Lincoln Hospital in an RMP from the Four-Oh. Driven by a member—"

Johnson read it from his memo book. "Kholer, NSU seven. Badge seven nine nine three."

"Yeah. Weisberg says you left around two hundred hours. Where were you from two to five?"

Keogh felt anger and fear. What the hell could he say?

They saw him looking for words and each man drew a private conclusion.

"What the hell is this about, Zeke? You doing family counseling now?"

Pulaski was watching him the way a man would watch someone taking apart a pipe bomb.

"Where'd you go, Frank?"

"What the *fuck* is this about?"

Zeke's black face was full of pain and rage.

"Where'd you go, Frank?"

"Where'd you go?"

CHAPTER 9

**Wednesday, August 22
1230 hours
Manhattan**

Sonny wasn't impressed with Myron Geltmann's son-in-law. He was one of those yuppie-puppy types, in his early thirties and never been put to any kind of test by life, just surfing along on the opium dream of America, racking up cash with his industrial cleaning company as if God had woken up one day and said, Man, we gotta do something special for Joseph-call-me-Joseph Levine.

The four of them were sitting around in a restaurant on First Avenue in the Fifties, at a table in the window. The place was all white. The table had a paper tablecloth on it. There was a glass full of crayons on the table, along with a thin vase with a daisy in it. Lyle was leaning over the table; apparently the idea was you could draw cute things on the paper, and that's what Lyle was trying to do. Sonny hadn't seen much of Lyle other than the bald spot at the top of his head for the last ten minutes.

Myron Geltmann was sitting silently across from Sonny with a mildly embarrassed expression on his pouchy white face, his eyes wet and restless behind the rimless bifocals. He slouched in the bony metal chair and looked too small for his blue cotton shirt. There was a patch on the pocket.

It said *Myron* in script, above a computer-type logo that read PELHAM BAY INDUSTRIAL SERVICES.

Joseph-call-me-Joseph Levine was in a suit, a double-breasted gray, which he had opened when he sat down to show everybody his bright-red suspenders and his eel-skin belt. Joseph was deeply tanned, with intense black eyes, a thin black moustache, and very good teeth. He was wearing contact lenses and when he spoke he had a way of forcibly crinkling his eyes in what Sonny had realized was a conscious attempt to look hard and capable.

Levine was talking, a little too loud, leaning forward over his chicken soup and making points with his spoon, staring into Sonny's eyes without blinking. Now and then Sonny would look down at the thing that was floating in the middle of Levine's soup and wonder what the hell it was. It looked like a scoop of mashed potatoes. Sonny wondered if Levine was going to eat it, and if so, when.

"It's a matter of timing, Sonny. I know you're thinking, well, this guy's not experienced in this kind of work. True. I freely admit that. I'd be totally wrong to try to convince you otherwise. I know my limitations, don't I, Myron?" He didn't wait for Myron to answer. Myron didn't try. Sonny doubted that the kid knew his limitations. They hardly ever do.

"Yes, I know them. But you see that's the essence of this . . . project. I have the necessary connections, and you and your brother—you have the technical skills. You come well recommended by my father-in-law. I know we can . . . take this project to . . . fruition." He was trying to speak around the point and was sounding like it. Sonny wasn't happy with the location either. There were people all around them and here they were sitting right in the window next to a street full of more cars and people than Sonny had ever seen, a torrent of yellow cabs and slick-looking people, and it seemed that every ten seconds a siren would go off and some blue-and-white NYPD car would go whooping off up a cross street. Sonny wished Lyle were paying more attention, but he didn't want this Levine kid to see a division between them. It wasn't good to let people see where you had trouble.

"I'm not . . . persuaded." Sonny used the word deliberately, mocking the kid's style. "I'm not persuaded that you understand the results here, Joseph. If the project comes off successfully, you're still going to have to deal with a certain amount of questions. It would be natural for them to come to you with . . . questions."

Levine waved that away. Sonny noticed the gold Rolex on his wrist, a little too big for him.

Levine took a red crayon out of the glass and started to draw a random series of arrows on the paper. He didn't look down as he did it, keeping the eye-to-eye going with Sonny.

"You ever been through a major audit, Sonny? I'll bet you haven't. I have. Three years ago. I was only twenty-eight, just a smartass kid, but the IRS threw a major audit onto me. Went over me like a combat proctologist. They got nothing. Found nothing. Some asshole I was in business with, he put the word on me. But I rode it out, never cracked a bit. And those guys are hard. Nasty. I'm telling you, you go up against those guys, you're blooded!" His face was flushed under the tan. Sonny could see now why the kid was getting into this. He wanted to see himself as a risk-taker.

"I had double-booked a whole contract. The site manager was paying off like a slot machine. It was all over the books but they missed it. And they knew something was there. I can take some heat, Sonny. I've made a lot of money in the nastiest town in the world. Don't you worry about that. Anyway, it'll never come to it. I've got that covered."

He was still cranking out those little red arrows. They looked the way a silent alarm would look if you had to draw the sound.

"Yeah? How'd you work that?"

For once, Levine lowered his voice. "You really want me to go into that here?"

Sonny didn't want another curbside chat. It was now or never. "Yeah. Just the basics."

Lyle had stopped doodling. Now he was staring around the restaurant with a bored look on his face.

Levine wrinkled up his eyes. Clint Eastwood.

"Okay, Sonny . . . Down First here, there's a place called the King James. Huge old thing, couple of thousand apartments in it. Near the tunnel? No? Never mind. We got the contract for some of the tenants. There's a lot of money in there. Old money. There's a guy lives in the penthouse, has a house in Virginia, a condo in La Jolla. I'm not giving anything away if I tell you the guy's a close personal friend of Peter Lawford. Well, he was . . . and the Radziwills? You've heard of them? He's very connected to Los Angeles. Last time my crew was in there he was having a big dinner party, and the people there, man—Candice Bergen, a couple of ambassadors, Rudolph Giuliani—heavy heavy hitters, Sonny."

A residential hit. And he runs the cleaning staff. Levine would be first on the list when Holdup went looking for new assholes to tear. But they were here, so Sonny just let the kid talk. Maybe he'd hear something he could use.

"Now I'd give you his name. You'd know it in a flash. But first we gotta reach an . . . accommodation, right?"

"Joseph, what're we gonna do? Kidnap Candice Bergen? Force them to give us a screen test?"

"No. The guy's heavy into numismatics and philately. He's a world-class philatelist. Been in magazines."

That got Lyle's attention. "Philately? You hear that, brother? The man's a philatelist. I wanna meet him."

Sonny grinned. Lyle knew damn well what the kid was talking about. Even Lyle knew a jerk when he saw one.

Levine smiled back. "Coins, stamps, medals. Gold coins, rare stamps, mint-runs. Portable as hell."

True, thought Sonny. And he had a good idea who would buy them. At a reasonable discount. But . . .

"Yeah. Well, the trouble is, I'm not . . . ah . . . persuaded." He used the word with satisfaction. "I'm not persuaded that you understand the . . . complications. You're going to be in a position to . . . a position of power. We're on the inside, on the project. You're on the outside, having sushi or some shit uptown? Plus it's too obvious that it's limited information. Who else would have the information? And Myron here, he's already on their shit list. Myron's okay. But, Joseph, you're making a big mistake if you think the IRS is the same as talking to . . . It's the difference between a headache and a heart attack. How'd you get the information? You go there?"

"No. I own the company. I got guys do that for me. And I already thought of what you're saying. I got that covered too."

Here it comes, thought Sonny. What the hell happened here? All he wanted was to go back to Charleston, get a room in the Coeur d'Anjou, where he could watch the light change in the harbor and eat chicken-fried steaks. Pray for the Steelers to get somebody like Jack Lambert again. Make a deal with the *federales*. But no, here they are, Lyle and Sonny, the Pointy-End Kids, breaking bread with somebody whose idea of combat is cracking wise to the IRS. Curiosity was the only thing keeping him in the chair.

"Your point is well taken, Sonny. You're an obvious professional. I like that. I'm a pro too. Of course they'll think of the cleaners. So we use that. The best way to put a cop off the trail is to give him exactly what he wants."

Levine looked up and sideways at Myron, who took a deep breath and sat forward. He looked around at the people in the café, the well-dressed and self-absorbed men and women talking in fevered undertones, all at the same time, no one really listening, just holding their breath with their lips half-open, ready to start talking as soon as there was a pause. Myron's face was wet and gray.

"Me and Joseph here, we have an arrangement. In order to bond me, he had to register me as a convict. The bond company made him put up a surety. Anything goes wrong, even the hint, takes the surety. This . . . project . . . comes off, I'll be the first one they come to."

True, thought Sonny. So what's the trick?

Myron saw his expression. Lyle was now listening very closely. Levine's sleek face was empty.

"Sonny, Rose is in and out of the hospital. She's in bad shape. I need to set her up, take care of her once and for all. I need to do one last deal. This has gotta be it."

Lyle got it first.

"What is it? Cancer? You have cancer, Myron?"

Myron smiled at him. "Lymphatic. I'm . . . Yeah. So—"

Sonny wanted to say something but there wasn't much that wouldn't sound hollow. Levine cut in.

"Myron's a stand-up guy. He's worked this out. He's been inside this place, he's got a list of the alarm substations and the security boxes. The guy has showcases full of gold coins and stamps and lots of things. Myron has a list of what we should . . . acquire."

"I've been down at the library every day, Sonny."

"Yeah, he has. And he figures . . ." Levine used his red crayon to write a figure on the paper tablecloth. He wrote it upside down so Sonny could read it:

$800,000.00

Lyle looked up at Sonny. There was a yellow light in his eyes. Sonny was watching Myron.

"Myron, how long they give you?"

He shrugged. "Christmas, maybe. Maybe not."

"And you want to do it this way?"

"Well, Sonny, you have to admit it's pretty solid. They'd have come to me anyway. I . . . I go along. Joseph here will see to it that Rose is all set up. Hell, Sonny, I've been inside before. They'll treat me good."

Levine was all energy now, the final hard-sell.

"We fork out on the bond. The insurance takes the rest. I'm the outraged employer. The trust betrayed. My rep on the line. I go to this guy, I'm standing there on his fucking Aubusson; I'm drinking his sherry, using the Voice. 'One of my own. A family man. How can I make it up to him? I'll do anything. . . .' The shmuck will be trying to make *me* feel better." He circled the red numbers on the tabletop.

Sonny looked around at the people. Such a cold-assed crowd. If Myron died right in front of them, falling over into his soup with the mound of whatever it was in the middle, these people would hold up cards: Nine point five. Nine point nine. And the Russian judge.

Sonny realized that he was homesick. Eight hundred thousand dollars would see Lyle safe into Mexico.

"Levine. Why is it you wear suspenders *and* a belt?"

CHAPTER 10

Wednesday, August 22
1445 hours
The South Bronx

Of all the things a detective hates in the world, and he
hates a lot of things, there isn't anything he hates more than
having to ride in the back seat of an unmarked Plymouth
four-door with those little moon-shaped hubcaps. But it was
Zeke's car and Butch wasn't going to give up the shotgun
seat, so Butler and Keogh got into the back and they pulled
out of the lockyard at the 46th in front of all the uniform
guys getting ready for the second platoon.

"Thanks, Zeke. The whole precinct thinks I've been
busted for killing a cop."

Butch Johnson turned around to stare at Frank in the
back seat as if Frank were something that came shrink-
wrapped air mail from Sweden. Butler kicked the seat-
back.

"All right, you dickweeds, we gotta talk."

Keogh sent a look to Butler that could have taken a year
off his life if Butler had noticed it.

Zeke didn't turn around. He just grunted and kept
driving. They were on a rising crest of hill that gave them
a view across the Harlem River to the massed projects and
threadbare parks of northern Manhattan. Keogh stared out

through the side window at the scene and thought about the last conversation he'd had with Art Pike.

There was a crowd around: harness cops who were there on other business, a couple of nurses, and an intern from Korea named Wong who looked to be about eleven years old. Pike was already in one of those no-back hospital gowns they use to keep you humble while they box and file you somewhere in the attic. Pike's teeth were out and his cheeks were hollow and gray. But he was smiling up at Frank Keogh as if his troubles were over. Maybe they were. They tried to wheel him away through the swing doors but he caught Keogh's hand.

"I see you looking at me. I can tell what you're thinking. But you have no right, Frank. You don't know what it is to be old. You think it's just a matter of carrying the weight. But it's not like that. It's like after twenty years, the weight doesn't weigh anything, like what was holding you down when you were a kid, you took it seriously. But when you get older you see it ain't shit. You see they're all just as bad as everybody else. Cops, the assholes. What are you gonna do about that, Frank? None of it means a thing, kid."

Did Pike still think that, when whoever killed him came into the room in the middle of the night? Did he hear the footsteps in the hall? Was he awake and thinking about it when it happened?

"Frank, are you gonna tell these mopes, or am I?"

"Shut up, Pat."

"Shut up Frank, you are such an asshole. Zeke, have you talked to Myra Kholer yet?"

"Who the fuck is Myra Kholer?"

Butler looked across at Keogh and raised his eyebrows in a question. "Keogh? Frank? Come *on!*"

Butch Johnson fumbled through his memo book. "Yeah, I got a Myron Kholer, was the cop who drove Keogh home. Took an RMP from the Four-Oh off the computer at Lincoln. Weisberg says this Kholer dropped Keogh off in Yonkers and went back to check in the RMP. RMP is down as back in the yard by oh-three-hundred hours."

"That's *Myra*, Butch! Frank, Zeke here isn't gonna bust some PW for using a Department vehicle for personal use. All Zeke wants to do is clear the case—right, Zeke?"

Zeke turned around to stare at Butler.

"This Kholer guy's a broad? A cute broad?"

"Does Miss Piggy have a hand up her skirt?"

Zeke and Butch looked at each other.

"Ahh, shit. Let's go get something to eat."

The B and V Steakhouse used to be one of John Keogh's favorite places in the Bronx, back in the days when the Hunts Point section wasn't a reasonable facsimile of Beirut or Mexico City.

Back then it had been a pretty nice part of town, a slope of residential apartments with some trees and some parks and kids playing football in the alleys. It had gone through some changes now, and the B and V was a last outpost of civilization in a brutal landscape of ruined buildings, barred-up and caved-in shops, rusted car hulks decaying into the gutters, wolf-eyed men and boys carrying on business out of vans and in the reeking basements of fading projects. At night the lights were dim and yellow and the sound of sirens was as steady as smoke from a stack.

The woman who ran the B and V was Argentinian. She and her husband had been serving up tapas and chilies rellenos and back ribs in napalm sauce to a couple of generations of NYPD detectives assigned to the mid-Bronx sectors. Frank remembered sitting around in the dark red-and-black interior with his father many years ago, watching his father talk to his buddies, listening to the stories, seeing his father as an elemental force, trying to stand in his presence with some shred of dignity, seeing the cop world as a dark terrain lit by unexpected eruptions of passion and violence, seductive and repellent.

Now, in the ruins of the neighborhood, Keogh and the others came back to the B and V partly out of loyalty to the woman who had run it as a police club for so many years. They knew that if the neighborhood realized the cops had gone elsewhere, the little family business would go down in days.

Zeke Parrot sat on his haunches like a tired bull in a corner of the back booth and stared hard at Keogh as Keogh tried to tell his story without making himself look like too much of a complete bastard. By the time they got through a bottle of Glenmorangie, Butch was relaxing a little and Butler was getting a laugh out of both of them ending up with policewomen on the same night.

Butch said that as a family man he thought Frank was dicking around with some very dangerous stuff and it was too damn easy to fuck up a marriage. Zeke Parrot looked like he was prepared to believe that Keogh had spent the whole night with Myra, but Keogh knew that as soon as he got the chance, he'd be off to call Myra and find out just when it was they'd finished up with the flesh trading, and whether that left Keogh enough time to do whatever it was that Keogh had done. Finally, Zeke pushed himself up and out of the booth. When he came back about ten minutes later, he was a different man, relaxed, wry, just a little embarrassed.

Zeke didn't really give much of a damn what other men did with their body parts, as long as it didn't include killing people they didn't have permission to kill. He and Butch had spent most of the morning watching Peter Zouros— they all called him Zero—take Art Pike apart down at the Medical Examiner's offices.

Butler came out with it finally, asking for details. It wasn't really any business of his, but in the way of cops, Zeke and Butch were prepared to talk about the thing in general terms.

Butch, who was something of an autopsy fan, told them about it with his mouth stuffed full of chili, his unshaven pink cheek stretched out like a spinnaker.

"Man, you don't know how old a guy is until you seen him on the table, you know? Last time I saw Art was in the elevator at Thirty Rock. He looked *good*. Nice suit. Pink."

Zeke shook his head. "What? The suit?"

Butch gave his partner a look full of Christian forgiveness.

"Nah! His skin. His *skin* was pink. 'Course, then he was full of blood, right. It's your blood that gives you your pink color, y'know?"

Butler looked at Zeke. "What about Zeke here?"

That stopped Butch for a second.

"Well . . . underneath."

"Underneath what?" asked Butler, apparently puzzled.

"Zeke's pink . . . underneath."

Zeke looked away, sighing. Butch pulled his brows down to make the point. He didn't want to come right out and say anything about Zeke's color.

Butler leaned forward and asked with intense seriousness, "You did that?"

"Did what?" said Butch.

"You checked underneath Zeke to see if he's pink?"

This stopped Butch.

"Underneath Zeke's what?"

Zeke let out a long slow sigh.

"Jesus," said Butler, "how would I know? You're his partner."

Keogh was suddenly tired. This was the way cops usually handled death, any death that was close. But he needed to know what the Homicide guys knew, if anything.

"Look, Butch . . . how did it . . . how did Pike get it?"

Butch raised his massive shoulders in a shrug, lifting his hands up in front of him in a classic Zeke Parrot gesture. They've been together a long time, thought Keogh.

"*Ugly*, Frank. Pike died ugly. Man, we seen some shit, you know. Zeke, you remember that bathtub thing, guy was tortured by some kids, they sprayed paint up his nose, cut him up? Finally drowned him face-down in a tub? Most killings, it's like a reflex thing, unless it's a gay killing, which are pretty bizarre. This one, well, I can tell you the guy was in no hurry. Also, he knew something about anatomy. Also, a joker."

"How so?" said Butler.

Zeke answered that. "The nurse, the night nurse who got it. Sharon Zeigler? Whoever did this, he did a number on her was exactly, I'm saying *exactly*, like the stuff Jack the Ripper did in England. Opened her up like a can of sardines and flipped her out all over the bed. Right down to the position of the legs."

"Exactly?" said Keogh. "How do you know?"

Zeke nodded to Butch. Butch said, "Frank, I got a book tells you all about that thing. Shows drawings. Gets into all the short strokes."

"Why the fuck would a man do something like that? You gonna go to Quantico on this? See if anybody at the BSU has caught a guy mimicking old killings?"

The FBI maintained a special research and stats-analysis unit at its training academy down in Quantico, Virginia. It was called the Behavioral Science Unit. The specialty was serial killing. The psychologists and detectives assigned to it had worked on most of the major homicide cases in the United States and Canada. They collected data from every law enforcement agency. If killings similar to this had taken place anywhere in the world, they'd have the cross-index on it.

"Damn right," said Zeke. "Going out today."

"What about Pike? He . . . get some knife work too?"

Zeke didn't answer Keogh's question. He seemed to be thinking it over. Butch waited a bit and then said, "Well, Frank, he got some. But we can't really get into the details. I mean, we trust you guys, but we got this thing sealed up. We can't have some asshole coming in and confessing and giving us scene-of-crime details, and then later his lawyer asks us who did we tell, and boom goes the confession. We had cases killed that way."

Keogh knew they were right. Intimate knowledge of the homicide details was a critical means of testing a confession. And it had happened that killers who had later regretted their admissions had found lawyers who could get the confession squashed in court by showing that some of the details had been discussed with other cops.

Keogh had a brief stroboscopic image of a glittering blade in a path of blue-green light, and Art Pike's face surfacing into the light like a gaffed fish. He tried to shake it out of his head. Zeke caught the gesture.

"You okay, Frank?"

"Yeah. Anything we can do?"

The two Homicide cops looked at each other. There seemed to be a flicker of tension. Something was decided in a set of the brows and a twist of the mouth. Finally, Zeke looked at Keogh.

"There is something we could ask you guys. You ever catch any ligature cases when you were working the task force?"

"Some," said Butler. "Nothing special. Frank?"

"Yeah. Clotheslines. Panty hose. Once a tie some guy got for Christmas, he used it to strangle his wife next day. Fishing lines. A coat hanger. Can't remember anything else. Why?"

Butch answered that. Keogh had the impression this was a routine, something they had thought about and were now running out in front of Keogh and Butler. Why they would be doing this, now that Keogh's alibi had been pretty well established—that was something else.

"Weirdest thing I ever seen, Frank. Some kinda thin cord, like silk or something. Only it's not. Had a knot in the middle, a weird kind of braided thing. Like chink pigtails. Only more complicated. The knot was right in the center of Pike's Adam's apple. Like it was there to crush it? Pulled from behind and knotted in the back. Tied together. Pulled in hard."

"Lot of muscle in the pull," said Zeke.

"Yeah," said Butch, glancing at his partner as if looking for some sign. "Damn near took his head right off. Cord was out of sight in his throat, and there was a lot of swelling around it. You got the idea the thing was done . . . slow, if you get what I'm saying. The guy . . . you get the idea he enjoyed what he was doing."

Butler was thinking about it. "What do you mean, like a ritual or something? Satanists?"

Zeke cut in. "We can't get into all of this, Pat. You know that. We're doing the usual shit: medical records, personnel files, got the parking attendant to go over all the tickets, get the license number of every car in the hospital lots, public and staff cars. We're running all of them through CATCH and FINEST—for once the Feds are helping, looking for perps and skells. We dusted the room, and the CSU guys tried for latent prints on Pike."

"Get any?"

Zeke looked cagey. "Some. They fumed him, the iodine gun? He'd been undressed by the nurses, so there were latents on his upper arms and his ankles. On his back. We got prints of everybody who got near him, everybody on the staff. They all had a good reason for putting their hands on him, and they all came up with pretty good corroboration about where they were. So far, we got dick."

Keogh was trying to keep the picture of Art Pike's naked body on the table out of his mind, Pike's body cracked open like a lobster, shiny slick shapes in a blue light from a lamp, and Pike's face staring up, black and surprised.

"So the cord, the rope, whatever? It was still on him? You get anything off that?"

Butch looked at Zeke before answering Keogh.

"It's called a ligature. Yeah. Weird, right? Zero had to dig around a little for it, because we wanted it off in a piece. You can't untie something like that, because the ligature, the way the knot is tied—everybody does it different. Everybody has his own way of tying the knots. You know, you learn it in boot or scouts and for the rest of your life you're tying your shoes or the roof-rack on with the same knot. So the lab has it for fibers and shit, and we got a couple of strange prints off Pike's forehead. So it all comes down to who would want to ace Pike. Sorry about thinking it was you, Frank."

Zeke looked at him. "The Feds get this. They file the prints until we can give them some better information. But I'm asking them to go through the computer to see has anybody else used this modus operandi, right? They got a record there of all homicides nationwide. The VICAP system? If anybody else has used this kind of knot, used a cord like this, then it'll kick out a buncha names."

"You think it's some psycho from out of state?"

Zeke's mouth was full. Butch answered for him.

"Nah. We just do that shit to cover it off for the boss. He'll ask us for sure. You wanna know what we think, you keep it to yourself, guys? Okay? We're looking at the family of those kids you and Pat took out last week."

Butler and Keogh had already thought of that, but they kept quiet. It was rare enough for Homicide cops to be this open about a case without trying to stunt-fly around them. Butler ordered another bottle.

"The Rodrigues kid has an older brother in the Ching-a-Lings, and the Goncalves kid has cousins. We were looking at the news videos of that thing. By the way, Frank, that was a nice piece of work. You, too, Pat. Anyway, that Lewis guy from the *Eyewitness* station did a long thing about the hostage negotiator and they even had a picture of Pike on the news. Ran it twice."

"Shit. How'd they get that?"

"You'd never believe it, Frank. They used a telly lens to get a shot of Art in the truck. Some dildo left the doors open. They had a good shot of Art talking on the phone."

Zeke wiped his face with a big cloth napkin. "Yeah, and a good one of you, too, Frank."

That shook him. He hadn't seen the news videos. And Tricia hadn't said anything. "What shot? Where?"

"You was coming down a stairway. How come you wear that blue suit anyway? I thought all you ESU guys had to wear those flak jackets and the Buck Rogers suits with your ball caps on backwards. Anyway, it was you. Showed you clear as a mug shot, and the Remington and everything."

"They name me?" This was not good news.

"Damn right they did, the cocksuckers. Right out loud too. Man, those news guys are real dickheads. Voice-over said Detective Frank Keogh of the Emergency Services Unit. And there you was with the rifle and everything. I thought you knew."

Butler's face looked a little pale as well.

"Me too? Was I on camera?"

"Just the back of your head. You don't dress as nice as Frank here. You was wearing those cowboy boots, the blue ones. Man, you looked like a drug dealer or something."

Butler and Keogh thought that over while Zeke and Butch argued about dessert like a married couple.

If the person-or-persons-unknown who had killed Art Pike were doing it for some Latin vendetta, and they knew who the sniper was, then Keogh was in danger and so was his family. Butler and Keogh could get some police protection for their families, a regular squad car past the front doors or even an officer staying with them in their houses, but in the long run there was only one reliable way to deal with the problem. Zeke and Butch could see the idea taking shape in their faces. Zeke Parrot held up a huge black hand the size of a pot roast and looked very sternly over it at them.

"Now wait just a fucking minute, you guys. You go messing around in this investigation, we're gonna nail your nuts to a stool, the both of you. This is a homicide investigation, not one of your cowboy stunts. All we need is for the D.A. to hear you been whacking around our chief suspects and we'll have the ACLU and all those maggots on us like shit on a hamster! Butler, I know you. You half-killed that Armenian guy last year and all he did was phone you at home."

"You tell Pulaski about this?"

"The boss did. Pulaski's already got the C.O. at the Four-Five running extra patrols by your place on City Island. And, Butler, the Yonkers cops are sitting on Junie, so just relax, will ya? We're just trying to warn you—watch your asses. But none of that Tombstone Cops shit you guys are famous for, huh? This isn't Bronx Vice, you know."

Whatever Keogh and Butler planned to do about the Ching-a-Lings, the idea was not to have to go to war with Zeke Parrot and Butch Johnson over it. Keogh and Butler had been together long enough to know what the other man was thinking, and they'd been cops long enough to know how to fake absolute sincerity.

Keogh's eyes were wide and innocent.

"So you're saying the Yonkers cops are sitting on Pat's wife?"

"Yeah. All day."

Butler smiled at Keogh.

"Well, Junie'll like that."

There's a school of philosophical thought that holds the view that God is a kind of cosmic adolescent who got the keys to the universe while his parents were out having dinner at the in-laws' and that the last sixty quintillion years of the space-time continuum has been run by God in roughly the same way a brainless teenaged boy would handle a turn at the wheel of his father's Testarossa.

Another school maintains that the devil is only God when he's drunk.

Keogh was a lapsed Catholic—most Catholics are lapsed Catholics—who was usually of the opinion that God was paying no more attention to the universe than his son Robbie paid to the ant farm he had stoutly maintained he would love and cherish for eternity only a year ago, and which was now running energetically into chaos at the south end of the family lawn up in City Island, half in and half out of the very pricey aquarium that Tricia had brought home one day from the pet store.

This view of celestial malfeasance was about to be irrefutably confirmed. Tricia had noticed that the RMPs from the 45th were going past their bungalow on Schofield Street about three times as often as normal. She also noticed—as she sat in the sunny front room of the tiny red-brick house with the long rolling front lawn that led down to the clean white curb—that the cops in the cruisers were paying more than the usual perfunctory attention to passers-by on the sidewalk and that they were staring a lot at the driveway and the shrubs around the house.

So Tricia, who was a cop's wife and who knew a lot of other cops' wives, decided to find out from one of them why it was that the Commanding Officer of the Four-Five had given orders to his patrol cars to keep a close watch on Frank Keogh's house.

She had about a half hour before she had to report for O.R. duty at the cardiac unit at Bellevue, in midtown Manhattan, so while she dialed and talked, she kept an eye out for Custer, who was still missing. There was a picture of Custer up on the wooden mantel over the living-room fireplace, side by side with pictures of Keogh in various styles of uniform, Tricia in her nursing school graduation gown, Robbie as a kid, sitting rather unsteadily in front of a cloudy backdrop in his first long pants, an idiot grin on his chubby face. It was this chubby face and the idiot grin that Tricia still saw whenever she looked at Robbie now, and it was that gift which allowed her to ride out her son's current incarnation as Teenager From Hell. There were pictures of John Keogh, Frank's bulldog father, in his dress blues a year before his wife's death. Another shot of him in plainclothes being honored by the city at a Mayor's dinner, John's crew-cut hair bristling with his pride, and his immobile cop's face twisted into a parody of gratitude.

There were black-and-white photos of John's wife—Frank's mother, Madelaine—a forties-style black-and-white of her leaning on her forearm, her lips full and pouty, her heavy black hair shining, a softness in her eyes that suggested she was looking at or thinking about someone she was very much in love with. Tricia liked the shot of Frank's mother, and felt that Madelaine was someone who would have understood what it was like to be married to a Keogh and the NYPD. But she had never known the woman.

Frank sometimes tried to get Tricia to take the pictures

of his father down, but she always refused, as gently as she could. Frank wouldn't talk much about his father, so the pictures stayed there as Tricia's way of keeping the memory in the air. She felt that it was unnatural for a father and a son to have such animosity between them after all these years, after all the brimstone of adolescence had cooled and their lives had solidified into definable shapes and patterns.

The room itself was all Tricia, done in deep greens and the cherry-red of mahogany panels, here and there a vase of silk flowers she had arranged herself. It was a very English room, down to the patterned Persian rug and the bow window and the huge flowered sofa and the brass screen in front of the fireplace. She had worked very hard to make it a sanctuary for them, away from the brutality and the ugliness of Frank's job.

That was why Tricia was in a way offended and angry when she noticed the unusual attention from the local precinct cars. Maybe there was a good reason for the protection, or maybe it was just officiousness and drama. But whatever it was, the sight of those blue-and-whites rolling slowly up and down in front of her house bothered her the way weeds in her carefully tended rock garden offended her, as crude eruptions of the subterranean in the quiet green glade of this house and her life.

She called Bert Pulaski's wife, who was sweet to talk to in the way of sheltered cop-wives but who knew little of her husband's work, and no, Bert had not said anything to her about cars for Keogh's house in City Island.

Tricia tried to reach Pat Butler's wife in their house up in Yonkers, but Junie had the answering machine on, one of her cute little tapes with a Barry Manilow song in the background, Junie sounding like a cross between Garbo and a cabbie, saying she wanted to be alone today. Junie Butler was Tricia's closest friend in the incestuous substructure of the NYPD, but Junie's relationship with Pat was on rough ground. Frank never said anything, but Tricia suspected that Butler was sleeping around a little. Tricia's job down at Bellevue put her in contact with a lot of young healthy males. She had been attracted to a couple of them, and had even gotten into some steamy fondling at a staff party last year, but she believed that infidelity would crack an already strained marriage. And, when she looked at it head-on, she was in love with Frank, even if he was a clone of his hard-nosed father.

Well, so far no results. She decided to dig a little deeper into it for another ten minutes, then give it up and go to work. Frank would tell her when he got home. Maybe.

Butler and Keogh had both worked Vice in the Bronx area a couple of years back, so they had a pretty good idea of where to start looking for Flavio Rodrigues's older brother Fausto. Fausto was a middle-level consignment crack and coke dealer whose franchise territory covered the area around the El Niño Bar and the Concourse to Third, and from 160th down to 149th Street, an area of the South Bronx known as Melrose to the city planners and as Little Lebanon to the NYPD cops assigned to keep the lid on it.

This part of the South Bronx mainly consisted of ragged red-brick buildings jutting up out of vast expanses of rubble-covered vacant lots surrounded by chicken wire and the rusted remains of stolen cars, patches of scrub grass, and mud. Even the dirt here was dangerous; hard clay shot through with shattered glass and broken bottlenecks, tin-can blades, old needles, the occasional bullet case.

Back in the days when Frank and Pat had gone hell-for-leather over this territory, hard on the heels of some fleet little gentleman of the street, Frank or Pat would sometimes look down at what they were scampering across and think, Jesus, what are the archaeologists going to think of us when they dig through this stuff in a thousand years. The earth of the South Bronx was packed with the throwaway dreams of America: bottle caps and switchblades, condoms and blood, Coke bottles full of piss, cans of Bud Lite and Coors, slabs of concrete and jutting spars of girders, slat fences, stands of goldenrod and Queen Anne's lace and ragweed, a wheel rim, a cat with its legs cut off and a trail of its own blood fifty yards long, black birds dead in the storm drains. Kids like coyotes set fires in the basements; crack dealers and cops flew across the face of this landscape like wild dogs in God's Own Junkyard. Vice had been sweet that way—"intense" was how Butler described it in those days, after they'd just gone boot-first into a room full of cranked-up Puerto Ricans or brought down some kid with a flying tackle, and Butler would pick himself up or check Frank for bullet wounds and they'd look at each other with the dust coming down and say, well, that was intense, huh, Frank? Yeah, they'd say it like a koan or a prayer, putting the seal on it, adding it to the list. That was intense.

They were rolling down Third in Butler's grass-green Riviera, listening to the radio talk and playing Tom Waits tapes. Butler thought that if there was anybody could write the theme song for Little Lebanon, it would be Tom Waits, and he had practically every tape the man had ever done. They were listening to him do "Blind Love" and going down Third at around 150th, looking out for Fausto Rodrigues.

Butler was pretty convinced that Pike had been killed by a Ching-a-Ling, maybe a hired hitter doing it for his *pachuco compadre* Fausto. You could never tell about the Ching-a-Lings. They were a very bad crowd. A Ching-a-Ling had gotten into a small argument at a candy store over in the 46th Precinct area a year back. The owner of the store had told the biker to get out and backed up the threat with a tire iron he kept under the counter. The guy was a family man, one of the last surviving Italians from the old days, and he was sick of taking attitude from some Mohawk-headed biker who couldn't speak English, let alone Italian.

The Ching-a-Ling went out to his bike and tugged a Mac-10 out of his saddlebag. He stood on the steps of the little candy store and emptied a full magazine into the owner. When the guy's kid came running around from the back to see what was happening, the biker shot him twice in the head.

Another Ching-a-Ling was suspected of the execution of a detective who was giving them a hard time. The cop had been sitting in a tavern near Fordham when a couple of bikers walked in and lit up the place with machine-gun fire. It wasn't out of the ballpark for a Ching-a-Ling to decide that Pike and the others involved in the Bolsa Chica shooting ought to pay for it. It would be a good PR move for the gang, show the street that not even the *lajaras* could fuck with them. That was why Keogh and Butler were about to fuck with them in a very memorable way.

Butler had pulled a CATCH shot of Fausto Rodrigues from the computer room at the 46th. CATCH was an acronym for Computer Assisted Terminal Criminal Hunt. You asked the operator to find the NYSIIS or Criminal Ident number of the guy, and then the machine would refer you to a microfiche file of possibles. Then you got a blowup of the microfiche and went looking for him.

Keogh had a good idea of what they were going to do to this Fausto character. He was a little worried about the paper trail.

Butler waved it away, singing "Walkin' Spanish" to himself. "No problem, as Alf says, buddy. I know the operator. She'll dump the request. Anyway, all we're gonna do is talk to the guy, explain how we would appreciate it if he and his buddies would assist us in our inquiries."

"Assist us, huh?"

Keogh picked up the file on Fausto. The boy was beautiful, fine-boned and black-eyed, with expensive white teeth, a certain style about him, as though at some point in his line there had been some quality. But he was strictly middle-management for the Ching-a-Lings.

He had a credit line of five grand a week on coke or crack, whatever was selling. He'd pick it up on Sunday from another level of supply. They'd front him against his credit line. The supply would put a "5" down beside Fausto's name in his debt book. Fausto would take the drugs to one of his storefronts, a transient hotel, a room in a tenement, a basement somewhere. There'd be a slot in the door and the door would be reinforced with steel or wooden beams.

Fausto would leave the drugs in the care of one of his

girlfriends. Up until last week, his younger brother Flavio would help out in that area.

Then Fausto would put on some nice threads and go cruise his franchise, looking for people who were looking for him, keeping an eye out for competition, for people trying to sell in his protected franchise. Cops he could give a shit about, because Fausto never carried any dope and if you wanted to buy from him, it would go something like this.

Fausto would be hanging out in El Niño or Franz Sigel Park, he'd be working on his chill and staring slitty-eyed at the girls going by, and you'd come up and say, Hey Fausto, how's it goin'?

If Fausto knew you, he'd look away around the park to see who's watching. Then he'd say, Hey, *pachuco, que tal?*

You'd say, Well, you know I doin' this and that.

Yeah? *Un poco poquito*, hey?

The talk would go 'round.

So . . . Fausto. You know anybody holding?

He'd say, Hey, man, I don' know personally. Not into that no more, you know?

Yeah, well, I am, man. You think of anybody?

Fausto would look pained, staring into the sun.

Hey, man, I don' know. I hear maybe you could get some *hielo*, some ice.

Hielo? Hielo would be good.

Well, you know, man, you ain't heard it from me, but you could go over to Los Lobos, you know?

Sure, man. On One Fifty-fourth? The place with the roses on it, in the yard?

I heard some guy say maybe you could get something.

So you go over to Los Lobos and line up with the rest of the guys in the hall. When you get to the door you say what you want and you hand the cash through the slot.

Somebody in there will drop something into your hand and you don't stand around testing it or asking about the Knicks, and if you take it home and red-flag the works into your arm and it kills you, well then, you just found out the cost of a ticket to heaven.

At the end of the week Fausto will go back to his supply with $5,000 in cash. Whatever Fausto has been able to get over and above that amount is his to keep. A good week will see him make $3,000. Sometimes as much as $5,000. Everybody is happy. Unless Fausto were to get busted and then tell Vice about *his* supply.

But that wasn't likely either. Even if Fausto were to get popped in a SNAP program, Fausto's supply is protected by the Ching-a-Lings, the same people who guarantee his franchise area in Melrose. If Fausto tried to burn a Ching-a-Ling supplier in return for some plea-bargain leverage, it would be a very bad trade.

Drug gangs in the South Bronx punish informers by cutting their throats and letting them bleed to death while a couple of the boys sodomize them. Then they leave the bodies propped up on their knees, naked. Then the guys at the 48th Precinct, maybe Zeke Parrot and Butch Johnson, get a call from an RMP and they have another name for their Green Book. Most of the names in a Homicide cop's case file get there because of a drug dispute.

It was the Ching-a-Ling connection, and the way Pike died, that had brought Keogh and Butler out looking for Fausto Rodrigues. The idea of a Ching-a-Ling vendetta against a couple of SWAT cops and a precinct negotiator was business as usual. But wives and children called for some direct action. It called for something massive.

"Lincoln Hospital."

"Hello, is Marjorie Reyjak there?"

"She's in E.R. Who's calling?"

"It's Tricia Keogh. Can you call her?"

Bored sigh. "Yeah, just a minute."

Tricia listened to phone Muzak for three minutes, looking around her room, wondering why she was being this persistent. Sometimes she didn't know the contents of her own soul, let alone her husband's. But there was something.

"E.R. Hello?"

"Marjorie, this is Tricia."

"Well, hello. How *are* you?"

"Oh, good, good. How's Mirko?"

"Rotten. He hates Albany. How's Frank doing?"

"Well, he's okay."

"Not when I saw him last. They were pulling little metal balls out of his ankles last night."

"Yeah. Well, he's okay. Marjorie, did something happen last night? Anything you know?"

A pause. "Cops are such *pricks*."

"Why?"

"For God's sake, Tricia. Didn't Frank tell you about Art Pike?"

"Yes. About the fight they had."

A longer pause. "Tricia, didn't Frank tell you that the guy was murdered last night?"

The familiar room faded and came back.

"No. No . . . I haven't heard from Frank. How?"

"Messy. I wasn't here. I got off around two this morning and when I got back in here this afternoon, there were crime ribbons all over Three West and there was Zeke Parrot standing around looking like thunder and Butch Johnson and it looked like every cop in the precinct. I can't believe Frank wouldn't tell you!"

Tricia could. So *that's* why the extra patrols. Any time a cop died, every cop connected to the case put extra cover on his own family. And it was like Frank not to say anything to her about it until he could do it in person. She felt a little relief at knowing. Poor Marian.

"Margie, they have any idea who did it?"

"God, child. You think they'd tell us? They've been up in Records all day, and everybody had to fill out a form saying where they were, and anybody who couldn't prove it had to talk to them in the cafeteria. It's a zoo!"

"But Frank . . . Frank would have known about it last night, wouldn't he?"

"No. It didn't happen until later. They sewed Frank up and sent him home. I saw him go. This thing happened much later. They say around four or five in the morning."

Tricia's heart began to pound in her chest and her throat filled with ice.

"What time did he leave?"

Silence. "Well, honey . . . it's hard to say."

"Margie, don't shit me. You just said you got off at two last night."

"Yes . . . but it could have—"

"He got here at six-thirty."

"Tricia, that's nothing. He could have—"

"Who drove him home?"

"I don't know."

"You just said you saw him leave. Who was he with?"

"I don't know. Some cops from the Four-Oh."

"Any women?"

"Frank wouldn't sleep with a cop!"

"Why not? I do."

CHAPTER 11

Sonny and Lyle took a tower room at the United Nations Plaza Hotel, high enough to get a look at the King James a couple of blocks down First. Sonny could see that Lyle felt better as soon as they walked into the lobby. It was all mirrors and green marble and little rows of pin lights along the ceilings. A bellboy in a green uniform carried their bags to the elevator and the concierge welcomed them to the hotel. Lyle and Sonny were wearing the best they had: Lyle in his dark-blue Italian suit with the baggy pants and Sonny in jeans and a leather jacket. Lyle had the idea that everybody thought he was maybe an entertainment lawyer in from the Coast and Sonny was his bodyguard. Looking at the way the bellboy was watching him in the mirrored panels in the elevator on the way to the thirty-zillionth floor, Sonny figured maybe Lyle was right. Lyle was doing all the talking for a change, mainly for the bellboy's benefit.

"You've called Jason over at Fox? His position on this whole thing is horse shit. I'm giving him four days—then we go to Paramount and that's it."

Sonny wished Lyle wouldn't feel it necessary to try to con bellhops. Bellhops could give a dead bat about who they were. Only thing you got from trying to con a bellhop was that when you wanted something from him, he charged you twice as much. Sonny just hoped that Lyle would remember not to call him Sonny. They were registered in a two-bedroom tower suite as Dennison and Bolt, Lyle being the Bolt. Lyle had loved the name when they got the gold cards in the mail: Maxwell Emerson Bolt, a gold American Express card, not stolen, a legitimate alias Sonny had worked out for them before the Lawton disaster. Sonny was Paul Dennison. Right away Lyle had started calling himself Max Bolt and dressing the way he figured an entertainment guy from the Coast would dress.

The suite was as big as the prison infirmary, with a carpet deep enough to lose your car keys in. Lyle went straight for the mini-bar and opened it up the way Billy the Kid must have opened up that bank vault in Juarez, his chubby face all lit up. Sonny gave the bellhop a five and walked over to the window to get a look at the city.

Jesus, he thought, what the hell am I doing here?

The lights were coming on all over the city—what looked like a wall of glass and steel glittering with lights and neon, a gridwork full of buildings and streets packed with red lights and headlights, traffic on the big broad dirty gray river, bridges going across, and far out there past the slate-gray flatlands of Queens and Brooklyn, maybe a glimpse, a slice of hammered tin that Sonny figured had to be the sea. The size of the place, the numbers of strange faces and the sirens in the streets, the sound of it, made Sonny feel pinned down and pointless. He felt he could fall a long way in this city and nobody would notice or give a damn or call his people in Charleston to say what had happened to Sonny Beauchamp. These were not feelings he was used to having. Lyle called him from his bedroom.

"Sonny, you gotta see this. There's a TV in here bigger than the Rio!"

"Yeah, just a minute." Sonny was looking at the King James. It was big, the size of a city block, a massive pile of brown brick with English castle touches, and on top of it there were two huge English mansions, maybe three floors

each, with big leaded windows and terraces and even grass
and trees. It looked a little run-down, but most of New York
looked a little run-down. Sonny was learning that people in
Manhattan who had any money knew damn well how to
keep it. The guy they were looking to hit was living in the
penthouse apartment down there. A soft yellow light
glowed behind the big leaded windows. Sonny imagined
oak panels and green banker's lamps, and lots of oil
paintings about three hundred years old, swords and spears
on all the walls. A family crest. Some white-haired gent
with a cane from Burma engraved THANKS OF THE REGIMENT.

How to get in and get out, that was the question.

Sonny got his Bushnells from his flight bag and looked
the place over carefully. There was the sound of a game
show coming from Lyle's room, and Lyle saying, "Greasy
Grass, you dickheads! Greasy Grass!"

No outside escapes, no fire ladders. No pipes, no ropes.
Maybe three hundred feet to the ground from the terrace
walls. They'd have to go down the elevator. Place might
have a private elevator entrance. He could see the cap of
the shaft on top of the pitched roof. There'd be the usual
perimeter alarms, trip-wire alarms. Maybe a heat sensor.
Assorted weight-sensing devices. A motion detector.

This wasn't like a county bank, ground-floor walk-in,
wham bam thanks for the cash *adios*. They'd have to get in
a back way—that was possible. That little shit Levine could
get them in, maybe wear cleaning-shift uniforms. They'd
have keys; they'd know the man's schedule. The trick would
be picking their way through the alarm systems. That
would take some research, maybe access to the guy's
insurance company. Levine could get that. Myron would
know all about that—it was what he did for a living. Sonny's
problem was how to get them out once they had the stuff,
not just out of the building but out of the state.

He could see how easy it would be for the cops to lock up
Manhattan island. It could be like Alcatraz. Lock up the
bridges and the tunnels. Cover the airports and stations.

Have men on the subways. There were 28,000 cops in the NYPD, an army.

Well, shit. If it was easy, everybody'd be doing it. There was always a way to do every job. He'd done harder ones, with less help.

Jesus, though. This was one hell of a big city. When they figured out how to turn sea water into concrete they'd make the whole planet look like this. It'd look like a big disco-glitter ball hanging in space, all bright lights and neon, spinning in the middle of nothing.

Lyle was laughing now. He could hear the TV going.

"I *told* you! Greasy Grass! Shit, you coulda won!"

CHAPTER 12

**Wednesday, August 22
1600 hours
The South Bronx**

"Jugo, lemme in there, I gotta talk to you!"

The door was four by ten, plate steel. It looked a foot thick, including the planks. ESU had an armored personnel carrier with a ram that could go through this door. But Keogh and Butler didn't want to drag the whole of Charlie Section into this. It was personal. It was up to Fausto here.

It was a good thing there weren't any cameras in the hallway. Old Jugo in there would see how Fausto looked.

Fausto looked like he'd just tried to screw a bobcat and hadn't given her any flowers or candy first. His Armani suit was covered with dog shit, his face the color of a ripe plum. Keogh and Butler had their backs along the wall on either side of the door. They were standing in the basement of an abandoned tenement on Vyse Avenue. The place smelled bad: piss and old stone.

Jugo was talking back through the slot in the door. "Fausto, you come back. I can't let you in now."

Fausto was putting everything he had in the sell.

"Look, Jugo, this is important. The cops, man, they're going to take this place down. I gotta get in, see Roberto. Roberto's got problems, man. This is no shit."

Jugo's voice was hesitant. "Look, Fausto, I can't let you

132

in. Man, Roberto's with a broad. You know how he is. We go in there, he's gonna be pretty mad."

"Jugo, you fuck! You think the cops are gonna wait till he gets off? Man, open up. We got no time."

A silence. "You alone, man?"

"Yeah, fuck yeah."

"Lemme see your face, man."

Fausto looked at Butler. Butler nodded once.

Fausto bent down and put his face at the slit.

"*Hijo de la chin-ga!* Man, what happened to you?"

"Fucking cops, man. Come on!"

"Jus a minute." There was a sliding sound, iron against steel. A series of snaps and clicks. More bolts being pulled back.

It's not easy being a dealer, thought Keogh, his heart spinning in his chest like a fan blade. Butler's face was white and set, the skin across his cheekbones glistening with sweat, the big Ruger revolver in his right hand, his eyes wide. This is crazy, thought Keogh as the door started to open up, and then he thought about Robbie and Tricia and Art Pike, and then they were going in.

Keogh had Fausto up in front of him, on his toes, the Browning over Fausto's shoulder, shoving the weapon into Jugo's face. Jugo went limp and his skin flushed as he fell back into the room, the shotgun dropping out of his hands. Butler was on his heels, moving around to the right. Keogh raked the muzzle across Jugo's Mohawk haircut, slicing his scalp open. Jugo went boneless and slid into a heap on the ragged rug. Fausto went after a bagful of cash. Keogh kicked him in the head. Butler was already going through the thin wooden door, smashing it down in front of him, his Ruger out, going in like a pit bull.

Roberto was on his feet in the corner, naked, his big belly wet with sweat, his skin pink and raw, bringing up a shotgun. There was a naked girl in the far corner of the room, up against the corner.

Butler was in the air over the bed as Keogh got to the door. There was a blast from the muzzle of the shotgun. It

shattered the doorframe a foot from Keogh's head. Butler
hit the floor a foot from Roberto's right knee and drove the
muzzle of the Ruger into his crotch. The force of the blow
lifted Roberto up onto his toes, on his face the look of a man
seeing a new sun behind his eyes. Butler jerked the
shotgun out of his hands. Roberto was already going down,
three hundred pounds of wet bone and fat, a bald head,
tattoos and black hairs plastered to his body, his mouth
opening and closing but no sound coming out. Butler was
wiping off the muzzle of his Ruger and looking sick.

Fausto was standing in the doorway like a priest watching
the Goths sack his village. This was heresy. Roberto was the
war leader of the Ching-a-Lings, a power in the world.
Fausto used to think that if they wanted to sign a peace
contract between the U.S. and Russia, they'd have to come
over and see if that was all right with Roberto. And now
here he was, naked and down in the corner like a pile of
pink skin, holding on to his nuts and his mouth going *oh oh
oh* like a fish on a rock.

Keogh and Butler heaved Roberto up onto the bed,
rolled him onto his belly. Keogh used a length of yellow
nylon cord to tie his wrists and ankles in a hobble. Then he
ran a length up between Roberto's ankles and looped it
around his neck. Then he pulled it tight enough to take the
slack out of the line. It lifted Roberto's ankles up about a
foot. Roberto started to groan a little, and he raised his head
to take the pressure off his throat. He looked up and
sideways at Frank Keogh, standing there at the head of the
bed. Roberto's face was shiny red and his one visible eye
was hot and full of a kind of wild-boar hatred. He said a lot
of things in Spanish into the sheets while Frank looked
down at him, his right eye very blue and his green eye
hidden in a trick of the light, a hard plane of light across his
ruddy face.

Butler was staring at the muzzle of his Ruger. He
reached into his back pocket and threw a package of
something across to Keogh. It was a brown paper bag.

Keogh reached inside it and pulled out a package of
Ronzoni spaghetti.

"Roberto, you hungry?"

Butler was still looking at the Ruger.

Roberto closed his eye. His head went down, but then he
felt the pull of the cord and he raised it again.

Butler looked over at the girl in the corner.

"Hey, lady, you got any soap around here? I gotta wash
my gun."

Keogh drew out a single strand of the spaghetti and
snapped it in front of Roberto's widening eyes.

"You're not gonna *believe* this part, Roberto."

CHAPTER 13

Wednesday, August 22
1940 hours
The South Bronx

They were coming down in a swing through Crotona Park—Keogh and Butler feeling a silence on them, puzzled the way men are when the skin of life comes off and something shows underneath that is not what was expected—when Zeke Parrot and Butch Johnson caught up with them. Zeke's face was black and thick. They came to a stop in a stand of trees, Zeke was out of his car and coming at them, Butch calling to him, Keogh and Butler staring at him as Zeke came around the Riviera at Keogh. Keogh got out of the car fast but Zeke's fist caught him in the side of the head above the ear and he went down.

Zeke Parrot stood over him, fists up, his chest going like a bellows, his shirt torn at the belly. "Get up, you mick bastard!"

Butler pushed Butch out of the way and came over the hood after Zeke Parrot. Keogh got to his feet again, his ear burning, working his jaw, stepping forward to come in at Zeke. Butler had Zeke wrapped up, lifting him off the ground with his arms around Zeke's chest. Zeke could see nothing but Frank Keogh's eyes, Keogh in front of him.

"You trying to fuck up this case? Is that it?"

"No, Frank! Wait. Zeke, what the hell—"

Zeke twisted himself out of Butler's grip and squared off

136

in front of Keogh. Keogh looked up at him and held his place, his feet apart, his blunt Irish face giving away nothing.

"The Ching-a-Lings, you assholes! That's what this is about. Butch and me said stay away from them! But no, you two got hard-ons, have to go play movies. You couldna fucked this case up better, you been trying to!"

Butler moved around between Keogh and Parrot, facing the Homicide cop. Keogh moved to the side, where he could see Zeke's hands. Butch stood watching, his face uncertain, his hands up in front of him.

"You talking about Roberto?"

"What the fuck you *think* I'm talking about? I got a snitch said he could put two of those suckers in the area at the time. I'm trying to get a warrant on Roberto. And you wanna know where the fuck Roberto is now?"

Butler and Keogh said nothing.

"Cowboys, that's what you guys are! You're always gonna be cowboys. Botched Casualties and the Some-Dunce Kid. You're a fucking pair, ain't you?"

There was a long silent moment. Then Butch Johnson began to laugh. Butler had to smile. Parrot and Keogh were still looking at each other hard, but Keogh could feel a smile coming.

"Not bad, Zeke. Botched Casualties—I like that. Is that me, or is it Frank here?"

"The point is, the guy is down at the Civil Liberties lawyer right now. Guy's swearing an Information. They're naming you, Frank, Butch, and me, and half the task force. I got the D.A. on my ass, he's saying Miranda, Mallory, Elstad, Fourth this, and Weeks that. Tainted Evidence! Fruit of the Poisoned Tree. The case against those guys is dead in the water. You're letting a bunch of cop killers walk!"

Keogh moved away a couple of feet and turned around to look at the three of them standing there in the hollow of land, surrounded by worn-looking oaks, the sun coming in through the leaves, a hazy dappled light on them.

"It's not them."

Zeke Parrot's face darkened again.

"It's not them, huh? Who the hell is it then? Is it you, you cocksucker? You got this little pussy police broad to lie for you? You go in there, choke out Pike yourself? I can see it. You're crazy. Fucking sniper. Man, I can see you doin' it!"

Butler shoved Zeke back onto the car.

"You're starting to sound like a real dickhead, Zeke. What we're trying to say here, we don't think the Ching-a-Lings have anything to do with whoever took out Pike." He looked over at Keogh. "Roberto—"

"Roberto had nothing to do with it, Zeke," Keogh said. "Best thing you could do, stop fucking around with that theory. Pat and me don't think any of those guys had anything to do with it." Keogh smiled at Zeke, a slow twist of his mouth. "Zeke, if Roberto had anything to tell us, he'd have told us. Believe it."

"Roberto says you guys pulled some weird army shit on him. What'd you *do* to him, anyway?"

Butler looked away from Keogh. Keogh's face was empty now. "We made an impression on him, is all."

Butch spoke up. "That you did, Frank. He also says you stole all of his cash. And some guy named Jugo is in the hospital, got a concussion. And this Fausto guy, he wants four hundred bucks for a new suit."

Butler laughed outright at that.

"New suit! You want the money was in Roberto's bank, you go ask Fausto."

"That what you guys are saying? That Fausto scooped the Ching-a-Ling bank?"

"How much Roberto say was stolen?"

"Twenty-eight grand, old bills."

Zeke and Butch were looking very carefully at Frank and Pat. One of the great moral dangers of working in Vice was the amount of untraceable cash you tended to come across. Zeke and Butch knew that both Keogh and Butler had worked in Bronx Vice. Sometimes you took the cash; you told yourself you were just doing what the courts would do.

You were fining the dealers, putting them out of business.

Butler's hand was very close to his Ruger.

It got very still in the little clearing. A sound of sirens and children playing came drifting in the air. A candy wrapper rustled along the pathway.

"You calling us Buddy Boys, Zeke?"

"Buddy Boys" was the code name a group of bent cops had used a couple of years back. They had been busting dealers and splitting up their bank. One of them committed suicide when he was charged. The rest of them were simply destroyed by the Department, forced to wear wires against their own men, turning evidence against one another.

Zeke turned away and sat down under a tree, putting his head back on the trunk.

"Fucking job, man. Fucking shootout."

Butch Johnson walked around to the back of their cruiser and opened the trunk. He reached into a cooler in the trunk and pulled out some Stroh's. He threw one at Frank Keogh, who caught it without looking away from Zeke and Butler. Butch cracked his, cold foam arcing out in the sunlight.

"So, Frank. If it ain't the Ching-a-Lings did it to Art, then who the hell *was* it?"

Butler took a beer, and Zeke caught his on the fly. Keogh took a long pull and looked around the clearing.

"I don't know, Butch. Something's happening. I just don't know what the hell it is."

Zeke took off his suit coat and slipped his tie off over his head. He exhaled slowly and took another drink of beer. Butler came over and sat down facing him, on grass as worn as an old carpet. Butch walked away from Keogh and went to the car radio.

"Sergeant Four B to Central, K?"

"Sergeant Four B?"

"Central, we're gonna be sixty-two at Crotona Park and Charlotte with ESU Single Six, Butler and Keogh, K?"

"Any problems, Sergeant Four B?"

Butch looked over the car top at Frank Keogh. Keogh was looking past him at the woods, at a couple of black kids playing Frisbee with a big yellow dog. The dog went high for it and took it out of the air as neat as Roger Craig, coming down in a spin and racing back toward the boys on the long green lawn. A soft wind moved in Keogh's thick black hair.

"Nah, Central. No problems."

The four of them sat around on the grassy slope off Charlotte Street, drinking cold Stroh's out of Butch's cooler and saying pretty much nothing for a while. They were all feeling a little shaky, feeling that they had come pretty close to shooting at one another in the middle of Crotona Park. It was crazy and they were a little scared.

Finally Zeke opened his eyes and looked over at Pat. "Okay, what'd Roberto say to you, made you so sure he had nothing to do with Pike?"

Butler ran the cold can over his forehead. Whether he told Zeke about what they had done to Roberto depended a lot on how long it had been since Zeke and Butch had been off the streets. Life was different for Homicide cops. It was kind of a technical exercise for them, the main player in the thing being dead and just as likely to stay dead. It gave them the time to think strategically, to make moves and set up traps for suspects. It was a rare Homicide detective who ever actually terrified the truth out of a man, because there was a limit to how long a man could be terrified. No matter what you did to him, sooner or later he'd try to put himself together again and change what had happened in his mind. Most of the hardcases knew their rights better than the cops. But in Vice, things had been different. All that mattered then was the bust, and being the force on the block. You did whatever it took to make an impression on the man, and he told you what he knew. Then you went to the next man up the ladder and you took away his illusion that he was safe, that he had some real power. Butler believed that if power corrupted you, then having no power at all, being broken on the hard spur of that, made a man pure for a while, and he'd tell you the truth in that sudden clear time that came over him when he saw where he was and what was real about him and what was only luck in not being broken before this. But how did you tell this to guys who could afford to worry about due process?

Keogh told Zeke and Butch exactly what it was he had done to Roberto. Butch and Zeke listened in absolute silence. When Keogh had finished, both Butch and Zeke stared at him for a long time, seeing him from a distance.

Finally Butch said, "You learn that in Vietnam, Frank?"

"You could say that."

"Shit! Who would think of that?"

"They did. Charlie did. They used bamboo."

There was nothing to say to that. Zeke shook his head to get the image out.

"Okay, Frank. You think Roberto doesn't know anything about Pike. That's good news. It means that the Ching-a-Lings aren't going to war with us. I can tell my wife and kids to come home. But that leaves us nowhere. It leaves us with some completely unknown guy who comes into Pike's room and he strangles him for reasons we may never figure out. That's the worst kind of case there is. And you know what? In eight years working Homicide, I have never once come across the kind of case you're telling me this is. Not once. It was always somebody knew the guy, always somebody had something to gain. If it's like you're saying, we're never gonna solve this one."

"What about Forensic—fibers and all that stuff?"

Zeke and Butch started to laugh.

Zeke said, "Frank . . . this isn't the movies. All that stuff can do for you, it can say where something might have been, or it can tell you yeah, this guy was there. You get something like bite marks, that's good, like a clear fingerprint. But none of this stuff is going to tell you your guy is right now taking a piss in the phone booth in the back of a restaurant at First and Fifty-first. You send forensic to Quantico, they'll do miracles with it, and when you actually put your hands on the guy and you drag him into Central Booking, man, these guys they'll say: Well, yup yup yup, that's the man okay. Then they look at you like you should kiss their butts because they solved your case for you."

Butch threw his can at a couple of crows sitting on a rock at the top of the slope. "Damn right. Don't matter what you know about the guy, you still gotta find him. And finding him is still the same old shit, the shit you guys made a hundred times more complicated. Cop gets killed, okay, we got a task force and all the time we need, we got a budget, we got the Feds, we got Albany and Langley and Quantico, we can pull a whole platoon, fly off to Iceland if the case goes there. It's not like Pike's some addict, we find him smoked in a dumpster, who gives a shit. But you tell us: Hey, Butch, I didn't do it, and the guys with a clear motive didn't do it. It was some total fucking stranger did it. We're like fucking stable cats in a barn full of blind horses."

Butler wanted to know what the hell that meant.

Butch raised his hands, made a gesture that took in all of the park, all of New York City. "You ever seen a stable cat when they're bringing the horses out? I grew up on a farm. Huge horses come out of the stalls, hooves the size of a sledgehammer. These crazy little cats are walking around in and out of the hooves—the horses don't step on them because the horses can see them. But New York, Pat, all the horses are blind. We're ducking around, hooves are coming down like hammers. We're not gonna make it."

They were all staring at Butch. Zeke said, "Butch, what the hell are you talking about?"

"I don't know, Zeke. But that's how I feel. We're just cats chasing rats in a barn full of blind horses."

Keogh walked over and handed him a can of Stroh's and patted him on the cheek. "Don't you worry, Butch. You and Zeke'll hurl the glove of defiance into the jaws of destiny and the dragon of fate will throw up the fur ball of truth onto the pool table of life and the pool shark of justice will knock the eight ball of evil into the . . . the . . ."

"Dumpster of destiny?" said Butler.

"No. Keogh already said *destiny*," said Zeke. "The . . . the . . ."

"Anyway," said Keogh, brushing his jeans off, "things will work out okay, Butch. Me and Pat'll leave you to it. Anything you want us to do? Other than stay the fuck out of your way?"

Zeke smiled up at Keogh.

"No, that's enough. Just stay out of the way."

CHAPTER 14

Wednesday, August 22
1600 hours
Manhattan

There was a pretty little park, surrounded by a wrought-iron fence, diagonally across the street from the entrance to the King James. The park fascinated Sonny and Lyle, because neither of them had ever seen a park with a dress code posted on the gate: MINIMUM ATTIRE: SHORTS OR SKIRT, FOOTWEAR. It was a nice park, with maples and oaks and alders and cool green grass and ivy, flower beds and pebbled walks. Here and there in the park, mothers were sitting watching their kids play, or nurses were pushing elderly people around in wheelchairs. Sonny and Lyle were sitting on a bench in the park, waiting for Myron to come along. They'd had a fine meal at a place called Il Mondo, Lyle explaining to Sonny that *Il Mondo* meant "world" and making a real production out of the wine and the sauces. Sonny had picked up the bill, reeling a little at the price.

Then they'd taken a stroll around the neighborhood, Lyle expounding in a carrying southern drawl on the differences between a Burgundy and a Bordeaux while Sonny got a sense of the terrain.

The King James was even bigger than he'd thought. It occupied a raised, somewhat isolated section overlooking First Avenue. There was a staircase that led down beside Il

Mondo to First, but cars would have to go east on 41st and
west on 43rd. There were more stairs running down onto
42nd Street. But it was a box with only one way out if you
were trying to run in a car. Any police trouble at all, they'd
be trapped.

The main entrance to the King James gave you no idea
that there might be real money in the place. Gothic arches
framed the oak doors, but the lobby was dark, the rugs
worn, and the front desk was just a counter with a couple of
bored men sitting watching a Sony portable in front of a
wall of pigeonholes for residents' mail. The switchboard was
an old-fashioned plug-style. There were four elevators,
ancient, creaking relics with expensive brass fittings and
patches in the woodwork. The lobby smelled of dust and
mold, airless and hot.

But Sonny had watched the people in the little park
carefully, watched their wrists and necks, studied the
clothes. Gold Rolexes, Piagets, solid chunky diamonds,
clothes cut with a scalpel and fitting like mist, walking sticks
and careful hair and faces heavy with years of self-satisfied
living. Nurses and nannies and servants all over the place.
No. It was here. You could sense it in the air, in the quality
of the light.

Lyle could feel it too.

"Sonny, I do believe I've found my city."

Sonny looked at Lyle, sitting back on the bench, one leg
up on his other knee, his arms stretched out on the back of
the bench, flushed with good wine and stuffed with veal, his
belly showing, blue suit and black Italian loafers and the
gold chain with the Krugerrand on it that he'd bought with
some of his cash from the Lawton job.

"You've found your city? I thought you wanted to go back
to Charleston. Live at the Coeur d'Anjou and eat every day
on the promenade."

Lyle sighed theatrically and patted his belly. "Now here's
the thing, Sonny, difference between you and me. I'm the
kind of man, you can't tell from looking at me what's going
on inside. I'm a complicated man. I know that's been a

thorn in the side for you, and don't you think for a minute I don't appreciate all you've . . . tried to do for me. Not your fault it worked out like it did. Take you—you're more the action-oriented guy. Always were. You never did know what was going on at home. Pap was dying of that cancer, you never even noticed it. Now I did. Mother and me, we'd have long talks. She'd ask me what'd I think, y'know. I'm the one got her to sell the house—"

"Lyle . . . she gave you the money to buy into Carl's Cars and where the hell did that go?"

Lyle raised his eyes to heaven. "Sonny, Sonny . . . see, that's where you go wrong. Negativity, that's your problem. That was a high-concept capital-intensive operation. It took vision to see Carl's Cars going from just a little dealership to a chain of used cars, absolutely quality-guaranteed, state-wide North and South Carolina—but all you can see is the negative side."

"Yeah. You lost the dealership to Trickem, Dickem, and Dumpem. Those bastards sheared you like a lamb."

"Negativity, Sonny. Always your problem."

Sonny heard a truck coming up the hill. He watched a brown panel truck pull around the corner, *Pelham Bay Industrial Services* in gold script on the side. "Lyle, you notice the price of that fine meal we just ate?"

Lyle waved that away. "See? Once again, oblivious to the . . . essence of the thing. The wine, superb. The sauces, exquisite. Milk-fed, lovingly harvested—"

"Harvested! . . . Shit, Lyle. The tab was one thirty-eight sixty-five, plus you gave the guy thirty bucks on top. Does that give you any idea how much it would cost you to live in this city?"

Myron Geltmann was climbing out of the driver's side of the van. He didn't look over at the bench where they were sitting. He went around to the back of the van and started to take out some cleaning gear. Myron was moving like a man in some kind of physical unease.

"That's the point, Sonny! It costs to sit in at the high-stakes games. This city—you can just feel the opportunities here. It's a town full of possibilities!"

Myron had taken a clipboard out of the van. He was holding it up against the side of the door, writing on it. He shook his head, scratched something out, ripped the sheet off the pad, and threw the sheet at his feet.

Something . . .

"What'll you do here? These high-stakes players—you know any of them? It's like everywhere. You deal with who you know and who knows you. It's got nothing to do with your ideas, not when you're getting in. And in this place, I figure you can't get in unless you're in. What would you do here? What's your specialty?"

Geltmann's left foot moved to pin the torn sheet under it, keeping it from blowing away. His foot was tapping on it to some kind of nervous rhythm Myron was feeling.

"Look at Myron over there, Sonny. That's *your* future, you're not careful. Now me, I'm thinking entertainment, communications, maybe film. It's all happening here. My theory, the Japs, the Koreans, the Germans, they're going to be running heavy manufacturing in the next century. But America, we'll be the marketing and entertainment center for the whole planet. It's what we do best—we sell you on the idea of a product. Who cares if the product is cars from Hyundai or microwaves from Braun? And film, books, television? That's the American genius. That's where we oughta be heading in the next century! Why *make* something when you can make it *up* and the whole world will love you. It's the purest form of creativity—we're not selling a *thing*; we're selling the *idea* of a thing. Nobody does that like us."

Geltmann was walking into the doorway of the King James carrying a toolbox and some mops. The pink sheet torn from his clipboard was wedged into the gutter at the back of the van. Myron had jammed it in as tight as he could.

"Lyle . . . Lyle, hold off for a second. I want you to get

up now, walk away toward the restaurant. Shake my hand like we just met, get up—"

Lyle's face went slack. "What, what is it?"

Sonny held him down on the bench. "*Sit!* Don't get up and start fluttering around like a shot duck."

Sonny looked up and down the street, checking cars and faces and places. But there was nothing out of place, no Con Ed van, no ice cream vendors, nobody on a motorcycle playing with the controls and keeping his helmet on, no men in the park, no man on the roof.

Sonny became very aware of every window in all the buildings surrounding the square. A box with a lid.

"Sonny . . . what'll we do? What'ya want me to do?"

"I count to seven. At seven, you shake my hand, you get up, you walk off slow toward the stairs down by the restaurant. You look around a little like you're strolling. You go down the stairs and you catch a cab on First and you take the cab to Grand Central. You go through Grand Central and you take another cab on Vanderbilt and you go—"

"Slow down, Sonny. I'll never remember all this!"

Sonny smiled at Lyle, calming him. "It's just practice. Just take a few cabs, then end up . . . Go to that Pussycat place on Forty-second. Near the Port Authority? Watch some flicks. I'll find you. Now get up and go slow."

Lyle's face was wobbly and loose but he got up and shook Sonny's hand. He gripped it hard.

"Don't look around, Lyle. Just say goodbye."

"Goodbye, Mr.—"

"Goodbye, and enjoy the movie."

Sonny watched the street as Lyle made his way down the walk under the maples, scuffling in his Italian loafers, his body as rigid as a post.

Myron was coming back out of the King James.

A nurse went by, hitting hard on her soft rubber soles, her hair flipping as she walked, her hips working.

No cars started up and pulled away.

This was scary. Usually Sonny could tell. If there was surveillance, he could always pick it out. But here, nothing was showing. If they were here, they were very very good.

Myron shoved the tools into the van, slammed the doors, and walked unsteadily around to the driver's door. He kept his head down and never looked at Sonny once.

An elderly woman came out of the front of the building, a huge flowered hat on her blue hair, a heavy brocade dress on, makeup like Bette Davis as Baby Jane.

Myron started up the van, slammed the side door shut, and started to pull away. A yellow cab came around the corner.

The old woman raised her hand, a mammoth purse dangling from her wrist, tottering on her heels, waving.

The van was almost at the corner. The driver of the yellow cab was a black guy, slouched low in the seat, a head-scarf on, reggae music coming from the battered old cab. He accelerated down the street after the van. The old lady flagged him.

He passed right by her, looking down the street at the van. There was no one else in the cab.

Sonny stayed very still for another five minutes. The old woman went back inside. Phoning a cab, Sonny figured.

He waited another twenty minutes. The wind plucked at the sheet and moved it about fifty yards down the street. Sonny watched it carefully, thinking if it got any windier he'd have to go after it and wondering how to do that. But the air felt different, less pressure in it.

Sighing, he got to his feet, stretched, and strolled off down the road toward the pink sheet fluttering at the base of a fire hydrant. He reached the fire hydrant and stopped to light a cigarette, dropping the lighter at his feet. In one fluid motion he bent down to get the lighter, and the pink sheet disappeared into his left hand. He stood at the hydrant for another minute, one boot resting on it.

Sonny flagged a cab on Second and listened to the driver bitch about fares that wanted to go to Grand Central and didn't know what the traffic was like at this time of day and who didn't know enough to leave a guy a decent tip, fucking town was a crock, no place for a working man. . . .

Sonny unfolded the pink sheet.

DUST
TAPS
CLAMPS
REPAIRED WIRING
FOUR HOURS
INVOICE $2,241.49

Sonny smiled at the back of the driver's head, thinking that it was a poor man who never learned anything from what life was doing to him. Myron's code was pretty simple, the kind of general-association thing they'd put on the underside of plates going in to guys in solitary at Santa Fe prison.

DUST meant something coming after you, probably a tail or some kind of surveillance. TAPS was clear enough: If there was a tail, there'd be phone taps as well.

CLAMPS puzzled him for a while, and he thought about it while the cab butted and bluffed a path through the intersection of Third and 42nd. Sonny looked up and down the canyons of Manhattan and felt a certain kind of homesickness for places in the Southwest where the sky came all the way down to the horizon. CLAMPS?

Well, it was a guess, but CLAMPS was probably a way of saying "hold on" or "don't move" or something of that kind. That stood to reason. Myron needed this job to set his wife up in a chronic-care hospital, and Sonny's reading of Joseph Levine was that he was the kind of guy who would go right on taking chances and grabbing what he could until something from the real world stopped him. That oversized gold Rolex was a clue. A man buys a Rolex, why buy one too big for his wrist? A man gets offered a stolen Rolex, he takes what he can get. And then he leaves it that way, on a band too big for him, because the thing itself, oversized and all, it stands for the bandit he thinks he is, and when it moves around on his wrist he can feel it and think: Man, I'm a player. I gotta be watched.

REPAIRED WIRING was easy. Myron had somehow taken care of the alarm systems. He either had all the blueprints, or he had gotten the cancel codes, or he had figured a way around the problems. That was what Myron did for a living, and in his time there'd been no one better at it working in the Southwest.

FOUR HOURS would mean a meeting or a contact four hours from the time Myron wrote the note, which was around four in the evening. But where?

INVOICE could mean what it said, or it could mean a phone call: IN VOICE. So the "$2,241.49" was a way of telling Sonny the address, the place where he'd wait to get a phone call from Myron or from Levine.

It would be too cute for Myron to use some algorithm or a matrix code. Myron knew Sonny well enough to know that it was all Sonny could do to add up a list of expenses.

So these numbers meant . . . ?

How about 224 149th Street? Sonny had been all over the city maps, looking for routes out of town, alternates in case of a chase or traffic trouble, and he was pretty sure that 149th Street was well up into Harlem and that there was no East 149th Street around there, where the island tapered off.

A couple of white guys hanging around in some bar or a shoe shop or some bodega up in Harlem, waiting for the pay phone to ring? That wouldn't be too smart. Might as well send up a flare: *Yo, cops! Robbers here. Come and get it!*

No, the numbers meant . . .

TWO TWO FOUR ONE FOUR NINE?

Something Myron knew he'd know. What'd they both know about? Santa Fe prison. All right, what were the blocks in Santa Fe prison? One Block. Two Block. Three . . .

They'd been built in a pentagon. One Block was . . . the eastern side. In the east. So ONE meant . . .

Okay. It's 224 East 49th Street. A phone booth in a public place there, or a phone on the bar.

Grand Central was coming up on his right. The street was packed with people, blacks and whites, office people, these strange Manhattan women wearing suits with sneakers and carrying their purses under their arms like a halfback going slot right, faces hard as prison muffins. Sonny realized then that he hated New York and that no matter what it took, he and Lyle were going to be out of this place by Sunday afternoon at the latest.

The cabbie was slouched in the seat, staring in his rearview at Sonny. "Grand Central, buddy. Outa the cab!"

Sonny said, "Thanks very much," got out and closed the door quietly and gave the man the exact fare and a dime.

He could still hear the guy as he went through the big glass doors and down the ramp into the massive station, looking at every face, seeing no one reacting to him. He'd walk over to 49th, check out the address. Do whatever it took.

CHAPTER 15

Wednesday, August 22
2100 hours
City Island, the Bronx

Frank Keogh climbed out of Pat Butler's green Riviera outside his house on City Island. The house lights were on and the neighborhood was settling down into a summer night. He waved to some people he knew sitting on lawn chairs across the street. The air smelled of woodsmoke and fresh-cut grass. Butler rolled down the window.

"You going to be okay, Frank?"

"Yeah. I'm getting the Plymouth back tomorrow. I'll see you at the station at four. You going home?"

"Yeah. Junie's gonna want to know what the hell's going on. They'll be doing something for Marian Pike, I guess. You better have a story ready for Tricia."

Keogh turned to look up the driveway toward the house. Tricia's car was in the garage. He could see Custer lying on the asphalt in front of the car. Sleeping off a bender, no doubt. But home safe. It came to Keogh that coming home was what he wanted to do, settle this out with Tricia. Stop fighting over Robbie. Get things back to the way they used to be. He looked back at Pat, slapped him on the shoulder. "Pat, I'm thinking of telling her the truth. About Myra, the whole thing."

Pat shook his head slowly. "Not a good idea, Frank. A

153

man screws around on his wife, that's one thing. He goes home and tells her about it, that's just plain mean. You feel bad about it? Then don't do it again."

The house seemed very still. Custer hadn't moved. It was as if the place were waiting for him to come home.

"Maybe, Pat. But she's hard to lie to. She's got real good antennae for a lie."

Butler put the car in gear. "And a nasty temper. You better hope you can get this one by her. Call me."

Butler pulled away down the street. The low growl of his Riviera woke Custer, and the dog came down the driveway toward Keogh at a dead run. Keogh met him halfway and braced to take the impact. Custer hit him hard and was all over him. It was nice to be met that way, made to feel you were exactly what was needed.

"How you doin', kid? Is your momma home?"

Custer sat back and made a low keening sound in the back of his throat. He looked up at Keogh, and Keogh could see the trouble in his eyes.

A cold wave ran over him. There was a hell of a lot that he could worry about, and he went all the way down the list in six seconds, going for the door with his heart blipping like a needle skipping across a record, and when he reached for the screen door with the blue heron scene on it he could see his hand was shaking.

The Hopi say the world's a wheel and Pat Butler says what goes around comes around, and it came around to Frank and Tricia sitting at the little round table in the kitchen across from the counter where Keogh used to find his sandwich waiting for him when he came in from a thirty-six-hour shift. Tricia was looking at him, waiting for an answer to her question.

Keogh was thinking that there were two possible answers to that question and that the one you picked depended on the kind of man you were.

Some men would hear the question and they'd pull it together and reach out to touch her, put a hand on her wrist or her cheek, look at her as steadily as she was looking back, and in the voice there'd be nothing but conviction and he'd say, No, no I'm not, not now, not then, you got it wrong although I can see how it would look like that but no. And he'd see to it that he would never have to lie to her about something like this again and he'd thank his angels for letting him slide by this one and still have his marriage.

The other kind of man was a Catholic prick hungry for absolution and he'd say yes.

Keogh thought he was neither but he said yes anyway, feeling two things at once, feeling a deep and cutting sadness for his wife, for what she was going through right now, and under that a thin hot wire of anger at her for . . . For what? No idea. But there it was.

She'd never looked finer to him than at that moment, her strong face and the deep green of her eyes and the skin like bone china and the head up straight, the lips hard and red. They sat and listened to the numbers on the stove clock flick down and the sound of kids in the street coming in the kitchen window.

"What's her name?"

That surprised him. It wasn't what he'd expected her to say.

"You need to know?"

"She knows my name. I ought to at least know hers."

"Myra."

"She's on the job?"

"A trainee. Patrol."

Tricia's face showed something like contempt. "A kid. How old is she?"

"Twenty . . . twenty-eight?"

"What is it? I'm too old. Is that it?"

"No . . . no, it wasn't that at all." A fleet shimmer of Myra's throat and her smooth white belly.

"Do you love her?"

"No . . . no, I don't."

"Then why? Why do it? Why do it so I can find out?"

"It wasn't like that."

"No? What was it like, Frank? I'd like to hear you say what it was like. Did she do things I won't do? Does she go down on you? Is that it? The big-time male fantasy? Does she say, Oh, Frank, you're so good?"

"Shit, Tricia . . . don't do this."

Then it broke. Her eyes changed color and tears showed in them and a muscle in her left cheek started to jump.

"Do what? Don't be too hard on you?"

"No. That's not what I meant."

"No? What did you mean? Don't be too hard on myself? Don't look too close at my husband, the great street cop? Why is it you take all your promises so seriously except the marriage promises? Did you tell yourself anything? Did you say, Well, shit, we're fighting all the time so what the hell? Did you say, Well, she doesn't understand the Job? Did Myra understand the Job? You're so goddammed *easy* on yourself, you know that? The thing that gets to me is, what, six years or something you worked all these secret narcotics squads without anybody finding out about it and here you are, looking as sorry as can be, and you know what gets to me is, you couldn't even have one party fuck without me finding out about it. Don't say anything. I've watched you working up to it, feeling sorry for yourself and taking it out on Robbie and using it as an excuse, and all you ever wanted was everything you ever wanted. Look at you. I'll bet you think you still want to be married to me. I'll bet you think you still *love* me."

"I do. I don't want to lose you."

"No? Then why is it all you think about when you're home is being back on the job? Why is it you couldn't come up with a good lie when it was never more important? No. You just sit here and look at me and I can see underneath you're thinking how *bad* you feel and how *awful* this is for *you*."

"No. That's not how it is. I want—"

"You want. Frank, who cares what you want? That's what you're all about: *you* and what you want. Just once, why can't you bastards just grow old with style. It's not . . .

seemly. You look stupid, an old married man and some little girl. It's such an *old* story. I thought you had more to you."

"You're hurt. I can see that. But things haven't been too good with us for a long time—"

"Oh, yes. And how did you handle it? Did you try to talk about it? Don't you think I know what a pain in the ass Robbie is? And all the stuff on the Job? What about *my* job? I spent two hours last Thursday holding an anencephalic baby while it died—two hours it took, the little thing holding my finger and the breath going in and out. I could feel it on my cheek and I thought of how I used to give you butterfly kisses, remember? It was like that. I *needed* you then, Frank. And where were you?"

"I'm here now, Tricia."

She shook her head, her eyes glittering in the downlight from the Tiffany lamp over the kitchen table.

"No, you're not. You're here, but you're not. You're thinking how *hard* this is for me but it isn't. You know what it *is?*"

He said nothing.

"It's a goddammed relief."

Tricia gave Keogh a half hour to pack some things and get out of the house. Frank stood in their bedroom with his suitcase in his hand, breathing her scent in, seeing the pictures on the dresser. There was a place on the far wall, up high near the corner, where he had missed a spot while they were painting the bedroom last year, and Tricia would lie in bed some nights and look over at it and say, Well, Frank, when are you going to get to that part? And Frank would slide a hand down her belly and say, his face buried in her neck, her scent very strong, he'd say, As soon as I get to this part, and Tricia would laugh.

Robbie had come home as he was packing. He was sitting in the kitchen, his face scalded-looking and white, Tricia saying something to him in a soothing voice.

Keogh stopped at the door with his suitcase and looked at

them, trying to understand why all he was feeling was a dull, centerless, and consuming anger.

Robbie pushed back from the table and stood up and walked around to his mother and put his hands on her shoulders.

"Do you want me to—"

"Just fuck off, Dad. Mom doesn't have to take any shit from you anymore. Just fuck off!"

No, thought Frank, even as he came across the kitchen on his toes, a black bile in his throat, Robbie coming forward and Tricia on her feet saying, No, Robbie! And then a wild crosscut sweep from Robbie that Frank took on the left forearm, and with his right foot back and his left forward, Frank hit Robbie hard in the solar plexus with the heel of his right hand. He felt the rib cage bend, felt the breath come out of Robbie, and saw his son's face white and stunned as Frank stepped back away again and Tricia was in between them, her face as hard as bone. Robbie was settling onto the tiles beside the kitchen sink, not yet even ready to gasp, still in that terrible middle time where the nerves are tight as tangled wire and you think no breath will ever come again.

"Get out," said Tricia. "And take your goddammed dog and never come back here."

"Tricia," he said, watching her on the floor holding Robbie, not even looking at him now.

"Just go, Frank."

She was crying. Frank saw that, saw the tears on her cheeks, and he wondered, Why can't I care about that? Why can't I feel some of this? This is real. This is you screwing up your life again, Frank.

Where the hell are you?

Why aren't you paying attention?

CHAPTER 16

All day Thursday the sun burned like a match head in a dun-colored sky. Myra kept the curtain down and watched Keogh sleeping, his thick black hair tangled, a black scatter of beard on his ruddy cheek, his eyelids fluttering as he dreamed.

Keogh was dreaming about Pinkville. Charlie had mined the whole of the flatlands around Pinkville and their unit was doing sweeps around the lock-and-load line, months of sweeps in the Pinkville territory, the sun riding high in the sky and the heat coming down so hard that a man in the saw grass could feel the cotton of his jungle shirt burning and smell the shirt cooking, a hot dry scorch-smell that made Keogh think of his mother's kitchen back home, his mother moving around in the kitchen, Keogh at the kitchen table, drinking chocolate milk and watching his mother cooking dinner and trying to get the ironing done. The iron would sit on the fabric and cook it, the hot dry cotton smell of it exactly like the smell coming off his jungle shirt as he crouched in the saw grass and tried to get up the nerve to go forward to where Max and Blueboy and Top were lying.

The thin black thread of smoke from the mine rose into the pale-blue sky, straight up into it like a black post, into

159

air as still as Top and Max. Max's Prick-Two-Five radio was squawking and crackling from the static and the damage the mine had done to it.

Keogh was still holding the cigarette that Max had given him during the rest stop before Top had told Max to get up there beside him. Max had handed Keogh the last of his C-rats Marlboros, crushed and bent but still smokable, and Keogh had used his Zippo with the crest of the First Air Cavalry on it to light it up, Max watching him carefully, that look in his soft brown eyes.

Max had been with Keogh since the beginning of Tet and had saved his life once during the fighting around Hue, street fighting and house-to-house work. Keogh's M-16 was one of the old ones, no "C" on the underside of the barrel to mark a piece with a chromed chamber, and Keogh had used the old rounds with the red dot, the ones that burned dirty and kicked a lot of smoke back into the chamber, so when the firing had come from the roof across from the temple and Keogh's M-16 had jammed, the round stuck in the chamber, it was Max who came up with his old M-14 and it was Max who put two rounds into the sniper up there and saved Keogh's life.

Now it was Max's blood on the saw grass, and the cordite smell of the mine in Keogh's nostrils. Max was crying a little and Keogh knew he should go up there, get to Max and give him a field dressing, maybe some of the Darvon he had traded from the ARVN unit last week. Only there were mines and Keogh didn't know where the mines were. He was looking down at his boot and he couldn't move because one mine up there had taken out Top, and Blueboy, and Max. Blueboy had gone up in the air, his hips slamming up into his lungs, pink foam coming from his throat and his mouth, his flak jacket spreading out around him like wings. Top's head and shoulders were lying in a bloody pile about a yard from Top's legs. But Max was saying *Boot, Boot, Boot*, in a soft whisper, the whisper that a mortal wound gives you, air bubbling out of the holes in his chest, the blood cooking on his cheek in the saw grass under the hot sun.

Keogh was trying to get up and go to Max but there were mines and the whole thing was to get up the nerve to move your foot and lift it up and put it down . . . where? Here, by this stone? Would Charlie put it under the stone? Or would Charlie decide, Well, the man will *think* it's under the stone so no, he'd put it next to the stone. Or would he? No, it's under the stone.

And the Prick-Two-Five radio saying "Hotel Five actual, Hotel Five actual, this is Six Hotel Five . . ."

Boot . . .

Keogh listened to Max say *Boot* until he stopped, his weapon in his hands and the smell of cotton burning in the sunlight, the gunpowder stink and the smell of a C-rats Marlboro, and the smell of peaches in the air, the peaches that Top and Blueboy had shared at the last break, and Max's breath bubbling in his lungs.

"Frank . . . Frank . . ."

Boot. Boot.

Myra was leaning over him, a cool look in her soft eyes, her hair falling around them in a way he remembered very well. But the room was wrong, not the hotel room up in Yonkers, but a nice room, with bamboo shutters drawn against the hot yellow sun and white cotton everywhere, Myra in white cotton, her tanned skin dark against it.

"Whoa. Nightmares. What time is it?" he said.

"Who's Blueboy?"

"Jesus . . . Blueboy . . . What'd I say?"

Myra handed him a tall frosted glass full of orange juice and a couple of Tylenol with codeine.

"You said, Six six Top is hit. And something about Blueboy?"

Keogh swung his legs out to the side of the bed and sat up. His clothes were in a tangle on the floor beside the bed. His head was full of iron filings and his chest hurt. There was an empty bottle of Dr. McGillicuddy's Peach Schnapps lying under the bamboo night table.

Myra was pushing it. "Who's Blueboy?"

"Blueboy . . . Blueboy's dead. So's Max and so's Top."

That slowed her down for a bit, long enough for Keogh to get on his feet and go into the bathroom and get a long breath while the water poured down around his ears and into his mouth, bringing yesterday back into sharp focus.

When he came back out, Myra was in the kitchen, working at a gas stove, stirring eggs, still in her long white cotton nightgown. Keogh could see her body in the glow from the sunlit front room. He wiped his face with a thick red terry-cloth towel and stood at the stove, watching Myra cook the eggs.

"How'd I get here?"

Myra laughed, an undertone of bitterness.

"Jesus, Frank. You sure know how to sweet-talk a girl. Pat and Ruthie brought you here around three this morning. You were in bad shape and Pat said you were asking for me. Ruthie called me from the B and V. She asked me if I could take you, and I said yes. I gather Tricia knows about you and me?"

"You could say. She called Lincoln Hospital. Put the thing together."

"What'd you say . . . about us?"

Keogh watched the eggs cook in the pan for a while, thinking what to say to that.

"I told her I got you drunk and took advantage of you, that you woke up and threw me out. I said it would never happen again, that I was under a lot of stress and I had been drinking too much."

She smiled at him then. They had breakfast in a little dining area. The apartment was small and collected, a single woman's place, pictures of her parents by the bed, something in the place that reminded Keogh of a teenage girl's bedroom, full of light and flowers and the keepsakes of a family home only recently left.

"How old are you, Myra?"

"Twenty-eight. Why?"

Twenty-eight . . . fourteen years younger than he was. Jesus, Frank, what's happening to you?

"Seems old for someone just out of the Academy."

"I didn't like working for the Chase. I wanted to do something more . . . real. The Department seemed like the answer. I saw you once, you know?"

"Yeah?"

"At John Jay. You gave a lecture about weapons, about combat shooting. You were very convincing. We all thought you'd seen some of it for real. You and your buddy Pat. You're quite well known, you know. All the grads in my year knew who you were, knew all about your breast bars, the Honor Society, everything. When you . . . When I drove you home, I was pretty impressed with you."

"So you figured, chalk one up and tell your friends, is that it?"

"Yes. At the start."

Her hands rested at the sides of a plate with blue cornflowers on it. There was a soft dusting of fine blond hairs on her forearms. At her neck an artery pulsed under an arc of tanned skin. Her eyes were full of a soft morning light and she seemed to glow in her white cotton shift. Keogh was suddenly very aware of her body under the cotton, and of the smell of her, a soapy smell, shampoo and toothpaste and coffee. He wondered what Tricia was doing now, and pulled away from the thought like a man who has cut himself.

Myra could see this going on in him.

"Why did you come here last night?"

"Why did you let me?"

"I don't know. You're the last thing I need. I can see that. You're bad news for your wife—you'll be bad news for me too. I have a good life here." She looked around the room, as if seeing it from the outside.

"Yeah. Well, don't worry. I'll get out of here. I'm the last thing anybody needs. . . ."

Keogh saw Myra gathering herself for something. He let her do it and tried not to wonder how it was that his life had come apart so easily. It was as if there were a thin skin on the surface of things, and if you floated on it, like a swimmer in a pool, and didn't look down, it would hold you up and you could pretend you had a life. But you should never look down into the pool, because there might be something down there looking up at you.

"Frank . . . Burke Owens is coming over here."

Oh, Christ. She was reading him.

"Now why the hell would I want to talk to him, Myra?" Frank tried hard to keep his voice level. It seemed that just about everyone in his life wanted him to talk to Burke Owens.

Owens and Young, that shrink. They had been in on Art Pike's hearing after he got Stockholmed at the Bolsa Chica. Weisberg had been there as the officer responding. According to Weisberg, Owens had put up a pretty good case for Pike, arguing long and with apparent heat and making some headway. Then Young had gotten up and pronounced Pike a classic post-traumatic stress case, and from that point on it had been a straightaway into the rubber-gun squad. Weisberg had seen Owens and Young in the hall outside at headquarters, Young standing there stiff and cool as a frozen fish, Owens circling him and snarling at him in a low and carrying whisper.

Well, it was all history now. After the racket for The Paz, Pike had pulled his Last Stand at the gun shop, maybe because of what Paul Young had done, maybe not. Then Pike was dead. And the nurse. Whatever Young had done to Pike and whatever Owens had tried to do to stop him, it was over now. Poor Pike.

Poor Frank.

What the hell . . .

Myra was watching him go through this as if she knew where he was headed.

"When's he due?"

At that moment the downstairs buzzer rang and they smiled at each other and Frank began to be very afraid that he was in love with Myra Kholer.

Owens arrived in the sunlit room like a bulldog coming into a tea party, in the usual biker's denims, carrying an old Lion helmet, looking a little like Santa Claus's wastrel brother Bear.

He shook Keogh's hand and gave him a huge sardonic grin that somehow encompassed all that had happened to Frank up to this moment and made it almost funny. Frank felt a little lighter.

Myra was smiling too. Frank could see the charm in the man.

Myra put some coffee on and went into the bathroom to shower. They watched her go and Frank was aware of Owens's look, seeing Myra in her nightgown, her hair loose and golden and the insinuation of her walk.

"Where do you and Myra know each other from, Owens?"

Owens shrugged and gave Keogh a half-apologetic sideways smile. "Well, you wouldn't like it. Myra and Ruthie Boyko and a lot of the Bronx policewomen go to a weekly meeting at the office, supposed to help them get along with all the guys, deal with some of the resentment. What you call 'touchy-feely warm-fuzzies shit,' I think."

Frank had to laugh, hearing himself quoted so accurately.

"You don't strike me as your typical shrink, Burke."

Owens seemed to think about it for a while. He had a good capacity for silences. "Well, I got here the hard way. It wasn't the way I saw my life working out. What do they say? Life is what happens to you while you're making other plans?"

"Yeah. I can see that."

It was an opening into a talk about Keogh and his troubles. Owens didn't take it.

"I was all-star back in Sturgis. You know the place?"

Oddly, Frank did. "It's that place where all the outlaw bikers get together every summer. In North Dakota?"

"South Dakota. Yeah. I got into Harleys there. But football was the plan. Got scouted by the Cornhuskers and

Alabama. Might have made a decent linebacker. I was still waiting for the letter when I got the other one first."

"Uncle Sam?"

Owens chuckled into his beard and shrugged, a massive subsidence of shoulders and barrel chest.

"Oh, yeah . . . right into the shit. In sixty-nine." He tugged a big Colt automatic out of his belt and turned it in the light.

"Got this in my T.A. fifty at Camp Alpha. Still have it. Got a carry permit. Shoot sometimes with the guys up at Rodman's Neck. I was Mac-V'd."

"Mac-V?" Keogh tried to say it politely. MACV stood for Military Assistance Command Vietnam, and it usually meant a nice safe rear-echelon job.

"What? Rear Echelon Mother Fuckers, Frank? In The Rear With The Gear? No . . . I got my bush time with the Ninth at Dong Tam and then they slammed my ass into a MAT team and I spent the rest of my tour in the Plain of Reeds. Ambushes. Some shit with the Tango Boats. Mostly I got crotch rot and dysentery. It was a great war. Took an AK round from I never found out where. Blew a lung. Got a Purple and a bong. I ended up in Honolulu on a fifty-percent disability. There was a ward there with a lot of guys worse off than me. I sort of drifted into helping them out. Got to like it. It sort of made up for the shit. It just went on from there. A lot of the guys were like you, got into the police after the war. I just came along and the PBA offered me a job. You heard this already, Frank."

"Yeah. Well, it was a rat-fuck from the get-go. Shin-loy."

"Pegasus. Khe Sanh, Relief of. Hue. Some I-Corps work in the Song valley. Co Roc. Firebase Hooker. C.A.'s all over the place. You saw some real shit, though. Into the mine fields around Pinkville and the My Lai's . . . saw three guys ride a step-and-a-half. You were the real thing, Eleven Bravo all the way."

"So why are you reading up on me, Burke?"

Owens stopped smiling. "Okay . . . you wanta get into it, I will. First place, I don't work for the Department. I work for the Benevolent Association and the Sergeants Association and the Detectives Endowment Association, so what you tell me doesn't end up in your personnel file at One Police. But take a look around you, Frank. Where are you sitting? Is your life unfolding as it should, man? It looks a little wrinkled to me."

There was nothing to say and Frank said it.

"Yeah . . . see what I mean? So this week the D.A.T.F. was looking at you for a cop-killing and a job on Nurse Zeigler. Your partner thinks you're a little strung out. And your wife just pitched you out for . . . for this scene here. You know what they say? If you can keep your head when all about you are losing theirs . . ."

Frank smiled. "Then you obviously don't understand the situation. So I'm fucked up. What the hell can you do about that? Talking about shit never makes it any better. You just lose your rhythm and the shit gets deeper. Remember in the war, the guy most likely to get dinged was the guy trying to be careful. That's the trouble with you guys. You want to drag it all out, root through it."

"That what you think I'm doing, trying to get you into some group therapy thing? Because I'm not. But I can talk straight to you about what's going on and maybe get you some slack from the bosses. I don't think you're fucked up. I think you're overworked and tired and you're being a real dickhead about your family but so what, who isn't? I'm just saying look at it, Frank. Think it over. Ask yourself—am I having any fun? Man, from the look of you, I'd say no. I'd say you're in the deep end."

Deep end. Did this guy know about his mother?

But Owens was still talking.

"So okay . . . you think this is all touchy-feely shit. Most of it is. Take the Good Doctor Young—you remember him? He used to be about something. He worked in a hospital. Did some good. Worked with the truly fucked-up, and now and then he made some private purgatory a better place. But now he consults with the Department and advises the Behavioral Science Unit. Partner in a very pricey private practice for the worried well, up in Albany. I just came from a breakfast meeting with him. That's the kind of guy he is. He has breakfast meetings and he jogs and he plays squash with the rest of the assholes in the Hunt Club. . . . He's a real useless piece of shit."

Keogh had nothing to say.

Owens looked at him carefully for a moment. Myra had come into the room and was now leaning on the counter with her arms folded, watching them. Keogh could smell the soap and the perfume and he was painfully aware of her body under the white cotton gown.

"Okay . . . I think maybe the time has come for you to quit being a sniper."

Frank had not expected that. Owens held up a thick blunt hand and shook his head.

"Not quit being a cop. Quit being a sniper. Think about it. You were a sniper for the Sixth in the war. They put you to work here as a good street cop. You got a rack of breast bars. You and Butler had some fun in Vice. Then some hammerhead downtown says, Hey, we got us a sniper, and they take you off the streets and put you up on some rooftop to take down poor bastards from two hundred yards. One thing, it's a bad job. Got no honor to it. No honor in shooting a guy who can't see you doing it. And second, it puts you where?"

Altitude and distance, thought Keogh, but all he said was "Where?"

"It puts you back in the war. On some level, being a sniper here is bringing it all back and you're having God's own time trying to cope with it. Tell me something . . ."

"Tell you what?" Keogh was angry.

"When you pull . . . how does it feel?"

"It doesn't feel at all. It's a job. I'm a technician."

"Horse shit. When did things start to go sour with you and your wife?"

"None of your fucking business."

Owens closed down fast and for a moment a current of anger seemed to move across him, a surface eddy from something down in the deep of his being, but then it cleared.

"Sorry. I'm rushing it because I don't know if you're gonna talk to me again. The thing is, Frank, I see it that way. It happens to a lot of good guys. Why not you? All I'm saying is, think on this."

Owens got to his feet and walked over to give Myra a kiss on her cheek. Myra slipped an arm behind Owens's back and hugged him. They both looked at Frank.

"Well . . . I had my say. Sorry if I pissed you off. I think you'd be a hell of a lot happier in a task force doing good honest street-cop work, or over at the Department of Investigations. Bust a few of those fat cats. Maybe get the Mayor, huh? But it's your life, buddy, and you got the right to go to hell in your own way. We all do, huh, Myra?"

"Thanks, Burke."

"Yeah." He put out his hand to Frank.

"No hard feelings, Frank?"

The hand stayed out there for a long time, unwavering, and Owens waited patiently without any visible resentment other than a kind of ratcheting vibration in his eyes as he looked from Myra back to Keogh. Finally he pulled it back and walked to the door.

"Well, you're a hard man, Frank. Guess it runs in the family. You change your mind, I'm always around somewhere. Myra, see you at the meeting."

Keogh watched him go out the door with the feeling that he had missed a chance to help himself here, but not quite sure what that chance actually was.

Myra closed the door and walked into the bedroom. Keogh followed her in.

"Thanks," he said. "Sorry about—"

"Forget it. You ought to call Tricia."

Keogh didn't like hearing Myra say her name, and he didn't like himself for resenting it.

He had a dim recollection of dialing his number in a pay phone at the back of the B and V, of Butler giving him quarters, of Ruthie Boyko's face above him as he lay on the sidewalk. The phone call had never been answered.

"You mind if I call her from here?"

There was a flicker of hurt in Myra's eyes, and her lips tightened. She walked away. It reminded Keogh of Tricia and he began to get an idea of just how rotten he was going to be feeling in the next few weeks, a dropping-away and falling sensation, as if he had finally done it, finally destroyed the best thing in his life by applying torque to it until it snapped so he could stand here in this woman's bedroom and say to himself, See, I *told* you the bitch would never go the distance. Maybe Owens was right.

The phone was by the bed. He sat down, playing with the nine-mil which he'd left by the bed, and listening to the phone ring in his house, ringing as if it were a phone in a stateroom on a sunken liner a mile down in the ocean.

After a time, Myra passed very close to him, leaning over the night table to get a comb. Her scent was very strong. When he put his hand out to touch her hip through the fabric, she straightened and looked down at him. He felt the bone in the socket and the strong muscle over her hip, felt the young life in her like a red river. Her scent, the soap scent and the coffee scent, was all around him.

She stood looking down at him for a long while. Then she reached up to undo the buttons on her nightgown.

"You're the last thing I need, Frank."

"Yes," he said, watching her hands.

CHAPTER 17

Myra came up out of sleep like a swimmer rising to the surface of a pool, and she lay there in the striped blue darkness of her bedroom, trying to separate life from her dream. Something had changed in the quality of the night, in the filaments of normality in which she had been wrapped and dreaming. It was as if there had been a sound, a regular sound like a heartbeat or a drumbeat, and now it had stopped and the mind, which had tricked the sound out of her consciousness, now failed to shield her from its absence. Suddenly chilled, she came fully awake.

She was alone in her bed. Some time in the night she had been dreamily aware of the way his weight on the mattress lightened and she had smiled to herself, recognizing the too-familiar delicacy of the departure, the man telling himself that he just wanted to leave her happy, the woman awake and feeling him going but letting him play it his way, all the while both of them knowing that it wasn't the sentiment that counted. It was the going.

Well, he had tried to explain it to her. Why not stay here the night, she had asked him, watching him dress in the bars of moonlight.

"If I stay the night," he had answered her, not looking at her, his face in shadow, "if I stay the night, then it means something . . . serious. We'll talk. Talk's dangerous. We'll talk over breakfast and . . ."

"Yes," she had said, not saying that she always thought that making love was something serious too. "Very admirable. So go." And she had rolled away and not watched as he left the room. She had not heard the door closing.

Now this sound had wakened her. The sound of . . . what? A low hissing murmur was coming from the doorway of her bedroom. Wind? No. Something more familiar? Something electric . . .

Christ. The television set. Why the hell would the television set be on? Myra looked over at the alarm clock. It was a little after four in the morning. Frank. Probably out there on the couch, sound asleep with the television set on.

Poor Frank, up against his conscience. Dreaming of hearth and home and the little lady. She felt a small frisson of anger. Typical modern scenario. Girl gets fucked. Guy gets fucked. Girl gets sticky. Guy gets guilty. Grow up, Frank. Accept what you are. Well, time to go in and play the supportive and sensitive woman. . . . She slipped out of bed and walked toward the dark rectangle of the bedroom door. She passed the robe on the floor. Better to arrive naked. It would shake him up a little, change his mood.

Yes, it was the television. She could see the blue-green flicker of the screen as she came down the hall toward the front room. The hissing sound got louder and louder. Christ, Frank must have it cranked right up to the top of the dial. The light strobed and flickered, coming off the white walls of the apartment, casting a blue aura over her. Myra came around the corner looking like a ghost, a nude woman wrapped in a pale suffusion of slimy blue light. The room looked as if it were full of water.

The couch was empty. The massive Sony Trinitron was on. There was no transmission, no all-night cable. She hadn't paid the Cablevision bill and it had been cut off weeks ago. She pulled in what she could from a flat wire antenna one of her brothers had set up. Now there was nothing on the screen but that dead-of-night static and snow. It lit the room up. Myra came into the room. Frank's suitcase was on the floor beside the couch. The coffee table had a couple of glasses on it, half full of red wine. The kitchen was dark. The bathroom door was half open. She could see that his dog was gone, that big silent golden retriever that followed him around wherever he went.

Myra turned to shut off the television, thinking what inconsiderate bastards men could be. A man was standing in the hall leading to the bedroom, the hall she had just come out of. She straightened and stepped back, hitting the edge of the coffee table with her knee.

The man was shining. When he stepped forward, he crackled and shimmered.

Myra looked at him as he came into the light.

"You . . . what the hell are you dressed up for?" She started to smile. "What the hell are you doing? What the hell are you wearing?"

He smiled back at her.

"This? It's a total-body condom. Like it?"

Myra laughed, and remembered she was naked.

"Well . . . getting a good look?"

"Yes," he said, with a slow sideways smile.

"What are you wearing that for? We driving through plutonium later? You look like a Hostess Twinkie."

"That's from *Annie Hall*," he said, coming forward into the light of the television set, the blue-green light racing across the torqued surfaces of the plastic like a kerosene fire on water. "I loved that movie. Hold this, will you?"

"What?" said Myra, and then she felt a blow against her ribs and there was an arc of blue-green light, and the television crackled like something in flames.

Myra stepped back from him. There was a stick or a handle or something wooden stuck to her ribs, low on her right side. She touched it, puzzled.

"Man," he said, watching her, seeing her like a ghost wrapped in a pale aura of blue-green light, this woman naked in the center of it, staring stupidly at the thing in her ribs. . . .

"Man," he said. "I kill myself. I really do."

CHAPTER 18

The concierge in the lobby of the King James never looked twice at Myron as he walked past his station on the way to the elevators. Myron was in his Pelham Bay uniform, carrying a toolbox, with a clipboard work order ready to show the guy if he asked, but the clerk had seen Pelham Bay Cleaners come and go so often that he couldn't have cared less about Myron. Myron even called out hello to him as he went by. The guy's bald head glistened in the downlight from a ceiling lamp. He just raised a bored hand and kept his face buried in a copy of the *Post*.

Myron felt pretty good. Levine's plans were right on the money. There was a doorway at the rear of the elevator hall, and the key fit perfectly. Myron opened the door and there were Sonny and Lyle and Levine smiling at him, Levine looking a little feverish, but steady enough.

Nobody spoke in the elevator going up to the penthouse. Sonny was going over the plans, the route timings, the alternates he had figured out. He knew every staircase and elevator shaft in the building, knew which doors opened out and which doors were chained shut, which doors let out onto a street and which doors opened up in the parking level. Myron had mapped out the alarm system and Levine

175

had made certain that the owner was gone for the weekend. Levine had insisted on coming along, and Sonny had let him do it. He was a risk, but it was better to have him right there where Sonny could see him than to have him off somewhere else telling a hooker all about what his boys were doing.

Lyle was having a hard time with this. Back at the hotel room, as Sonny had been going over the blueprints and the escape routes and cleaning their Smiths, Lyle had fussed and worried that they hadn't done enough preparation, that maybe they should wait until all the problems had been figured out. Sonny had thrown a clean stainless Smith on the bed beside Lyle and stood in front of the television where Lyle was watching *Geraldo*.

"Look, Lyle, there's no way in this business that you can take all the risk out of something. We know more about the job than most of the banks and armored car hits I've ever done. We're covered here under solid IDs. I know every route into and out of the area. We've done everything we can do. All that's left is to do it."

Lyle's hands were plucking at his shirt button. He kept looking at the TV past Sonny's hip. "But the cops, aren't they watching Myron? They'll be watching him tonight?"

"Look, Lyle . . . Myron's an ex-con. New York State law is an ex-con who moves into New York City, parole board has to report him to the nearest precinct. It's routine for the cops to put surveillance on ex-bank robbers. They've got these guys sitting around on the payroll, sometimes they send them out fishing. That's all this is."

"But when the cops find out that this guy was robbed, aren't they going to go straight for Myron?"

"Lyle, that's the idea. Myron knows that. He's not trying to hide that from them. He just wants to keep them off him until we can get the merchandise and get out. He gets popped for it, and we see to it that his wife is taken care of."

"What if he talks? What if they make him talk?"

"Myron isn't going to talk. Look, Lyle, it's like it's a professional thing. The cops know Myron is dirty. They'll come and get him. He'll be sitting in the front room of his apartment in Park Slope. He'll have his suitcase ready, his wallet on the table in front of him, his piece out and the bullets lined up beside it. Have his going-to-prison suit on, and a couple of letters from his doctors. He'll be sitting right in the front so when the cops knock on the door, Myron says, Afternoon, gentlemen, I believe the door is open. They come in—shit, he probably knows the guys."

Lyle had that old look on his face, the how-could-you-get-me-into-this look. Sonny held his temper and kept trying to make the point.

"See . . . it makes sense to the cops too. They have nothing to connect Myron with anything we did in Oklahoma, so they're just going to see a dying man who put together a last hit to take care of his wife. If nobody is hurt tonight, they'll write him up and take him downtown. Myron tells them he did it himself but he's sent the stuff away. They'll know that's not the whole story, but it's enough to tell the insurance boys."

"But, Sonny, he knows who we are. I was thinking, you know, since he's dying and all . . ."

That rocked Sonny. He came around to the side of the bed and put his hand on Lyle's soft cheek, turning his face up. He put a fair amount of force into what he was saying.

"Lyle, I don't want to hear you say something like that again. You say it again, I'll cut you out right now, shove you out into the hall, and you can go make your way in the entertainment industry or whatever the hell it is. Myron is something to me. Only one I'm worried about is you. You're a hell of a lot more likely to blow this than Myron. How'd you like it, Levine says to me, Sonny, I'm worried about Lyle there. Dogs who get up on the table looking for meat ought to remember that in a lot of places, they *are* meat. You following me?"

That had been the last of that. They had dressed up like two business guys going out on the town, down the mirrored elevator and out through the lobby, smiling at the concierge at her desk, and out onto the side street. They walked a few blocks up to where the Pelham Bay van was parked, Myron and Levine inside it. They put on the overalls on top of their street clothes and drove over to the King James. Myron went in the front door and let them in the back way.

Sonny watched the numbers flicker on and off and tried to stop worrying about Lyle and Joseph Levine and New York City and get into that frame of mind where he was right here, inside the actual, ready to see what there was to see and not be blinded by what might happen.

One of the things there was to see, thought Sonny, was the gun pushing out the waistband of Levine's overalls. Well, that was interesting. It fit Sonny's reading of Levine as a guy who wanted to be a risk-taker, but it might also fit the image of a guy who had made other plans for himself than the ones they had talked about. Levine would have to be watched carefully tonight.

The elevator stopped one floor below the penthouse level. Myron took out a complicated steel key and held it up in front of them. It shone in the dim light of the elevator.

"Okay. This is Lock One. It gets us up to the penthouse level. It also triggers a sequencer alarm down at Intertec, right?"

They nodded. "Right . . . so how long do we have once we're inside the apartment to send the cancel code?"

"Sixty seconds," said Lyle in a calm voice that surprised Sonny. Maybe Lyle would be okay.

"Yes. Sixty seconds. This week's code is A771B53RZR. Sonny, you're backup on this. Have you got it?"

"A771B53RZR, sixty seconds, and the code box is in the library on the underside of the banker's desk, immediate right hand, first door on the left as we go in the front hall."

Myron smiled. They'd been over this drill fifty times. No one complained.

"Well, my last hurrah, gentlemen. Let's make it smooth." He put the steel key into the lock and the elevator began to rise to the top floor. The doors pulled back and they were standing in front of a pair of massive oak doors ten feet wide and twelve feet high. Heraldic devices were carved into the panels. A huge brass lion head snarled at them in the glow of a spot.

Lyle stopped in the vestibule.

"Levine, you sure this guy isn't home?"

"Benson Saltell was on the eight o'clock shuttle to Washington last night. I watched him get on it myself. I've told you this six times since yesterday, Lyle."

Reassured, Lyle took a breath. Myron put another key in the brass lock, and the oak door opened silently into an apartment the size of which neither Sonny nor Lyle had been quite able to get ready for.

Sonny went down the main hall with Myron, heading for the library. The hall was a lot bigger than he had imagined, and it ended with a split staircase that went right and left up to a landing where stained-glass windows rose up three floors, the Gothic windows Sonny had seen from the room in the U.N. Plaza Hotel. To the right and the left off the main hall were a music room, and a huge living room with a massive white marble fireplace and what looked like a walk-out through French doors to a large terrace.

Lyle and Levine went straight into the living area, where a series of glass cases held the collection they were looking for: rows of gold coins in blue velvet cases, medallions, silver pieces, shimmering in the light from the terrace. There were other cases along the rear wall, full of an array of stamps in airtight glass presses, each series in its own case, cards describing the provenance in a fine black script. Weapons and gilt-framed paintings covered the paneled walls up to the second-floor windows. It was an exact duplicate of an English country home, sitting on top of an apartment building in midtown Manhattan. Lyle found the whole thing a little overwhelming, but Levine had seen it a couple of times before. He stopped in front of the largest glass case and unrolled a long section of black velvet cloth on the floor. He pulled a thin jimmy out of his back pocket.

"Wait for it, Levine," said Lyle, looking back at the door,

waiting for Sonny and Myron to come through it and say that the alarm had been canceled.

Myron came in through the doorway right then, waving at them to hold on.

"Joseph, have you checked for anything new since we were here? Look at the cases—look at the backs."

Levine pulled a voltmeter out of his overalls and passed it over the tops and sides of the cases. Myron examined the floor around them and used a compressed-air can to puff a thin stream of powder into the air around the cases. There was nothing.

Levine slid the jimmy into the first case and twisted it slowly. There was a tinny pop, and the glass top lifted an inch. Lyle and Levine lifted it back carefully. There was a lot of gold lying there in front of them, rows and rows of coins and medals, bars and ingots stamped in every language, heads of kings and queens, worn irregular discs with crude designs of falcons and ships, anchors, daggers, a head of Marcus Aurelius, Vespasian, Tiberius. . . .

"Mercy," said Lyle. "This is history here. We're not melting this down, are we?"

Myron smiled at him through his half-frames.

"No," he said, looking down at the case. "These coins—they were minted to be stolen. I imagine half the coins here were stolen from someone else's collection. Saltell will claim half or a third of what this is worth. And he'll be vague about what was taken, you can rest assured, Lyle."

Levine and Myron began to lift the coins out of the cases, delicately placing each one in a slot in the cloth, going slowly and reverently, as men do around gold. Lyle stood and watched them for a while, and then began to wander around the huge room, looking at the paintings and weapons on the walls. At the far end of the room a small oil painting floated like a blue pool in a downlight. Lyle saw it from twenty feet away and went straight to it, drawn by the light in it, and the scene.

It was a little oil, no more than six by ten inches, in a gilded frame, a scene of men driving posts into the ground in a hazy atmosphere of light and color, grays and blues and auburns, the paint a sensuous swirl of pigment and motion. Something about the scene reminded Lyle of country roads in the Carolinas and it hit him that here was something he ought to have. He stood in front of it for a few minutes, thinking about it, considering what the consequences might be if he tried to keep it to himself. It was such a small painting, three men working on a row of posts or stakes, a dappled blue-gray sky, behind them a field of wheat or rye with touches of green, and a dusty Carolina road running along beside the stakes, receding into a blue distance. There was no signature anywhere. It was probably worth nothing, since it was unsigned. Even in the frame, Lyle could see taking it without a lot of trouble.

Sonny was back in the room, over at the stamp cases, helping Myron pack the little books and packets. They were about to go. Why the hell not, thought Lyle, and he reached up for the picture just as Sonny turned around to look for him, Sonny's face going white as he saw Lyle's hand coming up. . . .

Keogh and Butler were parked on Vanderbilt Avenue next to Grand Central Station, sitting in the blue Plymouth listening to cross-talk on the radio and trying to explain the death-poo story to a couple of harness cops from Midtown South. The harness cops were leaning in the side windows with their hats pushed back, a couple of weight lifters three years out of the Academy. Frank and Pat were in the Midtown area because Special Agent Duffy wanted the Department to have its best Emergency Service guys downtown instead of stuck up in the Bronx, where Duffy figured there was nothing Sonny Beauchamp would feel like taking. In the psycho-hydraulics of police power, Duffy's pressure came all the way down the tubes to Pulaski. It was a little after seven on Friday night. Keogh and Butler were enjoying the change of scenery, and so was Custer, who was sitting up in the back seat watching the crowds passing by on Forty-second Street, taking it all in, the Westchester teens and the screamers, the tourists out of the Grand Hyatt holding on to their ladies and spinning around every fifteen feet to see who was following them, pushcart peddlers selling Italian ices on a hot summer evening, all the lights and the cars and the trucks. . . . Keogh looked back over the seat and saw Custer sitting up there, his eyes wide, his mouth half open. He reached back to scratch the dog's throat, trying not to think about where he was going to sleep tonight.

"So we get the call—this is what, Frank? Middle of September? Temperature had been running close to a hundred for two weeks. Dog days, you know, where it's hot enough to make people ugly but not hot enough to keep them from doing something about it?"

The harness cops were nodding, one of them, the black guy, eating a burned pretzel and looking around the inside of the car, at the rifles on the back seat and the shotgun upright in the dashboard rack.

"So, Central says possible Barricaded Emotionally Disturbed. The Four-Eight guys are all nervous, since they've had a shitload of trouble at this address. So we get a call, do the kick-in for them."

Keogh was sort of wishing that Butler wouldn't tell this story, but Butler loved it.

"So in we go, Frank first, me on his heels, Frank with his nine-mil out. What do we see?"

"What? They're gonna guess, Pat?"

"Not in a million. It's this Oriental guy, he's hanging from a steam pipe. Dead maybe four days. Get this: He's wearing a *scuba* suit—you know, one of those Jacques Cousteau suits, rubber? The attic is empty except for this guy hanging from the steam pipe in his diver's suit, swollen up like a balloon, face all black, tongue out."

"Not empty, Pat. There's skin mags all over the floor, and a stool lying on its side under him."

The black cop said, "Autoerotic death?"

Butler was a little upset at having his story accelerated, but he nodded. "Yeah. One of those guys, likes to get into bondage gear, rubber and the golf balls in his mouth, had his machinery out through a hole cut in the rubber suit. He's standing on a stool with the rope around his neck, playing with himself, looking at these bondage magazines on the floor, putting pressure on the rope."

The blond cop didn't get it. "Why the hell would he do that?"

Butler gave him an evil grin. "So when he comes, he's half-unconscious from the choking. If he gets it right, he almost passes out right at the same time as he comes. It's called autoeroticism. Supposed to be a major thrill."

The white cop was having trouble with it.

"So why did he kill himself?"

"He screwed up. Pushed it too far. He passes out, staggers a little, the stool kicks out, and bingo! He goes straight to Valhalla. Putz death of the month, we called it. But he'd been there for a while, so I'm outa there. I'm gone. Can't stand the smell, you know?"

Keogh had to laugh at the memory. "Yeah, Pat was out of there and down the stairs and on the sidewalk shaking. So I think, Well, let's open a window. There's a window on the other side of the guy, across the room. The roof slants down to it, and the guy's hanging in the middle on this pipe. So I go over, step around him there, and I jerk this window open. I'm standing there—"

"He's standing there, his head hanging out the window—I can see him from the street. He's green, right?"

"So I hear—"

"So he hears this noise? Creak-creak-creak—"

"Like someone is sneaking up on me?"

"Keogh spins around. We hear him scream. He starts to shoot at something! BlamBlamBlamBlam—that Browning nine-mil hammering away. BlamBaBlamBaBlam."

The cops were riveted. "What was it? Some psycho?"

Keogh shook his head, thinking about the scene.

"I spin around and here's this dead guy swinging back and forth on the rope and he's coming right at me. All I can see is his face all black, tongue sticking out, bare feet hanging out, arms all puffed up, and he's swaying from side to side and sliding down the steam pipe at me." Keogh twisted his face and blew out his cheeks. "Gah . . . eek eek eek, this creaking sound I heard, it's the rope slipping down the steam pipe—it runs right above me. But all I see is this *thing* coming at me. So I shot him."

"*Shot* him? Frank, you vaporized the sucker. Frank here puts fifteen rounds into the guy. We come racing up the stairs, there's Frank leaning backwards out the window with his nine-mil out in front of him, digging around in his flak jacket for another magazine."

"Of course, they called a Thirteen, so out in the street we have every car in the Four-Eight screaming up the road at us."

Butler laughed. "Yeah. Quite the scene. Anyway, we get it all straightened away and we lead Frank here—he's a little upset—we lead him down the stairs and I put him in the car. Pat him on the head. There there, Frank. The bad man he's all gone away."

"That was no lie," said Frank. "Fifteen rounds."

"Anyway, I come around, get behind the wheel and we're driving away, and there's this . . . smell. . . ."

The cops looked over at Keogh, grinning.

"No, not Frank. This guy, he takes fifteen rounds of nine-mil, he's already under a fair amount of internal pressure. He must have . . . Anyway, we look at Frank's cuffs and his pants. He's covered with—"

"Pat points at me and starts screaming. *Death poo! Death poo! You got death poo on you!*"

"Can't stand that stuff," said Pat by way of explanation. "Freaks me out."

Keogh gave him a look. "No kidding. He flips out, he's screaming, *Death poo death poo* at the top of his lungs, not looking where he's driving. People on the streets are looking at us, at this squad car going by, this big blond dickhead here, his face all red, pointing at the floor of the car and screaming *Death poo death poo!*"

"Yeah, true. I . . . overreacted. Anyway, I get the car stopped and I say to Frank: *Outa the car, outa the car!*"

"I'm saying, What? What?"

Butler had tears in his eyes. "Jesus, Frank won't get out of the car. So—"

"So he pulls that goddammed Ruger out—"

Pat lifted his huge stainless-steel single-action revolver to show the cops. "I wouldna shot him. I was just trying to emphasize my . . . distress."

"He emphasizes his distress so well I get the hell out of the car—it's still rolling."

"I made him ride on the roof. Took him over to the Two-Eightieth Firehouse. Made the firemen get out a hose."

"Stood me up against the back wall and they hosed me down. At gunpoint."

"Yeah," said Pat. "They never even charged us for the service, either."

"Archangel, Archangel, K?"

Keogh grabbed the radio handset.

"Central, this is Archangel, K?"

"Archangel, respond immediately, the King James for a Ten-Thirty-three. Units of the One-Seven request assistance. This comes from Lieutenant Pulaski of the Emergency Service Unit. Be advised, Lieutenant Pulaski will Eighty-five you at the scene. K?"

The two foot-patrol cops jumped back from the car as Keogh started it up. Butler stuck the gumball on the dashboard. "We're outa here, guys."

Keogh pulled an illegal U-turn, hung a left onto 42nd Street, and sped east, pushing the traffic. Butler pulled his flak jacket out from under Custer. Custer was up against the side window, moaning to himself. This was like the good old days for him. He felt great.

Keogh thought about the King James. It was the highest building around, nothing higher within a couple of hundred yards. That meant they were going straight up inside the place. Depended on how high the trouble was. "This sounds like a kick-in, Pat."

"Yeah," said Butler. "I hate those."

They had the stuff in canvas bags slung over their shoulders to leave their hands free, Myron pretty cool but Joseph Levine looking like someone had just kicked him in the throat, swallowing, staring at Sonny and Lyle in the crowded elevator. Levine fumbled at his waist, trying to get out of the Pelham Bay uniform. Levine's hand hit the little .32 in his belt. He jerked it out and stuck it in Lyle's face.

Sonny was watching the lights: Ten. Nine. Eight . . .

"Sonny!"

He looked around, saw the little auto in Levine's hand.

"This son of a bitch—" Levine was saying.

Myron hit Levine with a jimmy. Sonny pulled the gun out of his hand, lifted Levine up, and held him in the corner of the elevator, his face up close to him.

"Settle out. Listen to me. There's a fire stair in the middle block. Where does it come out?"

Five. Four. Three.

Myron shook his head. "It's no good. They all come out on the ground."

Two. One. Sonny hit the STOP button.

"All right. Stay here. Hold the elevator. I'm going to see what's in the lobby."

Lyle said, "No, Sonny. They'll be all over that!"

Sonny was calm. "I got to look, Lyle." He handed him Levine's little auto. "See this guy behaves."

Myron said nothing. Sonny pushed OPEN and the door started to move. The little hallway was empty. Sonny stuck his head out in the hall. There was nothing in sight. He could see a section of the main lobby. He stepped out and started to walk up the hall, trying to see around into the entrance, his Smith in his right hand. A uniformed cop jumped out from the corner and fired point-blank at him, hitting him three times in the chest. He staggered back toward the elevator. Lyle was calling his name, the door started to close. More shots hammered off the marble wall, zipping and zanging around off the exit door at the back of the hall. Sonny made it back to the elevator, tumbling through the doorway just as the door closed, hearing heavy boots coming down after him, a cop's voice saying, *Stop, stop right there*.

Sonny was on the floor, Lyle tearing at his overalls. Sonny was trying to breathe. He felt a weight on his chest, and a numbness. Lyle got the overalls ripped open and there were three crushed slugs stuck in the material of Sonny's Kevlar vest.

Lyle pulled him to his feet. They were going up again. "Well, that way's out," said Sonny, grinning.

Out in the street it was a cop carnival, units from the 17th Precinct every this way and that on the curbs, harness cops running around the property line, going around to cover all the exits, more cops going in through the front lobby at a dead run, guns out, hats back on their heads, blue lights flashing, lighting up the whole scene. Keogh and Butler came around the corner in a slide and stopped by a crowd of uniformed cops.

"Where's the CP?"

"Who the fuck're you?"

Keogh pulled out his gold shield and ID.

"ESU. Where's the brass?"

The cop stiffened up and pointed to the park gate.

"There. The Mobilization Point's that RMP."

Keogh and Butler got out of the car carrying their Remingtons and strapping up their flak jackets. Butler had the Ruger in a shoulder rig, and Keogh had his Browning.

"You're not dressed for this, Frank," said Butler.

Keogh looked down. "Yeah. I don't think this is going to be a formal anyway."

Butler had his head back, craning to see the spires and terraces on the roof. "What you figure, twenty floors?"

The top of the building was divided into four huge penthouse complexes. There was nothing around that would give them a higher position. ESU regulations were pretty clear: No sniper assignment in a built-up area could cover a greater distance than two hundred yards. The nearest tall building was more than two hundred yards away. They'd be going up inside.

When they got to the Mobilization Point, Lieutenant Pulaski was waiting for them, along with Special Agent Delmore Duffy of the FBI. Duffy's two-button suit set him apart from the city cops who were milling around.

Pulaski looked up from a clipboard.

"Frank . . . Pat. You know Delmore here?"

They nodded to Duffy. Duffy was a thin balding man in his forties with deep-set eyes and a lot of nervous tension.

Pulaski pointed to a brown van parked on the street.

"Pelham Bay Industrial Services. We figure it's them. The Beauchamps."

"Yeah?"

"Yeah. This is going to a Ten-Forty-six, a Rapid Mobilization. I'm the C.O. We get eight more sergeants and forty troops. The Zone Commander has already given it to us. We have the exits sealed and they're clearing out the top floors now."

Keogh looked up at the building again. "You know where they are? That's a hell of a big place."

Duffy spoke up in an angry tone. "The Intertec alarm was in the Saltell place, right on the top of the tower there. We watched the elevator come down—it made no stops until it got to the main floor. One of your guys put three into a big blond guy. He thinks maybe it was Sonny Beauchamp. But the guy made it back to the elevator and it went all the way back up. We pulled the switch on it, and there's no other way down. The stairs are all covered and all the doors onto each floor are one-way locks. You can get into the stairs, but once you're in, you either go all the way down or to the roof."

The ESU van pulled up, and Moxie and Pepsi got out of the front of it. Moxie went around to open it up and let out the rest of Charlie Section. Bravo Section, the ESU unit for Midtown, was already in the building.

Slick Ryan, Finn Kokkannen, Charlie Boudreau, Peggy Zacco, Arnie Sayles, Joe Langosta, and Nate Zimmerman were all waiting for the signal from Pulaski.

Pulaski leaned out the car door to look up at the roof line. "This is gonna be a bitch."

They got back inside the Saltell apartment, Sonny still trying to get his breath, Myron walking away from them all as if this had nothing to do with him. They had broken up into three units: Myron apart from all of them, Levine slouched in the corner staring at his Rolex, and the Beauchamps looking out at the huge terrace on the other side of the French windows, the city lights glittering through the gauzy curtains.

Lyle was in bad shape, but he was trying to hold himself together. He was looking to the right, toward the next penthouse. There were lights on in the windows.

"Hostages, Sonny. We could go over there, get some hostages. Make them bring us a chopper or something."

Sonny shook his head, looking out over the city, hearing the sirens in the street below, seeing in his mind what was going on down there. They were well and truly trapped. It had gone as wrong as it could ever go. He put a hand on Lyle's shoulder.

"I don't take hostages, Lyle. It's not polite."

Levine slid down the wall and put his face in his hands. Myron walked over to a wheeled cart full of crystal decanters and poured himself a long shot of something labeled GLENLIVET. It was very good. He poured another.

He called over to Sonny and Lyle.

"Drinks, anybody?"

Sonny smiled at Lyle.

"Hey. Can't hurt, right?"

It took Charlie and Bravo sections about an hour to clear the other penthouses and the floor beneath the Saltell place and another two hours to make sure that there were no other civilians lurking around in unexpected corners. The CP tried to reach the Saltell phone; it was off the hook. The stairs were controlled, and the Saltell place was very effectively cut off in all directions except straight up into the night sky. And they had an NYPD chopper up there, one of the last two Hueys in the Aviation Unit. If Pulaski wanted to drop some of his ESU team onto the roof of the King James, they'd do it from the Huey up there. The 34th Street Heliport was only a couple of blocks away down the river. But the building was in an airspace the NYPD called Kamikaze Corridor, a stretch of sky along the East River that was uncontrolled by the FAA. A lot of unscheduled and random flights in the air, as well as some very tricky winds. After the NYPD lost Jim Rowley and Charlie Trojahn there a couple of years back, most of the ESU teams preferred to use the stairs instead of the Hueys, Keogh and Butler included.

Pulaski called them together in a hallway on the twenty-first floor. Since Pulaski was the first ESU boss on the scene, his team was getting the actual assault assignment. Bravo Section and Able Section were stationed in all the stairways and passageways. The harness cops from the 17th had the residents located and were keeping them in their apartments. The families who lived in the other penthouses had been escorted downstairs and were right now getting coffee and Cokes at the CP van, having a pretty good time, all things considered. It was the Alexandria factor. Many people lead lives so arid and claustrophobic that they can hardly wait for the plague or the enemy troops to come along and shake things up.

"All right. Keogh, you and Butler are going through the penthouse next to the Saltell place, get up over the roof, and take up positions here . . ." He indicated two Gothic spires, one on either side of the broad, flat, pillar-lined terrace that led into the apartment through a set of French doors. The terrace was a good fifty feet wide and forty feet deep, with plants and a red tile flooring. Anyone walking out onto the terrace would take fire from either Keogh or Butler.

". . . and here. Use the Starlite scopes, in case they kill the lights out there. Bukovac and Kowalczyk, you and Arnie and Charlie Boudreau will go in the front—stun grenades, flash, the whole drill. Peggy, Slick, and Finn will take the elevator and provide covering fire. Nate and Joe, you back up Keogh and Butler. You hit the terrace as soon as you hear Moxie and . . . Bukovac and Kowalczyk get the word. We have no information as to how many people are up there. They've been in touch with Benson Saltell in Washington and he confirms that, to the best of his knowledge—that's what he said, fucking lawyers—there's no civilians up in that apartment. Only way out of the place for the guys in there is here"—he pointed to the elevator exit—"and here"—he indicated the terrace, which provided a route onto the steep pitched roof and a possible way out to another one of the penthouse apartments. "And here, where a guy might be able to jump this gap and make it to the next terrace. But nobody's going anywhere. We've tried to phone in to them. They don't wanna talk."

He stood up and looked at their faces, people he'd picked himself, men and women he knew and liked. Pulaski looked over at Butler and Keogh. "So . . . we're through waiting. We figure, they'll hear Moxie and Pepsi coming in, they'll run for the terrace. You guys saw the video. These assholes like to shoot. At least one of them is as good with a Heckler as either of you two. You give the big guy a chance at you, he'll blow you both out of those spires. It's a long way to the street from there. You just think about that Oklahoma trooper and do what's right."

Butler smiled at Pulaski.

"Hell, Bert. Maybe they'll just give up. Maybe they're up there now, getting pissed and writing to their moms."

Pulaski shrugged and looked at his watch. "Yeah, Pat. We'll ask them when it's over. Now go."

Lyle was standing a few yards back from one of the big leaded windows. A tall glass tower, blue and shining, rose up out of the ragged roof line around them. The United Nations Plaza Hotel. Sonny put his glass down and walked over to where Lyle was standing. Myron was sitting in a pile of gold coins in the middle of a silk rug, flipping them into the air and skating them at a collection of glass figures on the mantelpiece.

Levine was nowhere around.

"Have a drink, Lyle. It's damn good."

Lyle's hand shook a little, but he took it.

He inclined his head, indicating the glass tower a few hundred yards away. "I left the lights on in the room—you can see from here. And the television." He looked at his watch. "It's nine-thirty. We're gonna miss 20/20."

"They'll run it again, Lyle. Anyway, it's summer. Nothing but repeats."

"Yeah. So, little brother, what happens now?"

Sonny exhaled slowly, feeling the bruises in his chest where the slugs had hit him. It was like taking a five-pound boot right in the ribs. Three times.

"Well, Lyle . . . there's a couple of ways this can go. We can do what Myron's doing over there, play silly-bugger with the gold coins. Drink up all the scotch. Wait for them to come through those big oak doors. Or in from the terrace over there."

Lyle looked back toward the French windows. There were yard lights on out on the terrace, and the skyline of New York beyond that. It was the most magnificent view Lyle had ever seen, the quintessential American dream. He was already feeling like he lived here, they'd been through so much this evening.

"What happens when they come in? What do we do?"

"We're either shooting or we're lying on our faces on the rug there, our weapons on the floor about twenty feet away. One way, we maybe live. Other way, we never have to spend another day in prison."

Lyle shuddered. "I've never been in prison. You think they'd put us in the same prison, Sonny?"

"Not much chance of that, Lyle."

"What's it like, in prison?"

That was hard for Sonny to answer. Sonny had done all right. He was big enough and he knew how to handle the yard, knew the rules. Knock down the first man who steps up in front of you with that brain-dead look, daring you to go around him. You always had to go through him, hit him with whatever you could reach and anywhere you could reach him. Otherwise . . . well, after a while it wouldn't be safe for you ever to leave your cell. If the guards could be bought, it wouldn't be safe there either.

Sonny looked at Lyle standing there staring out across an unbridgeable expanse of Manhattan toward their hotel room in the United Nations Plaza Hotel, thinking about missing 20/20. How did you tell a guy like that what prison would really be like, especially for him?

Lyle seemed to pick up some of this.

"Hey, Sonny, lighten up. I'm sorry about the stupid picture." He looked down at the little oil, still in his hands. "Well, anyway, don't get all brotherly with me, will you? I'm a grown-up. I always knew the way home. Okay . . . ?"

Sonny was looking for something to say. Levine came racing back into the room.

"The elevator doors! Sonny, I got the doors open. We can get into the shaft, get out of here!"

Sonny and Levine ran back to the elevator. The steel doors were open about a foot. Forty feet of black shaft and cables, and the top of the cab down there at the twenty-first floor.

"Levine, can you slide in there, get those two wires there, coming out of that black fuse box? There's four. Take the white one, if you can. Don't pull the black one. Think you can do that?"

Levine looked down the shaft. "Yes. Let me try."

Sonny wriggled out of the way. Lyle watched Levine working at it. "Sonny, what're we going to try?"

There was a loud clanging noise from the elevator cab

down the shaft, then the sound of a big electric winch. The cab started to move up.

"This is it, Lyle. We're going to ride the cab roof."

Lyle's face was blank, and then it hit him.

The cab was moving up now. Thirty feet and rising.

Levine jerked a bit, and said, "There."

Sonny heaved at the safety doors and they opened up wide. The shaft was massive. They could see the cables straining, see the counterweight running down. The cab was closing fast. Sonny knew it would be full of SWAT cops, cops with Uzis and Remington 1100's or those stubby little Franchi assault guns. They'd last about fifteen seconds. Levine went pounding back into the apartment.

"Lyle, you got no choice. Come here."

Lyle stared at the shaft, his lips moving, his face gray and wet. "You don't understand, Sonny—"

Fifteen feet away and rising. Levine came racing back out of the penthouse with a canvas bag. It jingled as he ran. When he dropped it in front of the doors, it landed with a heavy metallic chunk.

Levine's eyes were wide, focused, getting ready to step onto the roof of the car as it came up into the open doorway. "Come on, Sonny. Lyle. Myron's not coming."

Lyle moved back a step. Sonny put a hand out, bunched a fist in the material of his Pelham Bay overalls.

"Lyle! Do it. You're not gonna like jail. Now come *on*!" He started to heave Lyle forward. Lyle ripped himself out of the way and took two steps back into the apartment, staring at Sonny. The top of the cab was level with the floor below. They had seconds left.

Levine pulled himself up onto the stanchion, his face wet with fear, dangling ten feet above the rising cab. It looked like a freight train coming up at him. The bag cut into his neck.

"Sonny—hurry." His voice was a raw whisper. "If the door's open when they get up here, they'll—"

Sonny shoved the outer doors shut, cutting Levine's voice off.

He went after Lyle, pulling at his Smith.

He was twenty feet down the wood-lined corridor leading to the main room when the elevator doors slid open.

The cab was full of cops.

Sonny went down on his right knee, turning sideways to narrow the target he was showing, and brought the Smith up.

There were four men in the elevator. Something was in the air, coming at him. A grenade.

He got his sights on a black cop in the doorway, bringing up his rifle.

An M-16, thought Sonny, and he squeezed off three rounds.

The black cop's face disappeared into a ragged red flower.

Sonny fell to the right.

The grenade hit the carpet, bounced, tumbled away from Sonny.

Three cops in the elevator got tangled up in the door, struggling with the black man's body. One lifted his Ingram and put out a burst of automatic fire. Wood chips flew into the air by Sonny's head. The sound was hard and punchy in the narrow hall, and then there was a white light and a massive silence, and Sonny felt a hammer blow on his chest that knocked him down the hall and his ears stopped working.

The stun grenade.

Moxie was sliding another magazine into the Ingram.

Pepsi and Charlie Boudreau were lifting Arnie Sayles's body.

Arnie's face was gone. Moxie could see bones and a flap of pink muscle. When Pepsi moved Arnie up, Arnie's head hung from his neck like a sack of wet meat.

"Jesus," he said into the intercom, his voice packing up in his throat. "Arnie's dead. They got Arnie."

Every member of Charlie Unit heard that.

Keogh and Butler heard it at their stations, wedged into the terrace railings with their backs to a three-hundred-foot fall, Remingtons braced and aimed at the glass doors fifty feet away, Butler at one corner and Keogh at the other.

Keogh had the Starlite scope mounted, his scope image a field of greens and blacks.

Sonny was back on his feet now, running through the main hall of the Saltell place. He saw Lyle as Lyle ran toward the glass doors leading to the terrace. The room was full of light. Sonny hit the switch and the room went black, the only light now coming from the terrace, from the city itself.

"Lyle!" he called, his own voice just a distant buzz in his deafened ears, but Lyle never looked back. He was carrying something. Lyle reached the doors and pushed them open. Sonny saw him there in the doorway, a black figure against the city skyline, and then he was through the doors and gone.

Myron was sitting on the floor in the middle of the room. In the hard light coming through the terrace doors, Sonny saw Myron smile, wave. Myron was staying.

More sounds from the front hall. The entry team from the elevator, cleared now and coming down the hall.

Another white flare and a massive shattering bang.

Concussion waves hit Sonny's back.

He turned and fired three rounds back at the hallway, his Smith kicking in a ringing silence, cleared the cylinder and reloaded. The entry team took cover and put semi-auto fire back up the smoke-filled tunnel. Sonny kept running for the terrace, not able to stop, knowing it was useless.

In his night scope, Frank Keogh could see a man in overalls come running out through the terrace doors, a short man like a green flame, his face a green pool, something black in his hands.

Arnie, he thought. Arnie at the rackets, playing "Willow Weep for Me," Arnie in the squad car last summer when he was in Auto Theft, going up Fordham Road past them, playing that stupid trumpet, waving.

The short man skidded to a halt. He brought up his hands, opened his mouth.

Keogh saw him do it. Saw the fear there, and the thing in his hands. It was as if Frank were standing right in front of him.

Butler's voice was in Frank's ears, a rasping burst of radio static, saying . . . what? Saying *no*?

No what? thought Frank.

The Remington kicked back into his shoulder; hot muzzle gases blurred the green field, pale flame in the scope-sight.

Who's firing?

Christ, thought Frank. I am.

I'm firing.

The Remington bucked again.

He couldn't remember working the bolt.

In the ringing silence, Sonny saw the rounds taking Lyle high, saw Lyle make a childish gesture, holding up that thing in his hands like an offering in front of him, saw the muzzle flashes from a rifleman out at the end of the terrace. A sniper. Some goddammed cop sniper. He brought the Smith up and put the thin red bar of the foresight over the blue-white flash.

Frank felt a great sadness for the little man he was killing, felt a kind of connection each time he squeezed the trigger, with each round he put out. Here, he said, firing. Take these and call me in the morning.

Lyle's head came up as shreds of cloth blew out his back, the rounds plucking at his body like crows feeding.

A section of the stone railing at Frank's shoulder blew apart. Chips of stone burned into his cheek.

There was a flame and a heavy boom from the darkness inside the French windows.

Frank jerked and another round hit the pillar.

Someone was shooting at him from inside the apartment.

Move. He shifted and flinched and then another round came in with a rock-hard crack, and his left foot slipped off the terrace ledge and he went over, the Remington snagging on the pillars, and he was hanging in the thick night air, midtown circling beneath him like a bright burning wheel, red and blue lights, white blurs of faces staring up at him, a distant swell of noise from the crowds below him, his left forearm tangled in the rifle sling, his shoulder socket a dull red coal and his heart feathering.

No more time, thought Sonny. He never looked at Lyle's body on the tiles out there. Fire came from the hall and the other corner of the terrace—another sniper over there. The terrace doors began to shatter.

He raced for the door leading to the kitchen, clearing it as Moxie and Pepsi and Charlie Boudreau came in on the run. Boudreau saw a dim figure low in the middle of the room and he put two shells of double-oh into it.

Moxie and Pepsi were already past him, down into the ruin of the massive room and running for the hall leading into the dining room and the enormous kitchen beyond that.

Keogh had his eyes shut, but he heard the flat crack of Butler's rifle and then the scuffle of heavy boots coming across the terrace after him.

Butler's voice. Very close.

"Christ, Frank."

Strong hands were on him and he was being pulled up. Butler lifted him right over the railing and they tumbled back onto the terrace tiles.

In the sudden complete silence, Frank could hear Butler's heavy breathing.

"Jesus, Frank," said Butler. "Don't *do* that!"

A half hour later they were watching as a couple of EMS paramedics strapped Arnie Sayles's body onto a gurney. There was no special rush. Moxie and Pepsi and Charlie Boudreau stood back. Pulaski and the FBI man, Duffy, were talking to the Zone Commander and the Commanding Officer of the 17th. Pepsi was crying, huge in his SWAT fatigues and his flak jacket.

"What the fuck happened?" Butler's voice was low and soft.

Moxie was looking at what was left of Arnie's face. The black body bag was swallowing him up like a snake eating a rat. The EMS man tugged at the zipper and it closed over Arnie's face.

After a time Moxie said, "We fucked up. We come out of the elevator, all jammed up in it. The doors are slow. Pepsi pitches the stun and it's in the air and we see this guy kneeling there steady as a brick. He gets three rounds off, some big double-action piece. Maybe a Smith and Wesson."

He stopped and took a long ragged breath.

"I felt something on the vest. Arnie goes down and back. I saw . . . I saw the back of his head coming apart. I pulled on this guy, but we're all . . . tangled up. We shouldna tried to help Arnie. We should've gotten right out of the elevator . . . but we . . . choked. Then we go in. The hall's narrow. The stun goes and I can't think straight. Me and Pepsi and Charlie get more fire as we're coming down the hall. We hit the floor and put out some shit. We have to come up the hall in overwatch. You know? Charlie puts out another stun. We get around into the main room there and the guy has killed the lights. Charlie takes out a target on the rug there. You saw him?"

They had. A huge baronial hall. Armor and a big marble fireplace. A man on his back in a litter of gold coins. His name was stitched into the pocket of his Pelham Bay overalls. *Geltmann*. His head was gone. Literally gone.

"Was it the same guy?"

Moxie thought about it.

"Could be. I thought the guy was bigger."

Butler said, "One of the harness guys put three into some big guy down in the lobby. This guy have any impact marks?"

"He has a Kevlar Second Chance on. But Charlie messed him up pretty good. He did have a three-fifty-seven Smith on him. I guess we'll have to see if the M.E. can get a decent slug out of . . . out of Arnie."

"Yeah."

"Anybody have a count? A target count?" asked Keogh.

Moxie shook his head.

"We had some guesses. We got two to bag. The guys have been all over the place. We even checked all the window ledges. Place is fucking huge. Lots of hidey-holes. If there's somebody else on this job, he's outa here. We got the chopper lighting up the roof. It's a steep fucker, though."

"Think he jumped for it?"

"I don't know, Pat. If he did, he's cherry Jell-O in some backyard down there. Hard to miss that."

"We're talking about Sonny Beauchamp here," said Butler. "He's a hard guy. That's his brother out there on the terrace. I don't think that mess in there on the Persian rug is Sonny. Looks like an old man. I figure it's Geltmann, just like his name tag says."

"Yeah," said Moxie. "So do we."

"Then," said Frank, "let's look again."

They did.

They didn't find him, and they couldn't rip up a rich man's house looking for him, either.

Pulaski and Duffy and some harness blues were waiting for them out on the terrace, gathered in a circle around Lyle's body. They all got quiet as Butler and Keogh came over.

Lyle was on his back, one leg caught under him. His mouth was open and his skin was blue in the lights from the city.

"Nice shooting," said Duffy, not looking at Keogh.

Pulaski grunted and looked hard at Frank.

"We got a problem here, Frank. The Commissioner is on his way. I think you ought to get the fuck outa here."

The harness cops shuffled and started to drift away.

"What's he got there?" asked Butler, looking at the dark rectangle still in Lyle's hands. In some sardonic twist of circumstance, the thing was untouched, although the body on which it rested was a ruin.

"Crazy," said Pulaski, picking it up and handing it to Keogh.

"Whaddya think, huh, Keogh?"

Frank looked at the shape in his hands.
He could hear Butler breathing and feel Pulaski's look.
"It's an oil painting, Frank."
"Yeah?" said Keogh, not looking at anyone. "Crazy, huh?"
"Yeah," said Pulaski. "That's what we were thinking."

CHAPTER 19

Saturday, August 25
0200 hours
Manhattan

Joseph Levine had a lot of time to consider the error of his ways riding up and down on the top of that elevator in the King James. He gripped a support strut, his stomach churning and freezing, his heart slamming against his ribs, and his throat working away, sweat and oil and fear marking his face. Now and then he'd look at the canvas bag between his feet and the thought would come to him that maybe he'd still get away with it.

Then the cab would move again, and there'd be voices in the cab and he'd hear the talk, low and competent but angry voices. In those first wild seconds of the SWAT assault, the rounds going off a few feet away had brought dust off every surface and the shaft had been full of rolling echoes, Levine with his head down between his knees, his arms over his head, wishing as hard as he could that he had never tried anything in life more snaky than shaving the weight off a shipment of paper towels.

After the first exchange there had been the sound of men running, and more shots. He pictured Sonny somewhere in the huge apartment, with men hunting him, and when he heard the solid boom of rifle fire he knew in his heart that Sonny had been killed, and Lyle, too, and certainly Myron, and he felt a terrible solitude that brought him close to

knocking on the cab and getting himself caught, just to
break the tension. But the weight of the canvas bag and the
fear that the cops might just kill him anyway stopped him,
and in the end he simply waited there and rode the elevator
cab up and down and tried not to think about the pressure
in his bladder.

He heard men talking in the cab. A cop had been killed
or hurt badly, somebody named Arnie. And there was talk
about somebody named Frank Keogh, and his partner,
Butler. From the talk Levine gathered that these men had
done some shooting from somewhere out on the roof. It was
confirmed for him that Myron was dead. And Lyle, brought
down by the snipers out on the roof.

And the hours passed. At one point someone in the cab
started to fumble with the escape door in the roof of the
cab. Levine could feel it under his hip. He slid off to one
side and watched the hatch the way a man might watch a
fuse burning down. But the escape door was stuck, warped
by years of neglect. The man in the elevator gave it up after
three hard slams with a closed fist failed to move it. Levine
spent another panicky interlude waiting for someone to pull
open some door overhead and shine a light down into the
shaft. But no one did.

Finally, unaware of it, drifting, Levine slept.

CHAPTER 20

Saturday, August 25
0200 hours
The South Bronx

Keogh and Butler were sitting in the back booth at the B and V Steakhouse a couple of hours after the King James go-round, drinking Stolis and working their way through a platter of ribs. Custer was on the floor under the table. They could hear him cracking down on a beef bone. The bar was almost empty. Maria had been closing it for the night when they had pulled up in the Plymouth, Butler using all his charm to get her to stay open and feed them. When they told her another policeman had been killed this evening, she pulled the doors open and went back to the kitchen to do something special for them.

Neither of them felt much like going home. Keogh had called his house on City Island. He stood there in the booth waiting for somebody to answer. Nobody did. He could picture the phone ringing on the wall above the microwave. The night light would be on over the sink. But he was pretty sure there was no sandwich wrapped in aluminum foil waiting for him on the counter top.

It had taken a while for the harness cops at the 17th to get things straightened out again. The citizens got back into their apartments by midnight. Benson Saltell hadn't bothered to fly back from Washington. His lawyer had come by, poked around through the destruction, shaking his head, scuffing at the broken glass with the toe of his Mauris, saying "goodness" and "well well" and looking at the ESU cops as if they had done it all on purpose.

Homicide cops from the Midtown South Task Force had come over to write up the PD-424-151's and work out just how it was that Lyle and Myron and Patrolman Arnie Sayles had died in this place. Some spooks from Internal Affairs rode along with them, but it was all fairly routine. Nobody was too proud of the operation, and this killing brought the total to four police officers killed in the last eleven days, three line-of-duty—Laputa, Paznakaitis, and Sayles—and one homicide, Art Pike, killed by person-or-persons-unknown.

Pulaski and the Commanding Officer for the 17th had to stay around to wrap up the paperwork for the Zone Commander. The Commissioner was supposed to be coming over from a fund-raiser in White Plains, and there were camera trucks and press people all over the landscape, so Pulaski sent the rest of Charlie Section home. There wasn't going to be much of a post-op cool-off anyway. They were all sick of not looking at each other. It would be easier to go home and not look at themselves. Moxie and Pepsi had already asked Pulaski for transfers out of the Emergency Service Unit and back to Patrol.

Keogh had been on the phone to Myra's house, trying to tell her that he wouldn't be coming back there to get his bag, he'd drop over in the morning. Some guy had answered, saying Myra was busy and who was on the line?

Keogh slammed the phone down, thinking, well, that goes to show you, Frank. You're not as unforgettable as you think you are. Butler was watching him from the car and that's when he said, Frank, let's go to the B and V. They'd ridden over in silence. Nine Stolis later, Butler pushed the plate away and patted his belly, sighing.

"So . . . where the hell was the big guy—what's his name? Sonny?"

Keogh had been wondering about that. He drained his glass, wincing at the vodka burn. "Beats the hell out of me. I talked to that cop who got the shots off in the lobby and he made a positive ID from CATCH. The guy he shot at was Sonny Beauchamp. Hit him three times—says he saw the dust coming off the overalls."

"So how come no blood?"

"Easy," said Keogh, patting his own ribs. "Second Chance Kevlar vest."

"Yeah. So where was he?"

"You want to know what I think? I think we fucked up. I think we must have run right by him. That's a hell of a big place—he could have been hiding somewhere."

"Frank, two sergeants and ten cops went over the place after the assault. He wasn't there."

"Yeah . . . tricky fellow. Hard to kill."

There was silence for a while. Keogh saw Butler checking his watch under the table.

"Hey, Pat. I'm keeping you up. Why don't you turn in? I'll be fine. We have to do a complete report by noon tomorrow . . . today."

Butler kept his eyes down on his wristwatch. When he looked up, Keogh had the feeling that something had been showing in Butler's eyes, but now he had it under control again. "Pat . . . about Arnie. If it was a safe job, everybody would be doing it."

"I'm gonna miss that stupid trumpet playing at the unit racket this year. He was just getting good."

"No, he wasn't. We were just getting used to him."

Another silence. What was there to say?

"Frank . . . where you planning to sleep tonight?"

Not at Myra's, thought Keogh, remembering the man's voice on the phone, a rough, hard voice. Not somebody who would take kindly to a guy showing up at the door at four in the morning with a smile and a hard-on.

"I don't know. Probably at the Thunderbird up in Yonkers. They'll let me take the furball into the room with me. Then I guess I'm looking for a place."

Butler's eyes were down again. "You not going to see Myra again? I figured you and Myra were kind of an item."

"Why'd you figure that?"

"Way she lit up when Ruthie and I brought you in."

"Yeah? Well, you know . . . once they've had Keogh—"

"How could they go back to a full-sized guy."

"Well, tell you the truth, Pat, I don't really want to torque the marriage. This stuff, I don't know where it comes from. It seems I just have a flair for putting the blocks to anything good in my life."

"It's been a rough season. I was going over the book for June, July, and . . . what's this? The twenty-fifth of August. Almost the end of the summer? Charlie Section rolled on an average of one thirty-three every thirty-six hours. Plus the Joint Task Force thing with those peckerwoods from Albany in the spring. What a crock that was. And now it looks like Moxie and Pepsi are throwing it in."

Keogh ordered up two more Stolis and a pitcher of Red Stripe in honor of the memory of Art Pike and Arnie Sayles, Arnie being from Jamaica originally. Drunk looked like as good a place to be as any tonight. He looked over at Butler. Butler looked like hell.

"Hey, Pat. Fuck it. Moxie and Pepsi been talking about walking from Charlie Section for a year now. They'll get over it. They always do."

"Maybe. What about you? You staying?"

"Hah? Where would I go? The CIA's only taking Mormons this week. I'm too old to become a real cop. I get out of here, I'd try for First Grade and go work Major Crimes on a task force. Nice brainy work, like Zeke and Butch. Wear those Midtown suits, punch out every day at four."

"You've been a good cop, Frank."

"What's that? That sounds like an obituary."

Butler's uneasiness was getting more obvious. Keogh was suddenly aware that Butler was trying to work himself up to saying something he didn't want to say.

"No. I don't mean it like that. It's just, some guys, they dogged it their whole careers. Not you. First time I saw you, back in seventy-two, three? You were on that PEP thing, chasing the dealers around Jefferson Park. You brought Speedo into the station, had him stuffed into the icebox of that pushcart. You remember?"

"I remember. I was out of cuffs, I had to put him somewhere. Speedo ate three Drumsicles and a Polar Bar. Best meal he had in weeks he said."

"Yeah . . . You ever miss it? Miss those days?"

"Yeah. Sometimes, Pat. Things . . . seemed clearer then. You had your shits and your cops and your citizens. A citizen was just a shit who was still in the larva stage. Life was pretty simple."

"I know what you mean. Take tonight. One way you could look at it, those guys were quietly going about their business, stealing gold coins from some uptown fixer who probably did things to get them would make a weasel go running into the bathroom with a paw over his mouth. The guy had insurance up the ying-yang. Nobody was getting hurt except the insurance firms, and fuck them."

"I'll drink to that," said Keogh.

"Yeah . . . so along we come, full metal jacket, brass balls, and all. Stun grenades, automatic weapons. You and me out there on the terrace, waiting to blow some poor hopeless dipshit out of his Reeboks. What worries me is, who was doing the escalating, you know?"

"I can't believe I'm hearing this from . . . what'd Zeke call you? Botched Casualties?"

"And the Some-Dunce Kid? I think he got that out of *Mad* magazine. That's too good for Zeke."

"Point is, it's not about stealing. Society is real clear about stealing. They've set up all kinds of ways to steal from other people legally. You can raid their pension funds on a legal pretext. You can arrange a stock market 'correction' and scoop a billion or two. You can vote yourself a pay raise if you're a congressman. You can see to it that your buddies get all the great contracts. You can charge the government six hundred bucks for a hammer. I don't give a damn about the stealing. It's the guns that bug me. These guys tonight—you saw that Smith the guy was carrying. And how about that trooper back in Lawton? Is he supposed to die because some hammerhead wants to get something for nothing?"

"Frank—" Butler stopped. It was clear to Keogh that his partner had slammed a lid on something he was about to say.

"What? Get it out, Pat."

Butler's hands were tightly interlocked on the table between them.

"Jesus, Pat. Loosen up."

"Okay. You're saying it's about guns and stealing. How about us? You and me? The Department?"

"You're talking about the pad?" said Keogh.

"I'm talking about having to pay off that cockroach sergeant at the Two-Five to get off the street and into a patrol car. Fifty bucks a month from each man in the platoon. I'm talking about the humps down on Mott Street and the little packages we used to pick up, take them over to the captain. I'm talking about grease. There are cops in this town, not so far from where we're sitting, they get so much grease it takes them half a block just to change direction."

"You got a point here?"

"Yeah . . . Who are we to do what we're doing?"

"Civil servants, that's who. You know that."

"Sure. Poor motherfucker tonight, he comes running out onto that terrace like a bull into the ring. Waving that picture around. I had him in the Starlite. So did you."

Keogh was silent for a long time.

"I couldn't see what he was holding. I thought we had the green light."

Butler slammed a fist onto the table top. Custer jumped out from under the table and stared up at the men.

"You *thought*? Fuck *you*, you *thought*! You got the balls to tell me, you maybe heard the green? And you couldn't see what that poor mope was carrying?"

Keogh said nothing. He played the thing out in his mind, a green movie, the man running out, stumbling, that black thing in his hands, and the rifle kicking, and the image jumping as the recoil took it, the man jerking like a piece of meat when the dogs get it. What had he seen? Was there a green? What had he felt?

Good—that's what he had felt. It was good to pull on a target. How was that wrong? The green was irrelevant. Wouldn't it be worse to feel nothing?

"What's the point, Pat? What's the point of all this?"

"The *point*, Frank, the goddammed *point* is, how much is left of us after we go on the pad, after we do shit like you did to Roberto? After we take down poor dumb shits like that guy tonight? What gives us the right?"

"Pat . . . nobody . . ."

"Man, I can't get by that thing with Roberto, buddy. I just can't get by it. It worries me."

"This is horse shit, Pat. . . . Come on, buddy. You're pissed. You're tired."

Butler's eyes were bright and liquid. He was crying. Butler was crying. Keogh felt the shock go through him.

"Pat . . ."

"Know what sucks, Frank? What sucks is, we used to be *about* something. Both of us. Now . . ." He made a large sweeping gesture, taking in the wreck of the B and V, the Bronx, New York. "Now what the fuck are we? Killers, Frank. This is the city of the Big Fix—the whole fucking *place* is on the pad. How the fuck you blame somebody for doing what he can to get his own in a game that's fixed, and I mean *fixed*, from the start?"

"I don't blame them. That's not what I do. I get paid to stop them. I stop whoever they aim me at. You got your head stuffed full of . . . What's the word?"

"The truth. The whole truth."

"Fuck the truth. Cop work isn't about the truth. It's not about just being a good guy and wearing the good-guy hat. You and me, we're grunts, foot soldiers. We're expendable. In the war they had this thing they called *dee-ross*. Date of estimated return overseas. It was supposed to be like a promise from the army to all the mothers: Don't worry, your kid will be back in exactly one year. Like it was a big favor they were doing, sending the troops back in exactly one year. But the trick was, the joke was, after a year in combat you were useless anyway. They figured: Most a guy ever was useful for in a combat zone was about sixteen months. They were burned-out units. Expended. Empty as a used round."

"So . . . what's the point?"

"Point point point. No point. Say a war zone is ten times more fucked-up than a cop zone. So if a grunt wears out in a year and a half . . . ?"

"A cop'll wear out in—"

"Fifteen years. They know that, downtown. They send you out, figure they'll get you to do the shit that has to be done. Figure it'll either kill you or it'll make you another sick hairbag. Important thing is, Pat, that the Job gets done. That's what we do. We do the Job and you know what, Pat, you know the fuck what?"

"What the fuck what?"

Keogh took a long pull from the glass.

"The fuck what is, you have ta stop talking to this stress guy and going to his . . . sessions, and sitting around taking apart your life so you can see how truly fucked-up you are. All those guys—the shrinks. Burke Owens—all he's going to do is break up your rhythm. Most things in life, thinking won't help you. It's a dance, and you can't dance while you're *thinking* about dancing. You follow?"

Butler was pulling back. "If you had any sense at all, you'd have taken Burke up on it, gone to some of those meetings. Okay, yes, I go. Okay, yes, I didn't tell you, and the reason is this here now. I have ta sit and listen to you give me this cop shit. Other guys in Charlie go. Not just me."

"Other guys? Who?"

"Slick Ryan. Moxie was going."

"Slick. *Slick*?"

"Hey. There's more to Slick than you know, Frank. More than just the song and the smile. He's been fucking up too. If you could pull your head outa your own ass, you'da seen that."

"What's happening to Slick?"

"Ah, shit. Never mind."

"No. I want to know."

"You know those nights he says he's always out porking some chick? Supposed to have porked Finn even?"

"Yeah. So Slick's a swordsman. People say that about you, too, Pat."

"Yeah. Only he isn't."

"Isn't what?"

"You know Hardesty?"

"Hardesty? Jimmy Hardesty? He's with Armory, isn't he?"

"Yeah. He was out at the Neck last week, way late. Past midnight. He was gonna check out those parabellums we were gonna get. Guess who was out there all night long, down on the two-hundred-yard range?"

"Slick?"

"Slick. Hardesty says the range boss checked the log, and Slick goes out to Rodman's Neck *every* night. Know what he's shooting? Wanna know?"

"So tell me."

"Remington. Three-oh-eight. Big Leupold."

"That's not his weapon. He's on the entry teams. They use shotguns and the M-sixteens."

"That's right, Frank."

"The Remington . . . That's *us*, Pat."

"Yeah."

"So . . . he's got ambition."

"So why lie about it?"

There was a long silence. Custer rolled over under the table and settled down with a low groan.

Finally Frank shook it off.

"So what? So what about all of it? It's just the Job. You ask life for too much and you might piss it off. We might wake it up, get its attention. We don't want to do that, do we?"

"No," said Butler, leaning back into the booth. "We wouldn't want to wake up anything that ugly. We had a good time, though—right, Frank? Some good times were had by all. Here's to that black bastard and his horn."

"To Arnie," said Frank. "And Art."

"And here's to Myra, Frank."

"Myra? Pat, I don't even want to *think* about Myra."

"No? Well . . ." He drank it down. "You better start, my friend. Because everybody else is thinking about her."

"Myra? Why?"

"Because she's dead, Frank. That's why."

Frank was looking at his glass. It came in and out of focus. It seemed to complete something. He felt like a man at the edge of great revelation, seeing movement in the deep water.

"How? How is Myra dead?"

Butler's face showed three or four warring emotions.

"She was stabbed, but that didn't do it. That was just to keep her busy. No, Frank . . . she was strangled."

Pike. Myra. Keogh wanted to get up and go to the phone and call Tricia, wanted to hear her voice and know that she was alive. But he couldn't move.

"Strangled with a thin red cord, Frank. Like the thin red cord you don't know dick about."

"When?"

"I don't know, buddy. Ask Zeke Parrot."

"Who was the guy at Myra's, Pat?"

Butler seemed surprised by that. "You called, huh? Probably Boo Blanchette."

Boo Blanchette worked Homicide with Zeke Parrot and Butch Johnson at the Four-Eight D.A.T.F. Now he got it, got the picture of the room, maybe Myra's body on that bed, or somewhere on the floor, Myra dead and white except where the blood had settled, where there'd be a stain like a red-wine spill under her skin, and her face puffed and stunned-looking.

"You think I did it, Pat? Why do you think that?"

"I think a lot of things when my partner pulls on an unarmed guy. When he does things like you did to Roberto. When a guy fucks up his marriage like you are. We been trying to get you into counseling for a month, or haven't you noticed?"

"Who's we?"

"All of us. Pulaski. Junie and me."

"Tricia too?"

Butler said nothing.

He pulled an envelope out of his jacket pocket. It was a long white business envelope. Butler dropped it on the table between them.

There was an FBI logo on the upper left-hand corner of the envelope. It was addressed to:

DETECTIVE SERGEANT EZEKIEL PARROT
BRONX DETECTIVE AREA TASK FORCE
48 PRECINCT NYPD
BRONX, NEW YORK 10456

"Took a hell of a chance getting this. Zeke's got a copy. You better read this, Frank. It's a bitch."

FEDERAL BUREAU OF INVESTIGATION

Tenth and Pennsylvania NW
Washington DC 20535

REPORT EXTRACT
BEHAVIORAL SCIENCE UNIT
FBI ACADEMY
QUANTICO VIRGINIA

NYPD FILE NUMBER 19-779   08/24/90
FBI FILE NUMBER 88-217698   FAX MAIL
LIGATURE CASE NUMBER K-537   13/11/59

TO: Det. Sgt. E. Parrot
    Bronx Detective Area Task Force
    48 Precinct NYPD
    Bronx, New York 10456

RE: ARTHUR RANDALL PIKE
    LINCOLN HOSPITAL
    BRONX NEW YORK
    08/22/90
    LIGATURE HOMICIDE

REFERENCE: Federal Express Courier Package
            Telephone Requisition Chief of De-
            tectives

SPECIMEN: Red fiber rope one meter in length
            Six scale color photos of ligature in
            situ
            Tissue samples to laboratory

As per the request of the Chief of Detective's Office, Priority Four telephone request, an immediate computer search of our Criminal Incident Index File was undertaken by staff members under the supervision of Technician Aaron Friedlander and Reba Jannsons, Director of the Department of Justice Computer Analysis Unit.

The ligature was received with knots and stresses intact, as per your accompanying photos showing the ligature in place on the victim's neck. The Medical Examiner's Report was also received. The search parameters were confined to ligature homicides investigated by law enforcement agencies in the continental United States and Canada, accessing shared computer data banks of the RCMP in Ottawa.

The red fiber rope was examined by technicians at the FBI Laboratory in Washington. The material of the rope was cotton. The three-part interlocking spiral braid is typical of cords produced at the Matsukazi Dojo School in Kyoto, Japan. It was imported by six distributors in the U.S. (see appendix list) but importation of this particular cord type was suspended in 1966, when supplies of the Madras dye were interrupted by internal political disorder in India, at which time a substitute dye was obtained from sources within Japan. The specimen cord supplied by your department is of the older type of Madras dye, and has been unavailable in the United States for 22 years.

The ligature knots were examined by forensic experts and compared with all known knot styles. The knots are consistent with knots used by the Thugs, a cadre of ritual killers operating in India in the nineteenth century. The method and location of the cord on the victim's neck, the duration and pattern of impressions and contusions are all consistent with a ritual Thug strangulation methodology.

A search of the Criminal Index Files generated eighteen similar Thug-style ligature homicides in the past forty years. Of the eighteen cases isolated, seven of them involved the use of Thug-style strangulation technique identical to this homicide, but in two of the cases, the ligature in situ was not consistent in fiber, dye analysis, or braid style with the ligature specimen provided.

The five homicides which were isolated as being similar in ligature, fiber content, and methodology to this ligature homicide are:

Queens NY 11/13/59 CARUSO, JULIA WF aged 9 years.
Queens NY 11/27/59 CADMAN, DONALD WM aged 5 years.
Brooklyn NY 12/25/59 DOUEY, BRUCE BM aged 10 years.
Bronx NY 02/24/61 BENKO, GRAZIELLA WF aged 3 years.
Manhattan NY 08/04/61 VIGODA, BIANCA WF aged 13 years.

One homicide which was identified as identical in style, ligature, and method, but dissimilar in cord fiber content and color, was:

Flagstaff AZ 05/13/60 CHUNG, KEIKO OF aged 2 years.

An arrest and disposition was made in these cases, with the exception of the CHUNG homicide, in which charges were never laid, although connections were posited by the investigating officer. KENT, MICHAEL D'ARCY WM/ DOB 11/11/45 was arrested by the supervising investigator in this case, Detective John Keogh (GS#604) of the NYPD Seven Zone Homicide Squad.

KENT was examined on Monday, April 15, 1962, by the Bronx County Juvenile Offender Board. Defendant was confined to the State Psychiatric Hospital for an indefinite period at the discretion of the Board.

Periodic reviews of KENT, MICHAEL D'ARCY were carried out by psychiatrists appointed by the Board of Examiners and it was the considered opinion of each examiner that KENT, MICHAEL D'ARCY was suffering from a LATENT SCHIZOPHRENIA that constituted a permanent psychiatric disorder under the terms of the related statutes of New York Penal Law.

KENT, MICHAEL D'ARCY is currently being held in secure custody at the State Psychiatric Hospital in Albany, New York.

Detective John Keogh (GS#604/NYPD Ret.)
ADDRESS:
Bahia Azul Marina
Slip 14
Matecumbe Key, FL 33036

Should you desire the assistance of one of the FBI's Computer Analysis experts, or the ligature specialists, we should be notified in ample time to permit the necessary arrangements. This report should be used, however, if legal considerations permit, in lieu of the appearance of our expert in any pretrial action such as a preliminary hearing or a grand jury presentation. Our representative cannot be made available to testify if any other forensic ligature expert is to present testimony on the same point, namely that this ligature is identical to the ligatures used in the above-cited homicides.

The ligature provided and the other enclosures are being sent to you by registered parcel delivery.

LIGATURE CASE K-537

Sincerely,

Warren Kite
Special Agent in Charge
FBI Laboratories
WASHINGTON DC 20535

Butler watched his partner read the letter in silence. Out on Hunts Point Avenue a car accelerated down the slope with a sound like a chopper going by. Angry voices came in on a wind smelling of smoke and rubber. Maria was standing in the kitchen door in her street coat, shoulders bent, leaning against the frame. Under the table, Custer whimpered in his sleep.

Keogh put the letter down. He looked at Butler.

"Pat . . . I swear to you, Dad never said a thing about this case. I never heard a word about it."

"Never? Frank, this had to be one of the biggest cases your father ever caught. Look at it—shit, serial killer, looks like six children dead. All over town and maybe one in Flagstaff, which would have brought in the Feds. It had to be all over the papers at the time. And you don't know about it?"

"What was I, fourteen, thirteen? This is twenty-eight years ago, Pat."

"Your father never said a word? Your mother?"

"Not a word . . . Anyway, you know my father. We . . . we didn't talk. By the time I was fourteen, I hated the man's guts."

Butler knew the story. John Keogh had been a Homicide star, one of the top cops in the NYPD. As with a lot of career cops, his home life was a disaster. Junie and Tricia had talked about it, about the contempt Frank's father had shown for his son. Butler and Keogh never talked about it. It was something men don't have a vocabulary for.

"So . . . so what you're saying is, you're telling the truth to Zeke and Butch? About the knots? The rope?"

"Yeah . . . yes, I am. For all the fucking good it's gonna do me, I'm telling the truth."

"They're gonna call your dad on this. Probably have already."

Jesus, thought Keogh. His father. Down in the Keys, his father had receded into a bitter memory. Frank hadn't seen the man or talked to him since one miserable vacation with the family, shortly after his father's retirement in 1975.

"So . . . what it is . . . is that Zeke has me figured for Pike and . . . for Myra too?"

"I don't know, Frank. No charges yet. But, man, it doesn't look good. You get into a fight with Art. He dies. You spend the night with Myra. She buys it. You don't know dick about the most famous case your father ever had. You never heard of the murder weapon. It looks bad. I think they got you figured for some kind of stress thing."

Keogh had nothing left to say. Butler looked at him, and for the first time in the long night, there was something in Butler's face that looked like sympathy. Like belief.

"Man," said Butler, smiling at Frank, "what was that you said? About not fucking around with the universe. Waking it up?"

Keogh remembered it.

"Well, Frank . . . I think we did. I think we woke up something. I think we got the attention of something ugly."

CHAPTER 21

**Saturday, August 25
0330 hours
Manhattan**

"**H**ey, Levine!"

Levine was deep in a dream where he was free and clear, and all of this was over. He woke up and he was still in the elevator shaft and still in the shit. Someone had called his name.

"Levine! Move over!"

A hoarse whisper from somewhere over his head. He looked up into the tangle of cables and machinery at the top of the shaft. The cab was up at the top floor again. It had been going up and down most of the night, but now it was parked at the top, outside the Saltell apartment.

"Sonny?"

Levine couldn't see a thing. There were no lights at the top of the shaft, and only a few dim ones here and there on the way down. But it was Sonny's voice, Sonny's Carolina drawl.

"Move, willya? My hands are slipping."

Levine moved and Sonny came sliding down the lift cable. He looked tired and dirty and his hands were bleeding.

Levine stared at him for a long time.

"How the *fuck* did you do that? I heard them shoot you."

Sonny wiped his hands across his face.

221

"No. They missed."

"They got Myron, didn't they?"

Sonny nodded in the dim light.

"And . . . Lyle. Right?"

"Yeah. They got Lyle."

They sat in silence for five minutes while Levine worked on his nerves and Sonny thought about what he had seen.

"You killed a cop, Sonny."

"I thought so. I saw one guy take a couple rounds. Black guy. He went down in the elevator door. Got them all tangled up. It's too bad. Too bad for everybody."

"We're in the shit now, right?"

Sonny grinned at Levine. "Oh, I'd say so. Major shit. How's it feel? You feel like a player now, Joseph?"

Levine had nothing to say to that. Sonny felt a transitory flicker of sympathy for the man. Life could be damned dull. Sometimes a man turns out to be no more than what he's been pretending to be. That's a hard thing to live with.

Still, Levine wasn't whining about it. And he had found the only way out of this place. All things considered, Levine had done pretty well for a cherry.

"So, how the hell did *you* get outa there?"

Sonny didn't answer. Voices rose up out of the well, men coming and going.

"Sonny . . . ?"

"You hear anybody talking? About the shootings?"

"Yeah. Guy you killed was named Sayles. And the snipers were right under me here. They were talking about the guy. Somebody was doing some crying."

"Tough. You happen to hear who the snipers were?"

"The snipers?"

"Snipers. The guys out there on the terrace. The ones who shot my brother Lyle. Lyle, remember?"

"I don't know, Sonny. You haven't told me how Lyle got it."

"They shot him down on the terrace while he was trying to surrender. He was out there doing his famous Blanche DuBois depending on the kindness of strangers, and they smoked him like a junkyard dog. I got off a couple of rounds but I don't think I hit shit."

Levine thought about what he had been hearing, off and on the past few hours, the talk in the elevator cab coming through the metal roof.

"What's a green light?"

"A green light?"

"Yeah. They were saying that this guy . . . What'd they say? Gimme a second. They said there'd be a shooting board. Something like that. They were gonna tear this guy's ass off for going . . . without a green light. That's what they said."

"That's a SWAT term. A green light is when they get the go-ahead to shoot. You saying this guy shot without permission?"

"Sonny, I'm buggered if I know. All I know is, the guy's up shit creek. The Commissioner was here."

"Where?"

"Right under my ass, Sonny! I heard him say that if this guy brings one ounce of shit down on the Department—"

"Who! What was his name?"

"Frank Keel. Keeler. Something like that."

"Keel? Or Keeler? Which?"

"No. It was Keogh. Frank Keogh."

"Yeah?" said Sonny. He was quiet for a long time. Men came and went far below them. Voices stopped and they heard locks being set.

Another hour.

"Sonny . . . what're we gonna do?"

"You're looking at it."

"How long?"

Sonny looked at his watch. It was close to five in the morning. There might be a guard in the lobby, but they could slip down the outside of the cab and get into the basement. There'd be a way out there, a coal chute or some forgotten exit in this old pile of stone. They could clean up in the janitor's room. Dump the clothes. Walk home to the

U.N. Plaza Hotel and ride the whole thing out. Stay indoors until it rolled over.

"As long as it takes."

"What happens to me?"

"You stay with me in the U.N. Plaza. Give yourself a day there. Then I stake you, give you some run money. A month from now—"

"A *month*?" It was an anguished bleat. "What about my business?"

"You don't have a business anymore. You got a Rolex and a one-third share of Saltell's gold. Myron's wife gets Myron's. One month from now, you run an ad in the *Post* classifieds. Call yourself Rolex. I'll get it to you."

"I can handle the cops."

"Whaddaya think this is? You think they're gonna sweat you for a couple days? Be *rude*? Maybe push you around a little? Fuck with your Fourth Amendment rights? We killed a New York cop today. I hear they lost two last week. They get ahold of you, they'll take you down to the showers and shove a nightstick so far up your ass you'll spit splinters, and that's just for starters, just to get your attention. These are hard guys. This is for *real*, Joseph! You'll give them everything you know. If I was a hard guy, I'd take you out right here. But I'm not. You wanted to walk the walk. Well, here it is."

"Jesus!" said Levine. "I got to piss."

"So? Piss."

Levine scrambled over to the edge of the cab.

Over his shoulder, he said, "So? You still haven't told me."

"Told you what?"

"*Where*, for fuck's sake? Where'd you hide?"

Sonny looked away again.

"Sonny?"

"Joseph. I tell you, you keep it to yourself. I'm gonna introduce you to some people, get you some work. You're gonna need my recommendations. Yes?"

"Shit yes."

"In the oven."

Levine stared at him. "Where?"

"In the oven. I made it to the kitchen. The cops were right on my ass. I got into one of the ovens. One of those big steel jobs, like they have in restaurants."

Levine was still staring at Sonny, but his face was changing. A muscle worked at the side of his mouth.

"Yeah. I know that thing. Saltell has two of them. I clean the place, remember? You got into the Trane oven, that huge monster on the left?"

Sonny was still looking away.

"Yeah. That one."

Levine started to grin. "And that's where you've been? Until they all left the place? In the goddammed oven?"

Sonny gave Levine a hard look.

"Yeah. It was quiet for a while. I think they were down talking to some chief. I took a chance and made it to the shaft. So what?"

"So . . ." said Levine, and Sonny started to smile too. "So what?"

"So it's a damned good thing they weren't hungry."

CHAPTER 22

Saturday, August 25
0350 hours
The South Bronx

There were always some cabs around down by the grill on Ryawa, near the waterfront. Keogh pulled up next to a gypsy cab parked by the treatment plant and blipped the siren to wake the man up. It was close to four in the morning. The perimeter lights of Rikers Island prison were cold and clear across the flat plain of the East River.

Butler saw Keogh staring at Rikers Island.

"Hey, Keogh, come on. You're not gonna end up there."

"No? I bloody well hope not. I'd last about a day in there. Ex-cop? I put a couple of gang-bangers in there a year back. They'll be very happy to see me."

"You know where you're going to sleep? You can come with me—Junie'll be glad to see you."

Keogh thought about it for a long time. Butler let him, leaning in over the passenger window and watching him. Custer snored in the back seat.

Finally, Keogh said, "No . . . no, if there's no warrant out yet, I think I'll go home. Try to find out what Tricia's up to. See what I can do to put this back together."

"You're liable to run into Zeke up there. They're gonna want to toss your house. They'll get a warrant if you make them."

"They can go through anything they want, Pat. The point is, I haven't killed anybody."

"No?"

Keogh grinned.

"Okay. Anybody I wasn't being paid to kill."

"You'll give a call later today? Junie's doing some wings for her sisters. You could bring . . . You could come by, have some brewskis. Talk about this thing?"

Normal life. Now that he was in danger of losing it all, it seemed the most precious of possessions. His eyes blurred suddenly. Butler gripped his shoulder.

"Hey, Frank. What's Lamont always say?"

" 'Who knows what evil lurks . . .' "

Butler grinned and walked away to the cab. When he reached it, he turned with his hand on the door, a ragged grin twisting his shaggy moustache, massive in his cop blues with his pointy-toed cowboy boots on and that ugly Ruger at his hip. Wyatt Earp in the Twentieth Century.

"The Shadow do!" said Butler, and then he was gone.

When Keogh pulled into the driveway of his house on Schofield Street the drapes were drawn over the living room window, and the garbage cans were at the curb. The basketball hoop over the garage made Keogh flinch from internal pain. He came up the steps to the front door. Custer followed him up, whined a bit, and then ambled down onto the lawn to investigate the latest messages from the locals.

Someone, probably Robbie, had brought in fresh sod and cut the grass. The place looked painfully neat and orderly, as if it had been fixed up to somehow balance the chaos inside. Keogh pulled open the aluminum door with the blue heron scene on it and found, to his surprise, that his keys still fit the lock. He opened the door slowly, feeling like a man opening a crypt, and stepped into the hall.

He could tell that Tricia and Robbie were gone. It was hard to say how. A stillness on the place, a silence rising up

out of the carpets and the flowered furniture. Tricia
perfect English living room, shaded and dim in the ha'
light from the hall, gave off the stale scent of a tomb. He s:
down on the sofa and stared at the pictures over the mant
for a long while as the shadows receded and the growin
light of day showed him more clearly with each passin
minute the extent of his loss.

After he felt he had punished himself sufficiently for th
moment, he called in Custer and put some food out for hi
in a kitchen so dense with emptiness that it seemed hard t
breathe. He showered in a bathroom that still held th
scent of Tricia's perfume. He wrapped himself naked i
their bed and he went to sleep holding a pillow to his bell

He dreamed about Myra and Tricia. In his dream, My
and Tricia were drifting in a rectangle of blue-green ligh
They were naked. Myra was talking to Tricia but h
couldn't hear what they were saying. When they kissed an
Tricia's hand moved slowly down Myra's wet belly, he trie
to look away and found he could not move.

Around him the neighborhood lived its Saturday under
high blue sky. Lawns were cut. Kids on skateboard
clattered down the rutted walks and skittered crazily ov
the curbs. Cars floated by on the heat-lacquered asphal
Women talked across the fences and men smoked an
cursed in their basements and garages. Now and then a j
from La Guardia boomed across the skyline. A soft win
feathered leaves. The shadows under trees came down t
black pools and slowly grew long again.

On Keogh's bed a barred square of hazy light drifte
slowly across him. After a long while it warped an
stretched and spilled itself down the side of the bed an
pooled out across the deep-blue rug. Custer found it an
lay down in it, feeling the heat in his chest and along his r
cage. He listened for a time to Keogh's breathing and felt
kind of sadness.

A pounding. Keogh woke into a perfect blackness th
gradually shaded into a familiar bedroom that had onc

been his. Custer was out in the living room, barking and growling. Under the basso snarling from the dog, Keogh heard the sound of a closed fist on the front door.

"Frank! Open the fuck up!"

Keogh slid out of bed and pulled on his fatigue pants.

"Frank. This is horse shit. Frank!"

Bam-ba-bam-bam. The little house vibrated to the blows. Keogh had to smile. This was the first time he'd ever been on the receiving end of the formal cop knock. He'd done it himself a thousand times. He ran a hand through his hair and rubbed his face a couple of times and found himself staring at a picture of his father in the crowded mass of family photos over the fireplace.

Happy, you sanctimonious prick? Keogh told Custer to be quiet and walked over to the front door and jerked it open.

"Hey, Zeke. You're just in time for a beer."

Zeke Parrot filled the narrow doorway, a big black bull in a brown suit and a breakaway tie in a nasty pattern. Down at the bottom of the driveway, a squad car from the 45th was blocking Frank's blue Plymouth, a grizzled old uniform cop leaning on the driver's door and grinning up at them. Keogh knew the cop in a distant way. He was one of the cops who had come to the house to keep an eye on Tricia last week. Bortz.

It was full night out. All the lights were off in all the little houses up and down Schofield Street. Zeke's brown detective's car was parked across the road.

Zeke's face looked like a brick wall.

"Get that dog out of my face, Frank." Custer stood behind Keogh. A low sound like someone trying to jump-start a lawn mower was coming from his chest.

"Custer. Off." Custer drew back and padded into the living room to await developments.

"Where's Butch? Around the back, waiting to take my head off as I come flying out the back door?"

Zeke pulled out his handset. "Butch. Forget it. He's out

here." Zeke put the radio away and waited for Frank to step back from the door.

"Got a warrant, Zeke?"

"Yeah. You want to see it, I'll shove it up your ass. You can get the guys at Rikers to read it back to you."

Butch Johnson came around the porch with his little Colt out.

"Butch . . . how you doin'?"

"Not good, Frank." He came up the steps and Keogh backed away. They filed into his front room. Keogh turned on a couple of lights and stood by the mantel. Zeke and Butch faced him, standing. This was going to be formal. No breaks for an old friend. Zeke and Butch were radiating a kind of scalded rage. Something had changed in the case.

Zeke started it. "Frank Keogh, you have the right to remain silent and—"

"I know the song, Zeke."

"Butch, if he opens his mouth again, Mace him. And refuse to answer questions. Do you understand?"

"I answer, do I get Maced?"

"The subject replied in the affirmative."

Butch was writing this down on the back of a card from Frielich's gun shop on East 21st Street. Keogh used to hang around there and watch the detectives when he was a rookie going to the Academy across the street. He had about two hundred Frielich's cards in his top drawer up at the 46th.

"Anything you do say may be used against you in a court of law. Do you understand?"

"You forgot to tell me what the charge was."

Butch stopped writing.

"Shit," said Zeke.

"Do you want to go out and come back? We can start again?"

"Shut up, Frank," said Butch.

"Frank Keogh, you are charged under Section One Twenty-five, paragraphs two-five to two-seven Penal Law for the murder of Police Officer Myra Jane Kholer, in that at or about four hundred hours on the twenty-fourth of August, nineteen hundred and ninety, you stabbed and strangled her in her apartment at—"

"Zeke, I was out of her place by midnight. I—"

"Shut up, Frank. You are also charged with the murders of Sergeant Arthur Randall Pike of the New York City Police Department and Sharon Zeigler, in that you—"

"I spent the rest of the night driving around town. You can check this out."

Zeke stopped the litany.

"Yeah? Prove that."

"I can't. I mean, not right away. I can tell you the places I went. Somebody will remember."

Butch laughed shortly. "So what? Maybe you killed Myra earlier. Then you go out to make up your alibi. Anyway, let's cut the shit, eh, Frank? We found the suit."

"Butch," said Zeke, turning on him. "Shut up."

"The suit?"

"Oh, come off it, Frank. Whaddya think we are? The fucking plastic suit you wore to keep the blood off you."

"Butch, you're just helping him out."

"Fuck it, Zeke. We gotta give his lawyers all this shit anyway. I just wanna watch his face. I wanna hear what he has to say before his fucking lawyers get to him. You wore a clear plastic suit, pants and a pullover top, and gloves. Kept you clean while you went to work on Myra. What was the idea, Frank? She figure out you killed Pike? Figured you'd make it look like a psycho or something?"

Keogh had no idea what the hell Butch was talking about. Saying so would only sound false. He wouldn't believe it himself, if he heard it from a suspect.

Butch went on in a controlled kind of raging.

"Thing I can't figure, you take the trouble to rinse out the inside of the glove fingers so we can't lift a latent, and then you stuff the suit into your bag, and you walk out and you leave the fucking bag right there! Why the *fuck* would you do that? And the red cord again—what's that? An in-joke for your daddy?"

His suitcase. He had left it at Myra's apartment. He could see it there in his mind, sitting by the couch.

"Hey, fuck it. Don't tell me. I figure you were a little freaked out by how much bleeding you got little Myra to do. Man, you shoulda expected it. You don't want them to bleed a lot, you stop the heart first. But then, she wouldna been around to appreciate what you were doin', would she? Hah, Frank . . . would she? You got something to say, you fucking mick bastard?"

"Forget it, Butch," said Zeke, pulling out the cuffs. "Turn around, Frank. Put your hands on the mantel."

It hit Frank then. Turn around and stare at your father's face while a couple of family friends arrest you for murder. He tried to get himself to move. His chest was tight and his breath wouldn't come. He shook his head and stepped back.

Butch Johnson took the hesitation for resistance and lost his temper. He grunted something and came forward. He had a small spring-steel sap in his hand. Face distorted, in silence, he brought his arm up.

Custer hit his forearm in mid-swing, dragging Butch forward and down. The sap flew out of his hand.

Zeke Parrot drew his Smith, stepping into the struggling pair to get the muzzle up against Custer's head. He fired twice. Custer's brains and bits of his skull hit the brass fireplace tools and he went down in a tumble of red fur and blood, urine running out of him. Butch scrambled backwards, out of the mess.

Zeke and Frank looked down at Custer's body.

"What'd he think?" said Zeke. "This isn't fucking *Lassie*."

Keogh's fist caught him in the knot of nerves and muscle and bone behind his left ear. Zeke Parrot went straight to the ground.

Butch was on his knees, his mouth open. Keogh picked up the sap. Butch started to get up. Frank kicked out at him.

Butch went back onto his rump and stared stupidly up at Frank. Butch's eyes were dull and red. His right hand moved. Keogh saw the snub-nosed Colt, a blue shape in the yellow light.

Keogh came around from the right in a wide arc, moving as fast as he could, feeling his shoulder muscles working, feeling the snap, seeing the sap take Butch in his left temple, Butch's left eye bulging out, his face going rubbery, blood filling the eye.

Butch stayed where he was, on his ass in the middle of Tricia's Persian rug in the center of Tricia's perfect English room with the flowers and the prints. Butch sagging into himself, his face up and back on his thick neck, his left eye open and clouded with blood and fluids, his mouth slack. He had his hands crossed in his lap. Keogh took the snub-nose out of his hand.

"Butch?" said Keogh, kneeling down and touching his face.

There was a long slow exhalation. Keogh could smell ribs and hot sauce on his breath. They must have been at the B and V, waiting for it to get late. When you were looking for someone, the best time to come calling was in the middle of the night. Everything happened at night.

"Butch . . . ?"

Johnson's lips opened and closed. His breath grated in his throat like pebbles down a pipe.

"Frank . . . call a doctor, man. Call a doctor."

On the floor Zeke Parrot lay like a fallen pillar, breathing deep and steadily. The room smelled of blood and urine.

Shit, thought Frank. Custer.

There was a pounding at the door. Keogh remembered the uniform cop waiting outside. Bortz.

He stepped to the door and opened it and Bortz came tumbling in, his weapon out in front of him. Frank put the snubbie up against the man's temple.

"Man," said Bortz, looking at Zeke on the floor, at the dog with no top on his head and the blood running out of him onto the Persian rug. "They shot your fucking dog."

"Yeah," said Frank. "So imagine how cranky I am right now."

CHAPTER 23

Sunday, August 26
0200 hours
New Jersey

Keogh pushed the Plymouth at a flat seventy-five down the gray tunnel of I-95 with the luminous green squares coming up at him in the glare of his headlamps.

BAYONNE.

RAHWAY. CARTERET.

EDISON. SAYREVILLE.

PROSPECT PLAINS. CRANBURY.

NEXT RIGHT.

ARCO. SHELL.

FORD.

TRENTON. BURLINGTON. HADDONFIELD.

CAMDEN 15 MILES.

The signs burned green in the night, the pillars and spires of Manhattan no longer even a glimmer in his rearview mirror. He listened to the crackle and the cross-talk of the police radio in his dashboard, catching the frequencies of the New Jersey State Police talking slow talk about B & Es and Ten-Twenties and Seventeen all-arounds roger Central what's your ETA?

The bright-green signs flickered up and past his hood like sparks from a fire somewhere farther down the gray tunnel of his headlights, and the road went on ahead, racing at him, snaking this way and that in the long sweeping curves of the interstate, running this way, sliding that, leaning south and west and south again as New Jersey gave way to Delaware and Maryland.

And his home back on Schofield Street . . . By now, they'd be taking it apart brick by brick and slat by slat. Keogh had done what he could for Butch, wrapping his head in ice and bandages. Butch had dropped into unconsciousness while Keogh was tending to him. Zeke Parrot had never moved while Frank tied him up, snoring loudly on his face on the carpet in front of the fireplace. Bortz he'd left tied up and gagged in the bathroom, cuffed to the pipe by the toilet.

Keogh had gathered a few things, clothes, what money he had, and thrown it into his equipment bag. Then he went over the house and the yard and the garage, tearing through boxes and dragging out crates and ripping through old clothes and shoe boxes. He had to work fast. They'd send another car around in a few minutes—sooner if they couldn't get Bortz on the radio.

He found the red cords at the bottom of a box of Pennzoil at the back of his garage, a tangle of them, slick and scarlet and coiled neatly into a braid like a convolution of cobras.

Although he had expected to find them hidden somewhere, seeing the cords gave him a cold rush in his belly. This was enemy action, a visible trace of malice.

He piled what he could into the blue Plymouth and moved the squad car and pulled away up Schofield Street with the feeling that every darkened window was full of neighbors watching him run. At the corner he used a phone booth to call an ambulance for Butch Johnson.

They'd never have listened to him anyway. They were beyond reason. He was guilty. Resisting arrest had slammed the gavel down. Gold Shield Detective Second Grade Frank Keogh, son of Detective Retired John Keogh, cop killer and psycho and soon-to-be interstate fugitive.

The motion of the car soothed him. He managed to stop seeing Custer dead on the rug in front of the fireplace.

It was close to dawn when he came up a crest and down

a long hillside. There was a sign saying FREDERICKSBURG AND
SPOTSYLVANIA NATIONAL MILITARY PARK. Good enough. It was a
clear Sunday in the making, and he needed to stop and try
to figure out what the hell he could do about his situation.

Somebody somewhere was having a very good time
putting his life in a blender.

Somebody he knew.

Someone with access to police files.

Names started to come to him but he didn't like the
sound of any of them.

Police buddies from the department?

Who hated him enough to do *this*? The man—the
woman?—whoever, would have to have a psychopathic
hatred, something out of a private pit. . . . He took out
the FBI report and read the name.

KENT, MICHAEL D'ARCY.

Secure custody. State Psychiatric Hospital in Albany,
New York. Born on the eleventh of November in 1945.
Veterans Day. Christ, how old would the guy have been
when he started strangling these kids? Julia Caruso died on
November thirteenth in 1959. The kid would have just
cleared his fourteenth birthday. Fourteen years old!

Latent schizophrenia? What the hell is that?

Michael D'Arcy Kent would be . . . a grown man now,
forty-two, almost forty-three years old. That was a long time
for the psychiatrists to hang on to somebody, even a serial
killer who had strangled five, maybe six children in a
two-year period. Back in harness at the 25th, Keogh had
seen a couple of murders where the killer had been
released as "cured" by one of the psychiatric institutions.
Psychiatrists were always ready to see their patients get
better, go back to normal life. Nothing about the victim
survives except old photos and files. But the killer, he's
always around, isn't he? Always sitting there in front of you,
asking to be handled, asking to be cured and rehabilitated.
Alive and here in front of you. It was natural for people to
want to see the guy as human, as troubled, as something

broken that could be fixed so maybe *some* good could come out of the killing.

How did they *know* that Kent was still in secure custody? Did anybody drive up there, go see the man?

No. They took the word of somebody up there, some distracted bureaucrat. They would have spoken to him; he'd look down at his files, say, Hey, yeah, he's here.

Keogh could see the open file on the guy's desk. He remembered other cases, psychiatrists going on and on in a hot Bronx courtroom, the clerks dozing, phrases like "transient situational disturbances" and "dysthymic disorders." What was the best one? Oh, yeah . . . "dissociative states." Keogh imagined a reedy black-bearded man in half-glasses and a tweed coat with leather patches on the elbows, talking into the telephone saying, Oh, yes, Mr. Kent is coming along nicely, yes, sir. Hasn't tried to strangle any children in . . . God, it must be *years* now. Well no, we haven't actually put him in a room with one, but trust us. We can tell about these things.

Which was total horse shit. If being a cop had taught Keogh anything, it was that psychiatrists knew absolutely nothing about what a person *might* do, and whatever they had to say about what a person *had* done was gibberish.

His father had arrested this kid. His father would have been . . . how old in sixty-one? Forty-one.

Keogh was forty-two. He felt a current, a shock of recognition and connection go through him. His father was just a forty-year-old cop when this happened, around the same age as Keogh was now. He must have felt the same things, must have been watching his body change, maybe even wondering about his place in things. Not knowing he was going to lose his wife in a stupid accident only seven years later.

John Keogh must have felt a lot of the same things that Keogh was feeling right now. Perhaps he even felt himself judged and dismissed by his own son.

So . . . Frank couldn't go to Albany himself, to confront this Kent person. Owens might help him there.

Owens would be hooked into the whole shrink club. He'd know how to move around in it, if Keogh could get to him. Convince him that he hadn't done it, that there really *was* a mysterious stranger doing this to him.

And his father . . . Old Johnny Keogh would know where to start, who the players had been. Christ, it would have been his biggest case. He would have made his First Grade out of it. He'd remember everything about it.

And when Frank called him the Feds would be sitting at his elbow saying, Good, good, Mr. Keogh, now just keep him on the line and we'll get a squad out there faster than you can say Freeze, motherfucker.

He'd have to travel. Great. He had his gold shield and his NYPD identification card. An American Express card that was useless now. Use it once and he'd ring bells in every FBI office between here and Ultima Thule. And maybe seventy bucks in cash.

Time to get off the interstate.

He found a glade off the main road, on a hill with a view of the battlefield. The car fit in nicely under a stand of black oak, a dappled cool circle under the branches. He climbed out and stretched and walked to the rise.

He could see the valley as terrain, as a tactical problem for a foot soldier. Defilades and enfilades, where to set the beaten zone. How to mount the sixties. Bloop guns over here . . . forward posts to break up the assaults . . . Shit, it hadn't been like that for the men who had come across the Rappahannock in the winter of '62. Lee had the high ground and it was Burnside's men who got chewed up in the valleys. Twelve thousand Union troops in one day. It tended to put things in perspective for Frank, helped him see his own problems as just something off to the side of the stage, not really critical to the action. It was a calming feeling, and it felt good, and it lasted about fifteen seconds.

He walked back to the car and stood looking at it for a while. This would have to go. It said *cop* as clearly as if he had spray-painted it on the driver's door. And the trunk . . . Jesus, he had an arsenal in there.

He popped the trunk lid. Oh, yes.

Butler's Remington, in a tooled leather case, a cactus and sage pattern around the initials PB. An M-16. Boxes of ammunition. A black canvas bag. Keogh's own Remington, oiled and cleaned in a black leather case.

Keogh reached for the Remington. And stopped.

The black canvas bag.

The bag of Ching-a-Ling cash that Fausto had made a dive at when he and Butler had kicked in Roberto's drug shop. Keogh had kicked Fausto in the head. Butler had gone into the bedroom after Roberto.

He scooped the bag out of the trunk and set it down on the fender. He opened it.

It was full of worn and dirty currency, twenties and tens and fives, here and there a fifty.

There was a piece of paper folded into the side of the bag. Keogh opened it up. It was a typed note.

Frank:

If you're reading this then you have cut and run. I don't know what to tell you. I think Zeke and Butch have got some new stuff on you because Pulaski has been downtown to Internal and the Advocate Office has been phoning all day. They have the Communication tapes from that call at the King James and it looks like they are going to beef you for an unauthorized takedown on that Lyle Beauchamp asshole.

You're going to be pissed about the cash. I don't blame you but I have my own problems and if it ever comes to it I will take the freight with Internal as you know I will.

It were me, I'd go to Flagstaff. That's the case that sticks out. Maybe you can shake something out. I will see about the ones back here. If it isn't you then it has to be somebody on the job. I tried to get Zeke to go up to Albany, see this Kent asshole but he says no way. They already sent up Boo Blanchette and he says the guy's there all right. A real gork too. So that's fucked.

They will figure you to go to your dad. Junie talked to Tricia and she says that is where they have gone and Zeke will look there first if you try there. Tricia and Robbie are staying on his boat.

I think you should come in but I figure you won't. They will be all over me as your partner. When I was UC, I used a phone at a bar called Brews on West 34th. The number there is 555-2211. I will be standing by it at 2315 hours on Monday night.

Good luck. I will take care of Custer. He likes me.

Keogh looked up from the note. The valley of the Rapidan and the Rappahannock was all around under a cloudless sky. A couple of jays squabbled in the branches overhead. Down in the long slope of grass, yellowjackets zoomed and hovered. A moist dense heat was rising up out of the black earth.

There was a kind of pressure in his ears and he realized that it was silence. For the first time in years he was out of New York, away from its ceaseless rumors of machinery and cars. The silence pressed in around him.

Butler.

Butler was either trying very hard to help Keogh.

Or he was setting him up.

There was an old line from the war. How can you shoot women and children? Easy, was the answer.

You just don't lead them as much.

Who was leading him?

CHAPTER 24

Sunday, August 26
1700 hours
Manhattan

Of all the brass-balled things that Sonny Beauchamp had ever done in his thirty-six years on the planet, sitting around in this forest-green suite of rooms in the United Nations Plaza Hotel was about the brassiest. Now it was Sunday afternoon and he was lying on the king-sized bed in what he still thought of as Lyle's room, surrounded by a litter of room-service dishes and glasses, little plastic scotch bottles from the mini-bar, about sixteen pounds of the Sunday *Times* all over the room, the big Sony Trinitron all lit up in the corner, watching a Jacques Cousteau special about sharks, thinking, Okay, Sonny, one more day being Mr. Paul Dennison and then it's checkout time.

It had been a hard twenty-four hours, trying not to think about Lyle too much, listening to the sirens going whoop-whoop up and down the avenues and cross streets, expecting that special police bam-bam-ba-bam at the door any minute, with a canvas bag full of stolen coins and stamps in the hall closet and his stainless .357 Smith on his chest like the family cat, warm from the heat of his body, covered with potato-chip crumbs and Frito dust.

There hadn't been anything else to do. He had to assume that they had an ID on Lyle now. They'd be looking for him. Every rookie cop and part-time security guard would be driving around Manhattan with a black-and-white glossy of Sonny Beauchamp out there on the passenger seat beside him. Sonny had depended on staff changes to keep him anonymous; he'd stayed in his room and made it a point to be in the bathroom when the room-service waiter came up with another ice bucket full of beer or a tray of back ribs.

He'd listened to the news last night, and mercy, did this town love its news shows—had to be a good four hours of early news, news breaks, news briefs, new news, *Live at Five* news, *Eyewitness News*, twenty-four-hour news, cable news, midday news, and late news and midnight news and sunrise news roundup and noon news and . . . nothing ever seemed to happen in any of it; it just promised you that any minute now something was about to happen or that *wowie*, it *just* happened, you poor bastards, and you *missed* it because you were in there in that marble-and-glass bathroom taking care of nature and *whoops*, there it goes *again*, and you missed that too, but okay, don't worry, we'll have film at eleven. And at the end of all of that, Sonny still hadn't heard any more than that the brave NYPD SWAT cops had cornered a pack of crazed desperados in a midtown apartment and had, at great risk to life and limb, brought them to speedy justice, at the terrible cost of a brave policeman's life. They ran this cop's photograph about every fifteen minutes most of Saturday night. That had been hard to take.

He was a black guy, with deep-set eyes and a thin wry mouth. He was smiling up into a camera at what looked like a nightclub or something, holding a trumpet up in one long-fingered and oddly delicate hand. His name was Arnold Sumter Sayles, single, twenty-seven years old, a graduate of Fordham University, holder of several NYPD ribbons and citations. There was to be a funeral for him at Cypress Hills on Tuesday. Sayles was, according to the news reports, the third policeman to die in the line of duty in New York City in the last fourteen days. One of the talking heads, a black woman with drop-forged hair, kept referring to "a season of blood," dropping her voice a couple of floors and pausing a few heartbeats at the end of the phrase to telegraph her spontaneous and deeply felt personal anguish and then going on to promise more film of the bloodstains in the front hall of the Saltell apartment. . . .

Another news break. A photograph of a ruddy-faced Irish-looking cop with a trim salt-and-pepper moustache, and the type under it read COP SOUGHT IN KILLING.

Sonny plucked up the remote from the mess on the bedspread and shut off the MUTE button. A blast of sound came at him and he lowered the volume.

". . . are not giving out much information other than to say that this officer, a decorated gold shield detective with nineteen years' service, is being sought by authorities in connection with the death of a fellow officer earlier in the week. No information has been released about the death of this officer, but sources close to the Commissioner told *Eyewitness News* that there is evidence linking this officer's death to the man now being pursued."

There was a confusing succession of images: video clips of the outside of a hospital somewhere, squad cars parked with their lights flashing, a stretcher being hurried into a coroner's wagon, and then another press scrimmage inside some place called One Police Plaza, a barren brick hall with uniformed cops in the background and a harried-looking plainclothes cop, huge and black and full of resentment, blinking into the floodlights as a gaggle of TV reporters pushed their mikes into his cheeks.

"No, we haven't charged anyone in this matter. We are trying to get in touch with Detective Keogh. We believe he can assist us in our inquiries." This was said with a ghost of a grin, the classic Scotland Yard line.

Keogh? What the hell . . . ?

"Is this a murder investigation, Sergeant Parrot?"

"Hell, yes. What'd I just say?"

"Detective Keogh is wanted for murder, Sergeant?"

"Detective Keogh is wanted for questioning, I said!"

"How did he kill the other policeman? Was it a grudge

killing? Was it about money? Is it true drugs were involved? Is it true they were fighting over drug money?"

The big black cop was being backed up into the hall with questions—mikes sticking in his face, little tape recorders coming over his shoulders, sweat on his forehead, the questions flying around him like scraps of paper in a windstorm.

"No, it wasn't about drugs. No, there weren't drugs involved! What do you mean, is that an official denial? What am I denying? I'm not denying anything, I'm telling you—"

"Then you don't deny it was about drugs?"

"How big a problem is police corruption, Sergeant?"

"Is it true that Frank Keogh was on the take?"

"What's the name of the cop Keogh killed?"

"Is it true Keogh was using cocaine?"

"Have you contacted the FBI yet?"

"Yes, the FBI is involved."

"Do you know where Frank Keogh is now?"

"Not at the moment. We expect to hear from him momentarily, though. No, I can't say any more. That's all. That's it. No more comments. I said *no comments*—can't you hear what I'm telling you?"

They kept at him like jackals, thought Sonny, feeling a little sorry for the guy. The cop was trying to get through them. A hot floodlight brushed his cheek and then his arm came around, there was a blurred sequence of tilted images, feet, heads, faces open . . . . somebody saying, Hey, you can't do that, I'm a—

They brought the photo of that cop back, the black Irish cop with the salt-and-pepper moustache. It was a color shot. There was something odd about the guy's eyes. Mac was intoning on the voice-over.

"To recap tonight's top story: City and state authorities are currently seeking this New York City Police detective. His name is Frank Keogh. He is considered armed and dangerous and he is wanted in connection with the murder of a fellow police officer in what may have been a fight over illegal drug money."

The screen filled up with a cartoon of elderly men and women stumbling around on a giant diaper looking worried, and then a pair of disembodied hands poured a cup of blue liquid into a paper bowl and Sonny shut the damned thing off.

Keogh. Frank Keogh. Wanted for questioning in the death of a policeman? Drugs? How many Frank Keoghs could there be? How many worked for the SWAT team in this city?

And the eyes. He had one blue eye and one green eye. How hard could he be to find, with a mark like that on him? And now he was out of the club, over here on the far side of the street, where Sonny Beauchamp lived and where Sonny knew all the rules.

Mercy.

CHAPTER 25

Sunday, August 26
1650 hours
Applegrove, Virginia

Keogh was developing some sympathy for guys on the run from the law. First of all there was the wear and tear on your nervous system. He'd kept to the back roads all the way down to this small town called Applegrove and every time he saw a black Ford or a Plymouth grille in his rearview, his belly would clamp up and freeze and his pulse would hammer against the side of his neck. He'd watch the car come up in his mirror, thinking, yes, well, this is it—they're just gonna pull up alongside and stick a 12-gauge in your cheek, Frank.

Then the car would turn into a sedan full of farm kids or a couple of old folks on the way to Sunday dinner, and the relief was almost as painful as the fear.

Interesting effect. But what are you gonna *do* about it, Frank? So far you're not cutting much of a swath as a wild desperado on the run. It's one thing to cruise around the Bronx in a DT car or sit up in a room at the Pretty Kitty with a loaded Remington and a heart full of nasty intentions. It was a whole other thing to rabbit around the countryside in a stolen cop car with some vague idea of catching this asshole who has sabotaged your life while all the state troopers on this side of the Cumberland Gap were tear-assing up and down the seaboard thinking about gunfire and promotions and staring at your black-and-white glossy on the dashboard.

ID, Frank was thinking. How the hell do you get ID? Back in Harlem there was a guy running a bodega on West 116th who could get you anything you wanted: American Express, Visa Gold, a Jersey license with your picture, Green Card, Social Security . . . he even had a price list. But getting up to Harlem was looking a tad tricky.

Bad guys without a ticket to West 116th and an in with a Puerto Rican *zapatero* got their IDs in other ways. Two other ways, to be exact.

They bought stolen IDs from guys who steal IDs.

Or they stole one themselves.

Time for something clever, Frank.

Anytime soon would be good, Frank.

Applegrove was a dozy little ville lying in a curve of green hills a few miles out of Richmond, just north of I-64. Frank slid into the place in midafternoon, a slow Sunday summer day in rural Virginia. He found a turnaround off the road and left the Plymouth under a stand of black oaks. He walked two miles into the town itself. On the way to Applegrove's only motel—The Eagle Inn, a Spanish court-yard motel with a pool and a red tile roof—Frank passed a couple of gas stations, a Bob's Big Bite, and a rambling red-brick building with a painted wooden sign on the sloping lawn.

TIDEWATER HOUSE
A CHRONIC CARE FACILITY

By the time Frank had gotten past the solicitude of the motel owner—a sweet apple-doll lady who told Frank her name was Flora Jellicoe—and had himself installed in an upper room overlooking the pool and the square courtyard, he was working on an idea.

Flora hadn't blinked at Frank's false name, and she was prepared to accept him for whatever he said he was. It was a strange feeling, if you came from New York. In New York, nobody thinks you are who you say you are and they just stay back a ways until whoever you really are becomes clear.

"Tidewater? Oh yes. A cancer place."

"What, a cancer?"

"No—my, no. A place where they treat cancer patients. Very fine reputation. Lots of nutritionists and that sort. My niece works up there as a nurse. Such a sad place, though. All those poor people shuffling around in the halls and wearing housecoats. Some of them so sick they don't know who's talking to them. Up-to-date clinic, mind. Richmond folk come all the way out here to try the cure. Some do get better." She looked at Frank, her small brown eyes sharpening.

"You're not here for that, son?"

Frank said no, he wasn't. Just passing through looking for work. She seemed relieved to hear it.

After a long while, as the courtyard quieted down and people went to their dinners, Frank stepped softly down the stairs and out onto the road and walked the two miles back up to Tidewater House.

He went in with the visitors. There was a flower stand in the lobby. He bought a spray of lobelia dappled with hibiscus flowers and shuffled onto the elevator with a distant and troubled look on his blunt Irish face. The palliative care unit was on the sixth floor. No one paid a lot of attention to him. He had the drug cop's flair for looking ordinary and harmless.

There were twenty-eight people in the various beds of the section, old women, young men, mothers with photos of their kids and side tables full of houseplants. Cancer was taking all of them. They looked like members of the same family, wisps of bodies and blue skin, the same uneasy rise and fall of the sheets, wired together by machinery, chained to the planet by the pride of modern medicine.

Frank went through the rooms and down the rows of beds. Nurses avoided looking at him, keeping their heads down and their eyes on the middle distance, like waiters ducking the customers.

It took a while but finally Frank found a white male who looked to be roughly his age and body type. Black hair and pale white skin. His eyes were sunken into his face. An IV dripped something into a bony arm that looked like a piece of pipe. A clipboard hanging on the end of his bed said his name was GALSTON, BARNABY E. A home address in Utica, New York.

Jesus, thought Frank. Another New Yorker up against it in Virginia. How'd *you* get here, Barnaby?

Well, Barnaby wasn't exactly here, was he? Frank spent a while sitting on a white cane chair at the side of Barnaby's iron bedstead and watched the way the breath came and went in the ruined body under the cotton sheet with the letters THCC in army stencil.

Biology, Frank. Every day a trillion rolls of the dice until one day it goes sour for you, and here you are in the bed next to Barnaby. And in another part of his mind, the lizard part where the only calculations were safety and hunger, Frank had noticed the gray metal cabinet beside the bed. It had a channel lock in the face of it. Frank estimated that it would take about sixty seconds with a paper clip to spring the first two tumblers. The third one would go with a tug. There wasn't much to do until his chance came but to sit there and listen to Barnaby Galston breathing and try not to think about what he was going to do if he got it open and saw nothing in there but Double Stuff Oreos and a galvanized bedpan.

It was midnight by the time Frank got back to the Eagle. He sat down on the deck chair out front and thought about his next move.

It was cooler now. A little country music was coming from the next unit. Frank sat back and popped a can of Dixie beer. He had a pack of Winstons in his coat pocket. What the hell, he thought, reaching for them.

He'd have to buy a car with local plates from somebody a long way from here. Store the Plymouth. Then what?

He pulled out Barnaby's ID. GALSTON, BARNABY EARL. D.O.B. October 2, 1948. An address in Utica, New York. And a Social Security card. Born in 1948 would make him forty-two. The eyes were listed as brown. Could be altered. But the height and the weight were right. The hair he could fake with some Grecian Formula.

He wondered what Barnaby's relatives would think of the money he'd left in place of Barnaby's wallet. Three thousand dollars. Frank had figured it would be enough to bury Barnaby. The least he could do. Now, as long as Barnaby held out for a while, nobody would miss his license or his Social Security card.

And where will they take you, Frank?

Florida? They'd be ready for *that*.

Mexico? Take the Ching-a-Ling cash and bury himself in a backwater seaport down in Oaxaca state.

And leave this bastard to spend the rest of his life grinning into his shaving mirror every time he thought of Frank Keogh and Art Pike and Myra Kholer and Sharon Zeigler?

No.

Flagstaff? Maybe.

He cracked another Dixie.

After a while he cracked another.

The last thing he heard before he hit the tiles in the bathroom was a sound, a sad siren kind of sound, rising and falling in the full dark night. Clear as a brass bell in the winter. Pure as well water and liquid as a snake in a glade.

A siren? Maybe, he thought, lying on the bathroom floor not really caring, staring up at the underside of the sink where it said *DIXIE PORCELAIN WORKS* in an old-fashioned script.

But just as he drifted off, just as the room started a slow roll up and to the left, he realized what he was hearing.

It was Arnie Sayles playing his trumpet.

CHAPTER 26

Monday, August 27
0730 hours
Applegrove, Virginia

It took Keogh twenty minutes to get up from the bathroom floor and into a cold shower. He let the needle-sharp water rake him from neck to knees, feeling his sense of reality return slowly.

Afterward he used a complimentary shave pack with the Eagle Inn logo on it to hack his moustache off and cut way back on his sideburns, which he had let grow a little too long for the current fashion. Blood drops running from his snow-white and freshly butchered upper lip, he stood and stared at a new man in the mirror, thinking he hadn't seen this face for twenty years. That was how long he'd had the moustache. He looked younger by ten years, except around the eyes. There was crepy wrinkled skin under his eyes. Stepping back, he looked down at his body in the mirror.

Solid and short, with too much meat on the middle. He still had some tone and some muscle showing in his chest and belly, though. His legs were skinny and slightly bowed, his feet white and huge-looking. I look like a duck who lifts weights, he thought, and I better work on the tan a bit. Maybe pick up some of that tan-in-a-bottle to cover the white spots on my upper lip and at the ears.

Sitting on the unused bed, he flipped through the phone

book, looking for the storage barn he'd seen up the road.
Forgie Brothers—that was it, in a village called Cuckoo.

An hour later, wearing his jeans and cowboy boots and a
baggy shirt, Keogh was sliding carefully back up the
highway to Cuckoo, sipping a black coffee and blinking in
the flat yellow sunlight as the blue hills and red oaks of
Virginia rolled past him.

He found the Forgie Brothers Store n' Stash Warehouse
down a country road about a mile the other side of Cuckoo.

A bored teenager in a Red Man ball cap and worn denims
didn't pay much attention when Keogh flipped his New
York driver's license down on the counter top in a ram-
shackle gas station out in front of the barn.

"It's a private lockup, Mr. . . . Galston." The kid pronounced it Gawl-*ton*. "Bay nineteen around the back. Cost
you three hundred a month cash on the table top. Chain
and padlock extra. What you goin' to store in there?"

Keogh had his story ready.

"Well, I was just on a ramble, you know. Laid off up in
Olean . . . you know Olean? No, well, anyhow, called my
sister last night and it seems my momma . . ." Shit, he
thought, hearing his accent develop, lay off the drawl,
Frank. ". . . she's had a heart attack and I'm going to have
to fly out of Richmond to see her. Take too long to drive
back. I figure to leave the car here with you and come back
in maybe a week to ten days."

"Monthly rate only, in advance."

"That's fine. Do I get a rebate if I come back before a
month is over?"

"No, sir. You got to pay insurance on the lockup. Only
comes in a month rate." He pushed a form across the desk
and Frank filled it in with a worn pencil, trying not to
hesitate too long over his address in Utica. He needn't have
worried. Only the guilty feel this skinned-off and raw, he
thought, watching the boy stamp his receipt. This kid could
care less if I was storing a stolen tank in Bay nineteen.

Bay nineteen was one of a long row of prefab metal
garages with solid metal doors. The Plymouth fit in with

room to spare. Keogh rolled it right to the back of the garage and drew the door down behind him. They hadn't even asked him for the license on his car. The only problem would be if the Virginia State troopers had the energy to check every storage barn and lockup in the state. Somehow that seemed unlikely to Keogh, who knew something about the laziness of cops.

He stood at the back looking down at the gear in the trunk. Time to pick and choose.

He settled on his nine-mil and a box of ammunition. He had a crossover shoulder rig, which let the Browning ride flat under his left arm. Two spare magazines and a set of cuffs fit under his right arm. He sat for a while on the fender, holding his gold shield in his hand. It glimmered even in the twilight in the garage.

If you had half a brain you'd leave this in the car, he thought, looking at it, feeling the worn black leather case warm in his palm. The nine-point sunburst pattern surrounded a ring of blue and gold.

CITY OF NEW YORK POLICE and DETECTIVE on the banner across the bottom of the ring. The NYPD crest in the middle. And his number, 4558, in gold cut-out lettering on a plate at the bottom. Gold Shield Detective Second Grade Frank Keogh, badge number 4558. There weren't more than two thousand of these badges in the whole NYPD.

No, he said to himself, deciding. This comes with me.

The sunlight was straight down and brutal when he finally stepped back out into it. The heat burned into his back and shoulders and he could feel it coming up through the leather soles of his pointy-toed black cowboy boots as he crunched across the gravel toward the side road.

When he got to the road, he looked back at the garage, at the heavy chrome chain and the big brass padlock holding down the door to Bay nineteen. He'd miss that car. He walked away down the road for a couple of miles, breathing dust from pickups and gravel trucks going by, smelling hay and dry earth, listening to the cicadas in the bushes. Crows flew high overhead, black as bullet holes in blue silk.

CHAPTER 27

Monday, August 27
2200 hours
Lake Charles, Louisiana

"How come a man like you, can afford to buy all this stuff, you don't buy yourself a decent set of teeth?" said Sonny, tired of watching the man's cheeks fold in on themselves and his lips ride up into his nose. "Not right, a man in your position, living in a place like this." Sonny made a gesture to bring in the house, the big dock down at the beach running out into the bay, the huge Chris-Craft bumping up against the pilings out there.

Zeev smacked his lips again. The sound made Sonny's skin go ripple and chill all the way down to his belt. "Damn it, Zeev"—he pronounced the man's name *Zeef*—"you stop that. You just do it to put my nerves on edge, get me to take a lower price."

"You're lucky I'm dealing this at all. You tell me, Sonny, why is it you can't seem to carry out a simple operation lately without killing some poor man who happens to be in your way?"

There was nothing to say. What had happened was what had happened. Zeev sat back in his Castro convertible and pressed the button that made the thing vibrate. His huge fleshy body rippled like a bowl of water. Zeev's fat white feet stuck out of the bottom of his red silk bathrobe like the south end of a snail.

Gold coins arrayed themselves in front of him on a green felt table like regiments. Stamp cases were piled up on his left. A couple of reference books sat open on their spines, and Vivaldi was coming from a stereo console on the far side of the room. A silent man wearing a yarmulke sat on a high-back chair at the door, an Uzi in his hands, his face a stone mask. Zeev waved a pale fat hand over the table, over the gold and the tinted paper squares, taking it all in and yet somehow diminishing it at the same time.

Smack smack smack. Sonny held his peace. The time had come for a price, and Sonny needed the money.

"Little of this can be . . . salvaged. The insurance firm has been most uncooperative. People are watching the dealers. Sotheby's has made it clear they want none of it. What would you have me do with it? Add it to my collection? I think you might be advised to take this to someone a little less . . . scrupulous."

Sonny watched Zeev in the half-light from the overhead lamp. Zeev let his eyes close slowly and opened them, his pink tongue sliding wetly across his red lips. A dusting of fine white powder lay on his rounded cheeks like mold on a stone. Sonny wouldn't have been surprised to see Zeev's tongue flick out to catch a fly in mid-flight.

"Yeah? Who do you suggest? Fabrizzi, in Denver? I'm going there tomorrow."

"Fabrizzi would cheat you, Sonny. Perhaps . . . Mr. Joshua in St. Louis has expressed some interest. Leave this with me. If I realize something on the shipment, I will call you. On consignment, as it were?"

Sonny relaxed. Zeev wanted it. All that was left was the price. "No. Maybe I'll just take it, melt it down. There's about twenty pounds of solid gold there. I'll just melt it into ingots and move it over the counter. Yeah, that's safer."

Zeev's heavy-lidded eyes glittered in the lamplight.

"You have no sense of history, Sonny." He leaned forward, huffing with the effort, extending a white hand. He picked up a single dented and twisted coin with a brutal face on the obverse.

"Caligula. Little Boot. The first modern man—a man who understood the fundament of life: that sensation is all. This coin was in Rome when he had his grandmother poisoned. Perhaps some grain merchant had it from a centurion." Zeev put it to his nose and drew a long breath. "Smell it—you can smell the Tiber in it. Hear the voices in the streets. Over there, on the mantel, I have a piece of pottery from Judea. Picture the potter at his wheel, strong brown hands turning the clay, a simple earthen vase rising up between his hands. He is talking, speaking Aramaic to his wife. Say, there is talk of this man they have crucified in Jerusalem. The potter speaks close to the clay as it turns, his wife in the doorway. At her back the white sun of Judea burns. The air is heavy with the scent of sandalwood and woodsmoke. Children dead two thousand years play in the square. Women are drawing water. The sound of this is sinking into that clay, like grooves on a recording. Someday they will find a way to release the sound hidden in ancient clay jars. We will play them like records, listen to ancient voices and winds, hear music and songs thousands of years old. This coin comes to us like an arrow from the past. Its presence here is a miracle. Sonny, you have no head for this. This coin is not antiquity. *We* are antiquity. We are the elders. This coin, that piece of clay, they come to us from the youth of our world."

"Yeah, I'm just one in a long line of thieves. And every thief who ever stole this coin wanted a fair trade for it. If you give such a damn about tradition, pay up like a man—pay up the way a thousand men before you have paid up when the thief brought it to him. Stop trying to cheat an honest thief."

Zeev laughed, a liquid turbulence in his heavy body. The red silk slipped away from his calf, revealing his white leg all the way to his thigh. Sonny looked away.

"You make a point, Sonny. You make your position. Fair enough. Let us say . . . a hundred thousand?"

Sonny smiled at Zeev, a wolfish gleam in the dim light.

Sonny's teeth were wet and white, his face strained and thin. He had lost weight in the last two weeks.

"Let's say three hundred thousand. Fabrizzi would give me that."

"Take it to him then, and hope he won't just kill you and keep it for himself. Fabrizzi is a slug."

"This is horse shit. I need three. What about it?"

Zeev turned the coin in his fingers, watching the light on its burnished surface.

"Let's be concise. Let us say . . . two?"

"It's worth a half million."

"Puerile. Nothing is worth anything if no one will buy it. That's what value means, Sonny."

"No. Value is what someone will do for something. My brother died for an oil painting."

"You described it. Too bad you lost that. I think it was the little Seurat, 'Peasants Driving Stakes.' The Loebs had it in New York, or so I thought. Perhaps this Saltell person had it stolen from them. Strange, isn't it? How the finest things an artist can do, the attar of his soul expressed by force, becomes a commodity for trading. It's quite exquisite when you think of it. How corruptible it is. Van Gogh died in penury. His paintings are bought by Japanese corporations with no faith in the American dollar. Your brother had a good eye. I hope that when he was shot, the painting wasn't damaged in any way. Such a pretty work, if I recall it."

"Three hundred thousand, Zeev. I'm sick of this talk."

"Very well," said Zeev, raising a hand to the man at the door. "You have an emotional attachment. I respect that."

"Cash."

Zeev raised his hands in a supplicating gesture, his eyes on the heavy wooden beams above him. A black night with stars rode above the beams through the glass. The smell of pines came in through the open door as Zeev's man left.

"Vulgar. You stink of the street, Sonny."

"True," said Sonny, walking away. Zeev never looked up. When he reached the door, Zeev was running his pink tongue over the gold coin, tasting it.

CHAPTER 28

Monday, August 27
2200 hours
Richmond, Virginia

It was full dark by the time the big silver bus growled into the bus station in downtown Richmond. Keogh expected to see a couple of troopers waiting for the bus, and one of those FBI voidoids with the sunglasses and the brown suit.

But no one was waiting for him.

In the big wooden hall a monitor listed bus connections to points all over America. He could make a connection to Flagstaff through a Trailways subsidiary. It left in two hours.

And he was being filmed right now. He could see the video cameras up against the ceiling, behind the ticket counters. They were there for security reasons, and to let management watch the clerks. But the tape would be checked daily by a low-grade FBI man working for the Richmond office. He'd be looking for anyone who vaguely resembled Frank Keogh. By the time his connection got halfway to Flagstaff, they'd have the bus stopped and Keogh would be pulled off it in handcuffs.

No. Buy a car, cash.

He booked a room in a walk-up hotel called the Beulah, a block from the bus station. Dinner was a tuna sandwich he ate lying on his back on the chenille spread while he stared

260

up at the red flocked wallpaper overhead and ran through a list of possibles.

Slick Ryan? Why was Slick keeping his nights at the shooting range a secret? That wasn't like him. Did Slick have a problem with Frank? They rode him about being "in the rear with the gear" during the war, but there was never anything in Slick's face that looked like he wasn't taking it just fine.

Moxie? Moxie was from the old neighborhood. Did Moxie have a problem?

Charlie Boudreau?

Joe Langosta?

Peggy Zacco? Pepsi? Pulaski?

Who could have the access?

Christ, it could be anybody with a connection . . . someone he used to work with . . . someone who worked with his father . . .

Somebody who was close. Somebody who was around to watch Keogh leave Myra's place in the middle of the night . . .

Owens? He'd be in on all the gossip. Ruthie Boyko was part of his little therapy group and . . .

Owens and his . . . what did he call them? His sessions?

Who attended those sessions? What did they talk about?

And what about Owens himself? Well, he'd gone to bat for Pike, according to Weisberg. If he wasn't a stand-up guy, he was damned good at faking it. Better than anyone Frank had ever seen. And the Department would have run so many checks on him that he'd have looked like a plaid suit before they'd let him get near any Department members with stress problems.

And . . . what about Pat?

The money. The cash bag. All he had to prove that he didn't take it was a typewritten letter without a signature. If Pat was really going to take the heat for stealing the drug money, why not give Frank a signed letter?

And the typewriter it was written on? Keogh wasn't sure,

but the print looked familiar. Butler and Keogh shared a machine at the squad room. They'd just say Keogh typed out the letter himself.

Prints?

Keogh's were sure as hell on it. Were Pat's prints on it too?

Pat. What about you, Pat?

The Hamilton on Keogh's wrist showed eleven o'clock. Right now Butler'd be waiting for him at Brews, next to the pay phone at the front. The bar would be full of cops and talk, guys leaning on the rail and throwing a ball cap at the boar's head behind the bar. Out in the night, 34th Street would be full of kids going to the movies, cabs honking and squealing, and the city would smell of diesel fumes and popcorn.

Who else would be waiting for that call?

Angry with himself, knowing it was a bush stunt, he rolled off the bed and went down the back stairs of the Beulah and found a pay phone on a side street.

He hit the last number when the minute hand clicked onto the three. Exactly eleven-fifteen.

"Brews."

"Yeah?"

"Shit . . . Frank?"

Good. Use the name. Was this a signal? Was some tech punching it into the ANI-ALI right now?

"We don't have much time, buddy," Pat said.

His voice was steady and clear. Frank could hear the sound of other voices in the background. Bar sounds.

"Yeah, well, I'm a little pressed myself, Pat. Anything?"

"You're not gonna like it."

"I haven't liked much lately."

"Myra was a mole. One of Internal's little spies."

"Myra? A Field Associate? She was still in the Academy. A cherry."

"That's where they scoop them. Fresh outa the Academy."

"Who told you?"

"You're not gonna like this either. I saw her name on Moxie's list. You know, chicks he claims he's boinked."

Frank had to smile. Boinked. He's on the run with a psycho trashing his life, and Butler's still talking like a frat kid.

"Yeah. And—"

"I asked Moxie where he'd met her. He says he saw her with Slick. Says Slick was real heavy into her in the spring."

"He never said."

"He didn't know you were seeing her until after all the shit happened."

"Far as we know, Pat. Slick make her as a mole?"

"That's what Slick says."

"You asked him?"

"Damn right."

"You ask him about the midnight shifts out at the range?"

"No. Keep something up the sleeve."

"So what's it mean?"

"Fucked if I know, Frank. You comin' in?"

"Seems I'm running with a bag full of Ching-a-Ling cash."

"Yeah . . . Well, your credit cards are a little warm, kid."

"Yeah. You heard about Custer?"

"Shit yes. Well, Zeke, he never was much for Bambi either. Cheered when they popped his mother. Sorry about that."

"How's Butch?"

"Fucked up. What'd you hit him with?"

"A sap. He gonna be okay?"

"Yeah . . . well, maybe. I sure as shit hope so."

"Yeah . . . Pat, can you get the mole list for the Bronx units? See who else is working two jobs?"

"The *mole* list! There isn't one. That shit's buried so deep in One Police it'd take a backhoe to dig it out."

"Okay . . . Just get one name."

"Whose?"

"Pike's."

There was a long silence. Frank heard music and voices and a siren from out on 34th. It made him feel lonely.

"You think Pike was a mole?"

"I think something was working on him we don't know about. He was pretty fucked up, and now you say Myra was a mole, and well, it just looks hinky to me."

"Give me a day."

"I'm not calling you at this number again. I already talked too long."

"So where?"

"You know the Thunderbird?"

"In Yonkers?"

"Yeah. There's a pay phone outside the lounge there. All the Yonkers bulls use it to call their wives. I have the number. I'll call you there, say . . . twenty-one hundred hours."

"Tomorrow?"

"No . . . Wednesday."

"What're you gonna do?"

"You asking me, Pat?"

"No. Fuck no."

Frank hung up the phone and walked back to the Beulah.

He lay awake all night and in the morning he walked a couple of blocks down to a used-car dealer called Bobby Durkel's, where Keogh paid cash on the trunk lid for a 1975 Coupe de Ville with a fresh coat of midnight-blue metallic and white sidewall tires.

"Where you headed, mister?" The salesman could just be making conversation. Keogh was acquiring the chronic paranoia of the hunted man.

"South," he said, thinking: I-64 to St. Louis, then I-70 to Denver, then south on I-25 to Albuquerque, and then west on I-40 to Flagstaff.

He tried not to think about south. He could be in Valdosta, Georgia, in twenty hours, and well into Florida in twenty-four. In Pat's note he said Tricia and Robbie were there, down at the far end of the interstate. Interstates

were like that—black cables connecting you to everything
and everyone. But they'd be ready for him in Florida.

Myra.

Myra a goddammed Field Associate.

Taking names and making anonymous phone calls to the
Bronx Internal Affairs branch.

That's great, Frank. Think with your dick like that, it's
small wonder you ended up in a very tight place.

CHAPTER 29

Wednesday, August 29
Noon
Denver, Colorado

Denver, Colorado, smelled pretty much the same as Chicago, Illinois, these days. It used to smell of mesquite and woodsmoke and cold winds down from the Rockies.

Now a superhighway ran right up the spine of the city on a long rise from south to north, splitting a tangled web of tract homes and restaurants, gas stations and shopping malls and warehouses. Denver was one of the reasons Sonny stayed in Santa Fe when he could. It was also a good reason for missing Charleston, but there was no sense in letting those feelings run. Charleston was closed to him, unless he wanted to serve twenty years upstate before he could have a drink in Old Town or go for a walk along Murray.

A chubby kid in a lime-green rodeo outfit was holding the door for him, waiting for a tip. Sonny pushed by him and went through a lobby packed with tourists in loud shirts and shorts, sitting around in padded plastic chairs sipping drinks that looked like salads.

Waiting for the elevator, he checked for coverage. There was nothing. If Lucas Poole had drawn surveillance here, they were better at it than they had been the last time he and Lucas had worked in Denver. They'd helped a couple of Israelis clean out a Palestinian banker who had a big house down on the South Platte. Lucas and Sonny got to keep most of the cash. The Israelis had taken the banker.

Sonny knocked on the door of 317, standing a little to the side. Lucas Poole hadn't been the type to shoot a man through a door, but Lucas hadn't been shot in the chest before. The latch was off. Sonny heard Lucas's voice saying, "It's open."

Lucas Poole was lying on the big double bed, propped up on a couple of pillows, holding a little Ingram auto on his belly. He looked like a skull on a stick, cheeks sunken in, his eyes yellow and red, his skin hanging on his ribs and slack in the hollows of his neck. Cords stood out as he smiled and raised his hand.

Sonny kept his mouth shut and his face blank.

Lucas set the Ingram down and levered himself up off the bed. Sonny took his hand and then he pulled Lucas into him, put his arms around him, feeling the body like a leather bag full of rods. Sonny slammed him a couple of times on the back and pushed him back to arm's length, holding Poole by the upper arms.

"Lucas . . . how you doin'?"

"You can see for yourself. One thing I don't recommend is Mexican medicine. Broca's cousins almost killed me, they took care of me so good."

"You took a hell of a round there."

"Yeah. I'm still waiting for the lung to come back. Doc inflated it a couple of times, but I take a deep breath sometimes, feels like I swallowed a cactus. Anyway, I'll be okay. You want a drink?"

Sonny watched Lucas carefully as he walked over to a dresser to pour them out a couple of fingers of Bushmill's. His hands were steady enough, and he didn't pour too much, and he waited until Sonny had his before tasting his own. Sonny nodded toward the puckered circular ridge just below Poole's right collarbone.

"Well, here's to you."

They drank it down in silence.

"You talk to old Eufemio?" asked Sonny, still trying to get used to the way Poole looked.

"Broca's dead. Texas Rangers boxed him up in a trailer park a couple of miles outside Del Rio. Come sunrise, they shot the place up. Killed Broca, Broca's little sister— remember her? Delia? Killed his father and a couple of neighbor kids sleeping over. Supposed to be something like a thousand rounds put into the place."

"Yeah? Sounds like somebody worked out an arrangement with the Rangers. Anyway . . . too bad about him. Eufemio was good."

"Yeah," said Lucas, smiling broadly, remembering the old drinking toast. "End of a long line. Here's to him . . . So, you work something out with Jabba the Hutt?"

Sonny opened his shirt and tugged out a tan canvas money belt. He tossed it over to Poole, who caught it in one hand. He hefted it speculatively.

"There's about a hundred thousand in there. One third. I put 50K aside for Myron's son-in-law. Send that to him in about a month. Also another 50K for Myron's wife. Put it in a trust for her. She's dying, so Myron said."

"It go hard for Myron?"

"No. I saw him. It was quick. He was dying anyway. Had cancer. In the end, I think he was just as happy to go out working. Save him some rat's-ass finish, tubes up his pecker and down his throat. He did a good job his last time out."

Lucas poured them another round. The liquor seemed to give him some blood and color.

"I read a little about it. What went wrong?"

Sonny shrugged. "We screwed up, is all."

"Yeah?" said Lucas. "That happens."

Lyle's name drifted in the air between them for a couple of minutes, but neither man was ready to say it out loud. Finally, Lucas said, "Sorry about the kid."

"Yeah. He always saw too many possibilities in things. It can hobble you, thinking that way. It was like he was always looking for just the right move to make—as if any one thing you did was going to change your life. Made it hard for him to pay attention to what he was doing. People would always take advantage. . . . You still pissed off with him, Lucas?"

"What? About me getting shot? Hell, Lyle had nothing to do with that. Sooner or later we're all gonna get something we don't want to get. No, I just . . . I always figured it'd be Lyle sitting here someday, and you who'd be dead, trying to save his sorry ass. No offense, Sonny?"

"No offense, Lucas."

"So . . . what you have in mind now?"

"You get that bulletin from your cousin?"

"Yeah. She's gonna be a real cop soon. Can you see it? My cousin, a girl cop in a uniform and everything?"

"No. I can't. She give you a hard time about this?"

"No. She's a good kid. I wouldn't ask her for anything that would . . . that she wouldn't want to do. But this is different. We find a bad cop for the Feds, that's okay with her."

"They even send these bulletins to places like St. Cloud?"

Lucas dug the sheet out from under a stack of magazines and papers and handed it across to Sonny.

"Nationwide, this one went. They haven't got him yet, though. I checked with her this morning."

Sonny flattened the sheet out on his knee. It was a standard Federal notice, a picture of Frank Keogh in his police blues, head-and-shoulder shot. Age, weight, any identifying marks. Wanted in connection with the murder of NYPD Sergeant Arthur Randall Pike at Lincoln Hospital, 08/22/90. Ligature homicide. Notice listed by a Detective Sergeant Ezekiel Parrot of the Bronx Detective Area Task Force. So on and so forth. Sonny read it twice.

"So you figure this guy's going to go straight to this place . . . Upper Matecumbe Key?"

"Yeah. Story is, the guy's father is a retired cop. Now get this: It seems the way this Pike guy was killed, it's exactly the same way a bunch of kids were killed maybe twenty years ago. Guess who was the cop on that case? The guy's father. Marlee says the FBI has the father's marina under twenty-four-hour surveillance. Man owns a boat down there called *The Madelaine*. Runs fishing charters out of the Bahia Mar Azul Marina. Drinks all the time at a place called Rotten Ralph's or something."

"So let me get this straight. This Frank Keogh, his father did the original investigation?"

"That's what she says. Caught some teenage psycho. The kid walked on an insanity plea. They slammed him into an asylum upstate. He's been there ever since."

Weird, thought Sonny. It bothered him that there were factors here he had no control over. What the hell was going on with this guy?

"Sonny . . . I have to tell you, I think you're out of your fucking mind, chasing this cop around the country."

"It's a personal thing, Lucas."

"Suppose I said it was a personal thing, Lyle fucking us up back there in Lawton?"

Sonny felt a thin red streak of anger, but he fought it down.

"I don't know, Lucas. Is that how you feel?"

"Hell, no. The point is, it makes no sense, you chasing a cop. The cop didn't know your brother. The cop was just doing what he was told to do. It was his job to shoot Lyle. If Lyle hadn't wanted to be shot, he shouldn't have been keeping bad company."

Levine's line. Bad company. Maybe they were. It had been a long time since Sonny looked hard at what he was doing for a living. Somehow he always thought of himself as one of the good guys, a man capable of keeping his promises and being faithful to his friends and family. It seemed to him that being loyal to a partner, caring about the death of a brother, those were the things that made up in a way for the stealing he was doing. He had no illusions about who he was. He was a thief, a professional thief. But he was also a man who had some good qualities. Going after Lyle's murderer was a way for Sonny to go on seeing himself as one of the good guys.

"Maybe that's true, Lucas. But I'm doing it anyway. Are you in or out?"

"No hard feelings if I'm out, Sonny?"

"No. I could use you, but no hard feelings."

"What is it you want me to do, anyway?"

That was a tricky question. Sonny knew that Lucas wasn't going to approve of what he had to say.

"Lucas . . . how healthy are you?"

Poole's thin face darkened. His throat flexed and he looked at Sonny in a flat way.

"I'm fine, considering I have half a lung gone. I'll be fine. If you don't think so, then say goodbye now and stop sitting around in my room depressing me."

"Well, there's no other way to say this. I need you to come along with me, help me figure out where this cop has gone. When we find him, I want you to help me take him out."

Poole said nothing but his eyes were changing, as if he was seeing Sonny in a way that hadn't been clear before, and he didn't like it.

"I don't do contracts, Sonny. Neither do you."

"This isn't a contract. This is for me."

Poole didn't like that either.

"Sonny, this is me. We never lied to each other in all the years we been through. Lyle's dying was business—that's all. For you to take it any other way is . . . mean. A man goes mean and there's no end to that. He just gets meaner and meaner until somebody stops him."

"That may be, Lucas. But Lyle wasn't out there on business. He was just standing around on that balcony with his hands up, waving a goddammed *painting* around. I don't think that Keogh bastard even had permission to take him out. That Irish prick did it because he *likes* it. You follow?"

"Yeah. Maybe he was mean. So you get mean too? You stop being what you are and start being something else, maybe even you don't know what that will be. It could be something you don't like. You got it in you, Sonny. It's never come out, but it's in there."

"You killed that kid in Lawton, Lucas."

"*That* was business. A man signs on to be a cop, he gets that snazzy uniform and the boots and the big black Ford, gets to carry a piece and a sidearm and wear that shit-kicking grin for all the citizens to see, part of the package is, now and then they get into something and they get killed. If it weren't for the fact that now and then one of them gets himself killed, they wouldn't like the job near as much. It adds spice, like Tabasco sauce. It's business. What you're talking about is ugly, mean-minded, and just plain stupid."

"Yeah," said Sonny, smiling at Lucas. "You gonna help me?"

Lucas said nothing. After a while, he smiled.

"Yeah. What the hell. Somebody got to be there to tell your relatives what happened."

They smiled at each other then. After a while they got into the Bushmill's and the talk rolled around to who they had worked with over the years, what had happened on this job and that. How Ronnie del Monica got himself shot by a security guard in Modesto while he was trying to get a scorpion out of his pants. And Hubie Ferris, who once lifted a rolled car off Sonny with his bare hands, by the side of the highway, the troopers no more than six minutes back.

And the time they took the bank in San Miguel down in Quintana Roo just because it was there, Lucas just deciding to do it and Sonny still at the teller's cage next door, Lucas pulling out his Colt and sticking it in the man's nose, saying later, Well, shit, he was a *rude* little fucker, you know? And the ride to Reno under a sickle moon, playing zydeco, the names and faces all running together, the kids who came to play, the hard guys who had gotten theirs in the big yard one way or another . . . Charleston and the family, playing football on the turf . . . Well, it had been sweet. It had been a good time.

Sonny woke up the next morning in the bathtub with

cold water running on his crotch. There was a note taped to the mirror.

Dear Sonny

You look so pretty there I had to leave you sleeping. I am downstairs having some coffee. You have a couple of aspirins and climb up on the sink there and reach up into the tiles. You'll see an old friend there I brought up to give you back. Take care you don't slip on the sink or you will give yourself a fearsome crack on the nuptials. This happened to me.

I forgot to tell you last night but before you got here I made a bunch of calls and if this cop you are looking for has one green eye and one blue and looks Irish as hell then it might be that he bought a 1975 Cadillac Coupe de Ville from Bobby Durkel's lot in Richmond on Tuesday. I told all of the guys who knew Lyle back when he had the car lot that there'd be money in it for anybody who could get some word about this guy. If it is the guy we send five c's to Chico del Monica in Atlanta.

The guy is using the name Barnaby Galston. New York ID. Plates were Virginia ZRG 334. Midnight blue sparkle.

Soon as you get yourself together, let's get the hell out of here. They're looking for us too.

Lucas

Sonny read the note three times. Damn, Lucas was good. There was more to him than you could see in a year.

He got up onto the sink and moved the sound tile. The package was short and bulky, wrapped in a Mexican blanket.

It was the Heckler, broken down and cleaned.

Sonny dressed and thought about Frank Keogh.

Richmond?

The guy was going to go down like a paralyzed falcon, dropping down the map all the way to Florida. I-95.

Dammit, they'd pick him off at a tollbooth if he kept that up. They'd have cameras all over that route. It was a big mule road—Sonny knew that from his brief run at the drug trade. I-95 from Florida to the northeastern seaboard and Montreal. The DEA and the FBI had funded surveillance cameras on some of the busier stretches. Keogh would be very hot. Somebody who was awake at the wheel would see the man, see that huge goddam car.

Sonny could see the panic in that kind of a flight and it made him smile. Different now, isn't it, Frank?

Not as much fun, being chased, is it? Gets on your nerves and you do stupid things.

The thing to do was somehow to get in front of Keogh before the *federales* got there. Once he was taken in, it'd be a lot harder to get to him. He'd have to subcontract the killing to somebody in the yard. That was expensive and risky because it linked him to the murder. Not a lot of men would pass up the chance to buy some reduced time if they had Sonny Beauchamp to sell.

Sonny thought about it all through a room-service breakfast. He had to get some very good information as fast as possible. His only advantage over the *federales* was that he knew what name the guy was running under, and the make of the car. It would take a lot of calling and he didn't want to hang around in this hotel room any longer. The Denver FBI would be checking the hotels regularly. Sonny was still hot from the Lawton robbery. Lucas was even hotter. Although Lucas didn't look like Lucas anymore. He'd dropped twenty pounds and aged ten years. He looked . . . old.

For a while, Sonny felt something like guilt at dragging Lucas into this. He put it to one side—something he'd think about later.

Lucas was down in the coffee shop, looking like a piece of chewed beef. They paid the bill and walked out of the lobby and into the hard clear light of Denver. Off in the west, over the ragtag sprawl of the city, a ragged blue ribbon marked the foothills of the Rockies. Three of the peaks had snow but it was ninety degrees and brutally sunny down here in the valley of the South Platte.

They found a little motel out on Arapaho Road. The room was cold and dim and mud-brown. Lucas had nothing to say and Sonny left him alone.

At the Safeway across the road Sonny picked up a couple of sixes of Lone Star and some sugar donuts. He worked out in the room for an hour, doing pushups off the bureau and crunches on the dirty shag rug. When he was sick and sore and shaking, he ate the sugar donuts and drank three Lone Star beers and started making phone calls.

CHAPTER 30

Pat Butler leaned on the kitchen counter in his Yonkers bungalow and watched his wife out in the backyard pool. Burke Owens was sitting in a deck chair with a cold beer in his fist, in jeans with his shirt off, a beefy mass of muscle and red fur, watching Junie in the pool with obvious enjoyment.

Junie was doing lengths in a slow steady Australian crawl. She'd been doing them for an hour now, her regular ritual, back and forth in the shallow pool, the sunlight breaking up in her wake, the water at the edges rocking and rising from the rhythm of her strokes.

Wednesday. Charlie Unit had been shut down all week, ever since Keogh had run. Nobody was saying so over at the Task Force, but most of the unit was being kept out of things so Zeke Parrot could keep an eye on them. Now and then Butler would look over his shoulder at the red wall phone by the fridge. He had a pretty good idea that his phone was being tapped. He was going to slide over to the Thunderbird to catch Frank's call around eight-thirty.

There was a lot of busywork going on across the street and down a ways, a New York Telephone truck parked beside a switching box. Two beefy guys in NYNEX uniforms were picking over the interior of the box. A driver sat behind the wheel and munched on a burger from McDonald's. Two days now this van had been out there.

Surveillance that handless and arrogant was an insult, clear and simple. Zeke must have persuaded Pickett, the Zone Commander, that Butler was in contact with his partner.

Jesus, thought Pat. Where would they get an idea like *that*?

Slick as a seal, Junie hit the far wall and rolled under to kick off again. She was a good-looking woman still, maybe better-looking now that she was older and her face was showing some lines. She had been a competition swimmer in high school, big-shouldered and tough, a girl who had settled on Butler with a single-minded dedication during his football hero days.

Hero.

Oh, yeah. Butler had tried to follow up on Pike, see if Pike had ever done any work for Internal. He had gone down to One Police to try to talk to a woman he knew in Intelligence down there. Six minutes into One Police he got called up to the Chief of Detectives' office. Pulaski was on the line.

Bert Pulaski had made it exceedingly clear to every member of Charlie Unit that whatever they planned to do for Frank Keogh, it had better not be something that included aiding and abetting.

Now Charlie was suspended. The whole damned crew. Unofficial stand-down, it was called.

There being nothing else to do, Butler and Slick Ryan and Burke Owens had gone along with Moxie and Pepsi to visit Butch Johnson in the hospital on Tuesday.

The homicide cop was cracked up in the temple, and the vision in his left eye was still in doubt. According to Butch, Keogh had sapped him there after setting the dog on him.

The Charlie Unit guys just let that go. Owens rolled his eyes but said nothing. Anybody who knew the dog would have to know that taking a swing at Frank was sure to set Custer off.

Zeke Parrot had walked into the hospital room while they were there, with a basket of fruit and a six-pack of Stroh's.

"Pat," said Zeke, nodding to Bukovac and Kowalczyk and Slick Ryan. He was cold and distant. They were on the other side as far as he was concerned. He didn't even look at Owens. Owens was a civilian. Owens could step off the ledge outside the window and Zeke wouldn't find it interesting enough to watch him hit the walkway.

"Zeke . . . how's it goin'?" said Butler, a half-smile tugging his mouth up sideways.

"You hear from your buddy yet?" Zeke was ready to push things.

"Hey," said Slick, grinning at Zeke, "you'll be the first to know, won't you, Zeke? I see Con Ed's on my street again."

"I wouldn't know. . . . You staying long, boys?"

Just to raise his hackles, Moxie said, "Well, Zeke, I'll have a Stroh's, now you're asking us."

Butler didn't like this. There was a hurt cop in the room. Scrapping like this, it made them all look bad.

As it turned out, Owens felt differently. Pat could see a kind of wave go through the guy as he watched Zeke across Butch's bed. Pat tried to head him off but Owens got right into it.

"Zeke, they must miss you in the enchanted forest."

Zeke didn't even look up at him. Civilian.

"I mean, it must have broken you guys up when Snow White pulled out. Shit, I'm glad to see there was work for Dopey. And shooting the dog—man, I *loved* that one. You couldna just given him a little tap on the nose, could you? Had to pop the dog. Get you a breast bar for *that*, hey?"

"Keep him out of this, Pat." Zeke was looking at Butler.

"*You* keep me out of this, Zeke," Owens rumbled at him. "You're a classic, Zeke. You know that? How far back do you and Frank go, and his daddy before that? Shit, Zeke, you even work in the same room John Keogh worked. Seven Zone used to work out of the Four-Eight back in the sixties."

Moxie said, "Hey, Burke, this isn't the place. Butch is—"

Butch finally spoke. "Stay out of it, Moxie. Zeke, whyn't you tell this asshole what Paul Young said?"

Zeke closed up and shook his head at Butch.

"*Young!* Zeke, have you gone to *that* dickhead for help?" Burke Owens said. "Man, I love it—it's like an idea gets into your head, it likes the dark and the solitude so much, it won't let anything else in. What'd Young tell you, Zeke? We're hanging on it."

"Go fuck yourself, Owens."

"I don't have to. I wait long enough, you assholes will do it for me. Let me guess—Young makes Keogh as psychologically unstable. Even money he hangs it on the war—am I right?"

Zeke said nothing, not even looking at Owens now.

Owens leaned back against the window ledge and started to laugh. "Man, I hate all that Vietnam bullshit. Young would go for that, though. Man, I can see him up there. Zeke, the guy's a courtroom whore. You ask him, is Frank crazy, he'll say, That depends. You'll say, Depends on what? He'll say, Depends on whether I'm being paid by the D.A. or the defense."

"*You* better buy it, Burke. Because otherwise that little fucker is going straight to Attica. You wanna get in on the precinct pool? We're betting Frank won't last one year in the yard, and when they bag him, his ass will look like the Lincoln Tunnel."

"That's it," said Butler. "Both of you, shut the fuck up. Butch . . . Butch, you take care."

Butch didn't look up. He watched his hands on the hospital sheet and tugged at his IV needle. Butler felt suddenly ashamed.

They left Zeke and Butch alone and shut the door quietly. As Pat reached out to pull the door closed, Zeke was handing the basket to Butch, and Butch was not quite able to say thank you. His hands were shaking in the late afternoon light coming in through the Venetian blinds.

The last things Butler saw before the door shut were the barred sunlight on Zeke's rough brown face, and Butch plucking at the ribbons on a basket of fruit like an old man.

Junie's slick sunburned arm came up above the edge of the pool. Butler could see her feeling around for her drink. He drew open the slide window over the sink and called out to her.

"It's at the other end, kid."

Her face appeared above the edge.

She looked at Owens in the deck chair.

"Get it for me, you sot. Or bring me a cold one. And, Pat, you get out here yourself. And stop brooding about Frank. He'll turn up." Junie looked at Owens again, at his furry barrel of a body, shirtless and reddening under the match-head sun.

She looked at him for a while.

Owens noticed it. His smile went down a couple of degrees.

"Hey. Stop undressing me with your eyes. You're making me nervous. Man, you suburban broads. It's all sex sex sex."

Junie laughed and pushed off the pool edge.

"Pat," she called from the center of the pool.

"Yassa, memsahib," said Pat. "What's your pleasure?"

"How come you never joined the army?"

Pat stuck his head out the window again, frowning. "Where the hell'd *that* come from? I fucked up my back at the Nationals. Banzai Pipeline, in sixty-six. I coulda been something. I coulda been a contender. Why you asking now? You want another zoned-out vet like Burke here, staring at your tits and chain-horking the Bud Lites?"

She shook her head, ducked under the water, came up half a length later, threw her hair back in a flare of spray.

"I don't know. Never mind. Know what I *do* want? How about a slow comfortable screw?"

Owens snorted at that, a basso rumble. She leered at Pat.

Butler leered back. Sloe gin, Southern Comfort, vodka and orange juice. Junie loved her sticky likkers.

Bam-bam-ba-bam.

Who the hell was that? Somebody slamming on the front

door like . . . That was a cop knock and no less. Butler slammed the fridge door and pit-patted through the hall in his rubber thongs and his flowered shorts, a nasty expression on his face and a certain tension in his belly. If this was Zeke dicking around . . .

He jerked the door open. An old man was standing there on his doorstep, a skeleton with thick brown leathery skin hanging on a rangy frame, the remnants of massive ropy muscle still visible under his purple Hawaiian shirt. He was wearing faded blue jeans and dark-green Sperry Topsiders and a hat that looked like a canvas bait bucket. The man stared at Butler out of a face as wrinkled and tough as a bull's elbow. A white beard rimmed the sunken cheeks and a shaggy white moustache covered the mouth. The eyes were hidden under bug-eye mirrored aviators.

"Christ," said Butler, stepping back. "It's Ernest."

The man was holding a faded canvas suitcase. He dropped it and reached up to take off the glasses.

"Ernest my ass, Butler. Are you asking me in or do we talk out here with those cocksuckers over there taking notes?"

Butler gave way, backing into the house. The man strode past, lithe and easy in spite of the years on him. He threw the bag into the middle of the room, gave it a quick and dismissive assessment, and faced Butler again.

"Oh Christ," said Junie from the hall. She was standing there in her wet suit, dripping on the tiles, Burke Owens standing behind her. "It's himself!" she said, coming forward.

The man turned and grinned at her and she ran to him and hugged him tight. Butler put out a tentative hand. The man took it over Junie's naked shoulder.

"Well, Pat," he said, not quite smiling at him. "What the hell are these poodle-fakers trying to do to my boy?"

Butler took a little time to answer. He hadn't seen John Keogh in ten years. The eyes were different. John Keogh's eyes had been drinker's eyes, a little yellow in the last years, and something of the wild boar in them. But now his eyes were steady and clear blue under bushy white brows, and the man did by God look like Ernest Hemingway. The effect was unsettling and it showed on Pat's face.

Finally he smiled and said, "Well, sir, the poodle-fakers have framed him for a cop-killer, sir."

"Zattafak?" said John Keogh, pushing Junie back and taking a long and mildly lascivious look at her.

He glanced over at Burke Owens, leaning against the dining room door, arms folded, a wide grin showing, his eyes careful.

Junie looked around. "Oh, John, this is a friend. Burke, meet John Keogh. John, Burke works for the Benevolent Association."

"Yeah?" said John Keogh, giving Owens a long calculating look. He stuck out his hand and Owens shook it.

"I've heard a lot about you, sir," he said. "Your boy's in a shitload of trouble, sir. We're kind of in a dead end here."

John Keogh looked back at Junie.

"We'll see about that, won't we, my darling. We'll have to see about that."

CHAPTER 31

Wednesday, August 29
1450 hours
Denver, Colorado

"Manny?"

"Just a sec . . . Manny, it's for you."

"Yello?"

"Jesus, I hate that."

"Hey, the voice returns. Hate what?"

"That—people who say *yello* instead of hello."

"Getting a tad cranky for a desperado, aren't you?"

"You heard about that?"

"Who hasn't? You run with the wrong crowd, kid."

"Maybe. How's Elvira?"

"Gone. You buy this? She doesn't like me anymore now
'm straight. She says I got no ambition!"

"Fuck her."

"No, thanks. I did that. Took weeks for the rash to go
way. Sorry about your brother."

"Me too. Thanks, Manny . . . Look, I need a favor."

"Name it, my son. I live to serve."

"You're still on the same job?"

"Even as we speak. I hope these things don't make you
terile. I'm sitting here right now, looking at little green
umbers and stuff. You wouldn't believe the kind of people
se Best Western. White trash. Here's one: Biff and Bop
Bunkley. Are we supposed to buy that? I mean, it's an

insult. Whatever happened to names like John and Joanie Smith?"

"Credit cards."

"Yeah . . . Well, listen, kid, the line's okay but my boss is a real bastard. What can I do you for?"

"A watch."

"Yeah? You looking for somebody?"

"Excuse me, I didn't know this was *Jeopardy*."

"Sorry. Got a name or do I read 'em all off to you?"

"I can't stay on the line. Here it is. Ready?"

"Hit me."

"I need a Galston, Barney or Barnaby. A G-1 of Barnaby most likely."

"That's Barnaby as in the teddy bear?"

"Yeah. There's a car."

"*Donnez-moi,* my child."

"Seventy-five de Ville, midnight-blue metallic. Zulu Romeo Golf three three four. Virginia plates."

"Got a time frame?"

"Seven days."

"Yeah. Alone?"

"Just the Caddy."

"Hah. Why not just carry a sign saying 'Yo, here I am. Come get me.' How's the nigra?"

"Middling. Gone home to rest."

"I heard he got himself a message from the Federals. I heard he took the big dive under the putting green."

"Who'd you hear that from?"

"Hey, what is this? *Jeopardy*?"

"Yeah. Well, no, that's not the case. He'll be fine."

"Okay. Glad to hear it. He still play liar's dice like he used to? Took five hundred away from me at the Helpy-Selfy Laundromat and Topless Bar in Lauderdale, back in eighty-three. He's the best liar I ever met, next to Elvira."

"Well . . . can you do it?"

"Oh, yeah. That's easy. Do you have anybody at the other chains?"

"I was thinking about Lillian at Holiday Inn."

"Forget it. She married a retired cop. A smoky for the state of Nebraska. Can you believe it? I can do Holiday Inns for you. I know a woman works in their Reservations office. That all right?"

"What will you tell her?"

"What is this—"

"*Jeopardy*? Yeah, Manny, it is. Go with God, my son."

"You want to give me a number?"

"No. You asking?"

"Give me an hour. Take care of yourself."

Sonny made the next call from a phone booth a mile down Arapaho.

"St. Cloud Police Department. Officer Pikkula."

"Can I speak to Officer Carasco, please?"

"Unit?"

"What?"

"What unit is he in, sir?"

"Oh." Christ . . . what was Marlee's last assignment?

"Communications."

"Thank you, sir. Just a minute. I'll put you through to Radio, sir. Will you hold?"

Hold what?

"Yes, thanks."

Muzak. All of America is afraid to be alone with itself. Oh, this is great. The Muzak version of "Nadine Honey Izzat You." Shame on you, Chuck. Shame.

"Radio."

"Hello, is Officer Carasco there?"

"Yes."

Smartass.

"Well, can I talk to her?"

"This a police matter?"

"No. Just a call."

"Call back at four. She's on duty right now. Goodbye."

Shit.

Here's something else. The remote control. Now how the hell could America let something like the remote control for the television set ever get invented? You don't like a commercial, you hit MUTE. The MUTE button on the remote control was the first sign that Sonny had ever seen that there might be intelligent life on this planet.

Mind you . . . see that? See the way the commercials use all that print? Even if you shut the sound off, they know you'll still watch the screen. You'll still get the message.

Now, there's a serious crock of shit. How come in all the beer commercials now, there's always some woman hitting some guy. There. She hits him with a purse. And in the other one, she's pushing this weight-lifter guy around and he's taking it.

What's the message there?

God. Mud-brown. This room is the color of shit. Why would somebody want to paint a room shit-colored?

The phone rang.

The sound went through Sonny as if he were wired into the instrument. He stiffened and stood up, staring at the thing as if it had turned into a toad.

Ring.

There's another thing. Why is it a good thing that any asshole anywhere in the world, if he has a dime he can make a bell ring in any house in the world?

Ring.

Ring.

It stopped. When Sonny looked up, the walls were about a yard closer. He was stuck in a shit-brindle room while things went on all around him. He called Manny Rizzuto back and was told that Mr. Rizzuto's line was busy.

At three-thirty he called Marlee Carasco in St. Cloud.

"Radio room."

Somebody different.

"May I speak to Officer Carasco, please?"

"Certainly, sir. Just a minute."

No Muzak. There's hope for the world.

"Hi?"

Lucas Poole's little cousin Marlee. The last time Sonny

had seen her, she was taking Highland dancing in a church basement in Buffalo. How long now?

"Still doing the sword dance, Marlee?"

There was a long silence.

"Can I call you back, sir? I'm on duty right now."

What the hell. He'd be out of this room in an hour anyway.

He gave her the number.

Thirty minutes later, the phone rang.

Sonny picked it up.

"Uncle Sonny?"

"Hey, kid. How's it going?"

"God. You should never call me at work. They tape every call that comes in."

"Are they going to ask you about that call?"

"I told them you were a boyfriend. They can tell it came from Denver, you know. They can tell in forty seconds. Even if you hang up. Don't do that."

"Marlee, I have a lot of faith in the incompetence of institutions. I need a little help and your uncle said he'd talked to you about this thing."

"Yeah. I hope they kill this guy. He sounds like a real psycho. Are you after him too?"

"I was wondering . . . the Feds will have a bulletin out on him. Is there anything on it that might help me out? I hate to ask, but he's pretty hot and I really need some slack."

"Yes. The bulletin came in on the FBI fax on Monday. But I gave all that stuff to Uncle Lucas. I don't know what else to say."

"Does it give you a list of departments they faxed it to?"

"No. It's a national fax. Routine stuff. Interstate Flight. A photo and identifying marks. He has one green eye and one blue one, if that helps?"

"No. I mean, thanks, kid. But I knew that. I was hoping they might have given you some sideband information. Direction of travel. Anything like that?"

There was a long silence.

"Yeah . . . Well, it may not be connected, but we're supposed to contact Washington if we see him. And also they asked us to let the Flagstaff PD know if we caught up to him. It seems there's a big alert on in Flagstaff, like they think he might go there for some reason. We're supposed to tell Flagstaff and the Arizona Highway Patrol as soon as we get any word, so they can stand down. It's costing a lot to keep troopers on the interstate and Flagstaff is all in a tizzy about him."

"Flagstaff? Why Flagstaff?"

"They don't tell us things like that. They just tell us. You know the FBI. They're as tight as a pickerel's asshole."

"A what? For Christ's sake, Marlee. Your language."

"Sorry, Uncle Sonny. It's these guys here. They're so gross."

"Flagstaff, huh? Okay, kid. That'll do. You okay?"

"Yeah. You're not mad with me, are you?"

"Over what, kid?"

"On account of I'm . . . you know. Me signing on."

Sonny laughed. "Not at all, honey, I'm proud of you. So's Lucas."

"Do you know where he is, Uncle Sonny?"

"Yeah. He's fine."

"I hope so. Aunt Marie saw him two days ago and she says he's real thin and doesn't look too good."

"Would I lie to you, Marlee?"

"I think so. Take care of yourself. 'Bye."

"'Bye, kid. Be a good cop."

"Talk to me."

"Can't you just say hello?"

"No. Derivative."

"Jesus, Manny. This is business."

"I think you're losing your sense of enjoyment."

"Second by second, Manny."

"Well, I'm not gonna make you feel any better. No sign of the guy. Nobody in this chain took a room anywhere under that name or anything like it. Lots of big blue Caddies, but wrong plates."

"How about your connection at the Holiday Inn chain?"

"She's still looking. I told her it was for the cops."

"She ask to see the case card?"

"No. She trusts me."

Sonny thought about it for a while. Manny hummed "Guantanamera." Did a good job of it too.

"Manny—you got any way of connecting with AMEX, Visa, MasterCard? Diner's, anything like that?"

"I know what you're thinking. You think he's stupid enough to use his own charge card? Anyway, even the dumbest desk clerk is going to say, look, how come you got one name here and another name on your card?"

True. Sonny was scrambling.

"It's a big country, isn't it?"

"Yeah," said Sonny, seeing it all in his mind.

"Well . . . you want me to keep on looking?"

"Yeah. And get on to your lady. He's got to be staying somewhere."

"Ahh . . . I hate to be crass, but this is business."

"One kay. You take care of the Holiday Inn lady."

"Sounds fine. But, Sonny . . . there's a lot of hotels and motels and rooming houses and flophouses. None of them on the system. Don't even take a charge card."

True, thought Sonny. And he could be driving all night and all day. Gas! He'd need gas.

"You have any access to the oil chains, Manny?"

"Sonny, you're not thinking too clearly here. If he's on the run, he's not gonna use *any* cards unless he got a stolen one, and that ain't as easy as it sounds, my friend. He's gonna be running on cash, pay cash for everything."

Sonny was silent.

"See?" said Manny. "It's a big country. He could be anywhere. Want some advice?"

"No," said Sonny, and he slammed the phone down.

CHAPTER 32

**Wednesday, August 29
1930 hours
Raton, New Mexico**

Keogh couldn't believe it.

He was sitting in the dining room of the Roughrider's Roadside Grill in Raton, New Mexico, with the sun going down like a radioactive dahlia behind a sawtooth ridge of purple mountains on his right. He was thinking about calling Butler, wondering if Pat had got anywhere with Pike's records, and staring at a plate of fries and gravy, the gravy being some kind of pale-white chicken gravy and not even a good rich beef gravy—which is what you were *supposed* to put on your fries.

He'd come all this way redball, with a litter of Bob's Big Boy wrappers in the footwell and three days of beard, deked out all the troopers and stayed away from every town, no sleep, running okay for an amateur, and here it all goes, 'cause there's two cracker assholes coming in the front door of the lounge and it was like they had a sign on them, or one of those big Felix the Cat balloons that say THINKS, and what it was these two crackers were thinking was ROBBERY.

Oh, yeah. The little one in the cattleman coat, the one hanging back now by the door—he'll have a shotgun or something under the coat. Look at him, thought Frank, feeling the weight of the nine-mil under his jacket. Look at he guy. Weighs maybe one fifty if you fill his pockets with change, and those reflector aviators, and the throat working away. Twitchy way about him, as if he's cranked up or something.

His partner halfway into the big room now, nobody looking up to see him, just a big room full of people eating, bunch of family folks by the plate-glass window, some truckers here and there, in off the interstate, some farmers, teenage waitresses in brown nylon cowgirl suits running around with drinks and dinners.

The little guy now at the door. Standing six, they'd call it in Robbery. Look at him. You could almost hear him talking to himself, like Goofy, saying Dum Dum Da-Dum Nossir Don't Mind *Me*, I'm Just a Harmless Old Dude Yup Yup . . . and the partner, a lanky thin guy with a forward lean and a kind of shuffle to his walk, jeans and a black silk A's jacket over a T-shirt with a picture of Kennedy waving and the back of Kennedy's head coming off as if he had just taken the round in Dealey Plaza.

Not too dumb, really, that shirt. The guy will go to the cash register, maybe even be quiet about it; he'll see it's the dinner hour and he'll show the old broad a piece. All she'll remember is the piece and the picture of Kennedy's head coming apart.

Frank looked around and saw no one paying any attention.

No troopers in the place either, or he wouldn't be here himself. God *damn*.

So keep your head down. Stick your face in the fries and the pale-gray stuff on them. Nobody sees anything, makes a fuss about it. They'll collect and pony on down the road.

Please let them be pros. Let them be at least *semi*-pros.

Well, he really featured his luck, and that was a fact. What was it Butler used to say when something went totally and mind-bendingly wrong on a job.

Shit happens, he'd say, and put his hands out to the side and open his eyes wide and grin at Pulaski.

Shit happens.

Shit happened.

CHAPTER 33

Wednesday, August 29
2200 hours
Queens, New York

Emil Pickett lived alone in a wood-frame bungalow out in Maspeth, where a lot of other senior cops in the Department had their homes. Maspeth was next door to Brooklyn, of which only the dead may speak. His house faced north, where he could see the green rise of Calvary Cemetery and Mount Zion across Newtown Creek. It was a nice little neighborhood of wood-frames and brick duplexes and tidy green lawns. New kids in the Department said that Maspeth was where the old hairbags and bulls went to die. In Maspeth, where they could sit on the verandas of their little wooden *boon-gallows* and see how the light changed on the graves across the creek.

Emil had never married. His house was a repository of everything he had ever done in the Department, from his days at the Delahanty Institute, before the war got in the way, and then back on the Job as a patrolman in Midtown, learning the tricks from Johnny Broderick, thumping the skells and perps like one of the boys. There was even a yellowed clipping framed over the fireplace.

POLICE SERGEANT CURSES THE KNAPP COMMISSION

God *damned* Knapp Commission—may those boys all die of testicular cancer, that weasel Serpico last of all. That

had been a hard year. A third of the Department chased off
the Job. The Pad dried up like the last of the water in the
Gobi. But Emil had ridden that out and gone on to glory.
Now he was the Zone Commander for the Bronx, buddies
with the Bronx Borough Commander. A few steps away
from Chief of Patrol. From *that* desk, you could see the
Commissioner's office, see that old black rascal up there,
drinking cognac with his toadies, slanging the Irish, dealing
out favors and ruination like aces slippery and slick off the
pink of his fat palms. That was Pickett's name for him: The
Ace of Spades.

The Commissioner's name for Pickett was "that fat fuck."

Pickett sat in a black leather wing-back in the middle of
his overstuffed living room, surrounded by pictures and
trophies and a miasma of stale cigar smoke and the fire-
and-cedar scent of brandy, in his slippers and a pair of
baggy blues held up by suspenders printed with the gold
captain's shields he treasured above rubies.

After captain, the Job had gotten to be purely political,
and he missed—somewhere in the barrel of his wheezy
chest and the yellow of his eyes, he missed—the Street and
the tip-of-your-toes feeling it had given him. Now he was an
old bull in a padded room waiting for something vital inside
to say, Well, fuck this, we're *outa* here, and then he could
go lie down across the creek with the rest of the boys . . .

. . . as long as this mick bastard didn't screw it up for
him. Ten years since he last heard from Johnny Keogh. At
a racket for the Chief of Detectives, back in '78.

They had circled each other like a couple of skaters, until
Keogh had given him a big grin and stuck out his hand,
letting him know in a silent way that neither of them was
going to bring up anything about how Jimmy Pelligrino got
himself dead.

Not that the bastard hadn't deserved it. Not that it wasn't
a long time coming. But it was an execution all the same,
and if it hadn't been for Johnny Keogh coming along when
he did in that alleyway and having a spare Astra to lend
him, it would have been the end of Emil's career.

It was a trick of human nature that we all come to hate the people we owe the most to.

Pickett didn't really hate Johnny Keogh.

But Keogh's wife had bailed out in some freak-ass accident and the Change had come over Keogh sooner than it came to most of the old guard. After that, there was more drinking and less work, and too many of Johnny's prisoners had to spend too much time in the hospital before they got to Central Booking.

Pickett looked at the clock over the kitchen door. Ten. On a Wednesday night, his bowling night. Then a few rounds at Flanagan's and maybe a blow job from one of the hookers over on Grand Street. Not tonight, though. Tonight he was waiting for Johnny Keogh. And as he thought this the doorbell chimed.

It seemed to him that Johnny Keogh looked old and shrunken in his jeans and that stupid shirt, standing there on the doorstep and grinning up at him, until Pickett stepped back to let him in and caught a glimpse of himself in the mirror next to the hall closet. A fat old man in slippers and baggy trousers, a red face and white fur all along his pale-pink arms.

"Emil," said Johnny Keogh, looking around the room.

"John," said Pickett. "Get you a drink?"

"A snifter out of that Remy I see on your sideboard over there and I'll not take up too much of your time, Emil."

"Not at all, John. It's good to see you."

He poured out the cognac in silence and brought it to Keogh. Keogh took it and they drank to each other.

"Here's to us."

"Who's like us?"

"Devil a one."

"And they're all dead."

They sat in silence for a while longer, Emil now oddly comfortable in it, letting the old days shuffle back into the room until the air around them was full of whispers and voices and half-remembered faces.

"Remember McCarthy? His horse died in the basement of that tavern down on Mott Street?"

"I do. How's he?"

"Good . . . good. Has a house up the street. We bowl in the same league. You want to go up there later, say hello?"

"No . . . not right now. Tonight's your bowling?"

Emil turned to look at the bag and the jacket by the door. He made a dismissive gesture.

Finally: "Sorry about your boy, Johnny."

"Yes. Bad business."

"That it is. Got him a lawyer?"

Keogh named him.

"That maggot? How can you go to him? You remember how he screwed us on that *gris-gris* killing? Then the pricks go out and do three more. Guy's a whore."

"Emil . . . you go to a whorehouse, you better get a whore."

"That's the truth. You're going to need one."

"That's the thing, Emil. This case . . . Why hang this jacket on my kid?"

"We ought not to be talking about it. It's an ongoing investigation in my own zone. You know the policy. You read the A.G. yourself."

"Fuck the guide. I know you, Emil."

A polite threat.

"Well . . ."

"Well what?"

Silence. Keogh let it run.

Emil sighed and sank a little deeper into his wing-back chair. "What can I do?"

"Tell me what's the motor in it. There's gotta be something to this that nobody's saying. No way they'd hang this on one of the boyos unless there was something wet and sticky at the bottom of the bag. What is it?"

"You're not gonna like it, Johnny."

"I haven't liked much since my prostate surgery."

"Okay . . . Story goes, Frank's turned himself into a

Buddy Boy. He and that cowboy partner of his. They been taking cash off the Ching-a-Lings. One of the dealers, a guy named Roberto, says they scooped close to thirty kay off them just last week. And the—you know he was porking a PW?—okay, the PW, Kholer, she was a Field Associate for Bronx Borough Internal Affairs. Way the D.A. sees it, she got onto him, got close. Maybe like Pike—"

"This is total horse shit. And Frank tries to make it look like a psycho killing and he uses an M.O. that only his daddy would know about?"

"They figure he's been into the powder room a few times. They figure he's a coke-head and the shit got to him, made him paranoid. Gave him delusions and stuff."

"Man, there's no way to keep yourself safe from the truly mean and stupid in life. Where'd that idea come from?"

"Pulaski's been worried about him for a long time. He thinks that maybe Frank enjoys his work a little too much. He's been trying to get Frank to go to a psychiatrist for a while. Even Butler says that. They got Burke Owens to talk to him, but Frank just told him to go fuck himself."

"Good for him."

"Well . . . it don't look good. All the SWAT guys have to be evaluated before they get the job and they have to talk to a shrink anytime the boss says to. And one of his own guys was talking him down at the racket for that nigra cop, killed last week?"

"The Paz? I knew that man. I don't think you'da called him a nigra to his face, Emil. Who was this guy?"

"Ryan. Slick Ryan."

"So what? Butler told me about Ryan. So Ryan's got ambition. Frank still doing the job?"

"Pulaski says he pulled on a guy last week without a get-go. They got a shrink, a specialist. He's been all over Frank's sheet. Figures him for post-traumatic stress—something."

"Are we fucked up, Emil?"

"What?"

"We're vets. You and me. Are we fucked up?"

Pickett thought about it.

"Yeah. Well, we had our troubles."

"We did that. All this post-traumatic shit—those guys are no more fucked up than we were. It was just the first war the fucking Yuppies had to fight. So naturally it's the Worst World War. I know my kid, Emil. This case is absolute crap, and deep in your heart you know it is."

There was absolute silence in the room. Keogh waited.

"Yeah," said Pickett, finally. "I think it is too. But the trouble is, they took all this to Gamboni and that wop has a hard-on to bust cops. They're easy and they get good media for the D.A.'s office."

"So what are you gonna do?"

"Johnny. What the hell *can* I do? You know the way it goes. They got everything they need to go to court. Indictment came down from the Grand Jury. You got a good lawyer there. Maybe they can plea-barg—"

"Do cop-killers get bail, Emil? Any jail time is a death sentence for a cop like him. Frank won't take an inch of crap, and some prison mechanic will take him out in the lunch line. He won't even see it coming."

"Get him to go for a diminished capacity defense. Christ, John, perps are walking away from homicides all over the country. It's *Let's Make a Deal*. You get this Young guy to testify to post-traumatic—"

Keogh was reaching around behind him. The gesture was unnerving. Cops carry their off-duty pieces in the back under their shirts. John Keogh's arm came around and he flipped a sheet of paper across to Pickett. He let him read it in silence.

"What's this?"

"It's a list of names. Butler and I put it together. It's a list of people who were in a position to set Frank up."

Pickett looked at it again.

"You got everybody in Charlie Unit down here. Shit, you even got Pulaski!"

"Has Zeke Parrot checked them out?"

"Fuck no! Why the hell *would* he? You catch a case, you

don't start off the investigation in the station house. Frank's the only one they're looking at. Christ, who can blame them?"

"How about the others?"

"These people? Patrolwoman Boyko? Who gave you that name?"

"Butler did."

"Butler! Butler's been porking that one. She's his latest."

"Yeah, I know that. He told me. But we're putting anybody we can think of on the list."

"And this guy? Owens? I ran him a long time ago. The PBA was putting him up as a stress counselor for the Department. We got the Feds to check him out. They shined a light up his asshole, Johnny. Grew up in South Dakota, someplace called Sturgis. Near the Wyoming border. High school hero. Vietnam vet. Purple Heart. Lost a lung for America. They ran him all the way back to the womb. It was a test project and we didn't want any weirdo civilian fucking it up."

"Zeke check him out for opportunity?"

"Johnny, Zeke checked out a lot of people. Frank just kept coming up. And then he ran. I told you this was an ongoing investigation. The fact is, it's open and shut. As far as Gamboni and the Homicide guys are concerned, they got the right guy. They're just waiting for Frank to walk into some roadblock. They got a bulletin out all over the country. Zeke's got the word out to the Flagstaff PD."

"Flagstaff! Why the fuck Flagstaff?"

"Zeke, his theory is, Frank's into some denial thing. Has himself convinced he didn't do it. So the only place Frank can go and act out—that's what they say, 'act out'—this delusion is Flagstaff."

"Shit. Who comes *up* with this stuff?"

"Things have changed since you been on the Job, Johnny. It's a science now. We even got consultants up in the capital."

"Who's the asshole shrink coming up with this?"

"All of them. Like I said, we got consultants."

"They figured Frank for Flagstaff?"

"No. Zeke did."

"Because of Keiko Chung?"

"Who?"

"Shit, Emil. Keiko Chung's the kid that asshole took out when he was out there. I went out to talk to the Flagstaff cops."

It struck him then that Frank—that his *son*—was now working on the same case. Maybe the case that he himself hadn't handled right.

"Well, whatever. Zeke's taking no chances. Any chance that Frank'll go to Flagstaff, Zeke has it covered. They even had people on your place down in Florida."

"Yeah. I saw them. I got Frank's wife down there, you know. And his kid. You dickheads are doing a lot of damage with this one. She's a wreck. So's the boy."

"It's hard, Johnny. What can I do?"

More silent thought. Then Keogh said, "Who went up to Albany?"

Emil stared at him. "Why?"

"Shit, Emil. Anybody go up there, see if this Kent asshole was still in secure custody?"

"I think Boo Blanchette drove up there. Yeah. He says the guy's a total gomer now. Got him Thorazined out. In a coma or something most of the time. That's a dead end, Johnny."

That stopped John Keogh for a while.

"Yeah," said Emil into the gathering silence. "That's a bitch, isn't it? But there it is, Johnny. What are you gonna do?"

"Will you give Albany a call? Tell 'em I want to see the guy myself?"

Emil held up both his hands.

"No fucking way, Johnny. That man's a patient now. There's not a hope in hell that they're gonna let the cop who busted him in the sixties go back there now and put him up against a wall. You'll never get near him. And I can't help you."

"Can't help me, huh? Jesus, and us old buddies. Been on the street together and everything. Why, we even been stand-ups together. Now I recall—that wop. What was his name?"

Emil made a face like a man with a hand caught in some machinery.

"Leave it alone, Johnny. I can't do it. You're a cop."

"A civilian, maybe?"

"You're not a civilian, Johnny."

"Been one since Knapp, Emil. Remember Knapp?"

"Am I gonna like this, Johnny?"

"I'll bowl you for it."

"What?"

"I'll bowl you. Right now. I win, you do it. I lose, I fuck off. Leave you to go to hell in your own way."

Old Johnny Keogh. Still the same shanty-Irish bastard.

The clock over the door clicked and whirred.

"Tenpin?"

CHAPTER 34

Wednesday, August 29
1940 hours
Raton, New Mexico

What did he think, Frank wondered, pushing the table back and getting up. Do a restaurant in the middle of dinner—sure as shit some civilian will be right next to you at the cash register waiting to pay his bill. T-Shirt had the jacket up and there was the piece.

Frank couldn't see it—T-Shirt's back was to him—but the civilian did, standing next to him, and he had to *do* something about it. Raised on stuff like *America's Most Wanted*. A clean-cut business type in a polo shirt and jeans and Topsiders, young, with a pricey Nautilus body.

Maybe he had a girlfriend back at the table, whatever. Frank could see him staring at T-Shirt, see the thought forming, see the guy thinking about it as his hand came up and he started to step forward into T-Shirt. T-Shirt saw it too.

T-Shirt took a half-step right and started to turn, the civilian still seeing himself on the eleven o'clock news, saying, Well, ma'am, this is New Mexico, not New York, lady, we don't let these outastate boys pull that shit around he—

T-Shirt shot him in the middle of the face, shot him so hard Frank could see the man's last thoughts come flying out the back of his blow-dried cut. A *big* round, must have been. It shattered a ten-foot-wide sheet of plate glass thirty feet away. Glass spears came down on a tableful of kids and moms.

Fuckfuckfuck, said Keogh, moving, going right.

The cashier, an old lady in a Fiberglas hairdo with a pin on her chest that said EMMA, starts to scream and the cash door drops right down behind the counter.

People all over the room are hitting the floor.

T-Shirt is still watching the civilian fall. Frank has the table out of his way and he's falling to his right, away from the line, away from the little guy standing six at the door.

Six is coming forward, the piece coming up from under his cattleman's coat, a big Ithaca shotgun, a riot gun.

Oh, Jesus, thought Frank, rolling under the next table and tugging at the nine-mil. Where'd he get *that*?

The civilian hits the ground.

The plate glass hits the ground.

Emma hits the ground behind the counter. T-Shirt hears the cash drawer fall, sees the bills scattering on the tiles, coins skittering. Two steps, turning now to face the room, Frank can see the weapon, a big black auto.

T-Shirt puts his right hand down behind the counter, comes up with a fistful of Emma's hair and Emma underneath it, face red, squalling in pain, real pain as T-Shirt gets her up in front of him and steps back away from the room, behind the counter.

Six still coming forward now, the shotgun out and rigid, the muzzle pointing every which way, covering everybody. He's screaming, too, out of control, screaming at his partner.

"Cash! Get the fuckin' cash!"

A door opens now, at the side of the room.

Frank starts to come up, the nine-mil low and in his right hand, coming up above the table line.

It's a bathroom door.

LADIES, it says.

Six puts two shells into it, two massive ear-slamming

bangs, the Ithaca held solid and hard against his right hip, his left arm over and rigid, his right controlling it.

The door disappears. A flicker of red and powder-blue, something going down behind the door.

Six is turning now, looking back at T-Shirt, starting to say *CASH!*" or something, the muzzle turning with him, Frank thinking, Well, damn, this guy's *good*, Frank now over the side of the table and firing at him, three times in the middle of his chest, three in a tight pattern, bambam-bam, the noise small after the sound of that big Ithaca, and then, an afterthought, Frank thinking about Kevlar vests and other Soldier of Fortune shit these assholes'd be into, two more into the side of Six's head, and Six is now on his way down.

T-Shirt gets Emma all the way up and puts three out at Frank, at the place where Frank isn't now.

Never stand and shoot was a rule of Frank's. A good rule. You've shot; now move. Turn up again somewhere else.

My, Emma's a big lady, he thought, seeing no piece of T-Shirt to try for.

T-Shirt's on that wavelength too.

"FUCKINDONMOVE!" He's shrieking it, voice going high and scratchy and his neck cords all wired and standing out. "I'll do her! I'll do the bitch!"

Jesus, thought Frank. Feature my luck.

Frank stood up, the nine-mil out in the combat position, instinct-centered on Emma's right breast, where most of T-Shirt's lungs would be. On the other side of Emma, of course.

"Drop the fucking gun, asshole!" T-Shirt's voice was going, but the thing in his hand was solid enough. Now that Frank was getting closer to it, he made it as one of those new Colt Deltas, a ten-mil with serious hitting power, twice the numbers of the old .45.

"I can't do that," said Frank, keeping his voice reasonable. Friendly. Cool the guy out.

Wrong thing to do. T-Shirt was way out there.

"Cocksucker," said T-Shirt, shoving the Delta up under

Emma's left breast. Emma's knees went, but he had his left hand in her hair and she came back up again, eyes big, sobbing.

"So what're you saying, fuckhead?" said Frank. Reasonable, but like he was losing his patience.

People were crying in the room, kids from over to his left. No noise from the ladies' room, though. It pissed Frank off, this shit. He was afraid, but there was only so much shit a man could put up with and then all he had was being *pissed off*.

"I'm *saying* I'll blow this lady to shit if you don't drop the piece, ass*hole*."

"Fuck it," said Frank. "I don't know the lady. Shoot her."

"What?"

"I said, shoot her. What's it say there? Emma? So shoot Emma. I could give a fuck. I'm new around here myself."

Frank didn't think he meant it, but on the other hand he wasn't going to let this asshole have his nine-mil. The world was full of Emmas but he had only one nine-mil.

"Bastard! Drop the piece!"

Frank had the nine-mil out in front of him. He knew that T-Shirt was looking right down the muzzle.

"You have a problem, son."

Emma's eyes were as big as boiled eggs. She was staring at the weapon in Frank's hands. Seemed like a nice lady except for the Fiberglas hair.

T-Shirt was looking around like somebody in the room was going to say, Hey, yeah, that's right, the guy with the hostage gets to say what happens. Like Frank wasn't playing fair.

Well, I better figure this right, thought Frank, and he shot Emma in the right shoulder, in the muscle about three inches from her little Peter Pan collar. Somebody screamed. T-Shirt grunted and Emma fainted, slipping down T-Shirt's body, and T-Shirt was standing there looking at the hole in the middle of his shirt, off to the left a bit, actually in the middle of Kennedy's forehead, Kennedy still smiling, now some blood starting to run out of Kennedy's head and into the famous teeth.

T-Shirt looked up at Frank again.

"I know," said Frank. "You never seen that done. You can't believe I *did* that, can you?" And shot him again, bambam, in the middle of his ugly face, and T-Shirt starts to go down, Frank turning to leave, and in the door there's a trooper coming in and Frank says, Well, fuck this, the trooper halfway into the room and—I don't believe this, thinks Frank—no piece out.

There. The sirens now, a long way off. But coming.

Man, this troop's here for lunch.

All this in a tenth of a second.

Frank puts the nine-mil on him.

"Stop it there, officer."

The trooper puts it together, sees the bodies on the ground.

Somebody says, "Bart—no! That guy, he *stopped* it."

Bart's frowning now.

"What?"

"He's a *good* guy, Bart!" Same voice, Frank's fan.

"The hell with that," says Frank. "Take your weapon out. Put it down on the floor."

Bart doesn't like that. "I can't do that."

"Yes, you can," said Frank. "You can do it. There's no shame in it. I don't want to shoot a cop."

"Who the hell're *you*?"

"Tonto. Take the piece out, put it down, Bart."

Sirens again. How long now?

"Bart, for God's sake, man. Do it." Another fan, in the back row. A woman's voice.

Bart takes his weapon out by the fingertips and sets it down on the floor.

"What happened here?"

Frank smiled at him, stepped around wide and came up behind him, and put him down on his face and cuffed him with his own cuffs, the nine-mil hard into Bart's neck.

"Shit happened," said Frank.

*   *   *

That made local news and then regional.

In Santa Fe one of the FBI special agents put the two descriptions together and got it out onto the wire.

It made the news in Denver too.

Lucas looked at Sonny.

"Well, he ain't going to Florida, Sonny."

They were on the interstate in fifteen minutes, going south to New Mexico, Sonny Beauchamp pushing his black Toronado into the gathering night, looking hard at every Cadillac he passed.

Lucas fell asleep in the back seat. His breath sounded, in the silent car, like somebody sharpening a knife. Sonny could tell he was sick, that the trip was wearing him down. He told himself that Lucas would hold out and everything would come out all right for his friend.

But he didn't think about it much. He put it down in the bottom of his mind. He had the car red-lined and that was all he really cared about right now. That and looking for a certain set of taillights.

The Toronado was one of the classics. Sonny hated the new cars. They all looked like suppositories. Aerodynamics had killed the American car. This Toronado rode as smooth and quiet as a crow over a river and there weren't very many cars built after 1983 that could catch it on a straightaway.

It had a radio. Sonny hadn't turned it on. Sonny didn't need the distraction. On his left the deepest blue night had risen out of the east. On his right, the mountains glided along with him, black and jagged on the horizon. Behind them the last of Wednesday the twenty-ninth of August had gone down in glory, and Sonny saw none of this.

On his blunt face the lights of oncoming cars flickered and faded away. Under his hands he could feel the steady rumor of the roadway, and in his ears was the sound of rushing wind.

Butler pissed away two hours in the Thunderbird, waiting for Frank to call on the pay phone by the doors. A lot of

Yonkers cops were there and actually he had a pretty good time, all things considered, watching an old video of the Big Wheel rally in Far Rockaway, wondering how Johnny Keogh would make out with Pickett, until around twelve-thirty, when a couple of patrol guys came in from the road for a Ten-Seven and a shot of Bushmills and saw Butler there and one of them came over, pushing his hat back on his head, savoring the moment.

"Butler. Why are *you* still here?"

"What?"

"Your buddy—Frank?"

"Yeah."

"Man"—he looked at his partner, grinning at him—"you ever go to high school, Butler?"

"Yeah. So . . . ?"

"So, you take Current Events? Or was you in Shop?"

CHAPTER 35

Thursday, August 30
0500 hours
Winslow, Arizona

Sonny and Lucas Poole went through Winslow, Arizona, like a black wind at five in the morning, doing an even 105 when they blew through the speed trap on the far side of town.

The cop on the speed gun was a nine-year veteran of the Arizona State Police, a rangy black man named Benjamin Dryer, with a wife on the force and a teenage son by the name of Rudolph, whom he hadn't seen in ten days, ever since a massive family blowup over the ounce of grass he had found in the kid's room. His buddies in the Winslow Sector called Dryer "Benbone," for no particular reason.

Benbone caught the Toronado in his Panasonic speed gun, fixing the glowing red numerals at 105 as he stood at the side of the interstate, resting the gun on the roof of his sand-colored Ford LTD just a foot in front of the bubble rack. Benbone was working alone that night because most of the other guys in the unit were spread all over the side roads looking for some runaway New York cop who'd shot the shit out of a couple of assholes back in New Mexico a few hours ago. Benbone said, "Christonacracker!" to no one when he saw the readout.

The black Toronado blew past him like a Cruise missile.

Benbone got a glimpse of two figures in the car. Something in the shapes suggested a couple of males.

Benbone slithered into the Ford, turning the key while he fumbled for the handset with his left hand. The Ford kicked gravel and dust as he shoved the pedal down, driving a passing Northstar into the speed lane.

The trucker hit the air horns, and the shock of that pushed Benbone's attitude needle from cranky to ugly. "Mother*fucker*," said Benbone. Now it was personal.

Other than the Northstar and the Toronado disappearing into the night a mile up, Route 66 was empty under a black night full of stars. Benbone pushed the Ford up to 100.

He looked down at the handset in his right fist.

Fuck it, he decided. I can take these assholes myself.

Sonny thought it might be somebody's taillights.

No. That red flicker in his rearview was no taillight.

There were two sets of lights about a mile back.

In the speed lane, a row of yellow lights over a set of whites.

A truck.

And next to that, passing it on the inside . . .

"Oh, shit," he said.

Lucas heard that. He sat up and looked out the rear window. "What are you showing, Sonny?"

Sonny felt his stomach tighten up. What an asshole he was.

"Over a hundred. We're fried."

"Damn right," said Lucas. "The limit's sixty-five. They'll run us for certain. Can you get by a check?"

Sonny thought about his Dennison ID. It was old. If they'd checked the hotels around the King James, which they damn well would have by now, there was a good chance there was a bulletin out on Dennison. "I don't know. What have you got?"

"I've got dick. A Green Card says I'm Noel Fearon from Toronto. And a hospital card says that too."

"That won't do it."

"Tell me about it. They'll have pictures anyway."

The troopers had their brights on. The bubble rack was flickering red and blue. Sonny could see the car coming up fast in his rearview. God *damn*. Now what?

"Lucas, what's the next cutoff?"

"Fuck, Sonny—I don't even know where we are *now*!"

"Winslow. What's next?"

"How far outa Winslow?"

"Couple miles."

Lucas riffled through the map in the light of a reading lamp in the backseat window.

"Leupp Corner's eight miles up. Someplace called Rimmy Jims is eight miles past that. But there's no use pulling off unless you can lose him first. Fuck it, Sonny— they'll have some cars on the road by now."

Sonny leaned over and pulled a black object out of the glove box. He flipped it over the seat to Lucas.

"Check the scanner. See if they've called it."

"There's sixteen frequencies set here. Which one?"

"Run 'em all." Sonny shoved the pedal to the floorboard.

Half a mile back, Benbone saw the smoke blur the taillights. The car was moving away. Yeah, he said, smiling. You *do* that.

CHAPTER 36

**Thursday, August 30
0700 hours
Albany, New York**

Sam Danziger filled his office in the administration wing of the New York State Psychiatric Facility at Albany the way a grizzly fills a pit. Surrounded by framed certificates and diplomas, his back to a slatted window radiant with early morning light, his massive desk precisely in the middle of a thick emerald-green carpet as deep as a lawn, Danziger stared across the rosewood expanse at John Keogh as if Keogh were something he'd found in his soup.

"I hardly see the point of it."

Danziger's big black head tipped ponderously toward an open file on his desk.

"I personally showed a . . . Detective Blanchette . . . of something called the Four-Eight DATF? Whatever? He came here last week and I took him down to the . . . quarters, where Mr. Kent is being . . . is under treatment. Detective Blanchette was quite satisfied. What's the point of running a few spectators past his window again? It strikes me as ghoulish. I'm particularly not interested in exposing Mr. Kent to the . . . interrogations, and perhaps the judgment, of the police officer who was responsible for his original arrest. It would be too traumatic."

John Keogh had gotten a letter from Emil Pickett giving

311

him the right to act as *amicus curiae* in the case. It was
pretty thin, nothing better than a bluff with letterhead.

Danziger was clearly deciding how and when to give
Keogh the bum's rush.

In his best professional baritone, Keogh said, "Dr.
Danziger, I have no desire to interrogate Mr. Kent. I'm
here simply to try to help my son. And to get at the truth."

Danziger permitted himself a thin smile.

"All I ask is that you allow me to look, and that's all I
mean. Just look at Mr. Kent. Let me see him. Let me
reassure myself that this is the same boy I . . . was
involved with in that case."

"I've read all the documents in this matter, Detective
Keogh. I'm sorry . . . Mr. Keogh. How do you expect to
recognize the boy of thirty years ago in this poor creature?
You have seen the fingerprints? The boy you brought in was
printed to verify his arrival here. The records are clear. I
have here copies of his assessments under the terms of the
Act. Every two years and always the same conclusions."

Keogh raised a thick white brow and tilted his head to the
left. Danziger took it as a question.

"In layman's terms, a very extreme case of schizophrenia
caused by excessive dopamine transmissions. Consequent
decrease in neurotransmitter activity. Chronic depletion of
serotonin and norepinephrine, probably rooted in enzyme
activity, the monoamine oxidase particularly. We're using
the phenothiazines and the tricyclics. He's in a rather
advanced state of tardive dyskinesia so he's not too pretty to
look at. In a fugue state most of the time. Seems to be
engaged in a permanent and gathering withdrawal from all
exterior stimulae. Can't be reached at all, Mr. Keogh.
Might as well be on Jupiter, for your purposes."

"What does that all add up to?" Keogh had heard most of
this stuff. It had been presented in the kid's defense during
the trial in '62. In his heart Keogh had always believed that
D'Arcy Kent was a brilliant psychopath with a flair for
deceiving the experts. In their few private moments, he

had seen glimpses of a cold and glittering clarity, and a trace of smug amusement.

And hatred. A hot bitter stream of bile-hatred, flowing in the kid's veins, sinking into the tissues, saturating his soul. In short, by any definition that John Keogh could gather, a monster.

Danziger sighed and looked down at the reports.

"It adds up to a man given to uncontrollable delusional states. Dissociative. Extremely dangerous. Incurable."

"Sounds to me like we're calling the same thing by different names."

Danziger frowned.

"Things *are* what we name them, Mr. Keogh. Naming a thing is the same as staking it to the ground. That's how we understand the world around us. What's your name for D'Arcy Kent?"

"I don't know, Dr. Danziger. I can't nail smoke to the ground. What do you do when something names itself?"

Danziger's frown cleared. "There's more to you than is immediately obvious, Keogh."

"There's more to this case than is immediately obvious, Dr. Danziger."

A square of barred sunlight had moved off Danziger's desk and was now lying on the emerald-green rug, a brilliant green jewel of sunlight.

"Well . . . John. Let's go look at our guest."

CHAPTER 37

Thursday, August 30
0505 hours
Rimmy Jims, Arizona

Frank ran out of back roads and dry washes around two in the morning and now he had no choice but to get the Caddy up onto Route 66 about a mile out of someplace called Rimmy Jims and redball it into Flagstaff, betting there was no roadblock on the interstate. He had twenty miles to go. He'd seen a lot of Arizona State cars here and there on the side roads but he'd run a good long way without his headlights on and jinked around the foothills like a crazed weasel. So far, they'd missed him.

Christ, that scene back in the Roughrider. Putting a round through a hostage like that. And the look on Emma's face. He'd see that look for a long time—could see it now if he closed his eyes. Now it was done, he couldn't get next to it. He had a feeling he was either cracking up or getting mean. Whichever it was, shooting a civilian would come with a hell of a price tag.

What now, Frank?

Redball it the last twenty miles, pull off somewhere outside Flagstaff. Cover the Caddy and walk into town.

Then what?

Call Butler, maybe? He'd missed his chance to get Butler at the Thunderbird last night.

In his heart he knew he wasn't really hoping for much out

314

of Flagstaff, that what he was doing was more or less running just to stay out of Rikers. Mexico was just south of him now. He had cash and a car and his nine-mil and a few cartridges for it. He could turn at Rimmy Jims and try for the border.

Yeah, only the most-watched border in the Western world, with infrareds and perimeter sensors and motion detectors and guard dogs and Border Patrol guys with M-16's, and even if he got through that, where'd he be?

Go to Guatemala? Belize? Costa Rica? Start to rot in the tropics with the rest of the wrinkled-white-suit-and-three-week-beard guys?

No. He was a cop and all there was to do was go to Flagstaff and see what Keiko Chung could tell him.

He'd had some luck so far. The chances were good they'd have their roadblocks back at the border with New Mexico, not thinking that he'd be able to snake around in the back country. And unless some civilian had made his car back at the Roughrider, they didn't know what he was driving yet.

Frank settled the Caddy into a nice polite fifty-five. There was nothing on the big black road ahead but starlight and moonlight and a broken yellow line and stands of pine and fir trees here and there. No headlights in his rearview and no traffic up ahead.

Yeah, trust to his luck and Barnaby Galston's ID and the sheer size of this country.

It wasn't a bad call. He was almost all the way right on it.

Sonny's leg was aching with the strain of holding the accelerator down. The car was full of the howl of the motor and the wind rush. Sonny could barely hear the cross-talk on the scanner. Laconic police voices talking about Ten-Forty's on a marker or going Ten-Seven for a burger out there in the Arizona counties. They could hear a couple of references to a roadblock they were setting up back at the New Mexico border.

Damned late for that, thought Sonny, looking in his rearview mirror.

Lucas was listening to the talk the way a man listens to his surgeon describe a dark shadow on the X-ray.

That red flicker was still back there. Dropping behind some. But not much. Sonny was doing a good 140 and the guy was still coming. And the Toronado's coolant gauge was climbing up. It was a hot night in the desert. The motor was red-lined.

"He's not calling in, Sonny. I don't hear a thing."

Why the fuck not? What're they doing back there?

What Benbone was doing was having as good a time as a man can have while being thoroughly pissed off. The Ford was a pursuit car, made for this kind of thing. He should have run that Toronado off the road back at the Leupp Corner cutoff. That was one fast mother of a car, that Toronado.

He hadn't called it in yet because he wanted the satisfaction all for himself, wanted to see that set of taillights coming closer and then he'd get alongside and roll the window down and stick this here Ithaca scattergun out the passenger window and just plain *enjoy* the change of expression on the driver's face.

He had a nitrous oxide canister hooked into the ports. It was for special occasions. On a flat, he might get 150 out of it, until the engine blew up. It looked to Benbone like this was a special occasion.

Now and then, he was thinking, as he went for the nitrous booster, this job was all right. It had its moments.

I should have stopped for this back in the boondocks, Frank was thinking, feeling the pressure in his belly. Now I'm gonna have to pull off on the side of the road and piss in the sagebrush and if some state car comes along, they'll stop for sure. Or some rattlesnake will bite me on the— How'd that joke go? All he could remember was the punch line: Doctor say you gonna *die*, boss.

Well, tactics are one thing and biology is another and right now it looked like biology was winning. He slowed the

Caddy on a curve and eased it onto the shoulder. The highway was empty and he got out and walked around to the passenger door.

Man, he thought, looking at the stars overhead, from one horizon to the other, what do they call this state—the Big Sky Country? Or was that Montana?

Well, he thought, letting go, they call this relief. Looking down, he missed the glow of headlights in the east.

Now this was more like it, Benbone was thinking, his speedometer showing 148. Under the hood the Ford mill was shrieking as the pistons hammered away inside the block and bits of metal burned off the valves. The Toronado taillights were coming up fast, filling his screen. He tugged the Ithaca shotgun out of the dashboard brace.

Poole was looking back. He saw the cruiser closing fast.

"If you got something brilliant to do, Sonny, now'd be a good time to do it!"

Sonny was fighting the wheel. He was losing power. A noise was coming from under the hood that sounded like a runaway drill. The heat gauge was off the board. A fast look in the mirror showed him a big tan Ford fifty feet back and coming up like Judgment Day, its roof a blaze of angry red-and-blue lights.

"Get the Heckler, Lucas."

Benbone saw the side window of the Toronado come down and he thought, Oh, Lord, this doesn't look good. He was going for the radio when the road lit up with yellow fire and his windshield blew apart. He saw little rainbows in the spinning glass. The inside of the cruiser was full of hornets.

Gunfire. And engines, big engines.

Frank was just finishing off the "D" in ROLAIDS. He shut it down and tucked it away and even as he was turning for the Caddy he saw two cars clear the curve two hundred yards back and ten feet apart, a big black cruiser and an Arizona State car with his roof rack blazing.

Christ. No time to start the Caddy. He reached in through the passenger window and snagged his nine-mil rig off the car seat, spun and jogged for the bushes, slip-sliding down the hardpan, tugging at his zipper and saying, Dammitdammitdammit, Frank, why didn't you go in the boondocks?

Benbone felt something cold hit his shoulder. He laid the Ithaca along the shattered windshield frame and fired. The Toronado shuddered left and began to spin.

"Fuck!" said Lucas. "The tires!"

Sonny felt the car going out of his hands. Up ahead he could see a big blue sedan at the side of the highway, driver door open, the inside lights on but no one in sight.

Something pinged in his mind, but then the right rear tire hit the dirt and the tail end began to come around. Sonny fought the wheel left.

Benbone got off another two rounds. The rear window of the Toronado disappeared. Shattered glass flickered like sparks in Benbone's headlights.

In the back seat of the Toronado, Lucas saw the pellets zip past above his head. He fell into the footwell. The spin held him there. He felt the flesh on his cheeks flatten. Sonny's blond hair was flying, a bright flare in the crazy white light, Sonny's shoulders working at the wheel.

When Sonny hit the brakes, the Toronado dug in nose-down and went into a 360, spraying rubber and smoke and stones.

Benbone was into a full four-wheel lock, standing on his brakes. He went past the Caddy and the Toronado, his tears blinding him, saying *shitshitshit* in a desperate hiss through his teeth.

The Toronado jumped the curb and slid to a stop on the median. Dust followed it and wrapped it up in a cloud.

Benbone got his cruiser stopped and kicked open his door and rolled out onto the pavement with his Ithaca tight against his chest and he came up into a low crouching run, jacking the pump one-handed and tugging out some shells.

He got three off at the black Toronado from fifty yards and thumbed the extras in and came on at a run, one seriously pissed-off cop, pissed at the Toronado, pissed at what they'd done to his cruiser, pissed at Rudolph and his grass, pissed at his wife, pissed at life.

Lucas was lying on the back seat feeling something grinding in his chest when Sonny jerked open the back door and tugged him out just as the first of Benbone's buckshot hit the front windshield.

Big buckshot. Bighorn rounds, or grizzly. Sonny could feel the car bounce when they struck. The sound came a second later, a thunderclap concussion.

One round hit Lucas in the left wrist, shearing his hand off, sending bone chips flying. Drops of red blood hit Sonny in the face.

Benbone fired again, hit nothing, and came up again at a low run, working the slide on the Ithaca, feeling like God's own hammer, his heart slamming against his ribs under his gold trooper badge, his throat so tight he couldn't get breath.

Sonny pulled the Heckler out of Poole's right hand, set it on the roof, and cleared a magazine at full auto, the piece bucking and jumping like a landed pike.

Benbone saw the automatic fire coming from the Toronado, saw red tracers flaring out at him and the blue-white flower of muzzle-flash from the darkness at the right-hand side of the car.

He dropped into the roadway and fired at the place where the flash was showing, feeling his belly go cold and tight, thinking, Dammit, Benjamin, what *are* you trying to do!

A cloud of buzzing steel skittered across the hood of the Toronado, and Sonny felt a shot go through his left hand. He looked down at it. Me and Lucas.

Christ, he thought, crazily calm. The fucking stigmata. Guess now I go straight to heaven.

Lucas Poole sat down in the road and stared at his stump, his mouth open, his eyes blank. A thin jet of heart's blood was arcing out onto the roadway.

"Put your fingers around it! Clamp it off!" said Sonny, and then he saw the blue sedan, saw the Cadillac, really *saw* it, and saw the Virginia plates.

Keogh. That was Keogh's car!

There was another magazine for the Heckler at Poole's feet. Sonny went down for it, and it bobbled on his fingertips, slippery and oiled. He caught it and locked it in.

Benbone got up again and came forward. Thirty yards. Twenty yards. He fired again as his right foot set forward, feeling the kick as the gun jumped in his hands, seeing the blacktop in front of him light up blue and pink from the muzzle flare.

Crazy, he was thinking. Charging a full-automatic? Stupid.

There was another burst of fire from the Toronado. More full-auto. Benbone saw more of those red lines snaking out at him, and he was still firing when his knee exploded and the ground came up and struck him in the face. His shotgun slid another ten feet.

Sonny pulled Lucas up off the road and started to drag him toward the Cadillac.

That was it, that's the car, he was thinking, not questioning it. But where's Keogh? Lucas staggered like a skater at his side. Sonny could smell Lucas's blood.

Down the road, Benbone was pulling at his sidearm. His knee burned like a crash flare, bone chips grinding in the rotator cup, blood running down his calf.

Sonny saw Benbone struggling with his sidearm and turned with the Heckler.

Benbone was up on one knee. He had the Colt up. The muzzle of the Heckler was like a black diamond in Benbone's eyes.

Fuck that, said Frank, watching it all from the trees. He had three rounds left in the nine-mil. He put the red bar over the men in the road and fired.

Sonny jumped as the mystery round came out of the purple shadows at the far side of the highway. He saw another red flare and heard the sound of it, a flat hard crack.

Poole's head got in the way of the second round. It came apart at Sonny's shoulder with a meaty liquid crack. Tissue blinded Sonny's right eye and Poole went down his side like running water.

Benbone was still trying to get a shot off.

Another concussive boom and another muzzle flare and another mystery round went past Sonny's head with a sound like a brass cymbal.

Poole was on the ground at Sonny's feet, an old black man in a puddle of bone and blood.

Sonny went for the Cadillac.

Benbone wavered, trying to track him, and tipped right onto his shot knee. A crystalline pain as clear and as sharp as cracking ice took his breath, rolled him over, and he passed out.

Sonny slammed the big blue door of the Cadillac and was into the road, the engine winding out. He missed Benbone by six feet.

Frank pulled on the Caddy as it blew by, seeing the big blond guy at the wheel. He got a dry click out of the nine-mil, looked down and saw the slide jacked back, and the Caddy was going away.

A name came into his head. Beauchamp? Sonny Beauchamp?

What the hell was going on here?

He shook his head and got sentimental about the Bronx as he walked out onto the pavement. Jesus, he was thinking, no wonder the NRA likes cowboys.

The black man who had been with Sonny was very dead. Most of the side of his skull was missing.

Lucas Poole, maybe?

The black trooper with the Ithaca was losing blood from a bullet wound in the knee. Frank used the man's belt to tie it off.

He sat back on his heels at the man's side. The trooper was wearing a name tag that said DRYER.

Way in the distance, down the lizard-skin glitter of the blacktop, in the east where a pale rose light was filling up the sky, a big Northstar truck was working up the grade.

Benbone's eyes came open at that moment. He looked at Frank.

"Who the fuck're you?"

Tell him, thought Frank. Why the hell not?

"Frank Keogh."

"Yeah?" said Benbone, looking up at him. He tried to move his leg. Pain thinned his wet face.

"Don't do that," said Frank.

"Keogh?" said Benbone. "Did you say *Frank* Keogh?"

"Yeah. Sorry about your knee. I couldn't do much."

"What the hell happened?"

"You got shot."

"You shoot me?"

"No. I shot the guy who shot you."

"Who the hell was he?"

"Some guy named Beauchamp."

"There were two guys."

"One's dead. Beauchamp's gone. He took my car."

"Man," said Benbone, "*everybody* got shot."

"Yeah." Frank looked around at the desert and the hills now rising up out of the night as the day broke over his head. The air smelled of gunfire. Frank's body seemed to weigh five hundred pounds and he wanted to lie down.

"Tell me something?"

Benbone stopped working at his knee and looked up at Frank. "What?"

"You people always shoot at each other like this?"

Benbone tried to laugh. "No. This is . . . outa my league."

"Yeah? They teach you to charge into full-auto fire here?"

Benbone looked down and then up again. "No. I guess I got carried away in all the excitement."

"I was back in Raton."

"Yeah . . . I heard."

"They were shooting at each other back there too."

"Well. I can't speak for them. That's another thing."

Frank shook his head slowly. "This shit's too weird for me. You guys are wingnuts."

"What're you gonna do now?" asked Benbone. "They'll be coming along directly. My view is, you're under arrest."

The Northstar was slowing down as it came up the long grade. The Toronado was a ruin. He'd get nowhere in a shot-to-shit state car. Anyway, this troop would need it to call Central for help.

"Guess I'm gonna hijack a truck."

Benbone made a face and said, "Well, what's one more felony?"

Frank patted his shoulder and eased him back down onto the highway.

"Also," he said after a while, watching the truck working up the grade. "I think I'm gonna need that Colt."

"Shit," said Benbone. "I was afraid of that."

CHAPTER 38

Thursday, August 30
0800 hours
Albany, New York

They came down a long, echoing corridor marked with steel doors painted white. Into each door a little wired glass window was set. An enamel number plate identified the room. Under each number plate a clipboard hung suspended. Down at the far end of the long green hallway, a glassed-in enclosure showed John Keogh a group of white uniformed male nurses standing around drinking coffee and watching something on a black-and-white television.

Danziger led the way, massive in his blue pin-striped suit, shuffling a bit in his slip-ons, saying nothing to the detective trailing behind him. It was as if the doctor were trying to distance himself from this exercise in prurience.

They stopped outside a door marked 222. Someone had scrawled an "X" and a "3" under the numbers. The computer printout on the clipboard showed the name KENT MICHAEL D'ARCY.

Danziger lifted up the clipboard and began riffling through the printout. Keogh resisted the desire to look in through the thick glass porthole.

"Go on," said Danziger, not looking up. "Or do you want to go in there with him?"

John Keogh didn't answer. Like a man putting his hand

324

into a black bag full of razors, Keogh looked into the glass.

The room was empty.

Straining, he put his face close to the glass and tried to see into the corners of the grubby white room. There was nothing in it but a high slit window crosshatched in wired glass, through which a thin milky light that might have been the sun drifted in. And, bolted to the terrazzo floor, a cot with a tangle of dirty sheets. And panels of gray-white canvas covering—perhaps *padding* was the word—the walls. In the upper right-hand corner a small convex mirror showed the room. Wrist and chest restraints trailed on the floor beside the cot.

Keogh was about to speak to Danziger when he caught a reflection in the convex mirror. A tiny figure like a spider was . . .

A wild red face hit the glass, contorting on the pane, dribbling spit across it, smearing it with reddened hands. A toothless mouth twisted and gaped an inch from Keogh's face. He stepped back six paces and brought his hands up.

The face in the glass disappeared and a thin low howling came out of the door. Danziger looked into the room and then stepped away to face Keogh.

"Go on, detective. Take a better look at it. Look all you want. This is the thing you left us with."

Keogh forced himself up to the glass again. The thing was on the cot now, grinding itself into the sheet, face turned up to watch the glass. Diapered, it fouled itself as Keogh watched, staring up at the glass, staring at Keogh without the slightest recognition. A bony furred skeleton of a man, almost transparent with sickness. The eyes were shaded and hunted and the mouth and cheeks jerked convulsively. The long tapered hands clutched the sheets and then sprang open again. A terrible low moaning came out of that wet red hole of a mouth.

Keogh stepped back.

"Jesus," he said. "Jesus and Mary."

Danziger said, "Is it him?"

John Keogh's face seemed to burn. Under his tan the

blood was racing. His hands fluttered in front of his shirt and for a moment it was clear to Danziger how old the man was.

John Keogh ran a hand across his face and seemed to gather himself. "Open it up. Please."

"No. Flat no. That's not going to happen."

"Danziger, I have to."

Danziger said nothing. Keogh let him think about it. Danziger was the kind of man who would do what he wanted no matter what you said. John looked at the numbers on the door.

Two two two. Under that, an "X" and a three.

Three times two two two.

Six Six Six. Sign of The Beast.

"No," said Danziger, his face set. "You've seen him. That's enough. Anything else is pornography."

"I don't know, Sam. . . . He looks wrong."

"Looks wrong? That's all you can say?"

"It's all I've got."

"It's not enough."

CHAPTER 39

Thursday, August 30
0900 hours
Flagstaff, Arizona

Flagstaff was an anvil under a hammer sun. Frank Keogh was in a motel strip on a street called Frontier Drive. A Holiday Inn blocked the slantwise sun and he stood in its shadow for a while, feeling hot and filthy and constructed mainly of road salt and gravel.

The car was gone, his Browning and his cash. He had his NYPD buzzer and a few bills and a borrowed Arizona State Colt and a license in the name of a dying man. It was in his mind to say the hell with it and go call the Flagstaff PD and tell them to come and get him. Then he thought about all the shooting these cowboys seemed to do and he thought, Well, no. Later. Maybe.

He walked a bit down Frontier Drive toward the center of town. Traffic was building in the four-lane road, cabs and family sedans and pickup trucks. He waved a cab down and climbed into the air-conditioned interior like a man slipping into a cool bath. The driver was wearing a massive black Stetson and listening to a radio evangelist cursing hellfire on the fornicators.

"You a fornicator?" asked the driver, looking at Frank in the rearview.

"Every chance I get," said Frank.

The driver smiled and said, "Me too, buddy. Where ya goin'?"

"I need a library."

The man thought while he cut hard in front of a Winnebago.

"Got the metropolitan downtown. Never go there myself. Go to bars."

"Bars? That depends."

"On what?" said the cabbie, punching the horn.

"On what kind of bars," Frank said, but the cabbie wasn't listening.

Fifty feet back, the driver of an unmarked Flagstaff car looked at his partner. His partner was a Flagstaff detective named Ewell Carson. They called him the Gibbon because of his first name and because he looked like a bald pink ape in his tan three-piece suit. "Now what do we do, Ewell?"

"You heard the FBI, Ozzie. We're not supposed to pick him up. We're supposed to follow him and see what he does."

"What's the connection between this guy and Sonny Beauchamp? Isn't Beauchamp part of that outfit took the bank in Lawton, Oklahoma, last month? Killed that trooper? What the hell is *that* guy doing in Arizona?"

The Gibbon sighed. "What do you want from life, Ozzie? You want it to make sense? We got every trooper in a three-state area looking for Sonny Beauchamp now. And all you and me have to do is trail this little mick. Don't put the spurs to God, Ozzie."

"How come all of a suddenlike we're just supposed to follow him? Late as yesterday *this* guy was a three-state bulletin."

The Gibbon didn't have to explain the mysteries of cop work to Ozzie. Somebody back East had put in a call and now the word was *follow him*. And somebody'd bag Beauchamp and then they'd put both of them in a room and see what happened.

Ozzie was quiet for a while. He seemed to expect no answer. It was a good trait in a partner, and a rare one.

"Where you figure he's going, Ewell?"

"Damned if I know. Downtown anyway."

"You think it's true, about him saving Benbone?"

"That's what the guy says."

"Doesn't make any sense."

The red cab pulled left onto the city parkway.

"He's going downtown all right."

"Yeah," said the Gibbon, pulling a huge plaid handkerchief out of his breast pocket and wiping his shiny pink forehead. "Maybe he needs some socks."

The death of Keiko Chung started small, a blurry nursery school shot no bigger than an inch square on page 17 of the Flagstaff *Eagle*. A headline, CHILD MISSING, and a few lines describing her and citing the concern of her parents. A call was made to the people of Flagstaff to assist the police in their search. That appeared on May 11, 1960.

Frank pressed the control and the pages flickered by on the microfilm reader, a dizzying stroboscopic flutter of lives and times and fashions from twenty-eight years ago. Watching it all go by made Frank feel his age. Sitting in the little booth in the main floor of the sandstone library, surrounded by the hush and murmur of air and voices and the padding of feet on the carpet, Frank felt isolated and somehow comforted.

Up on the second floor, leaning on the railing where he could keep an eye on Frank at the booth, the Gibbon chewed on a Jerky Treat and wondered about the guy. Why would a running man come all the way to Flagstaff to use the public library?

It didn't figure. It just didn't fit.

The Gibbon was uncomfortable with behavior that didn't fit his expectations. He was a good cop because he knew the basic cop truth: People Are All The Same.

A man kills a bunch of people, he runs like a pro or a putz.

This guy ran like both of them.

This guy has somehow made it all the way from the East and could no doubt have crossed a border, got his ass into Mexico, where anything and anybody that can't be bought can be rented.

But no, he runs straight into the arms of the Feds here in Flagstaff, which is running like a putz.

And what about this Beauchamp guy? The Gibbon had heard all about Sonny Beauchamp. He'd done hard time in Santa Fe, gone north to New York. Killed a New York cop. Now here he was, in a fire fight with a runaway cop on Route 66. Hell of a coincidence.

Curiouser and curiouser. The Jabberwock had come to Flagstaff.

Actually, shit like this made the Gibbon very happy.

He was always happy to have his expectations stood on their heads. It made him feel young again, made him feel that the world could still surprise him.

No, thought the Gibbon, chewing at the Jerky Treat, leaning on the railing and watching the little bulldog-type guy in the microfilm booth, watching the bulge at the side of his jean jacket where the Gibbon figured he was carrying a pretty sizable piece of iron, something's wrong. Something don't fit right.

And that call from Alvin Matthias, the FBI agent from New York, telling them just to watch the guy and not to scoop him yet. What the hell did *that* mean? The guy was protected?

No. It didn't fit and Ewell Carson didn't like it.

MISSING GIRL FOUND DEAD

There it was . . . May 13, 1960. A Friday. Christ, Friday the thirteenth. A front-page banner in the Flagstaff *Eagle*, pictures of a doll-like little Oriental girl with black hair and wide eyes and a tentative smile. Keiko Chung. Dead at two years.

The story was elliptical, as these stories are. A sexual

assault was denied but rose from the wording like the smell
of something rotting under the front porch. The Flagstaff
police expected to make an arrest within hours. Which
meant they had nothing. A Flagstaff detective by the name
of Dewey Schuyler was listed as the investigating officer.
Frank wrote his name down. Maybe Schuyler could help
him out.

Right, Frank. Excuse me, Dewey, but I'm a famous
fugitive cop-killer and I was wondering if you'd give me a
few minutes of your time?

The story went through the usual media cycle. Front-
page banner above the fold. Arrests pending.

Then, as the days passed and Dewey Schuyler labored in
vain, the coverage began to slide down and shrink until it
slipped off the front page and finally appeared as part of a
regretful editorial in the May 30th edition, part of a general
diatribe against the Flagstaff cops and Dewey Schuyler in
particular. All the media coyotes had gone yelping off after
some other animal's fresh kill.

Frank had the film for the first six months of 1962, the
year that D'Arcy Kent was arrested and tried. And in the
March 11th edition he found his father's picture staring out
at him.

NEW YORK DETECTIVE CONFERS WITH
FLAGSTAFF EXPERTS

In the photo his father was a thick-bodied man in a
two-piece suit, shaking hands with a lanky, egg-headed
detective wearing a white Stetson and a stiff-looking denim
jacket and jeans.

John Keogh was frowning and sullen, staring at the
camera in obvious resentment of the media attention. The
caption identified the other man as Detective Sergeant
Dewey Schuyler. The Keiko Chung case was mentioned in
passing. Apparently, John Keogh was in town to look at the
Chung case, and Dewey Schuyler was helping him out.
And they were being pretty vague with the press.

Yet, no charges had ever been laid in the Chung case.

The FBI letter was clear on that. Keogh fished it out of his jean jacket. Yes.

Queens NY 11/13/59 CARUSO, JULIA WF aged 9 years.
Queens NY 11/27/59 CADMAN, DONALD WM aged 5 years.
Brooklyn NY 12/25/59 DOUEY, BRUCE BM aged 10 years.

Jesus. The Douey kid was killed on Christmas Day. What a miserable prick this Kent guy must have been.

Bronx NY 02/24/61 BENKO, GRAZIELLA WF aged 3 years.
Manhattan NY 08/04/61 VIGODA, BIANCA WF aged 13 years.

How old would Kent have been in 1961?

KENT, MICHAEL D'ARCY WM/DOB 11/11/45.

Kent would have been just sixteen years old.

Too young. In those days anyway, too young to be traveling alone. It was too early for the shuffle of drifters that spread out across the nation in the high years of the hippie era.

Parents. He'd have traveled with his parents.

A vacation? Something like that?

Did the kid kill Keiko Chung . . . on his fucking *vacation*?

What supreme arrogance.

Whatever happened to old Mom and Dad?

In all the documents there was no mention of his parents. Yet they must have ridden out a season in hell over the killings, over the arrest and conviction of their son.

Where were they now?

*   *   *

The Gibbon pushed himself back off the railing. The guy was up and moving. Where?

The telephone books? The guy was going across to look at the shelves of telephone books from all over the nation. What the hell was he doing? The Gibbon got on to the handset.

"Ozzie, you awake?"

Crackle and some static.

"I'm here, sir."

A figure was waving from down on the main floor. Ozzie was standing behind a rack of magazines holding a newspaper up in front of him.

"Ozzie, the guy's away from that booth. Scamper on over here and see what he's looking at. Now."

"He'll see me."

"Ozzie, I can see him. I'll warn you. Now go!"

Ozzie sidled over to the booth. You look like a pickpocket making a lift, thought the Gibbon. Saint Jude preserve us.

The Gibbon could see his partner leaning over the microfilm booth. Across the floor the guy was riffling through phone books with obvious urgency in every motion.

I don't know, thought the Gibbon. It doesn't fit at all.

"He's looking at a picture of Dewey Schuyler, sir."

Crackle. The Gibbon digested that.

"Sir?"

"Yeah, thanks. Get the fuck out of there. And put that paper down. You look like a floorwalker at Woolworth's."

Dewey Schuyler?

Dewey Schuyler, who just retired off the force a year ago and who was now running Dewey's Dew Drop Inn, about a block from where they were right now?

The Gibbon started to smile, his large leathery lips pulling back over his long yellow teeth. He shook his head and grinned down at the top of Frank Keogh's head.

This is turning out to be a good one, he thought. He was gonna like this one.

Look at the guy down there, rooting around in the files like a dog at a rabbit hole.

What was he doing?

Why not just go down there, *ask* the guy?

Because the Fed would blow a testicle screaming at him. Jesus. Wouldn't want that.

CHAPTER 40

Thursday, August 30
0900 hours
Yonkers, New York

"Butler?"

"Yeah . . . Bert?"

"Look out your window, Butler."

"Out the window?" He waved his hand at Junie, who went through into the living room to check the street. In ten seconds she was back. She stood in the middle of the unlit kitchen and made flying motions with her hands.

"Nobody's there. What happened?"

"The surveillance has been pulled off you guys. You can ll go back to work."

"They caught Frank?"

"Not yet. But soon. An Arizona State car pegged him an our ago. You heard about the bullshit in . . . where the uck?"

"Raton, New Mexico. Yes, sir. I heard it from some onkers guys last night. It was on the news."

"Well, he's at it again. Fucking Billy the Kid, your artner there. There was some kind of fuck-up. Seems like e saved some cop's life. Then he hijacks an eighteen-wheeler. The driver says he took it into some place called Winona and left him there."

More shooting. Christ, Frank. Get a grip.

Pulaski coughed and sighed.

"Fucked if I know what's going on. Sounds like a real fire fight, though. Sonny Beauchamp was in it. They're still trying to ID a black male dead at the scene. One of the troopers is saying Frank saved his life. Makes no sense at all."

"Jesus, sir, can't you call off the dogs?"

"Something's being done. Pickett was on to Gamboni and Al Matthias. That's why I'm calling you. You know Johnny Keogh is in town?"

"Ah . . . yes, sir. He was here."

"Well, he's in Albany now. Doesn't wanna take Boo' word for it about the kid. He's wasting his time. Pat, you have any idea why Frank's in Flagstaff?"

Butler remembered the text of the FBI letter.

"It's a guess, sir, but I'd say he was hoping to kick out something on these killings. There was a kid killed out there. Her name was Keiko Chung. In May of 1960. I'd say Frank's hoping they missed something."

"Sounds like a guy who's innocent, huh?"

"I always knew that, sir."

Butler could sense that Pulaski was struggling with some decision. He left him to it. He could feel Junie watching him.

Finally, Pulaski said, "You might as well go back to work, Butler. I already called the rest of the guys. Hey, you know where Slick is?"

"Slick. He's in the Catskills. Went fishing with Charlie Boudreau."

"No. Charlie's in town. I just talked to him."

"I don't know, sir. I'll call around."

"Yeah. Well, I oughta let you know, I'm making Slick the A shooter for Charlie Company."

Okay. Here it comes.

"Slick? He's not qualified, Sir."

"He is now. I been sending him out to Rodman's Neck every night. He got his ticket from the shooting board."

"I heard something about it, sir."

"I figured you had. Can you work with him?"

"I can." The bastard.

"So . . . we're okay on that?"

"We will be, Bert."

"Okay. You telling Owens all this shit? About Frank?"

"He's been in on it, sir."

"Well, watch it with that guy, huh? He's a fucking civilian."

"Sir, can I go out to Flagstaff?"

"*No!* Forget that. We're doing what we can."

"Sir?"

"Yeah."

"Was Art Pike a mole?"

A long silence.

"Where'd you hear that?"

"What about Myra Kholer? She a mole?"

"Not any longer."

"Bert, what the hell's going on?"

"Pike was no mole. But he was worried about Frank. He talked about it to me. Pike heard the tapes, from that Bolsa Chica thing? You and Frank talking? He talked to the shrinks about it."

"Who? Young, or Burke?"

"Paul Young. Wanted to get Frank assessed."

"What? So Frank *kills* Pike for *that*?"

"Works for me, Butler."

CHAPTER 41

Thursday, August 30
1230 hours
Flagstaff, Arizona

"**M**aybe I can help you, Frank."

Keogh turned around in the narrow aisle. A big bald man in a tan suit was standing there filling up the far end, smiling hugely at Keogh.

"Ah, well, no thanks. I'm just loo—"

Frank. This guy called him Frank.

"Please don't do anything hasty there, Mr. Keogh." The voice came from behind him. He moved slowly to look over his shoulder. Another man, younger but capable-looking, was standing a few feet behind him. In between six-foot shelves, trapped at both ends. Obvious cops.

Frank felt a great wave of bitter sadness sweep through him. Rikers. The loss of everything. Robbie and Tricia and the rest of his life.

The big bald man in the tan suit held up his hand. There was a large revolver in it, the bluing worn off the cylinder, masking tape around the butt. The man smiled gently at Keogh.

"It ain't broke so don't fix it, I say. You wanna put your hands up on that there rack? Ozzie here will be stepping up there to help you comply with our local firearm ordinances."

338

Facing the phone books, Frank felt the younger man lift the Colt out of his belt. It was over.

"What now?"

"I'm Ewell Carson. This gentleman over here is Ozzie. Say hello to the man, Ozzie."

"Morning, sir."

"Now," said the Gibbon, "you won't be putting us in the embarrassing position of having to cuff you and all that TV stuff, will you, Frank?"

Frank shook his head. What was the point?

Ozzie and the Gibbon walked Frank out of the library and into the molten heat of the afternoon. The Gibbon stretched and yawned and wiped his bald head with a plaid hanky the size of a pillowcase. Keogh stood in between the two cops, trying to will himself into a dull zone where none of what was going to happen would touch him.

They walked him down the street to their car. It was an old Ford LTD, the black paint fading and slightly purple. Ozzie opened the back door and Frank climbed in.

Ozzie got in the front behind the wheel. The Gibbon maneuvered his bulk into the passenger seat.

"Ozzie, will you crank up the air conditioner?" He twisted around to look at Frank with wry sad eyes and a sardonic twist to his mouth. "Boy's a good cop but he's raw yet—right, Ozzie?"

"Raw, that's it," said Ozzie.

"Mr. Keogh . . . Okay I call you Frank?"

Strange sucker. "Yes, that'd be fine."

"You'll notice I ain't called you in yet?"

Frank had noticed. He said nothing.

"I'm trying to decide whether you gave yourself up, or me and Ozzie here nabbed you in a brilliant display of skillful cop work and raw courage. Maybe you can help me decide."

"I'll do what I can," said Frank.

"Ozzie and me, we been watching you since you got into town. You just don't fit into my experience of men in your situation. You got us both wondering about you. The main thing we been wondering is why the holy hell you're tear-assing around the Southwest like Pancho Villa, shooting up various assholes, and what concerns us *mostly* is what the hell you want with old Dewey Schuyler?"

Frank said nothing.

"I see you thinking there, saying to yourself *what's the point* or something. I can tell you this ain't New York and I got a different attitude to the law than you might expect. I seen it roll over a good man and I've seen it stop me from choking the living shit out of some asshole who desperately needs it. The law and me, we're like a couple been married for a long time. We're still together but I got my illusions pretty well under control."

Carson stopped and waited. Ozzie was cracking his knuckles and sighing. It looked like they were ready to wait a while.

So Frank told them.

They listened as the story reeled off, Ozzie sitting quietly and watching Frank's hands, and the Gibbon just slouching over the back of the seat and nodding now and then.

Frank came to the end of it. The Gibbon looked at him hard for a few seconds longer. Then he checked his watch.

"What's this Beauchamp guy doing in Arizona?"

"I think it's because I killed his brother."

"You kill him under the law?"

That was the question, wasn't it?

Carson and Ozzie saw him thinking on that.

"Ozzie," the Gibbon said, wiping his head again with that mammoth plaid hanky, "I do believe it's Miller time."

CHAPTER 42

Thursday, August 30
1300 hours
Flagstaff, Arizona

Ozzie and the Gibbon drove Keogh around the block to a bar set into a row of faded yellow brick buildings. The bar was big and dark and cold as well water. It took Frank a while to get his vision adjusted from the bone-white sun outside. When he did, he saw a long narrow room full of framed photos and antique rifles and big comfortable wing-back chairs. A long bar in battered rosewood curved around from the door and ran the length of the room. Bottles and glasses glimmered in the dark under a row of green-shaded lamps. The floorboards groaned and creaked as they came in. A few men were leaning on the bar, talking quietly, and they looked up as the Gibbon walked Keogh up to the bar and Ozzie stood a little way back where he could keep an eye on both of them. At the other end of the bar a leathery old man was polishing glasses and talking to a couple of uniform troopers.

"Innkeeper!" said the Gibbon, slapping the bar top. "Service here, for the working man."

The bartender looked up and bared a set of mail-order teeth.

"Ewell. Ozzie. What'll it be?"

"Soda for the recruit. I'll have a *mojiito*. And Mr. Keogh here'll have a pint of Pinto."

A rumor went through the room. The two state troopers got up and stepped away from the bar. Heads came around, white ovals in half-light. The bartender grinned and came down the bar toward them.

The Gibbon raised his huge pink hand. "Settle down there, Marcus. You too, Bob. This man here turned himself in voluntarily to Ozzie and me. He did it like a gentleman, and we're bringing him in for a drink because it's damned hot and I'm thirsty."

The lanky old barman with the mail-order teeth was standing in front of them, staring at Keogh with a kind of feline attention. He looked familiar.

The Gibbon said, "Frank, I want you to meet a friend of mine. This here's Dewey Schuyler, late of the Flagstaff PD."

Dewey Schuyler. Frank saw the remnants of the tall cop in the denims posing with his father. The same slight upturn at the eyes, the same birdlike bones and the flat light in the eyes.

Dewey Schuyler looked at Keogh for a very long time while Ozzie and the Gibbon waited to see what would happen.

Dewey shrugged, wiped his right hand on his apron, and stuck it out across the dented surface of the bar top.

"Welcome to Dewey's Dew Drop Inn."

The Gibbon felt the need to explain himself. Dewey let him do it. Most of the men in the bar listened as the Gibbon told Dewey about Frank's situation, the deaths in New York, the charges against him, and the reason for his arrival in Flagstaff.

Dewey Schuyler listened to it all without comment. When the Gibbon got to the part about the red cords, Dewey's eyes widened a bit and he moved his head slowly from side to side. But he let the Gibbon tell it and the Gibbon told it well.

He finished and picked up his *mojiito*.

"That's the story, Dewey. Ozzie sees him looking at your

picture in the paper. Frank here thinks you could tell him something about the case. That little Chung kid."

Dewey looked at Frank while he pulled on a can of Lone Star.

"You was in Raton yesterday?"

Frank nodded, bracing.

"What'd you get involved for? You coulda let it happen."

"They pissed me off."

Dewey smiled at that.

"I remember the Chung case. I remember your daddy too. Never seen a cop that angry. Coulda been a mean man, though. He had that in him. He comes to me about the Keiko Chung case, had to be March, sixty-two. He's got this suspect up in New York, kid was in Flagstaff when Keiko died."

"Why?" said Keogh. "What was he doing in Flagstaff?"

"His daddy brought him out. Kyle Kent. He was working for Barnes Business Machines and they were talking about moving him out here. Kyle brought the family—his wife Ruta and this D'Arcy Kent boy."

"How'd the little girl die?" said Frank, talking now cop-to-cop.

Dewey sighed. "Bad business. No rape, but . . . some knife work, you know. Done while she was still alive. Then there was that rope."

"A red cord . . . a ligature?"

"Yeah. We call it a rope around here. Tied in a knot so the knot would crush the larynx. Ugly piece of work. I was in the room when her father made the ID. Nice man. Killed himself the next year. You recall that, Ewell?"

The Gibbon nodded.

"Why didn't you pick it up on the FBI list? I know my father put it out. All serial killings get listed so any other Department that catches on can get in touch."

"They do now, son. But the VICAP program wasn't really started until after Gacey and Bundy. Those days, it never got this far. No computers in those days and if there was, this town wouldna sprung for one. It was all teletype and the Feds weren't any too generous with their information."

"You get any forensic from the Chung case?"

"Yeah. Some fibers and suchlike. So what? Forensic won't tell you *who*. It'll tell you *if*. We pushed it hard but finally we got nothing. Cases like that, all you can do is wait for the killer to do it again. And he didn't."

Frank said, "Not in Flagstaff, anyway."

"Yeah. That's how we finally figured it out. Your daddy had a short-list of possibles. One of them was this D'Arcy Kent kid. He'd gone through the records looking for any juvenile who might have been busted for cruelty to animals. Turns out this kid was on the list. Funny thing is, a few years later we get a call from a New York shrink about the same guy."

"A New York psychiatrist? Called you? Why?"

"About the kid. D'Arcy Kent. He called to ask about the Chung case, wanted to know all the details. Public Affairs put him on to me. Said he was doing research on the case for a . . . a paper?"

"When was this?"

Dewey thought about it.

"Jesus. I got this written down somewheres. I'd say, you was to push me on it, maybe sometime in sixty-eight. Or nine."

"You happen to remember the name of that psychiatrist?"

Dewey fell silent and stared down at the bar top. The two troopers had moved close enough to hear. One of the customers was behind the bar doing the drinks, a Spanish-looking man in a guayabera shirt and black slacks. Ozzie's radio started to crackle with conversation. Ozzie pulled it out and shut it off.

Dewey looked up at the rafters, where old rifles moldered in the heat and dust. "Sharps? I'm looking at that Sharps rifle up there. It was something to do with rifles. Come on, Dewey." He slammed a hard palm against the bar top.

"You make a note of that call?"

Dewey shook his head.

"No . . . Wasn't from New York City. Albany. But it all
come to nothing, Frank. I wouldn't get too worked up on it.
I asked the family and they said not to give him anything."

"Who? The Chungs?"

"No. The Kents."

"What? You called the Kents in New York State?"

"Hell no. Called them here."

"Here?"

"Yeah. Kyle Kent got the transfer from Barnes. Come out
here to live in . . . had to be sixty-six. Sixty-seven?"

The Kents. The disappeared Kents? In Flagstaff?

"Why? Why'd they move out here?"

"Can't really say. It was me, I had a son like that, killed
a bunch of children, I'd get out of the state."

Frank turned to the Gibbon.

"I have to talk to them. Just fifteen minutes."

The Gibbon was shaking his head but Dewey interrupted
him.

"You'll need more than fifteen minutes, Frank."

"Why?"

"They're dead."

The Gibbon pushed himself off the bar and said, "Killed,
Frank. August it was, Dewey? Seventy . . . ?"

"Seventy-nine. The seventeenth. We thought it maybe
was that kid, their kid. We called Albany. He was still in the
hospital. Anyway, the fire destroyed most of the evidence.
Only thing we could be sure of was how they died."

"In the fire?"

"No," said the Gibbon. "They were strangled."

"How?"

"Ropes. Burned off but you could see the marks in the
skin. Crispy critters, but you could see the . . . how you
call them?"

"Ligatures?"

"Yeah," said Dewey, savoring the word. "That was it."

"Red cord?"

"Like I said, you couldn't see that. Was all burned off."

"You put it together with the Chung case?"

"Well, we *knew* it was connected. We just couldn't *prove* it."

"You didn't solve it?"

"Nope. Still open, right, Ewell?"

"Open, yeah. Active? No."

"Yeah. But if the Kent kid went to jail back in the sixties—"

"And he's still there, far's we know."

There it was, what he wanted from Flagstaff.

"Look, Ewell. If the Kents were killed on August 17, 1979—"

"And with the kid's M.O.—you can prove *you* weren't in Flagstaff around that time, I figure?"

"Jesus . . . *yes*! August seventy-nine Tricia and I spent the whole month in Canada, at a lodge. Thunder Beach."

"Witnesses?"

"Hell, yes! Dozens."

"Then I'm gonna get on the wire to Al Matthias."

"No. Let me call my partner. He'll get them moving."

"Well, *somebody* oughta be in Albany tissue-typing this asshole in the loony bin there," said Dewey, finishing his beer. He straightened up. "Anyone for another round?"

The Gibbon smiled. "Yeah. But this time, mint in the *mojiito*."

Dewey looked hurt. "I put stuff in it,"

"Yeah," said the Gibbon. "Limes. A *mojiito* takes mint."

"Not lime?"

"Mint."

"Goddam fairy drink," said Dewey as he walked away. Then he stopped. Looked up at the Sharps rifle. "Damn," he said. "It was *hunting*!"

"What was hunting?"

"That doctor? One who called about Kent? His name was Hunt!"

Dewey was beaming at them. He picked up the Gibbon's *mojiito* and fished out a sliver of fruit.

"The limes. His name was Lyman Hunt!"

CHAPTER 43

**Thursday, August 30
1500 hours
Albany, New York**

Sam Danziger stood at the window of his office, staring out at the rolling grounds and the heavy oaks. People in groups of threes and fours drifted over the lawns under the sweet amber sunlight, talking, some laughing, some locked in the silent struggle of the lover to reach the lost.

"Who's Pat Butler?" he said.

"My son's partner."

"How'd your son get on to this information?"

"He's a cop. He did what Zeke Parrot and Butch Johnson should have done. He checked for similar killings."

"You're sure this . . . person we have under Kent's name isn't D'Arcy Kent?" he said to the old cop standing on the emerald-green rug on the far side of his desk. He asked the question without turning around.

"I'm pretty sure. But Al Matthias is sending a man down to print him. We'll DNA him if you want. But the eyes . . . they don't change."

Danziger didn't think that was true. Change the man and you change his eyes. And it had been over twenty-eight years. How could this old cop be so damned certain?

"How did you know to look?" Danziger's voice was a

348

basso monotone, a man bracing himself to face his professional ruin.

"D'Arcy Kent had very strong hands. Short and blunt. This guy, whoever he is, his hands are wrong. Doc, I have to ask you, how the fuck could something like this happen?"

Danziger was quiet so long that John Keogh thought he wasn't going to answer. Finally, Danziger turned around and sat down behind his desk and leaned over it, cradling his massive head in two large brown hands.

"Say you're right—and I want you to get him printed and be damned sure you print him right—then I would have to say numbers. That has to be it. We have eleven hundred people in here. There had to be a substitution at some point. But I don't know when. This . . . person . . . has been here for as long as I've been the director. I've written . . . Oh, Christ, I've written papers on him."

Ruin. Danziger's face was pale. His mouth tasted of salt.

"How long?"

"What?"

"How long have you been the director?"

Danziger looked at the walls covered with diplomas and board certificates. Framed photos and letters covered most of the wall above the rosewood sideboard. Danziger looked at one photo, a picture of himself standing on the front lawn at the entrance to the hospital, shaking hands with a white man, slender and professorial in a gray suit, a hawkish face with liquid eyes and a thin mouth.

"Nine years. Nine years I have been the director here. Kent was here when I arrived. I was briefed on him, on all the special cases. It was obvious even then that there was little hope. He was . . . out there. What the staff likes to call a *gork*—I believe that's the word. Unable to speak or communicate in any way. Violently assaultive. Unwilling to control his bodily functions. As you see, we have done little other than to . . . contain him. Actually, I'm . . . well . . . surprised he isn't dead. They waste, you know—cases like that."

"You know somebody named Hunt? Lyman Hunt?"

Danziger looked back at the photo.

"That's him. The one with me in the shot."

John Keogh walked over to look at the man. Something about him made John think of the plaster statues of Joseph in the church where he had gone as a boy. A pale man with flat liquid eyes and a thin mouth. Keogh had always thought of Joseph as a cuckold, and sometimes he had wondered at the anger that must have been in him, behind those painted eyes and that simpering saintly smile.

"Hunt . . . why do I know that name?"

"The Hunt family? He's quite well known now."

"Where do we find him?"

"He has a private psychiatric practice downtown. Does contract work for the government, mainly. Has several partners. The Hunt Club, we call it. At least six associates."

"You?"

"No. I've never been asked. I tan too easily."

"This Lyman Hunt. What's he like?"

Danziger thought about it. "What's the line? A confirmed bachelor?"

"Gay? . . . Let's go see him!"

"Why?" asked Danziger, in a worried tone.

"According to Butler, this guy was showing a lot of interest in D'Arcy Kent a few years back. Called Flagstaff to talk to the parents of Keiko Chung."

"He had every right to do that. Why wouldn't he call?"

"Why *would* he call?"

Danziger stared blankly at him for a breath. "The picture. I thought you read it. Under the photo? He had this job before I got it."

"Hunt was the director when Kent was sent up here?"

"Yes. This office used to be Lyman's. He used to counsel some of his patients. I haven't changed a thing."

Puzzlement and anger alternated on Danziger's blunt face like slides changing.

"Surely Lyman Hunt wouldn't have done anything irregular?"

John Keogh looked at Hunt's face in the picture for a long time while the afternoon sunlight crawled over the emerald carpet in a shimmering green square.

You son of a bitch, he thought. Why are you smiling?

CHAPTER 44

**Thursday, August 30
1800 hours
Albany, New York**

Lyman Hunt's consulting firm was in a sleek professional cube of mirrored glass in the heart of downtown Albany. The corporate logo was a steel Möbius strip over the name.

THE PROCESS GROUP
Psychological Resource Consultants

Danziger and John Keogh sat in opposite art deco chairs made out of wire and saddle leather and watched the receptionist punch buttons on her telephone with her mouth pursed up like a cranky trout. She was a pale creature with a bluish tinge to her skin and blue veins in her bony forearms. Just looking at her made Keogh feel cold. The place smelled odd and Keogh wanted a cigarette badly.

"Excuse me, Mrs. Beeton?"

The receptionist looked up at Sam Danziger, her mouth tightening.

"Have you had any luck yet? We've been sitting here most of the afternoon and you told us he'd be in any minute."

She pulled her lips and cheeks together and wrinkled her nose.

"Well, I'm sure the doctor will be along when he has the time. I believe I informed you that it is most unusual to try to see him without an appointment. He's a very busy man, as you—"

John Keogh tried to keep the snarl out of his voice.

"So're we, lady. This is official police business. You told us you'd called his service and that he'd be right along. Where is he now?"

"Well, it seems that he hasn't answered his beeper yet. You can't just expect a man in his position to come running whenever some . . . policeman calls him. There are channels."

Danziger said, "Can you call his house?"

Mrs. Beeton thought a while and then said she supposed she could. She picked up the phone with the air of someone calling Olympus to wake up Zeus. They waited while the phone light beeped on her machine. Mrs. Beeton seemed quite prepared to let it ring until quitting time.

Finally, Keogh said, "Ma'am, it seems to me that the good doctor isn't home. You think you might phone around and see where the hell he is?"

Mrs. Beeton didn't like his tone, but they badgered her into making a series of calls to Hunt's squash club, his banker, his broker, his accountant, his own analyst. Mrs. Beeton was breathless at the end of the circuit, fanning herself with a red file folder.

Finally, without a word, she got up and click-clacked down the marble hall to another office. They listened to a muffled conversation—Mrs. Beeton's birdlike chittering getting more and more insistent, and the muted burr of a male voice.

John Keogh got off the hard chair and went through the unlocked door into the inner office.

More art deco, very sleek and sterile and Japanese, a series of watercolors on the walls. No family photos. A huge blond wood desk. A row of pale-rose filing cabinets on the side wall. Keogh spent a few minutes riffling through the

K's, looking for Kent, Michael D'Arcy. Nothing. Nothing at all.

The click-clack sound brought him back out to find a near-panicked Danziger halfway to the door. They stood in the waiting room with blank faces. Mrs. Beeton came in followed by a small man in a perfect suit and perfect loafers with tassels and a wreath of brown curls around his slightly petulant face. The man seemed angry and nodded to them in a brief and dismissive way.

Danziger knew him. "Brewster," he said. There was a definite chill in the room. Danziger waved a paw toward Keogh.

"Brewster, this is Detective Keogh, of the NYPD. John, this is Dr. Carlyle."

Jesus, thought Keogh. Brewster Car-*Lyall*. What a name. Keogh wondered if it was real and decided it probably wasn't.

Carlyle didn't offer a hand. He looked at Keogh as if Danziger had asked him to give Keogh a flea bath.

"Sam. What's the fuss?"

"We need to see Lyman. It's important. Unfortunately, we aren't having any luck. Mrs. Beeton has been most helpful but—"

"Well, he's at home. I told Mrs. Beeton that."

"But he isn't answering, Dr. Carlyle." She was close to a faint now, and her concern was saturating the room.

Brewster Carlyle thought it over. Keogh watched the man. He had treated himself to a lot of cosmetic surgery.

"Odd . . . and he hasn't answered his beeper?"

She vibrated a negative.

He looked at Danziger. "Do you know his home address?"

Danziger said no. Carlyle did not seem surprised.

"Lyman's a private man. Perhaps you had better give it to them, Violet. Good day, gentlemen."

Violet did.

She was wiping the art deco leather down with a spray bottle of something green by the time they reached the

elevator. Danziger and Keogh watched until the elevator
door hissed shut.

"What's that about, Sam?"

"Disinfectant. Hunt's a bit of a case."

"Smells funny."

"Yes," said Danziger. "It's wintergreen."

CHAPTER 45

Thursday, August 30
1900 hours
Albany, New York

Keogh pulled in some favors and an hour later they met a couple of units of the Albany PD outside Hunt's low stone house on Delaware Avenue. The alarm service had given the cops a spare key. Danziger leaned on the doorbell for a long time, and then he shrugged and stepped back.

John Keogh looked at the uniform cops standing on the steps.

"Well, boys?"

They used the key and opened the door.

It was a nice big house, as spare and attenuated as Hunt's office, art deco throughout, pale-red marble pillars and Oriental touches here and there. A huge watercolor triptych ran the length of the main room.

The sound of a Jacuzzi burbling upstairs took them into a huge bathroom with a skylight and walls of mirrors. Three hot-white spotlights played on the tub and the onyx floor around it. The marble room reeked of wintergreen and chlorine and copper.

A video camera was set up on a tripod, aimed at the Jacuzzi. It was on but not running. No one noticed that until much later.

Danziger took a long look and lightened three shades to a kind of pale tan.

"Damn," said Keogh, seeing his face. "Don't hoop here! Do it outside in the hall."

Danziger went outside and leaned on the satin wallpaper.

Keogh stood and looked down into the Jacuzzi for a while. The uniform cops stood next to him.

"Lord," said one of the cops. "We better call Homicide."

"Call the Medical Examiner too," said Keogh.

He walked out into the hall and looked at Danziger.

"Is that Lyman Hunt?"

Danziger was staring at the opposite wall. There was a framed print on it, something Japanese. A samurai warrior was screwing a geisha girl. It was very specific.

"No," said Danziger after a while. "That's Paul Young."

Young was floating on his back in the churning water, held up by the gases in his bloated abdomen. His arms were stretched out on the surface, but his face was underwater.

The water was red with blood, and pink foam fluttered across the surface where the air bubbles rose. The marble room was wet and thick with steam. The smell of blood and wintergreen burned in their eyes.

Young's wrists were slit vertically on the underside of each arm. The deep pink slices opened the ulnar artery for six inches.

John Keogh stood there in the steam and the reek of it, staring down at the thing in the water, and thought, God damn you.

Talk to me.

CHAPTER 46

Thursday, August 30
2155 hours
Albany, New York

The telephone rang quite often while they were waiting for the Crime Scene Unit to finish up. But it rang only once for John Keogh. Danziger took it.

"It's for you, John."

"Keogh?"

"Yeah? Who's this?"

"My name's Ewell Carson. I'm with the Flagstaff PD out here. I got somebody wants to talk to you."

John Keogh's heart started to blip and his breath got short.

"Put him on."

There was some muffled talk.

"Dad?"

Keogh swallowed.

"Frank. How are you?"

"They told me where you are. How'd you get on to Hunt?"

"We didn't. We were just stumbling around and here we find this guy in a Jacuzzi."

"It's not Hunt?"

"No. His name's Paul Young."

"How'd he die? Was he strangled?"

"No. Looks like suicide."

358

"Where's Lyman Hunt?"

"Damned if I know, Frank. They're out looking for him."

Someone was talking to Frank in the background.

"Look. I have to go. You oughta know about this."

"What?"

Frank told him about the call from Hunt, about Dewey Schuyler and the death of the Kents.

"Okay. Butler already told me."

More talk as Frank spoke away from the phone.

Finally, he came back on. "Dad . . . I want to thank you. For what you're doing."

That was both hard to hear and hard to say.

"No, Frank. I owe *you* on this one."

"Well . . . you better push it hard. They're telling me I'm going to the cells until something works out."

"Why? Why the hell?"

"Christ, Dad! Interstate Flight. Felony Assaults. Theft of Departmental Property. Unauthorized Use of a Firearm. Theft of a Firearm. Assaulting Police. Resisting Arrest. What'd you think?"

He was off the line.

Keogh called Alvin Matthias in New York. The FBI man said, "Look Johnny, don't push it. Just see where all this crap ends up. Then we'll worry about your kid."

"You better," Keogh told him. Then he settled back to watch the circus developing around Lyman Hunt's place.

Red flashes from the cherry-top lights raced crazily across the rooftops and cast a hectic glare on the long, rolling front lawn and the knots and clusters of neighbors. The lights of the coroner's wagon turned slowly in the thickening night, pulsing a nameless blue.

The harness cops had seen to it that nobody touched the crime scene and then proceeded to track forensic white noise all over the porcelain and the tiles—tracking grass over the edge of the tub, muddying up the evidence, cluck-clucking over the smells.

Finally a pair of Homicide detectives looking more like

insurance salesmen dropped by on their way to a more clear-cut killing in Rensselaer.

The taller one told the shorter one that the cuts in the ulnar region were consistent with self-inflicted wounds and he'd bet that the County Medical Examiner would make this a suicide.

The shorter one allowed as how this was probably true but that they ought to let the M.E. reach his own conclusions.

The harness cops nodded and touched their caps and waited until the Homicide cops had driven away. Then they looked at each other, and one said Assholes to the other. Finally the M.E. dropped by to pronounce the body as seriously dead and set up a time for the official autopsy. Then the Crime Scene Unit dusted and photographed everything within a ten-yard radius and bagged the corpse's hands, and the coroner's wagon took the remains away in a black latex body bag.

The duty sergeant from the local station arrived to see to the details and the reports. John Keogh brought the video camera to his attention a couple of times.

The third time he did this, the sergeant asked him again who the hell he was, asked to see his ID card with the RETIRED stamp on it, and grumped away over to Sam Danziger to mutter in a corner about old harness cops who didn't know when to quit.

Danziger pointed out that it was this old harness cop who had been responsible for the discovery of the body.

The sergeant looked John Keogh over from head to foot, taking in the brutal-purple shirt and the forest-green Topsiders and the beard and the blue eyes full of sardonic amusement.

"Well . . . you were saying something about a video tape. Where is it?"

"It was in the camera, Sergeant Jenko. The camera in the bathroom."

"That's a crime scene, Mr. Keogh. The camera's sealed and dusted. We're not touching it."

"We don't have to, Sergeant Jenko. They took it out already."

"Took it out? Who took it out?"

"The detectives. They took it out earlier." A flat lie.

"What'd they do with it?"

John held up the videotape.

Jenko scowled, grumbled, and finally said, "Well, let's look at it."

"Good idea," said John. "Wish I'd thought of it."

Young was leaning back in the Jacuzzi, naked, talking into the video camera. The mirrored walls and the bright lights made him look like a pink spider trapped in a diamond. His erection projected from the surface of the water. He was stroking it.

"The collective conscience does not allow punishment where it cannot impose blame. That's from *Holloway* versus *the United States*. I think the decision was in 1945 or '46. I have the reference in my library, should whoever finds this care enough to check.

"These are noble words and noble sentiments. I have spent my entire professional career trying to live according to those sentiments. I have always believed that compassion was a more difficult emotion to sustain than passion, especially the passion for revenge which seems to animate the brutes who call themselves police officers in this nation. Well, I'm ahead of myself. . . . I'm making this tape as . . . What do they call it? A dying declaration? I believe it has force under the law. You had best listen carefully because, at the conclusion, I will slice my wrists with this little instrument here." Young held up an artist's cutting knife. The edge glittered dramatically. "Which should prove intriguing to watch."

He leaned forward to pick up a glass from the edge of the tub and drank from it slowly, still stroking himself.

"Well . . . I first met D'Arcy . . . in 1962. A well-made boy. Smooth and very sweet-smelling. Of course they had bathed him before they brought him to me, but still . . . I was the consulting psychiatrist in the case. I oversaw the administration of a complete psychometric analysis during the time he was under our care here. I had also been apprised of the circumstances of the . . . events which brought him to us. I had, of course, formed some opinion. Who of us can say with honesty that he does not form opinions? It is in our nature to do so. The test of a professional lies in his willingness to discard any opinion the instant that it cannot withstand empirical and rigorous analysis. . . . I'm ranting, I fear."

Another long drink from the glass. He refilled it from a bottle of Heidseck at his shoulder.

"Personality inventory. Minnesota Multiphasic. We looked for a causative propulsion. You're no doubt familiar with the facts of the case. It's well documented in the medical literature. I published a series of monographs on the case in *The American Journal of Psychiatry*. You can refer to my article in *The New England Journal*—'Smooth Eye Movements in Psychopathology,' I think it was. Well received. Also a collaboration with the estimable Dr. Danziger entitled 'Dopamine Transmission Dysfunction as a Result of Norepinephrine Depletion' . . . Well, it's all there. My bequest to the community, if you will.

"We even looked for Ganser syndrome. It was suggested that the boy was mimicking the symptoms to excuse his . . . behavior. As if the desire to mimic insanity as a justification for such . . . extremities of behavior would not in and of itself be tantamount to a critical systemic dysfunction . . . But no one wants to hear this. We will have our little crucifixions, won't we?"

More champagne. He was now almost fully erect. His voice was strong and insistent. Keogh and Danziger sat on the ocher sectional. The sergeant stood in the center of the room, as if to sit was to accept some kind of moral responsibility for what looked to him to be nothing more than the pornographic ravings of an obvious pervert.

"All of this is of course quite easy to speak of . . . until the child is actually in our . . . under our care. D'Arcy had been horribly abused. No, not sexually. We looked for that of course, and for cruelty of other kinds. I concluded that he was suffering from . . . There's no better way to put this: Stripped of jargon, I believe he was a classic failure-to-thrive baby and this continued throughout his adolescence. A simple matter. The boy had been born to parents incapable of loving him. A strict authoritarian Catholic mother. A father obsessed with career. No siblings. Small wonder that he had been pushed to such . . . extremes. Nothing more than a *cri de coeur* from a child locked in an adolescent body. A beautiful boy really . . ."

Young's voice grew faint and wistful. The activity in his lap increased.

". . . passionate. Quick. Immensely strong, yet gentle in his movements. Sardonic. Wry. Knowing. Well, his parents . . . Oh, let's not overlook Kyle and Ruta. This all started when Ruta found her boy masturbating and indulged herself in a paroxysm of religious mania. They called in the clerics. They . . . degraded him in the interests of some medieval dogma. Children died as a result. They killed those children, as surely as if they had done it themselves. But the children were dead and we had this broken boy. . . . Stress, you know, is the causative factor, given a chemical imbalance. There was some sign of monoamine oxidase activity. Also the aminos and the tricyclics. He developed tardive dyskinesia, and that was so hard to watch. That beautiful boy, his face wrenching and jerking, his mouth pulled and twisted.

"Oh, Kyle didn't like that and Ruta stopped coming to see him. Even the Board of Examiners lost interest. And the months and years went by and it came to me that I could do something . . . something decisive about at least one of my . . . captives.

"D'Arcy would come to Lyman's office—he liked the light in it. Lyman always knew how to take care of himself— And he'd sit in that chair in front of me and we'd . . . Oh, the *talk*! Talk is sometimes the *most* exhilarating experience!

When you find someone—what does the *age* matter? Someone who really *lives*. Who is *present* in the moment and yet contemplative. Aware! Oh, and yes, I'd kneel at his feet sometimes. Take him in my mouth. My lover and my . . . my son.

"In June it was . . . it was presented to us. Lyman and me. Oh, Lyman was jealous, but even Lyman knew what we had here in D'Arcy. Not some genetic freak. It was like having a predator, a tiger who could *talk* about it. The research possibilities alone were . . . But of course they'd want to lock him up. They wasted an opportunity in Ted Bundy. How could you *really* learn about a creature like D'Arcy while he was in . . . a cage? It was vital to . . . release him. We needed . . .

"Finally, a ruined street child admitted by a distracted social worker. The right physical type, a degenerative disease . . . technically it was progeria but affecting only the brain cells. Similar to Alzheimer's, but mimicking many of the symptoms.

"Lyman and I assisted—with hallucinogens. He was a lost boy anyway. I saw it as a soul transplant. Here was a body with no soul and a soul with no body. So Lyman and I locked up the body and I substituted his file for D'Arcy's, and Lyman handled all the workups himself. One night we took D'Arcy home with us."

Young looked up at the camera.

"I had my own place, of course. But Lyman and I shared this house and somehow D'Arcy liked the . . . Oriental touches.

"No one asked any questions. We'd send in our reports to the Board. Bureaucracy. You can always depend on the incompetence of institutions. No one cared about him anyway, especially after Kyle and Ruta moved to Flagstaff. Then he was truly ours. . . . Well, you can think what you wish. He's beyond you now. I will be soon. Lyman has . . . gone away. This . . . policeman has called from the city and we know that sooner or later it will come out."

Keogh and Danziger looked at each other. Jenko's face
as stiff and pale.

"But we worked hard at . . . his troubles. He came to
a understanding of what he had done. D'Arcy was very
rave. He was willing to recognize the symptoms that
dicated an onset of a dissociative state.

"We visited the graves of all the children. Julia Caruso
d little Donny Cadman. The black child, Douey. That
hinese girl in Flagstaff. Graziella Benko. Bianca Vigoda.
oor Bianca.

"Lyman and I made a terrible mistake. We were trying to
emonstrate that rehabilitation of someone like D'Arcy was
ossible. We were going to publish on it. Part of that was to
ncourage him to confront his parents. It went . . . badly,
ith Kyle and Ruta.

"When we returned to Albany—to Lyman's house—
'Arcy was cold. He talked about leaving us."

Young drained his champagne glass and set it carefully
own on the marble beside the Jacuzzi.

"Well, after all Lyman and I had done. Lyman and I—we
greed that D'Arcy was not really . . . fit to go into the
orld. And he had some . . . Let's say it was guilty
nowledge."

Young leaned forward and stretched out his left wrist and
ruck the vein with a knuckle. Then he cut, swift and
eeply.

"Shit!" said Danziger. John Keogh watched Young's face,
eling a sick and furtive joy. Too easy, was all he could
ink. And so much of the story is going with him.

A jet of purple blood bounded from the artery and then
owed as the cut widened, following the blade through the
ft white skin as a wake follows a boat. Calmly, with
eliberation, Young moved the blade to his left hand and
ened up his right wrist. The water began to color. He
wered his arms beneath the surface.

"So . . . you'll want to know where . . . where
'Arcy is. He's . . . here. In Lyman's house. We could
ever have let him lie in some . . . potter's field. No.

You'll find him in Lyman's garden. We were working on Shinto garden. We made it beautiful for him, a place whe he could find the . . . harmony . . . that he had alwa sought. Harmony we were never able to give him in h life."

Young was losing consciousness. His face was pale no He cupped his diminishing erection.

He seemed to recall his audience.

"Yes. You'll need to know about . . . these people New York. I suppose the simplest thing is to say that killed them. Lyman and I. Why? We have alwa hated . . . judgment. Police, lawyers. They judge. If th judge harshly or wrongly, where's the punishment them?"

Young stopped and his eyes closed.

Not yet, you bastard, thought Keogh.

"So Lyman and I . . . contrived . . . a little judgme of our own. To . . . remind the people who destroy D'Arcy's life—a life far more fine and more *exquisite* th any of you could *ever* understand—to remind you *all* the . . . complexity . . . of life. That vulgar animal co So *righteous*. Such presumption. And his own son follo ing, another animal, killing indiscriminately . . . a perhaps"—here he raised his arms and turned them in th light, showing his wounds; blood matted the black hairs his chest—"and perhaps to show them how easily one c lose everything. We . . . slide on the surface of life. Li water snakes . . . Lyman and I had the courage to below. And we took these people with us. We showe them . . . wonders."

Young slid down into the roiling scarlet water, a grea pink residue covering his face as he went under. Danzig sat transfixed.

Good, thought John Keogh. Couldn't have happened t more deserving son of a bitch.

Over at the doorway, one of the cops started to laugh

"This prick was exceedingly bent," he said.

"Yeah," said another one, smiling. "Instead of coming, he
ent!"

All the cops laughed at that.

Danziger did not.

Sergeant Jenko pushed FAST FORWARD on the VCR remote.
Vhat had contained some elements of the pathetic became
istantly absurd as Young's body jittered and jumped in a
ib of shimmering pink soup.

CHAPTER 47

Saturday, September 1
1100 hours
Flagstaff, Arizona

"Keogh." Something clanging.

Frank woke out of a perfect black space as blank an
silent as Zen. A blond kid in a Flagstaff PD uniform w
standing outside the cell. He dragged his nightstick acro
the bars again.

"Drop yer cock and grab yer socks, Keogh. The Gibbe
wants to see you."

The kid took him up out of the submarine and down
long white hallway with a red light at the end of it and the
up a flight of stairs to a screened window, where a woma
with the name TRUDY BENTEEN on a plate pinned to her le
breast pushed a big brown envelope across the ledge to hi
and said, "Check it and sign here, Mr. Keogh."

"I'm out?" said Frank, staring at her.

"You heard of bail? Or don't you want to leave?"

"Who bailed me?"

Trudy looked weary and tilted her head to the left.

"Golly, I just don't know, and frankly, Frank, I fear I do
give a fuck. Is your stuff all here?"

She tapped the big brown envelope.

Frank ripped it open. His Barnaby Galston license;
black leather folder with his gold shield in it; $116;

368

quarter and a dime, and a matchbook from the Eagle Inn in Applegrove, Virginia. Relics.

The Gibbon and Ozzie were waiting for him at the top of the stairs.

"Frank, you look like shit. Have a nice night?"

"Yeah . . . What's happening?"

The Gibbon smiled hugely and touched a finger to the side of his nose.

"Ozzie and me're going to Dewey's for a coupla *mojiitos*. Thought you might want to come along?"

"Yeah?" said Frank. "That's a nice thought. I take it I'm out on bail?"

"Looks suspiciously like it. Always the way, right, Ozzie? We snag the desperadoes and some slick suit comes along and sets him free to rape and pillage. Makes you crazy, right, Ozzie?"

"Who went bail for me?"

Ozzie looked out the window and the Gibbon shrugged as he pulled out his huge plaid bedsheet and mopped his bald head.

"Some commie, I think. Crazy—huh, Ozzie?"

"Crazy. That's it."

Out on the street it was a white-hot day that bleached all the color out of the city. They walked down the stairs to the old black Ford, Ozzie got in the back, and they let Frank ride up front with the radio. Once they pulled away, the Gibbon nodded his big pink head toward the glove box.

"Some stuff in there might belong to you, Frank."

Keogh opened the compartment. A set of keys was lying on a litter of old paper and candy wrappers. Cadillac keys.

"Yeah," said the Gibbon. "Auto Squad found it parked at the airport. Looks like this Beauchamp guy took a powder."

"He got away? How the hell?"

"Snaky guy. What can I tell you?"

Then Frank had a chilling thought. He had been traveling with a bagful of dope money stolen from the Ching-a-Lings. Christ.

"Anything . . . ah . . . anything else in the car?"

"Nah. Guy stripped it. Why?"

"I had . . . my Department sidearm."

"The Browning?"

"Yeah. How'd you know?"

"The Federal sheet said you had a Browning and a shitload of other weaponry. Where's the squad car you're supposed to have stolen?"

"It's in a storage barn. Place called Cuckoo, in Virginia."

"Man," said the Gibbon, shaking his head. "You sure been a busy boy. Got your hand well and truly shoved up the bobcat now, don't you. Seems to me you'da been better off sticking around the house there and not chasing pussy."

"Jesus, sir. You think so? Wish I'd thought of that. Why didn't I run into you years back?"

The Gibbon pushed the Ford through the traffic and in a short time they pulled up in front of Dewey's Dew Drop Inn. The big blue Cadillac was parked outside. It had been washed and waxed and it glittered in the Arizona sunlight.

Carson put out his hand. Frank shook it and found he still had nothing to say to this man. He tried to find it.

"Hey," said the Gibbon. "Never mind. Now and then we get it right. And anyway, you done us a turn or two out here."

"How is Dryer?"

"Benbone? He'll be okay. They'll give him a nylon knee. He'll have a hitch in his gitalong. Slow him down some, maybe."

He looked over his shoulder at Ozzie. Ozzie stared back, blinked, and said, "I'm staying. I got things to learn."

The Gibbon took a slow breath.

"I got something I want to say to you. Then Ozzie and me'll buy you a drink and then we're on duty so we'll say goodbye. Right? Well, once a few years back I caught a guy with about a pound of heroin and a briefcase full of cash. Had to be about a hundred thousand in the bag. Remember that, Ozzie?"

"Yeah."

"So we figured the hell with it, let's twist this guy's tail bit, and we took the bag and the heroin and we walked away down the road a bit. He had a road flare in his trunk and we set the heroin and the cash down in a ditch and we lit up the flare and burned it all. Then we let the guy go. Gave him his car keys and said, Thank you, sir, have a nice day. Be sure to drive careful now. A week later we found him nailed to a garage door out back of the Big Pine Lodge."

The Gibbon looked down at his pink hands on the steering wheel for a time and then he smiled.

"Traffic fell off in Flagstaff to a flat zero for six months. You want to know what I think about that now, Frank?"

Frank waited.

"I think that when you do something like that, it feels good for a long time. Like taking dope. It feels so good you just want to do it all the time. And the shit ain't worth it. The citizens aren't worth it. The courts aren't worth it. All the school kids in Arizona can die in their own puke from taking dope and it ain't worth one tiny bit of your word as a cop. Everybody's got to go to hell in their own way. They all make their choices. All you got as a cop is a list of things you won't do because you gave your word you wouldn't. Every time you knock something off that list, you lose a little more of what makes you a good cop."

He stopped and sighed and looked out the windshield.

"I hope you don't mind my saying this, Frank, because I think you were a pretty good cop. For an Easterner. Am I right, Ozzie?"

"Too deep for me, Ewell."

The Gibbon smiled again.

"Well . . . there was some talk about a drink?"

Dewey's Dew Drop Inn was as dark as always, with the same white ovals in the dim cool room and the pools of yellow light under the green shades above the bar. Dewey was leaning across the bar talking quietly with a short rangy man in blue jeans and green shoes and a loud purple shirt. They both looked up as Ozzie and Frank and the Gibbon walked in.

Frank saw the man look around, saw the leathery face and the blue eyes and the white beard and he stopped where he was.

John Keogh pushed himself off the bar and came all the way across to where Frank was standing.

John Keogh smiled and put out a hand.

"Frank. I missed you, kid. Will you shake hands with an old bastard?"

Frank looked down at the strong tanned hand and then up at the old man's face and saw his own eyes staring out at him and the withered muscle under the skin and the open way his father was standing there, ready to be hurt or hugged or told to go straight to hell, and Frank took the hand and felt himself pulled in and his father's arms go around him, and he hugged him tight, feeling the ribs and the age in him, and in spite of the surprise of it and the place, he felt like a swimmer coming up from the deep.

CHAPTER 48

**Tuesday, September 4
1700 hours
Matecumbe Key, Florida**

Sonny put the Heckler down on the table and rubbed his left hand. It felt like a radiator and looked like a ten-pound roast under the bandages. His eyes hurt from the Leupold scope and he was sick of the crying of gulls.

Sonny had been in Islamorada for three days and nights, watching the *Madelaine* at her slip in the marina. It hadn't been hard to pick her out. The *Madelaine* was quite a boat.

She was forty-eight feet of Hatteras sports fisher, gull-white, with a double flying bridge and a tower above that, a big radar array and a SatNav receiver, four big whip-style outriggers around the fantail. There were two brass and teak fighting chairs in the fantail and not a sign of rust or rot anywhere. A glittering jewel of a boat that must have cost $300,000.

Sonny's room in the Ramada Inn across the harbor was perfect for the job. A lot of drapes and a soft shag carpet in cool greens. A big sliding glass door that opened up onto a balcony that ran the length of the motel, ending in a stairway down to the docks. A window in his bedroom opened up over a ten-foot drop into a back lot that led to a side street. If he had to run for it, that would be his exit.

The room had a lot of sound-baffling to absorb the sound

of a shot. Sonny had pulled a table and a chair into the middle of the room. The range finder read out the distance at 150 yards.

During the days he'd sit out on the balcony watching the *Madelaine* and putting antibiotic cream on his wounds, sucking on vitamin C's and drugging himself with Percodan.

He could still smell Lucas on him, although he had bathed eleven times and scrubbed himself with hard soap. And the sound of his death, that liquid crack and the chuff of Lucas's last breath in Sonny's ear, like someone blowing out a candle, and the boneless weight that he had become in a heartbeat, half his skull gone, all there had been of all their times together spilling out onto the blacktop like fruits out of a basket.

Getting the hell out had been interesting.

Trucker's gloves had hidden the wound in his left hand. He'd cleaned himself up in the washroom of a service station and taken side roads all the way to the airport, with his back muscles crawling, waiting for a siren, seeing State cars here and there but nobody really looking for a blue Caddy yet. He figured he had maybe thirty minutes to dump it before the bulletin got out on the air.

He rolled the Caddy into a long-term lot. A shuttle bus got him to a private charter company. They knew him there. Two hours later he was on a point-to-point Learjet flight to Miami. It cost him $30,000 to help the pilot lose his memory and his records.

The best part of *that* was the cash he'd found in Keogh's car. Almost $20,000. It was sweet to think that Keogh's money was paying for this trip. The thought kept him happy all the way to Islamorada in a Hertz car.

He spent most of his time planning for his shot. He spent no time at all thinking about Keogh *not* showing up. It was all he had left. There'd be no other chance.

He was going to lay it out like surgery.

When he looked at the boat through the scope, he could see it was going to be a tricky shot. Sometimes a mast would

rock into the line. Winds and humid air would affect the
ballistics. And the damned boat tended to ride up and sway
in her slip every time another boat cruised by. He'd be
damned lucky to be able to use the bipod brace. . . .

Well, hell . . . he'd be damned lucky to have a shot at
the guy at all. He was buying the *New York Times* in town
and the Sunday edition carried a small story about the
suicide of a doctor up in Albany and a scandal in something
called The Process Group. There was talk about this being
connected to Frank Keogh. Then the thing had dropped
out of the papers.

There was no FBI coverage around, anyway. The marina
was wide open. Wherever they were looking for Sonny, it
wasn't here.

On Monday he had worked out the numbers. A 180-grain
.308 would kick out at 2,600 feet per second. The flash
suppressor would take some of that off. Even back in the
room, there'd be one hell of a bang when he tapped it off.
One shot. Maybe two. He didn't want to go firing a
senseless spray of rounds into the boat. There'd be gasoline. The guy would have his wife and the kid with him.

Any luck at all, he'd get a hit value of 2,000 foot pounds
out there at 150 yards. The round would shoot flat or drop
no more than an inch. There was a lot of stray light around,
from the boats and the dock lights and the Whale Harbor
Inn. It was possible. If Keogh showed, it was possible.

On Monday they'd been all over the *Madelaine*, cleaning
and washing it, running up the engines in the slip, doing
the brightwork—a full-bodied and graceful woman with soft
auburn hair and a lanky sunburned teenager with a shaved
head.

He had watched her with the boy. She had a fine-boned
face and a long neck and a way of holding herself that was
graceful without strain. She looked like a grown-up woman
and if she was Frank Keogh's, then . . . well, that was
hard.

Hard for the boy too. It was all hard. So what? Lyle could

use his life back, but he wasn't going to get it. Poole didn't want to be dead either, poor bastard.

Sometimes it would come to Sonny that Poole had been right all along. Maybe he *was* getting mean. If they'd just said, Hey, fuck it, back in Denver, Poole and Sonny would be in Costa Rica now.

Okay. He'd screwed up. But not to do it now—that felt like it had all been for nothing. If he finished it, it would be about something.

Too bad for the kid.

Anyway, the kid looked to be old enough to finish his growing on his own. And the woman was a classic. She'd have no trouble finding someone who would be damned glad to have her around on just about any terms.

When she'd walk down the jetty past the sloops and the cruisers, every man would watch her pass, and when she'd pass they would look at each other or down at their drinks and they'd shake their heads and each man would let out a long breath.

It occurred to him around three on Tuesday afternoon that he was watching the woman as much as they were.

It was strange to sit there in his room and feel as if he were floating off the transom, so close he could reach out and put a hand on her cheek.

Maybe it was the medication. Bone to stock on the Heckler, he'd settle the cross hairs on her breast and in the dim half-light of his hotel room he'd raise his right hand and touch the air where her image floated in his mind.

His hand would shake a little. His left hand throbbed and pulsed. His heartbeat would rise and ruffle in his chest. Out there in the bright sunlight, sitting in a deck chair on the fantail of the *Madelaine,* wearing a gauzy blue dress, tanned and talking to her son, she looked like a Carolina girl, like music over water.

Now she'd get up and say something to the boy and climb up the ladder to the flying bridge, and Sonny would watch her going up, see the way her hips moved under the thin blue dress, see the white panties under it, and when she turned at the top, her breasts would move, and her hair would touch her cheeks, and he would see a darkness in her eyes. . . .

Christ, he said, moving away from the scope, stepping back into the shadows of his room.

It's gotta be the Percodan.

That was on Tuesday afternoon.

That evening he watched her kiss the boy and walk along the jetty in the soft tourmaline of sundown in the same blue dress.

Where was she going?

Why did he care?

Still, he tracked her in the scope and he was still following her when she walked up the steps to the hotel and went into Rotten Ralph's bar.

He took the Heckler down and shoved it under the bed and paced the room for an hour, watching the light changing in the west.

He took two Percodans and lay down on the bed.

There were precisely 87 complete acoustic tiles in the ceiling. Each tile had 39 holes.

That would make a total of . . . 3,393 holes. Then there were the partials along the wall lines. You'd have to count them individually. . . .

He got up and looked at himself in the mirror.

Pounds had come off him. His cheeks were gaunt and his eyes were sinking. He felt hot and shaky.

Fuck it. This is a man who needs a drink.

CHAPTER 49

Tuesday, September 4
1800 hours
The Florida Panhandle

It was a good run, east on 66, stopping for a look at the place near Rimmy Jims so his father could see where all the gunfire had happened, then on to Albuquerque, New Mexico, and then south on I-25 to Las Cruces and a low swing into the east, and out into the flatlands of Texas on I-10 to San Antonio. . . .

Country music on the radio, Patsy Cline singing "I Fall to Pieces" and Roy Orbison with "Pretty Woman," neither Keogh saying much, the miles passing and the landscapes rolling . . .

Into the tangle of Houston and across the Sabine into Louisiana, through Lake Charles, the land changing now from prairie grass to old red oaks and Spanish moss, and a spicy smell like good brandy and woodsmoke from the Atchafalaya.

Then Baton Rouge and Mobile, with John and Frank singing "Nadine Honey Izzat You," stopping for the Stuckey's pecan pie and the Denny's Grand Slam breakfasts, the Cadillac growling away under the big blue hood, the car full of cigarette smoke and dented cans of Pinto and Dixie beer, and finally, like a big blue gull sweeping over the dunes, they broke out of Alabama at Pensacola and they were into Florida.

A hot Tuesday evening, just hours away from Matecumbe
Key, and Frank had to start thinking about what he was
going to say to Tricia and would she talk to him and what
was he going to do with the rest of his life: Would he have
Tricia and Robbie or would he be alone, one of those sad
old bastards who blow their families early and get to sit
thirds at everybody else's Thanksgiving dinner and play
horsey with kids who call him Uncle Frank and wonder
where he was the year before and don't miss him the year
after.

The closer they got to the Keys, the longer the silences
were between Frank and his father, and Frank began to
think that his father was getting around to saying something
important to him.

He felt better around him these days. The man was still
his father, but it was as if the game were played out now
and they were both on the sidelines, talking it all over.

Near the town of Lake Harbour, on the shores of Lake
Okeechobee, John Keogh took a deep breath and started to
talk.

"You ever think about your mother, Frank?"

Yes, he thought. Always.

"Some," he said. "Why?"

John Keogh wheezed out a slow sigh and looked out at
the flat Florida scrublands going by, the parachute palms
and the chrome-plated fast-food strips and the ARCO
stations and the deltas of saw grass and that peculiar soft
light of the Everglades.

"I miss your mother every day. Ever since she died in
that goddammed pool. That was twenty years ago just last
week. I can still see her going up and into the water. See
something of her every week, in the way a young girl turns
to wave or if there's a certain kind of blue in the sky or a
particular moon is out. Go to the hookers now and then, or
I let a drifter girl from the Islands on board for a week or
two. But I never wanted to take on . . . the risk . . . of
having a woman like your mother around again."

He raised a hand and moved it in the air like a bird flying.

"She was like one of those frigate birds you see down here. See how they ride out? No fluttering or flapping. Just all that natural grace, as if they were connected to the sea and the air all around them. Your mother had that kind of quality, and I always considered myself to be lucky that some momentary lapse of her good sense caused her to fall in love with a man like me. I figured my part of the deal was to keep her . . . safe."

Now it was out.

"Like it was my responsibility to see that something so perfect . . . I had to keep it from harm. Well, I didn't do too good a job, did I?"

"Dad. An accident . . . Who could know?"

"Yeah. Such a little thing. A little pool maintenance. See to the lights. But no . . . I was too busy being the big city cop to worry about the stupid pool. It was that—the *size* of the thing—that took it out of me. Such a huge set of feelings to come out of something like not taking care of the pool lights. It made it worse somehow. If she had died from cancer or in a plane crash, well, you could say that was fate, that was the end of the time I had been given with her."

He looked over at Frank, and Frank could see the question that had been grinding his father down for twenty-two years.

"But I always found it hard to believe that God would take Madelaine away from me by fucking with the wiring on a backyard pool. I just couldn't get next to it."

There was another long silence. What was there to say to any of this? Frank had seen enough of little deaths. Men killed because they carried a canteen half-full of water and the sound of it sloshing around got them shot by a sniper. An FNG dropped an M-29 grenade into his own foxhole one night while he was playing with it. They just filled in the foxhole and stuck his weapon into the red dirt because there wasn't enough of him left to scrape up and bag. Men died of dysentery because they didn't disinfect their water. They died of blood poisoning from the Crud. A kid from Little Rock who was 11 days short died of food poisoning in

Nha Trang after doing 351 days in some of the worst bush in the country. Sixteen fire fights, Lurps, sweeps, and ambushes . . . and he checks out over bad Nuoc Mam sauce with ten days and a wake-up.

"You really believe in God, Dad? After all those years in Seven Zone?"

John didn't hesitate.

"Yeah, kid, I believe in Him. I believe He's out there. I'm just not ready to testify to His actual state of mind. Or His intentions. I spend too much time alone on the ocean. It gets to me."

"I sort of wish you'd said all this to me back when I came home after Mom died. All we did was fight."

"Frank . . . I've thought about that, and all I can say is a man handles himself different when he's only forty. I took it that you blamed me for her dying . . . and I hadn't been able to keep you out of the army, so there was another important trust I had screwed up on."

"Well, that's horse shit, Dad. All due respect. Anyway, you feel responsible for every innocent kid you ever seen dead in a stairway?"

"Yeah. So do you."

Frank let that go.

"What about this Kent thing? How come you never told me anything about that?"

"When it happened you were just thirteen. And here I was investigating a boy not much older. Anyway, I never told your mother either. She got what she knew out of the papers."

He reached into the back seat and pulled out a big brown envelope.

"It's the file. It's all there. I dug it out as soon as I heard from Zeke Parrot. Wanted to know if I had ever told you about the case. I told him if he wanted to know who was doing this shit, he should go see if D'Arcy Kent was still in the hospital up in Albany. This was just his style."

John held up the file to the fading light and riffled through the papers, the original Information, the transcript of his talk with Dewey Schuyler, the lists of children with a record of cruelty to animals, the psychiatric assessment, the D.A.'s brief to the court.

"It was a hard case to work. And your mother was getting in between you and me at just the wrong time. I think I was taking a lot of it out on you because you were so damned full of yourself at that age. Nothing makes a daddy madder than taking shit from his kid at the table and the kid has his face all wrapped around some ten-dollar steak you're paying for."

"What do you figure happened to this kid?"

John Keogh thought about it for a while. Up ahead a road sign flickered in the headlights: MIAMI 50 MILES.

"I don't know. . . . Seeing what I saw of Paul Young and what I've heard about Lyman Hunt, I'd say they got into some kind of scrap—jealousy, fear of losing the boy. Homosexual fights are the worst you'll ever see."

"Where d'you think Hunt is?"

"Damned if I know. Pulled all his assets out the week before, right after Boo went up there. Lost a lot, but Al Matthias says he got close to four hundred thousand. He could be anywhere. Bury himself in some gay community somewhere. They don't ask too many questions in that crowd."

"You think that thing in the garden was D'Arcy Kent?"

Frank watched his father thinking it over. It was strange to look at another man and see so much of yourself.

"Hard to say . . . The bones were right. But when there's nothing left of the skull . . . They must have taken him from behind and then . . . just gone on beating him. Skull was pulverized. Face and forehead gone. No . . . I'd say it was him. It fits that kind of killing."

"I'm not happy with a lot of it, even if Zeke is. . . . And Myra. How the hell did they get to Myra?"

"Myra was taking a course from Young, at John Jay. All of her platoon. Young was in town all that week, after the funeral for The Paz. I guess he knew where she lived. My bet is she told him about you, or he found out some way

Why? I'd say it was just like Young said on the tape: They blamed us—me, actually—for what happened to D'Arcy."

It didn't fit. But it was all Frank was going to get.

"This kid . . . what was he like?"

"You know, the only time I ever got anything from that boy other than lies or some kind of self-serving shit was when I was taking him down to Central Booking and he says to me, well, did I think we could get this over with fast because he was kind of hoping to be back in school before the start of football season. Now I'd been pretty cool with him, just listening to him talk—they always love to tell you about it. They need the recognition. But when he said this, I just lost it and I said he'd be back playing football for his high school the day after all the kids he'd killed showed up at the prison gates and called his name three times.

"He turns around and comes at me, in leg-irons yet, his face all red and thick. He scared me then, Frank. I've been scared of him ever since. I'm glad he's dead. If we had any sense as a society, we'd kill things like that as soon as they get out into the light. Because they'll go on doing it as long as they can."

"Well, somebody finally did."

"Yeah," said John Keogh, yawning and leaning back in the seat. "I hope it was nasty."

They drove the rest of the way in silence.

CHAPTER 50

**Tuesday, September 4
1930 hours
Islamorada, Florida**

The crowded room was full of palm trees and Caribbean Flotsam and Kenny G. on alto sax.

Keogh's wife was sitting at the long bar looking out over the water and talking to one of the bartenders. She was playing with a long jade-colored drink.

Sonny took an empty stool a little down the bar.

The kid in the Hawaiian shirt brought him a Beck's beer so cold it hurt his hand when he poured it and he spilled a little on the wooden surface.

The boy looked at his left hand as he wiped up the spill. "Looks nasty, sir."

Sonny looked at it. He could feel Keogh's wife following the conversation and made damn sure he didn't look at her.

"Gaffed it."

"Jesus," said the kid, wincing. "Gaffed it yourself?"

"No. Just got in the way."

He turned his hand under the narrow downlight above the bar. There was some pink showing under the white bandage. It had been weeping for a couple of days now. His forearm was hot and a thin red line marked a vein running up it.

"You get some attention for it, sir? It looks pretty bad."

Great. He was here two minutes and already he was a topic of discussion. What the hell was he doing?

"Yeah. It's fine. Don't worry about it."

He'd have this beer and then he'd get up without looking at her and he'd go back to his room and lie down.

Men and women came and went around him. He had two more Beck's and he hadn't turned around on the stool. Out in the blue velvet bay, islands of glittering light drifted past. The music swirled like smoke around the bar. He could feel a vein in his neck like a hot wire but the Percodans and the beers carried him above the pain on a soft wave.

He knew, in a way, that what he was doing by not looking at the woman, by just sitting there under the pinlight spot and drinking quietly, was making it safe for her to think about talking to him.

In bars, the only man a woman alone wants to talk to is the only man who looks as if he doesn't want to talk to anyone.

Now the bar was clearing and there were two empty stools between them. He could hear her voice, low, saying something to the barman. His ears were still ringing—from the stun grenade or the Percodans.

"Excuse me."

He was thinking about another beer and wondering why the room was so hazy. Someone touched his right shoulder. She was standing beside him, looking down at him. She had lines around her eyes and the irises were a deep sea-green with slivers of hazel and her scent was spicy . . . something familiar.

"Opium."

"What?"

"Your perfume."

She took her hand off his shoulder and her eyes changed.

"Excuse me. I'm sorry to bother you, but you don't look well and I was . . . Well, I'm a nurse and I asked the bartender about your hand."

Sonny had a little trouble focusing on the hand.

"Hey. A flesh wound. I'll be fine."

Get out now. Get up, say thanks, and walk out. He pu
his hands down on the bar top. Pain sliced up his left arm

She saw the effect.

So did the bartender. "Sir, if you like I can call you a car.

Sonny stood up and pulled himself together.

"No. No, thanks. Look, I appreciate it. I've been mixin
my medicines some. I'll just walk home."

The woman shook her head.

"Will you have a coffee? Chris, will you get the man a
espresso?"

She held him lightly with her left hand. Now that he wa
standing she was looking up at him with the same worried
solicitude he had seen on her face when she was talking t
her punk son. It warmed him to see the look from thi
angle.

"Yeah. Yes, ma'am. I guess a coffee. A double espresso.

She didn't even look at Chris. He went to fetch it.

"That hand. You know what those red lines are?"

She traced one on his left forearm. Her fingertip was coo
and dry. She followed his vein up to his bicep, leaning
across him to do it. Her hair smelled of sea salt and
shampoo and cigarette smoke. Her blue dress floated or
her body like a mist over a pool and one soft arc of tanned
breast caught the downlight.

"No ma'am." He knew damned well. "What are they?"

She pulled back and gave him a clinical frown.

"They're a sign of infection. I think you should go to
clinic. I can drive you, if you don't feel up to it."

"I appreciate it, ma'am. But I can't allow you to trouble
yourself. I'll have a coffee and I believe I have some
penicillin in my room. I'll go along directly and take it. I'
be just fine."

He had to be reading this wrong.

She put out a hand. "I'm Tricia Keogh."

"Bolt," he said stupidly. "Dennison Bolt."

Her hand was strong and a little cold.

"You're southern?"

"Yes, ma'am." Why was he calling her "ma'am"?

"That's how I could tell. You're calling me 'ma'am.'"

The espresso came. Chris set it down and moved away.

No. He was not reading this wrong.

"You're down here on business?"

"No, ma'am—"

"'No, Tricia,' please."

"Yes, ma'am. Sorry. Ahh . . . no, I'm here for . . . pleasure."

She smiled and sipped at her jade drink.

"And you? Tricia."

She looked away and some emotion ran through her.

"No histories, okay? I'm a little drunk and I'm tired."

She pulled her shoulders up and a barely perceptible tremor went through her. She looked at him again. Sonny felt the look.

"Listen, I'm sorry. That was rude," she said, pushing her drink away. "I really do think you should get that hand attended to. It's been nice talking to you . . . Dennis."

She was leaving. It eased his mind and he smiled at her.

"Ma'am, it was my pleasure. You have a car here, or would you like me to call you a cab?"

She stood and looked at him for a long time.

"Very southern, aren't you? Too bad you don't give lessons. I'm from New York and the men there . . . aren't like you."

"Well, ma'am, there are days when I'm not like me either."

For the first time, her laugh was simple and uncomplicated.

Her breath was sweet and wine-scented.

"Sometimes, ma'am, it's good to be someone you're not."

Her smile flickered and dimmed and then it came back.

"Well then . . ." she said, her eyes darkening and her hand settling on his right wrist as soft and cool as snow. "Let's be someone we're not tonight."

No, he thought. Not a chance.

"Yes," he said. "I'd like that. I'd like that very much."

"Ma'am," she said.
"Yes. Yes, ma'am."

In his pale-green room in the indigo night with the se
sounding along the breakwater and the night wind rolling i
through the open glass doors, Sonny remembered ver
clearly how the blue dress had slipped away over he
shoulders, and how round and heavy her breasts were, th
nipples violet and hard as jewels under his palm.

When she came he thought she was going to cry, but sh
didn't and she came out of the bathroom with a nev
bandage for his hand. She dressed it in the half-light, sayin
nothing, her head down and her breathing steady.

He watched her get dressed and listened to the whispe
of the cloth as it slipped over her body. She came over t
the bed and leaned down to kiss him, and while she dic
while he felt her long hair around his face and her sot
hands on his chest, he thought about the Heckler in th
room like a thin black barracuda.

"You told me the truth tonight, didn't you?"

He didn't know what she meant.

"About not being who you are sometimes."

That was true.

"Why?" he said.

She touched his cheek and stepped away. "Why? I tol
you I was a nurse, remember?"

"Yes."

"Do you think I don't know a bullet wound when I se
one?"

Oh, Christ.

"Oh, don't worry. My husband is a policeman. I'm use
to it. I just think it's funny."

"How? How is it funny?"

She laughed once, and sighed, and walked to the door

"Oh, God, I don't know. It seems funny to me. Eve
when I have an affair, I have it with a cop."

She tugged open the door and stepped out into the light

In the aura around her from the hall, she turned an

smiled back at him. To Sonny she looked like something burning with a soft blue flame. Her body showed through the thin dress.

"That hand. It's very bad. And you have a fever. If you don't do something about it now, you're going to get very very sick."

"It's fine. Really."

"No," she said, her face hidden in the dark, her voice a soft vibration. "No, it's not."

She closed the door.

A sea breeze fluttered the curtains, and the cry of gulls floated into the room. He closed his eyes and lay back on the bed. In the darkness behind his eyes the gull cries glittered in his mind like kerosene flames on water, and an artery in his left arm burned like a coal seam underground. Hot, shaking, he felt the room rising and falling on the tides of his breathing. He tried to see Lyle the way he had been, but all he could see was Lucas walking in Old Town by the water.

"Emergency."

What was she doing?

"Emergency . . . hello?"

"Yes. A man needs an ambulance."

"Where are you calling from, ma'am?"

"Ah . . . the Ramada Inn at Bahia Mar. There's a very sick man in room two-eleven. He has a septicemic wound and possibly blood poisoning. He needs medical attention now."

"He can come in to the Emerg—"

"Dammit, I said he needs help now! He can't come anywhere! How about he dies on the way to the E.R. and they sue your ass off for it—how would *that* be?"

That did it. They always jumped when you got legal.

"What's the wound, ma'am?"

"I think it's a gunshot wound. In the left hand."

A pause and some muffled background talk.

"We'll send an ambulance and the police right now, ma'am."

"Police? He doesn't need the police. He needs a doctor."

"Any gunshot wound, ma'am, we have to send the police too."

God. Dennis would be furious.

"Well . . ."

"Can we have your name, ma'am?"

Tricia slammed the receiver down and walked away from the pay phone. She was almost down to the dock when she heard the sirens.

Well, she thought, he'll be angry at me. But he's a cop. They'll take care of him. Cops take care of one another.

The bastards.

When she reached the *Madelaine*, Frank was sitting on the taffrail gate with a fistful of dahlias and a cold bottle of Dom and a hopeful expression on his bulldog-Irish face.

CHAPTER 51

**Sunday, November 11
Noon
Cay Sal, the Caribbean**

The *Madelaine* rose as the swell came hard into it, riding up and onto the crest, the clean white bow slicing into the blue-green wall of the swell and the white foam flying like shreds of lace in a strong wind, then down again into the trough, the towers racing across the high clear blue, cutting across the sky in a slow eight, the way a skater cuts a figure.

The outriggers bent in the pull of the lures and there was a flash of silver in the blue-green water off the stern, like a needle in blue cloth, as the fish hit the bait and took it out, the rod bending and the line hissing out, skipping over the tips of the waves, snipping them off as the fish twisted right and left and then went down into the deep.

"Fight it," said Frank, leaning over the taffrail, watching Pat Butler in the chair. "If he gets your tip down, he's gone!"

Butler looked at Sam Danziger, standing by with the gaff.

"Tell Squire Trelawney to go screw himself, will you?" said Butler, fighting for the rod tip, feeling the fish in the line and in the rod, feeling the water vibrating as the fish cut through the green deep, forty feet down.

"Man," he said, grunting, "this fish is gonna take the whole rig right out of the deck!"

Danziger laughed and bent down to pull a cold beer ou of the locker. He threw it up to Frank. Frank fielded it on the fly and flipped it across to Slick Ryan at the helm.

"Damn," said Slick, snagging it at the side of his head "Give me a warning, Frank!"

"Whaddya want me to say, Slick? Look out! Beer!"

Slick kept his hands on the throttles. Frank's father wa sitting in the mate's chair watching Butler's line in the wate past the stern.

"Tell Butler to get his tip up," said John. "He's going t lose that fish."

Frank went back to the rail. Burke Owens was draggin a plastic bucket of ice out of the cabin. Danziger went t help him. The *Madelaine* dipped and labored down trough and he stumbled into the fish locker. Butler spun in the fighting chair, his muscles popping as the big ro dipped again and the reel hummed out another fifty feet o line.

Danziger looked up at Frank, his face half-hidden unde a big Bimini-straw hat.

"What's your father doing up there, Frank? Give us hand with this ice. I can't lift it. This is my holiday, not his You always make the guests do the work?"

Owens stood up and stepped back to the cabin door leaning on the bulkhead. He was dripping with sweat and his red beard glittered in the sun.

"Tell me about it, Sam. You don't know the Keoghs yet You'll learn fast. Here, let me do that."

He tugged the ice bucket up single-handed as the dec tilted again. In one motion, he toed the lid of the fish locke up and dumped the ice inside. Six big barracuda-lik wahoos lay in the insulated cabinet.

Frank watched Owens from the bridge, watched the siz and the power in the man, the easy way he moved.

Owens seemed to feel Frank watching him. He shade his eyes with a hand and looked up at him, grinnin through his beard.

"Hell of a vacation, Frank. Why'nt you bring the kic

along? I hear he's a hell of a mate now. He could do all this stevedore shit, and I could be up there posing on the poop deck alongside you."

Frank said something that got lost in the wind and the waves and the growl of the twin engines. Owens turned back to watch Butler fight with his fish.

Robbie, Frank was thinking. Robbie and Tricia.

The night before, when they'd been waiting for the men to arrive and cleaning up the *Madelaine* in Matecumbe, Tricia had come down to the engine compartment, where Frank was trying to torque on a manifold housing.

She had watched him struggle with it for a while, sitting on the steps with her arms around her knees and her face very still.

Frank wasn't trying to push her. She had a way of flaring up at him and then crying, and then it would seem as if things were getting better; there'd be a kind of . . . remembrance . . . of things the way they were when they were good. But he could feel her hurt and her anger not far from the surface. He tried to move slowly around her. He was hoping that if he just gave her enough time maybe it would come out all right.

Finally, he put the wrench down and leaned against the bulkhead. She reached behind her and handed him a cold beer.

"Robbie wants to go with you tomorrow."

Frank felt his nerves tighten up and he let out a slow breath to calm himself.

"Well, he's a great mate."

"Yes. Your father's very proud of him."

"So am I, Tricia."

There was not much left of the skinny kid with the shaved head. Even the tattoo of the skull was gone. According to John, Robbie had gone into a tattoo parlor in Key West and had the man cover the tattoo with the crest of the First Air Cavalry, a rounded yellow delta with a diagonal black slash and a horse head in the upper right of the crest.

Frank had taken that as a personal compliment. First Air

Cav was his division in Vietnam. Robbie was easier to get along with now. He was still full of attitude and opinions but it was a more polite attitude. Frank could live with that. Maybe time would show the kid that it was easy to be prideful when you were fourteen and all your failures and mistakes were still ahead of you.

"So . . . why can't he go along?"

"Tricia . . . we talked about this." Gently, Frank.

"Yes, we did, and I still don't get it. I thought . . . you know he's just getting used to . . ."

"Us?"

"You, anyway. And he's trying so hard. You can see that, can't you, Frank? Can't you and your buddies find a place for him?"

"Honey . . . I . . . need some time with these guys."

"Sure. The Boys' Club." Her voice was thinner now and Frank leaned forward to put a hand on her wrist. She tightened under his touch, and then moved her hand to place it on top of his.

"God . . . male bonding is so . . . What are you all going to do out there? Drink and tell war stories? Throw up and slap each other on the back and . . . He wants to be *inside*, Frank. Don't you see how important that is right now? I don't matter to him right now. He knows I love him. It's *you* he needs to be with."

"Honey . . ."

"You're going to do what you want anyway, aren't you, Frank?"

Damn, she's so beautiful, he thought, looking up at her in the yellow light from the bulkhead lamp, seeing the lines in her face and the way she was . . . changing.

The silence came back between them, but she didn't take her hand away and after a while it wasn't really silence but a kind of quiet and they were both happy to be quiet together.

Finally, she sighed and smiled and patted his hand.

"Oh, go, Frank. Have a good time. Go . . . bond."

"Men," he said, sighing the way she had sighed.

"Yes," she had said, looking at him, seeing the boy in him and the hardness as well. "Men. Can't live with them."

"Can't kill them. You . . . still think about divorce?"

There was a longer silence. Frank watched her face and felt the boat shift in the moorings and heard music from across the water. Her scent was in the air. Opium, saltwater.

"Divorce, Frank? No. Murder maybe. But not divorce."

"I love you, Tricia."

"Yes," she had said, "I know."

The next morning she and Robbie had helped them cast off and they'd watched on the quay as the *Madelaine* cleared the point. They'd made Boca Grande Reef by midday.

Now the boat was lurching and sliding in a trough. Frank heard his father calling to Slick at the helm.

"No. Don't force her! Port, Slick, port!"

Butler's line was slicing left through the rolling waves. In the bright noon sun they could see that flash of silver.

"What?" yelled Slick, still working at the throttles.

"Port! Left, damn it! Left!"

His father came back to the rail, grumbling about Slick.

"He's worse than you are even."

"Hard to believe, Dad."

His father grunted and stared out at the stern wake.

"What's that?" Frank asked, pointing to the wahoo on the line out there about fifty feet. "Behind it. That blue shadow."

His father shaded his eyes and watched the wahoo cutting and jinking through the foam, close to the surface now.

"That's a hammerhead."

"What? A shark?"

His father grunted.

"What'd you think? They're always around when you're fishing. The blood brings them. You go down there to the fantail, look over the side, you'll see fifteen or twenty of

them, down there about ten feet. Cudas. Blues. Lots
hammerheads. Carrion eaters, they are."

Great, thought Frank.

"I thought carrion eaters went after the already dead."

His father smiled at him, a ropy, hard-barreled old man
in a Red Man cap and faded jeans.

"Well, some of them have less patience than others."

Frank was quiet for a time, watching the hammerhead
chase the wahoo through the deep blue rollers.

"Now there's a fish with real problems, Dad. Hook in the
mouth, a hammerhead shark climbing up his ass."

"That's what they mean by the devil and the deep blue
sea."

Slick Ryan was calling them.

"Here—Jesus! Somebody take this thing off my hands."

He had the boat wallowing in a trough. He was fumbling
at the throttles. The engine beat was uneven and Slick was
tapping one of the RPM gauges.

John Keogh took the helm and pulled back on the
throttles. The boat rose to starboard and leveled out.

Slick watched him do it, and then smiled at Frank.

"Good at it, isn't he?"

"Yeah. He's been at it a while."

Slick cracked a can of Beck's and leaned on the mate
chair.

"Frank, I'm sorry about . . . you know, the job."

"What? You out at the range all that time?" He gave Slick
a shove and took the Beck's out of his hand. "Slick, I wish
you the best in it. It's nobody's month in the country."

Slick was nodding, reaching down to get another Beck's
and cracking it, pulling at it.

"Well," said Slick, "I better go downstairs there, get
some lunch on the road."

"That's *below*, damn it!" said John, looking astern, where
Butler was still working his fish.

Slick put his hand on Frank's shoulder and rolled his eyes
and went down the ladder.

"Have you figured out what you're going to do?" asked

is father, not looking at him, but giving him a sideways
ance from under his thick white eyebrows.

"No. Not yet. Tricia's got the house sold. She says she
ight look for work down here. There's a lot of call for good
rub nurses. Hospitals are always busy down here, thanks
the drug trade."

"I meant you. About a job."

"I talked to your buddy on the Coral Gables Department.
e says they could use me but I have to beat every felony
harge. Even one sticks, I'm gone. A lot of private security
rms are looking for people."

"They're mostly ex-FBI guys. Think you can work for
em?"

"If the D.A. lets me. Al Matthias says he'd put a word in.
hey dropped the Interstate Flight and the Weapons beefs.
wiped the departmentals by resigning. I might even get
y pension out of One Police. Zeke busted his ass trying to
ake it up, and Pulaski went all the way to the Advocate's
ffice for me. But I'm still looking at a felony assault on
utch Johnson."

"Butch gonna sue?"

"No. He even refused to lay an Information. But that
ther cop with Zeke and Butch—Bortz—he's got it in for
e and he's backing the case."

"How's Butch's eye?"

"Fine, now. Got it all back."

"Good. You hit him pretty hard."

"Yeah. Well, I'm not too proud of a lot of things I did
en."

His father shrugged.

"That Emma woman? The hostage you winged? What's
appening there? Tricia says she was going to sue too."

"Oh, yes. Suing my ass off. Litigation is the national
ort. But the Department is a co-defendant and the
etectives Endowment guys are providing a lawyer for me.
hat did I expect, anyway? It was kind of a bush stunt."

"He'd have shot you both, you know. If you gave up your
eapon, he'd have killed you just for balance."

"Yeah. Well, I guess all I can do is hope someday Emr
sees it that way too."

"And Beauchamp? Ever figure *that* out?"

"Some of it. Revenge. A . . . vendetta. Crazy."

"Lucky they scooped him. Ever find out who call
nine-one-one on him?"

"That was the funny part. Butler went to the Flori
State guys trying to get the tape of the phone call. But I
says they lost it. I keep telling him that's bullshit, they
have a backup system. But he says no. Funny thing, huh

His father wasn't looking at him. He was watchi
something at the stern. "Yeah. Funny thing."

There was a shout then and a burst of laughter from tl
fantail, Danziger's laughter and then Butler cursing.

"I'll bet he had his tip too low," said John Keogh.

Butler appeared at the top of the ladder with an emba
rassed expression on his face. Grunting, he flopped dov
on the deck beside Frank.

"That was a very bad fish. Good thing I had the sense n
to land him. He'd have eaten us all."

Sam Danziger and Burke Owens climbed up after hir
both big men clearly unhappy with the movement of tl
ship, slipping and holding on to each other, flopping in
the bench seat at the rear of the bridge.

"You see that?" said Danziger. "Show 'em, Burke."

Owens held up a length of line. A huge barracudalil
head hung on a hook, its jaws open, one yellow eye dull
death. The rest of the fish was gone, bitten off behind tl
gills. A crescent-shaped cut.

Owens's eyes were wide and his face was green under tl
burn.

"Goddammed shark comes up, no more than ten fe
back. Ate the whole damned thing. Four feet of fish, th
shark took it in one bite. Hammerhead. I could see h
eyes."

They said nothing for a while, watching the clouds ar
the sea all around them, feeling the boat ride it up ar

me down, running as solid and steady as a train through
field of spring wheat.

Slick Ryan came up the ladder with a tray of sandwiches,
ssed it around, and sat down on the deck across from
rank.

"How come this boat has an extra steering wheel, Mr.
eogh?"

"Call me John, Slick. I'm not *that* old. It's so you can take
e conn from below. In case we get weather."

"Take the conn from below?"

"Steer it from downstairs, Slick," said Owens.

Butler said, "I heard from Pulaski last night. Peggy Zacco
ent to the Department of Investigations. Moxie and Pepsi
t transferred to Citywide Street Crime out of Midtown
uth. They're all talking about a reunion but I don't think
s gonna happen. Anyway, Butch says hello. And Boo
anchette. Even Zeke."

"Yeah?" said Frank, tossing cans of Beck's over to Danger and Owens and Ryan. Owens was stripping his shirt
f and the beer bounced off his chest. "Hello to Zeke."

Butler said, "You remember Roberto? From the Ching-
Lings?"

"Yeah?" said Keogh, hoping that Pat wasn't so drunk he'd
t careless around Keogh's father. Butler grinned at
rank.

"Seems he found his cash and he was so grateful he
onated all of it to the Sergeants Endowment Fund, in
onor of Art Pike. Walked into the office himself and
anded it over to the receptionist. Asked for a receipt so he
uld claim a tax deduction."

"Walked in all by himself?" asked Slick.

"Well, no. Moxie and Pepsi came along. For protection."

Frank was pulling at his Beck's. He spoke into the can.
"Twenty-eight thousand? He say where he found it?"

"No. He was vague on that point."

"Well," said Frank, smiling back at Butler, "you never
now about a guy, do you?"

"That's a fact," said Butler.

"You never can tell what a man will do," said Slick Rya[n] grinning into his beer can.

"Nope," said Butler, "that's a fact, Slick. That's a true fa[ct] They'll always surprise you."

"Pat, you remember Fitz?"

"Fitz? Fitzpatrick? Yeah, I remember him. Lanky Iri[sh] guy, from Bronx Vice."

"That's the guy," said Frank. "Remember Bark Bark?"

Butler shifted his shoulders and grinned. "Oh, yeah."

"What's Bark Bark?" said Owens, balancing his Beck's [on] his big red belly and leaning his head back on the rail.

"Bark Bark was a thing Fitz did. We were doing stre[et] jumps, up along Third there. Taking out hypes and deale[rs.] We had us an observation post in the Blue Flame and t[he] hypes were buying like crazy. So Pat and me and F[ritz] and . . ."

"Grizzly," said Butler, letting Frank tell it.

"Grizzly. The four of us are street crew, so we see the[se] hypes coming out of the Blue Flame and they're coming [up] toward us. We know they're dirty but we want to take the[m] down someplace where we won't scare off the rest of t[he] hypes."

"Run like bunnies, they would."

"Yeah." Frank was talking to all of them now: Sa[m] Danziger and his father and Slick Ryan and Burke Owe[ns] just listening. The *Madelaine* had settled in for the r[un] home. The sun, full on their bow, was shining on Danzig[er] and Owens on the bench. Frank was in the shade, his fa[ce] hidden in the shadow.

"Like bunnies, Pat. So we all deke up this alleyway ahe[ad] of the hypes because we figure, hell, they'll come up he[re] to fix like they always do."

"It's night, Frank. Don't forget."

"Yeah. It's night, right, so the alley's dark as hell and v[e] run up about twenty feet. There's a big fence on one sid[e] next to a garage there, and this old Buick, a wreck, whe[re] the hypes like to cap up, you know? So Grizzly and Pat a[nd] me, we climb up onto the fence, we figure the hypes [will] come up to the Buick and we'll do a swoop on them, choke them out, take the caps—"

"Only the hypes are coming up too fast. So Fitz—"

"So Fitz doesn't have time to get up onto the fence with us. He looks around, and we can hear the hypes in the street. He gets down on his belly and slides under the Buick."

"Yeah . . . only the hypes stop at the entrance to the alley. They don't come up."

"They're standing there and talking. So Pat and me and Grizzly, we're thinking, damn, what'll we do, when we hear this sound."

"Yeah," said Butler, "this sound, like a little puppy—"

"Only it's hurt bad. It's yowling."

Frank put his head back and whimpered and yelped. Danziger and Owens and Ryan laughed. John Keogh watched the stern.

"Oowwowooo, it goes. Now the hypes hear this. And we can see them down there, going, Well, shit, that's a poor puppy somewhere and he's hurting."

"Hypes being your true humanitarians," said Butler.

"So up they come, and while they're coming, Pat and Grizzly and I realize this yowling sound is coming from *under* the Buick."

"Where Fitz is hiding—"

"Where Fitz is hiding. 'Cause Fitz is doing it. So he keeps this up, yowling and crying like this hurt puppy, and here come the hypes."

"He's reeling them in," said Butler, hooking his index finger inside his cheek and pulling it.

"Now by this time, we're all on the fence and I'm pissing myself laughing. Grizzly's a mess, he's leaning on Pat here, and it's all we can do to shut up and stay on the fence."

"And the hypes get up to the Buick—"

"The hypes get there—Who was it? Zorro and Bellhop and . . . ?"

"The little black guy with the butterfly knife. Tyrone."

"Yeah. So they can hear this puppy yowling. Fitz is really

into it now, he's *howling*, and the hypes get down on the
knees and look under the Buick, and what they see
Fitzpatrick down there holding this big Colt on them. He
shoves it into their faces, and he says owwwooowwooo
bark bark, motherfuckers!"

"We tried to jump them, all we could do was fall dow
and laugh, and Fitz had to slide out, start to choke them o
all by himself. The hypes're screaming, Hey, man, no fa
man—like we broke the rules. Frank's on his back . . .

"Yeah," said Frank, shaking his head, sighing, getting u
and walking over to where Danziger and Owens we
sitting on the bench, looking up at him, still smiling. Fra
pulled a little Smith & Wesson out of the back of his jea
thumbed the hammer back and shoved the muzzle hard u
against Burke Owens's forehead.

"So . . . Bark. Bark. Motherfucker."

Butler had his Ruger out, too, holding it easy in his le
hand. Smiling at Owens.

"Yessir. Bark. Bark. Bark."

"What's this shit?" said Owens. Danziger got up an
moved away from him, his face now grim. No one w
smiling.

"Come on, Burke," said Butler. "Show us some style.

Three minutes . . . A bank of clouds rolled overhe
and then it cleared again. The engines muttered an
popped in the wake, a deep and steady vibration they cou
feel in their chests.

Finally, Owens sighed and looked around and shrugge
a massive subsidence of beef and muscle.

"How? I mean, I *had* you, Frank. I had *all* you asshole

Butler said, "What's today?"

Owens thought about it, and then his face cleared up an
he beamed at all of them. "My birthday?"

Frank smiled. "Yeah . . . but what else . . . troop

"November eleven! *Veterans'* Day! So *somebody* final
noticed! Shit, you're not as stupid as you look, boys."

Frank stepped back, smiled at him, and moved the Smith down to his barrel chest.

"Took an AK round in the Plain of Reeds? Got a Purple? Lost a lung, you say? So where's the hole, D'Arcy?"

Owens thought that was funny.

"You know, I bet I can tell you the *day* one of you put that together. Butler, it was at your house. Frank here was on the road. Junie was doing lengths. Right? She's staring at my chest and then she asks you how come you never joined the army. Am I right? Come *on*. Indulge me, you pricks."

"Yeah . . . only she didn't tell us until later."

"*See!* A woman, man! I tell you, you can't get *around* those bitches. What about Vietnam? Don't you wanna know how I faked *that* shit? I know you guys ran me. All the way to Sturgis. And it stood *up*, didn't it? You all bought that one. Man, isn't there any intellectual curiosity here? Somebody?"

Danziger said, "Look, Frank, why don't we just take him in and leave it at that? He's already confirmed it. The rest is bookkeeping."

"*Bookkeeping?*" said Owens, staring at him. "Man, it was art, a masterwork, and you're calling it bookkeeping? What the hell have we got here? You all in on this?"

"Yeah," said Danziger. "All of us."

"Well, well . . . How long?"

Frank stepped backwards to the mate's chair and sat down.

"Since the middle of September. I didn't stop looking around just because I stopped talking to you about it. You're right about Junie. Junie also picked up on the way our eyes ratchet a bit. I saw you doing it back at Myra's, when you came by to talk to me about quitting Charlie Unit. It's one of the things that persuaded Sam to come long on this. What're they called, Sam?"

"Saccades. You see irregular saccadic movement sometimes, in some cases. Eye movements. You know what I'm talking about, Kent."

"Hey, can we call me Burke? I haven't answered to

D'Arcy Kent in years, and anyway I hate that little faggo
name. Yeah, I know. 'Smooth Eye Movements in Psych
pathology.' Lyman and Paul did a paper on it. Bullshi
mostly, for the Boards. Can I have a beer, Frank, or is th
a trial?"

Butler flipped him a can of Beck's.

"That's what it is, Burke. A trial."

"What—I make my case, you don't turn me in?"

"It's a possibility," said John Keogh.

"What's Danziger here for?"

"I'm the defense, I guess," Danziger said.

Owens watched Frank for a long time.

"Well, this oughta be interesting. I'm warning yo
though. You start asking questions, you never know *whe*
it's gonna end up. Where do we start?"

"We know most of it, Burke. You were never in Vietnar
You were in the army, though. You killed a kid in sixt
seven, while you were living with Hunt and Young
Albany. We think that's the kid we dug out of the Shin
garden in Hunt's house. His name was Maris Podnieks,
Latvian. A Podnieks joined the service, dodged an Eleve:
Bravo rating somehow, got into Graves Registratio:
Worked Records in Guam and Graves at Nha Trang."

"Yeah. That was me. Waiting for the right stiff to sho
up. And he did. Man, you shoulda seen what was left of th
Owens asshole when we unbagged him. He looked like
pizza-pocket full of road-kill and strawberry jam. He w
just what I needed, man. No family. Some backwoo
peckerhead from Sturgis."

"Before the army, back in Albany . . . you buried th
real Podnieks in Hunt's garden. Why?"

"Planning. It's a gift. Figured a stiff in the garden migl
be something I could use on those two if we ev
had . . . a falling-out. Like a dog buries something, fi
ures he may need it later. You shoulda seen Young's fa
when I told him. And Lyman, he fainted. I mean *droppe*
It was beautiful."

"Why set them up? They were helping you. They got you out of the state hospital. They covered for you."

"Oh, yeah . . . the good doctors. Hey, Sam, you know your office? Used to be Lyman's? You never saw it, Frank? Big rosewood desk, big window where Lyman liked to stand and watch all us poor dumb fucks stumbling around on the lawn, Thorazined out of our socks. Had this green rug in the office, emerald-green like a putting green, only *deep*. So deep, you drop your car keys into it, you're walking home—you follow?"

Danziger was nodding. He hadn't changed the rug. He would now.

"So three times a week that son of a bitch would ease off on my Thorazine and bring me up there for . . . therapy, he called it. Therapy. Man, what a guy."

Owens's voice was unsteady but his smile never shifted.

"Therapy . . . my therapy was to get . . . I'd be on my face on the rug . . . while he was doing me, you know? And the sunlight would crawl across the rug, you know? All bright hot and blue-green on that rug. I'd *see* things in that space there, see things on fire, hear it crackle, see flares and hissing like it was from the universe out there, like it was a TV transmission from Saturn, and I'd think how *far* this light had to come just to get here in time to see me being screwed by my God damned doctor!"

No one had anything to say to that.

"Well . . . it was a trip, Frank. I guess you hadda be there."

"Young confessed to the killings. He implicated Hunt. Then he killed himself," said John Keogh. "How'd you work that?"

"Like I said—once I saw *you* in town . . . By the way, you *never* made me at Butler's place, did you? Hotshot cop, huh? When you walked in and I heard your voice—man, I almost passed out. But there was nothing to do but walk in there, stick my hand in your face. . . . Anyway, where was I? Yeah, I just went up there, told Paul about the body in the garden. Painted a picture for him. Lyman had already taken a powder, but Paul . . . he figured he was responsible for me. Like I was a tiger or a pet anaconda or something and he'd set me free, and now . . . Well, it was my finest hour, seeing that putz weeping and crying in Lyman's hot tub. There's a shitload of mirrors in that room. I'll bet some smart video tech could pull a frame of me standing there in the doorway, grinning at him. I like to give the cops a chance, you know? But they're never up to it."

Frank asked, "Why kill your parents?"

"Hey, why Everest? Why Jupiter and beyond? Sam, you're my lawyer. I'm telling you, if ever two people needed killing, it was those two frozen fish. Only time they ever warmed up was when I torched them." He laughed at that, a quiet internal rumble.

He turned back to Frank.

"Myra had to go because you were porking her and it was a perfect chance to *really* fuck you up. I figured Pike was enough, but you mighta dodged *that* one. Never figured you for a run to Flagstaff, Frank . . . that was my mistake. You see the shots of old Mom and Pop? Actually, I guess that's Mom and Pop-*corn* now, huh? Get it? Jesus, Popcorn! I kill myself, I really do!"

Danziger cut him off.

"Why the killings? The children?"

"Jesus, Sam. You have no sense of history. Join the Book-of-the-Month Club or something. I'm in the grand tradition. I do what the race does best. I administer your basic randomized and totally mind-fucking death. I'm a Hall of Famer, Sam. I'm the Angel of Darkness."

Owens pointed at the sea birds wheeling off the fantail.

"See that, the way gulls fly? You know the way they have, they don't move, they just ride it and the sea brings everything to them. You ask *them* why, Sam? They do it because they *can*!"

"That's no answer," said Frank. "You to me, Burke. No

psychological bullshit. No sneaky-pete work setting up an insanity plea. Just us and you and the deep blue sea. Why the hell did you do it?"

Owens started to say something and stopped. They watched him while the wake rolled and churned away into the following sea. High above them a frigate bird called, riding a thermal into the farther blue.

"Truth, Frank?"

"Yeah. Just this once."

"What's in it for me?"

"Nothing. Maybe a chance to get the mask off. Show us how things are."

Burke smiled then. "Like Old Lodge Skins? 'That is the way . . . things are'?"

"*Little Big Man*," said Butler. "Chief Dan George."

Frank sent him a hard look. "Yeah, Burke. If you can."

"Ever eat oysters, Frank?"

"No."

"Damn right! Something slimy served in an ashtray, huh? But a lot of people do eat them. Ever think about who the first guy was who ate an oyster? I mean, what *balls*. And he probably *hated* it at the start. But then what does he do?"

"I don't know, Burke," said Frank. "What does he do?"

"He stays *with* it. He gets over his problems. He . . . develops a *taste* for it. It's a matter of . . . control."

"You saying you developed a taste for killing kids?"

"Yeah. It was *hard*. But I *stayed* with it. I worked at getting over my . . . nerves. Nobody becomes a killer overnight. It takes talent and . . . dedication."

"So what you're saying is you killed them because you liked it. Because you had a taste for it."

Owens raised his shoulders and held his palms out in front of him. "What can I say? I do it because I *can*! It's what I do."

"Man," said Slick, "what a piece of work."

"Thanks, Slick. So . . . you guys ever get the timing thing?"

"Timing?"

"Yeah . . . I took out the first little piglet on November thirteen, in 1959. Little Julia Caruso. Aged nine. Never made it to ten. You guys should have seen her face when she figured out what was going on. Talk about your world of wonders, boys. I showed her *wonders*. I bet, we dig her up right now, I'll bet they never got that look off her face. I'll bet it's still there, Frank. Talk about making your *big* impression."

"Timing—you were talking about timing."

"The thirteenth, Frank? That's a clue."

"Thirteenth . . . a Friday?"

"Good boy! Funny, you know, how traditions get started. It was Friday the thirteenth and I just woke up and said, Well, well, I do believe that this Friday is going to be some little piglet's worst Friday ever."

"Why the cords?"

"I was reading about the Thugs, you know? They were some very bad people. Kali? This mean anything to you guys? But I couldn't do the pickaxe thing. It was too quick. And all that shit about the sugar, offering it to Kali. Who's Kali to me? I was into karate then and the *sensei* had this system of rewarding you with these scarlet cords. So I just . . . improvised. I mean, I could give a fuck how I took out these piglets. I just didn't want it to be quick. I wanted to feel them going. The way some people like to feel that oyster sliding down their throats. Frank here knows what I mean, don't you, Frank?"

"So what about timing?" said Butler, to get him off that.

"Nobody put that together? Johnny? Donny Cadman bails out November twenty-seven same year. The Douey kid gets his—I loved this part—the two-five of December, same year. Christmas Day!"

"All Fridays," said John Keogh. "We knew that at the time."

"You did, hah? Smart son of a bitch, hah? Yeah, all done on Fridays. Not easy stuff, either. I tried to take a kid named Benny Glyde on the eleventh of December but his folks came home early. That was also a Friday. Screwed up again on March fourth, with a bitch named Mary Kugeluk. Tough little piglet. Almost got a look at me and I had to split. Made me wish I'd gone for the pickaxe. But rules are rules. Didn't score again until I got to that Chinese kid."

"Keiko Chung," said John Keogh. "May thirteenth, 1960."

"Yeah. Part I liked about that, it wasn't even my hometown! Then there was Graziella Benko. She went too fast. No stamina. February two-four in sixty-one. And then there was another fuck-up, I forget the kid's name, on July twenty-one same year. And—my introduction to your daddy, Frank—Bianca Vigoda on the fourth day of August in sixty-one."

He looked over at John Keogh.

"My trouble there, I broke my rules. Stayed around to try some new moves with her. Left some skin and some fluids. Next thing I know, I got old Johnny Keogh breathing down my neck. A real bulldog, old Johnny here. Nailed my ass to the outhouse door and never looked back. Should have, though."

"Should have put one in your eye a long time ago."

"That you should have. More than you know. What? You *still* don't *get* it, Johnny?"

"Get what?"

"Great . . . now it's getting weird, you want a *nap*? Come *on*, Johnny! Think! Fridays?"

"Shut up, Burke," said Butler, moving the Ruger.

"Shut up, Burke? Jesus, look at you. All of you. Sitting there, you think you got an edge on me. I'm the only honest man here. For chrissakes, I was the Department stress counselor . . . I *know* you dickheads. Butler, how about *you*? Fucking around on your wife? Scooping drug money? Crying to me about how fucked up your partner is. And Slick here, out on the range, sucking up to Pulaski for

Frank's job, talking him down around the squad room.
And you, Frank . . . how about *you*? Stone Irish killer,
you *loved* taking out those assholes as much as I loved
it. You're just a hired gun, Frank. You're on the run, what
do you *do*? You kill a bunch of poor dumb fucks on the road.
You're gonna *judge* me? We're the *same*, except I have the
balls to face it and you just drink and whine and screw
around on your wife and punch out your kid and feel *sorry*
for yourself. You had no green light on that Beauchamp guy
at the King James. That was a goddammed *murder*, sure as
my beer is empty. And Sam here . . . the great black
hope. *Hope* I don't piss off Lyman Hunt. *Hope* I get asked
to join The Process Group. *Hope* they don't find out I've
faked half my papers and my degree is from some grain-belt
diploma mill and all I know about psychiatry is Thorazine's
green and payday's Thursday!"

He smiled and leaned back against the rail, hands behind
his head, crossing a leg and grinning at them through his
red beard.

"And Johnny Keogh. The biggest asshole of the crowd.
Where'd this *boat* come from, Johnny? On a cop's pay? And
how about Jimmy Pelligrino? You and that sick fuck Pickett? And all the killers you've hunted down? Who the
hell're *they*? Brain-dead nigger dopers, starving Chicanos,
drippy-dick street hustlers hanging by their fingertips from
the tits of the most clapped-up syphilitic old whore of a city
in the Western Hemisphere. You slicking them around on
the Fourth, Mirandizing them a day late and a dollar short,
kicking their confessions out of them one word at a time,
and all along . . . you *still* don't get Fridays?"

"Leave it," said Butler.

"No . . . He thinks he's a fucking *man*. Let him hear
this. I'm talking the seventeenth of August, now. A little
ball-peen work for you? Come back with me now to those
golden days of yesteryear when men were men and women were getting themselves poached in the backyard
pool."

He looked around at the men in the following silence.

"Man. All of a sudden I'm on Easter Island. Now I got your attention? I was on you for days, Johnny. You and that wife, lolling around the pool. One night, I just snake on in there, use a ball-peen hammer on the lights. Did two of them, for the arc. Then I turn on the power and just . . . let it be. August seventeen in 1968 . . . a Friday."

Owens stopped and looked around at all of them. The frigate bird was turning in a slow circle in the high blue a thousand feet above them. A ribbon of cirrus cloud was sliding by the sun and the shadow hissed over the bridge and the men, cooling them. A breeze fluttered the pennons on the Bimini rig.

"I tried to tell you," said Owens, smiling at them. "But you don't *listen*. You start snuffling around in old graves, you never know *who* you're gonna turn up."

The *Madelaine* was six miles out on a long homebound reach with evening coming down and a flutter of white sails on the horizon, chasing a freshening wind. Where the breezes touched the sea the color changed from rose-pink and tourmaline to steel-gray. High in the fading sky, frigate birds soared and arced, pink in the setting sun. In the east a sickle moon rode above Mars, and the rising night was pierced with early stars.

Slick Ryan and Sam Danziger, Pat Butler and Frank Keogh were all leaning on the railing on the flying bridge, John Keogh in the mate's chair, no one saying a hell of a lot, just watching the way the light was changing. Frank was thinking about Vietnam.

Sooner or later we all get everything we want, Frank was thinking, looking at the light in the west, a soft gauzy light like the light around Cam Ranh Bay in the lowlands.

Up in the highlands there had been clouds like blue smoke that lay in the valleys, and they would climb through them, feeling the mist on their faces and seeing it settle into crystals of water on the barrels of the M-16's, and then the

patrol would break out of the cloud and they'd see moun
tains scaled with emerald-green jungle coiling and twistin
all around them.

There was a day, they had climbed to the top of
mountain called Co Roc, and they sat on that ridge of high
ground and for once, none of them gave a damn abou
Mister Charles and the ratfuck mission. It was enough jus
to be there, leaning against their packs with their hel
mets on the red earth under their boots, staring out acros
fifty miles of jungle, coiling into the blue distance like
great green lizard asleep and dreaming under a pale-gree
sky.

There was no talk, only the silence so they could hear th
rocks groan under them, hear the trees moving against th
sky, smell the sweat and cordite and gun oil and hot cotto
and the C-rats Marlboros, Max with his ham-and
motherfuckers, Blueboy eating his peaches, thinking *khon*,
xau khong xau, and Top on his back staring out at the jungl
with a warm can of bammy-bow on his skinny chest, and th
FNG they never got a chance to name, and Tully an
Buzzard and the rest, riding the ridge, riding the gree
spine of Co Roc under a pale-green sky.

A flaring chopper sounded like a heartbeat. A hog on ful
auto had a deep and chunky thudding syncopation they'
remember forever. All the belts were heavy and everybod
carried some to feed the hog. The brass rounds looked lik
gold and the links were flat black. Claymores were army
green and curved and when you hit the clacker three time
you heard the C-4 blast and under that the hiss of seven
hundred metal balls slicing through the leaves.

Arc Lite missions carried over the mountains like th
sound of a pounding drum. The M-16 chattered and had n
recoil but it climbed to the left. Our tracers were red
Charlie's were green, and in the night that was pretty, :
delicate flickering web of green and red threads. The M-79
had a comic pop but the round bit deep and had a re
flower at the center.

Incoming rounds sounded like scissors cutting paper.
Rounds on bone went crack. Rounds in the belly you never
heard unless they hit a buckle. The man would go puff and
sit down right where he caught it. Red blood looked purple
against army-green but it was always brown on Mister
Charles. Everybody dead was always blue.

Cordite smelled like the Fourth of July. The 50's sounded
like rock-and-roll. The sound of a mine was a slip and a click
and a half-step off, then, like a gas pipe blowing under
ground, a damp solid thud and the burst of red earth and
saw grass and the man going up into the sky, like a diver
diving into a pool of green sky.

Vietnam was beautiful but the ground was lethal. Frank
had learned to love the Remington because it was all about
altitude and distance, that shining circle in the scope like a
full moon, and the shooter still and perfect like a pool so
that a circle moon shone on a still pool and when you
pulled, the weapon drove you back and the muzzle flare
blurred the moon and in the faraway blue a tan man
crumpled and went down in silence like a cut puppet.
Looking out at the changing light, the *Madelaine* a steady
rumor under his hands on the railing, Frank could see how
a man could develop a taste for anything, but most of all for
distance and altitude.

"That's a serious blue," said Butler, staring up at the sky.
"How would you call that blue?"

Danziger said, "Don't be in such a hurry to name
something. It doesn't help anyway, right, John?"

"Not unless you nail it to the ground."

Danziger was silent for a while. Finally he sighed.

"I'm not happy about it."

"Who is?" said John Keogh.

"Everything he said. He was right about us. What gives
us the right to decide?"

Frank looked at him. "I knew a cop, back in Flagstaff—he
talked like that, Sam. And he was right. But I think,
sometimes, it's like a contract thing. The law says to

everyone, you give up these powers and we'll keep yo
safe, we'll do the right thing. But when the law can't d
that, or won't, then the contract is broken and what you'r
left with is—you have to keep your people safe and no on
else is going to do it."

"What does that make us?"

"It doesn't *make* us anything. It's not like that, like
switch gets thrown and you're one thing or another. Ever
day we all get up and start *being* something. At the end
the day, what we are is all the moves we made. Every littl
choice."

Danziger thought about it. "So all we have . . ."

"Is a list of things we won't do."

"Jesus," said Butler, going for a beer. "What the hell d
you guys want? Absolution? Call Pat O'Brien. Deal with
and shut the hell up. The world's a better place now than
was this morning. What else do you want?"

Frank said, "Everybody gets everything they want."

"What?" said Butler. "Who says that?"

"Co Roc says that."

"Who's Co Roc?"

"A lizard."

"Oh . . . Frank's hammered, men."

Slick Ryan was quiet. Butler watched him for a minute

"Slick . . . what's on your mind?"

Ryan took a long shaky breath. "What'll we tell them?"

Butler looked out to the east where the sea was rollin
into darkness.

"We'll say he went home."

They all smiled at that.

John Keogh watched the frigate birds in the blue for
while without speaking. He was remembering how the blu
light from the pool had shone around Madelaine, ho
her hair had burned blue and a blue aura had shimmere
around her hips and her shoulders as she stood there i
the light, smiling at him, calling to him from a sea of blu
light.

"So it wasn't my fault."

"No, Dad," said Frank. "It wasn't."

"Well," said Butler, "that *is* a serious blue."

"Yes," said John Keogh, answering no one who could hear him. "It is a wonderful blue."

ABOUT THE AUTHOR

Carsten Stroud has written two books of nonfiction, including the *New York Times* bestseller, *Close Pursuit*. In 1988 Stroud won the City and Regional Magazine Award for writing excellence. *Sniper's Moon* is his first novel, and he is currently at work on his second *Lizardskin*, also to be published by Bantam.

"*Close Pursuit* blows Elmore Leonard out of the water
and gives Joe Wambaugh a tight run for the money."
—*Toronto Sunday Star*

CLOSE PURSUIT

Carsten Stroud

Another night falls on New York City. A victim screams. A
siren wails. Eddie Kennedy is on his beat. He's a gold
shield homicide detective and a week of his investigations
is an electrifying journey into the heart of what it takes to
be a cop. From hookers to rapists to murderers, from
street-wise muggers to stationhouse rats, from the hectic
squad room to a bloody alley, Kennedy takes the reader
on a rare ride into a frightening hidden world.

"A strong, clear and admirable picture of
the working life of a homicide detective."
—Dorothy Uhnak, *The New York Times Book Review*

"An extraordinary work. Nothing I have read throws you
into the crucible of big-city police work the way this book
does. It is a gritty and gut wrenching piece of reportage
that reads more like a well-crafted work of fiction."
—Nicholas Proffitt, author of *The Embassy House*

"The best damned true-life cop book of the year."
—Bill Granger, author of *The Zurich Numbers*

When you're a cop, you have to draw
the line. Somewhere.

MICHAEL GRANT

LINE OF DUTY

In the tradition of Joseph Wambaugh and William
Caunitz, a debut already hailed as the most
gripping and authentic police thriller of the year.

When a major Harlem drug dealer is shot in the
forehead at point-blank range, the investigating
officer's initial reaction is, "Good." But as he picks
through the crime scene, he's surprised to find no
sign of a struggle, and nothing stolen from the
drug- and money-filled apartment...it just doesn't
add up.

Line of Duty is hard-hitting police fiction at its
very best. Politics, corruption, pervasive violence,
and the struggle of a few good men to maintain
their moral character in the high-pressure
environment of big city police work fill its pages.

*Michael Grant joined the NYC Police Department at
twenty-one years old. His first few years were spent
being dispatched in high crime areas from the South
Bronx to East New York. During the sixties he was in
the middle of every major upheaval from the race
riots in Harlem to the siege of Columbia University.
He was promoted to Sergeant and Lieutenant, and
his last four years with the department he was the
commanding officer of an internal investigating unit.
Grant brings unforgettahble characters, dynamic
action, and accurate detail to life as only a veteran
cop could.*

ON SALE IN APRIL WHEREVER
BANTAM BOOKS ARE SOLD.